reparation

a novel

ruth rodgers

Ruth Rodgers

Reparation — a novel

ISBN 10: 1-886104-64-6
ISBN 13: 978-1-886104-64-8

The Florida Historical Society Press
435 Brevard Avenue
Cocoa, FL 32922
www.myfloridahistory.org/fhspress

P•R•E•S•S

For my mother, Doris Everett, who always encouraged me to follow my dreams.

All that is necessary for the triumph of evil is that good men do nothing.

—Edmund Burke

We will remember not the words of our enemies, but the silence of our friends. The time is always right to do what is right.

—Martin Luther King, Jr.

Publisher's Note

The Florida Historical Society Press preserves Florida's past through the publication of books on a wide variety of topics relating to our state's diverse history and culture. We publish non-fiction books, of course, and our goal of disseminating Florida history to the widest possible audience is also well served by the publication of novels firmly based upon scholarly research. Teachers and students alike find that our high quality fictionalized accounts of Florida history bring the past to life and make historic events, people and places more accessible and "real."

In 2010, we published the novel *The Trouble With Panthers* by William Culyer Hall, which was a bit of a departure for the Florida Historical Society Press. Set in 2004, it cannot be properly called an historical novel. The fictional family depicted in the novel, though, has been in Florida's cattle industry for several generations. Their struggles with contemporary change very accurately reflect what many pioneer families are going though as they attempt to adapt from Florida's past to an inevitable future. The book is promoting thoughtful discussion about our state's pioneer history and its relevance to contemporary society. *The Trouble With Panthers* earned the 2011 Florida Book Award for Best Popular Fiction and the 2011 Patrick D. Smith Award for the best book of fiction on a Florida history topic.

Similarly, the novel *Reparation* by Ruth Rodgers is set in 2006 and features fictional characters. Told through the eyes of 62-year-old Katie, the story looks at changing attitudes about race relations in north Florida from the late 1940s to the present. As innocent four-year-olds, Katie, who is white, and Delia, an African American girl, become best friends despite societal pressures against them. In 1960, when the girls are sixteen, Katie abandons her childhood friend when she is needed most. In 2006, Katie is working to earn Delia's forgiveness in this suspenseful and exciting story. Although the events and characters in the novel are fictional, they reflect very real attitudes and actions that took place in Florida as the contemporary civil rights movement built to a crescendo in the mid-twentieth century.

As this book was being prepared for publication in the summer of 2013, the "not guilty" verdict in the shooting death of the unarmed Florida teenager Trayvon Martin sparked new discussions about race relations in America. In an impromptu address to the press following the conclusion of the case, the President of the United States, Barack Obama, offered context for the widespread negative reaction to the verdict:

> There are very few African American men in this country who haven't had the experience of being followed when they were shopping in a department store. That includes me. There are very few African American men who haven't had the experience of walking across the street and hearing the locks click on the doors of cars. That happens to me, at least before I was a Senator. There are very few African Americans who haven't had the experience of getting on an elevator and having a woman clutching her purse nervously and holding her breath until she had a chance to get off. That happens often. And, I don't want to exaggerate this, but those sets of experiences inform how the African American community interprets what happened one night in Florida.

Shortly after the verdict in the Trayvon Martin case, the nation commemorated the fiftieth anniversary of the historic March on Washington where Martin Luther King Jr. gave his inspirational "I Have a Dream" speech on August 28, 1963. The primary organizer of the March on Washington (along with Bayard Rustin) was Floridian A. Philip Randolph. An important civil rights leader, Randolph, who was from Jacksonville, also organized the Brotherhood of Sleeping Car Porters, the first predominantly African American union. At the fiftieth anniversary commemoration of the March on Washington, many speakers discussed how the event was not merely a celebration of the victories of the civil rights movement over the past five decades, but a continuation of the effort to reach full equality for all Americans. Many speakers pointed out that the recent Supreme Court decision gutting the Voting Rights Act of 1965 demonstrates that hard won victories of the civil rights movement must continuously be defended.

In the summer of 2013, the admission in a court deposition of Southern celebrity chef Paula Deen that she had "of course" used the "n-word" in the past also caused a highly publicized uproar over racial attitudes that still exist in this country. It must be noted that the offensive and racially charged "n-word" appears in this novel. While presented in an historically accurate context, its use may be too shocking for sensitive readers.

Clearly, a need exists for continued discussion about the history of race relations in Florida and the nation. It is our hope that this novel will help serve as a catalyst for such conversations. The story of Katie and Delia demonstrates that racism and bigotry are learned behaviors that can be overcome, even when they are instilled in children at a very young age and supported by prevailing societal attitudes. Beyond providing a particular perspective on racial attitudes in Florida and how they evolved in the last half of the twentieth century, this novel also offers a well written and suspenseful story. We hope you enjoy it.

Dr. Ben Brotemarkle
Executive Director
Florida Historical Society
August 2013

Acknowledgements

Although none of the events in this novel are based on real incidents nor the characters based on real people, the atmosphere of the time in which Kate and Delia grew up in two separate worlds very much reflects the culture of Southern segregation in which I was raised. I want to say thanks first of all to my mother, Doris Everett, and to my late father, Murphy Everett, both products of their time and place, who placed a high premium on education and made sure that I was able to go to college and fulfill my ambition of becoming an English teacher. Thanks also to my brothers, Jim and Bill Everett, and my sisters, Elizabeth (Libby) Hutto, Ann Olan, and Lynn Waller, who lived through those times with me and remember all too well what they were like.

I also want to thank the members of my writing critique group in Titusville, Florida—Southerners all—who read part or all the novel chapter by chapter as it was being written and gave me invaluable suggestions and advice. Their questions and comments spurred me on and opened fresh avenues for exploration as the novel progressed. My gratitude goes beyond words to Cathy Boyle, Irene Herring, Leslie Talley, Joe Richardson, and Kim Wendt for being my first readers and my cheerleaders whenever the going got tough.

Thanks also to the Florida Historical Society and all of the people there who shepherded the novel through the publishing process: to Kirsten Russell, Copy Editor, who read the manuscript with a discerning eye for errors; to Paul Pruett and Chris Brotemarkle, who designed the novel's cover; and most of all to Dr. Benjamin Brotemarkle, Executive Editor, who saw the novel through every stage of publication and kept me posted as to the novel's progress through its journey from first submission to finished product.

A final thanks to my husband Bill Rodgers, whose steady full-time paycheck over the years allowed me to have the best of both worlds by being able to teach part-time at Brevard Community College while raising a family and spending untold hours on the computer indulging my passion for writing. And to my three grown children, Matthew, Amy, and Will, the way of life depicted in this novel is one that you will thankfully never know. It is for you and your children that this novel is written.

Chapter 1

"Well, that was good news, wasn't it?" I opened the car door for my mother and waited for her to lower herself into the seat while protecting her right arm and shoulder. "Only two more weeks in the sling, and then you'll be able to start some therapy to get your shoulder joint working again."

"If I don't go crazy before then," Mama answered. "I hate to be such a bother to everybody. Roy taking time off work to build that ramp and you losing your whole summer vacation to stay up here with me. I know you need to get back home to your own husband and family."

I got in my driver's side door. "Don't you worry about any of that. We're glad to help out. And remember how you've been saying you wished I could come for a nice long visit? Well, here I am. What do you say we get some takeout cheeseburgers and fries for lunch? Then you won't have to manage a fork or spoon with your left hand." Without waiting for an answer, I swung the car into the parking lot of the Wachovia bank. "I'll get some cash from the ATM. It'll only take a minute."

Mama remained in the car while I walked up to the machine. A woman about my own age, early sixties, I'd guess, from the streaks of gray in her hair, was in front of me. I stood back at a respectful distance, waiting my turn. I could see only her back, but I noted that she was African American, like the majority of the people I'd seen in town

1

during the week I'd been up here. Had the black-white ratio been this high when I was growing up here? It hadn't seemed so, but back then society had been strictly segregated, and black people had taken pains to seem invisible.

Another car pulled into the parking lot, and a young black man stepped out, wearing a deputy's uniform, a star-shaped badge pinned on his shirt. He stopped a few feet behind me, opening his wallet to pull out his ATM card.

As the woman in front of me collected her money and turned to leave, I stepped up to the machine, inserted my card, and punched in my PIN.

The voice came from behind me. "Hey, Marcus. You ain't here to arrest nobody, are you?" Something about its tone sounded familiar, but, waiting for the cash to appear in the slot, I didn't turn around.

"Hey, Miss Delia," the man answered. "I ain't aiming to, but you never know. You better be on your best behavior just in case."

The woman continued walking away, a teasing lilt in her voice as she called back, "Oh, don't you know I'm too old to be misbehaving now. Them days are long behind me."

The deputy chuckled. "Oh, I 'spect you could still stir up some trouble if you wanted to. You take care now, hear?"

I took my card and the five twenty-dollar bills that came out of the machine. Delia? Could that have been Delia Adkins? Was Delia back in town? I felt a leap of excitement at the possibility that it was Delia who had just walked past me, close enough to reach out and touch. How long since I'd seen Delia? Not since we were sixteen. The old weight of guilt rumbled in my stomach, and I kept my face toward the machine, taking my time in retrieving my receipt, counting the bills, folding them, and sticking them into my pocket, giving my nerves time to calm. I had been trying for forty-six years to put that night out of my mind, but suddenly it was back gnawing at my conscience, the memory as fresh as if it had happened last week. Beads of perspiration formed on my forehead, and I wiped them away with one hand.

I could hear the deputy behind me shuffling with impatience, moving closer. I stepped aside. "Sorry," I apologized, risking a glance toward the parking lot. The woman was still there, stopped now beside the passenger door of my car. Mama had rolled the window down and was talking to her. So it *was* Delia. I had known it even before the man said her name—something about the way she held herself, something about her voice as soon as she spoke. I lifted one hand in a wave and stepped forward.

"Katie!" Delia widened her eyes in delight as I drew closer, then ran forward and threw both arms around me. "Golly, Miss Molly, it's good to see you." She stepped back, both hands still on my arms. "My goodness, you haven't changed a bit. I'd have known you anywhere."

I clasped Delia's hands, the same way we had held hands as girls and spun each other around until both of us collapsed in a dizzy, giggling heap. Seeing Delia made me feel five years old again. "You, too," I said. "You're looking great."

"Can't complain. I hear you're going to be staying a while."

"I'll be here through the summer, I guess, till Mama's got full use of her arm again."

"Then we'll have to get together, talk about old times." There were smile crinkles around Delia's mouth and eyes. "Lots of water under that old bridge."

"That's the truth."

"Listen, I gotta run, but call me, okay?" Another quick hug and Delia was gone.

I settled myself in the driver's seat, buckled my seat belt, and took a few deep breaths to calm myself. "Mama, you didn't tell me that Delia was back in Pine Lake."

"I didn't?" Mama looked as pleased as if she'd specially orchestrated this surprise reunion. "Seeing you two together just now, it sure brings back a lot of memories. When you were little, you thought the sun rose and set in Delia. Remember? Your daddy used to get so upset about the two of you playing together."

"Is Delia living in Pine Lake now? When did she come back?"

"He was always saying that no good could come of it, the two of you acting like you was sisters or even twins. He was worried that Delia didn't know her place. I admit, I worried about it, too, but—"

3

"When did Delia move back?" I asked again.

"Oh, 'bout a year ago now, I guess. Didn't I tell you? Silas was getting worse, and Maggie couldn't handle him by herself."

"The Alzheimer's?" Mama had told me about that, at least.

"You know how big and strong he is, and Maggie couldn't get him to stay in the house. He was always wandering off somewhere, and Maggie would have to call Theo or one of the colored deputies to find him and bring him home. Delia's got him enrolled in that new daycare center weekdays while she's at work, but nights and weekends he's at home."

"So Delia has a job up here? Is she living with her parents?"

"No. She's living with some man. Maggie says they're not married."

Mama continued talking, but I hardly heard her, my mind already back in the past, and I turned right at the traffic light, heading north, before I remembered that getting something for lunch had completely slipped my mind.

"We can scratch something up at home," Mama said. "I'm not that hungry, anyway."

But I was suddenly ravenous. "I want a cheeseburger," I said, "and French fries." I turned the car around and headed back to town.

Upon arriving home, we both walked up the new ramp that my brother Roy had built leading up to the front porch. When Mama had fallen on the front steps last week and dislocated her shoulder, he had taken two days off work to come over and construct it. "We can't have you stumbling on them high steps," he had said. "Next time you're liable to fall and break your neck."

A week ago yesterday, Mama had been coming back from an early morning trip to the garden with ripe tomatoes in both hands when she had stumbled midway up the steps. If she hadn't had both her hands full, she probably would have been able to catch herself, but in the split second that it took her to decide to release the tomatoes and grab for the railing, she had already twisted and fallen, her right shoulder slamming into the wooden banister. Fortunately, she'd been able to get inside and call 911, but as Roy reminded her, if she had broken a leg or a hip she could have been stranded outside on the steps for hours or even days, living out here in the country all alone as she did.

I had arrived late that afternoon, after getting word of what had happened, and Mama had been released from the hospital the next morning only with the provision that someone stay with her around the clock.

"How long?" I had asked the doctor.

"Depends," he had said. "She'll have to keep that arm and shoulder immobilized for about three weeks. Then we'll set her up for some therapy to get her range of motion back. If all goes well, she should be back to normal in five to six weeks."

"I can stay as long as I'm needed," I assured him. Russell could get along without me for a couple of months, and since I was a high school librarian, I was off work for the summer anyway. "Just tell me what I need to know to take care of her."

Even before Mama's fall, my two younger brothers and I had known that, sooner or later, this day was coming. After Daddy's death last year, I had tried to convince her to move downstate to Central Florida and live with Russell and me, but she had refused to leave home. "I was born here, lived here all my life," she'd told me. "I'm too old to up and leave everything and everybody I know." Roy was closer, only an hour away in Lake City, but he and his wife both worked full-time, and Zach, my youngest brother, lived way off in Colorado. So Mama had insisted on staying alone in this old farmhouse way out in the country, ten miles away from town, and now the dislocated shoulder and sling was payback for her stubbornness.

After lunch and her pain medication, Mama headed for her recliner. I put the footrest up for her, handed her the TV remote and the cordless telephone, and got a package of frozen peas from the freezer for her shoulder. "Here's your ice pack. Now you're all set for the afternoon."

With Mama engrossed in her soaps, I walked outside into the back yard. I'd been back here a week now, and was still getting reacquainted with this place of my childhood. Mama's clothes line had been gone for

5

years now, ever since she'd replaced it with a dryer, but I could still picture it between those two oaks — all the heavy, wet laundry I'd hung between those trees. The grape arbor was still there, and the pear tree, and the corncrib behind it. To the left was the pump house and Daddy's work shed with its winged roofs on either side, under which all the farm equipment had once been parked, and to the right across the lane the tobacco barn still stood, listing a little more to one side every year until it seemed impossible that it could continue to stand at that crazy angle. The next good windstorm would surely crumple it to the ground, like it had the house that had once stood beside it.

I could see that little square house so clearly in my mind — Delia's house, I'd always called it — and I could see Delia, too, at age four — brown eyes dancing, braids swinging as she raced across the yard toward me, eager for another day of play. I hadn't thought about Delia for years, but seeing her today at the bank had unleashed a flood of memories — Delia, my first childhood friend and confidant — Delia, whom I had failed on that beautiful, moonlit summer night of our sixteenth year.

Even after all these years, the memory still had the power to nearly bring me to my knees with shame and guilt. I had never told anyone about that night, not even Russell, not even in that intense soul-baring period of courtship when we marveled at how each could read the other's mind, could know what the other was going to say before the words formed into syllables. This was the one and only secret I had ever kept from him, the one secret that I feared would drive him away, would mark me as undeserving of his love.

I walked across the yard, opened the side gate, and stepped into the narrow dirt lane that led back to the pasture and fields. Nothing stood beside the tobacco barn now but a stand of pines — the little house finally torn down by Daddy after a windstorm had taken off its roof and left it open to the elements. It had never been much of a house — just an unpainted wood-frame square of four equal-sized rooms, but it had been home to Delia and her family during all of my childhood and adolescence. Delia's father had sharecropped for Daddy for years —

from the time I was four until the early seventies, long after I had gone off to college and then moved south to Titusville in Central Florida.

And now there was no sign that the house had ever existed. Once the lumber had been cleared away, Daddy had planted pines in the empty spot, leaving an unbroken stretch of woods between the tobacco barn and the pasture—a clear sign that time could not run backward, could not be rewound to give me a second chance to go back forty-six years and undo what had happened that June night of our sixteenth year.

Within a week or two of that night, Delia had been spirited away to Georgia to care for a sick grandmother, and I had not seen her again until today. Over the years I had occasionally heard snatches about her life from Mama: *Maggie says Delia's living in Atlanta now, working in one of them skyscraper buildings, Maggie says Delia had another baby—a girl this time*, but I had never probed for details, not wanting to know too much, not wanting to hear anything that might feed the guilt that nibbled constantly at the edge of my mind.

The only way to quell that guilt was to apologize to Delia—but simply saying I was sorry wouldn't begin to erase what had happened. Why hadn't I acted? My only excuse was that in 1960, conditions had been so different from the present, and I had been too afraid to speak up, too afraid of the repercussions that I myself might suffer.

If I could summon up the courage to call Delia now, to meet her for lunch at a restaurant in town, two equals sharing a meal at the same table, the same way we had shared milk and cookies on the back porch steps all those years ago, maybe then I could find the words to apologize to her, not just for that one night but for all of the past—all that terrible legacy of the South that had been instilled in me and all those of my generation, those old attitudes and habits ingrained and imprinted from infancy. Maybe then I could ask Delia's forgiveness.

Chapter 2

I walked a few steps down the lane, trying to pinpoint in my mind the exact spot where the house had once stood. Daddy had done nearly all the carpentry work himself, working through the late fall and winter of 1948-49, rushing to get finished before spring planting time. I had been four at the time, and deliciously excited by the house-building project. Every morning after breakfast I would scurry down the lane and watch as he sawed and lifted and hammered. Roy Jr. was only two and too young to be allowed to go with me, so I had felt extra important to be helping Daddy build the new house.

* * *

"Here, Daddy." I hold out a fistful of shiny new nails.

"Thanks, sweetheart. Now pick up all them scraps over there and put them with the others in your pile. That's a good girl." Daddy smiles at me.

I run to pick up the scrap ends that Daddy has sawed off the boards he's using for framing the walls. I'm making my own house with the end pieces, stacking them off to one side in the shade of the pines. Silas is helping Daddy, too. Silas is big — bigger than Daddy — and very dark, and he scares me a little with his loud laugh, even though he never talks to me or even looks directly at me. He is going to be a sharecropper for Daddy, starting in the spring at planting time, and he will be bringing his family to the house to live when it's all finished. Every morning Daddy drives off in his truck to pick him up, and at noon Silas eats dinner at our house, sitting with his plate that Mama fixes for him and his quart-sized Mason jar of iced tea out on the back porch steps, shivering in his thin jacket while we eat inside in the warm kitchen.

"He's got a little girl about your age," Daddy tells me one night at supper, "and two boys, one about the size of Roy Jr. and the other one a new baby, just starting to crawl."

"What's her name?" I wonder if she is as dark as Silas. Of course, I've seen lots of little colored children before, but always at a distance, and I haven't ever talked to one. Having one my size living so close to me is such a strange idea that I don't know what to think about it.

"His wife is Maggie. I don't know the names of the young'uns," Daddy says. "If you want to know so bad, why don't you ask Silas?" Daddy winks at Mama across the table.

But I'm not brave enough to ask Silas anything. At the new house, I try to stay out of the way and make myself useful so I won't get sent home, all the while listening to everything that Daddy and Silas say, storing away all the information that I can learn from their conversation. Most of their talk is pretty boring, mostly about the house itself and about the crops they'll be planting in the spring. Listen as hard as I can, I don't hear any mention of the name of Silas's little girl.

By early spring the house is finished. It has four square rooms, a tin roof, and a brick chimney and fireplace at one end for heat. I'm worried, though, about the missing porches — the wide covered porches that everybody else has on the fronts and backs of their houses to keep the house cool in the summer.

But Daddy says he'll add them later. "Right now," he says, "we need to get them moved in soon as we can. Fields need to be plowed and crops planted."

Moving day is like Christmas. I wake up early, not wanting to miss a thing. After breakfast, Daddy leaves in his truck to pick up Silas and his family and belongings. Silas doesn't have a truck. He and his wife and children have been living doubled up with Silas's mama and daddy and all of Silas's younger brothers and sisters, so they don't have much of anything to move in the way of furniture. "Silas says it'll all fit in one truckload," Daddy tells Mama.

When the truck finally comes rumbling down the road, I run outside and follow it down the lane to where it has stopped in front of the new house. Silas is sitting up front with Daddy in the cab of the truck; the rest of the family is in the back, squeezed in with all their possessions. I stand back and watch as *everybody piles out. Silas's wife hands the baby to Silas, who has already jumped out of the cab; then she climbs down herself and lifts out a little boy about the same size as Roy Jr. As soon as she puts the little boy down, he wraps himself up, out of sight, in the folds of her long skirt so I don't really get a good look at him. But that's okay, because I'm not interested in him or the baby, anyway. My eyes are fastened on the little chocolate-colored girl who is now peeking at me around the corner of a beat-up chest of drawers.*

Silas hands the baby back to Maggie and goes to get the girl. "Come here, Delia," he says. "Let me lift you down."

"Delia." The name sounds musical and exotic to me. "Delia," I whisper, quiet as I can, trying it out on my tongue.

"No!" Delia squirms away from Silas's outstretched hand. "I can get down all by myself." She turns sideways and squeezes between the chest of drawers and an old mattress speckled with sweat-stains. As I move closer to see her better, she takes a couple of steps to the tailgate of the truck and jumps to the ground right in front of me.

She is chocolate-brown, the color of a Hershey Bar, and her hair has been parted and plaited into tiny fuzzy braids all over her head. At the end of each braid is a barrette, all different colors and designs — green bars and yellow ovals and red bows and blue lovebirds. I stare openly, fascinated at the sight of so many colors and shapes on one head. Delia is barefoot, even though it's only March and still too cool to be going without socks and shoes. Her eyes are big and round, and as she spreads her mouth in a wide grin, I notice the gap between her two front teeth. She is the cutest thing I've ever seen in my life — a chocolate doll. Mama and Daddy have drilled it into me that "niggers" — that's the word Daddy and Mama and all the other grown-ups use — are different from white people and that I'm not supposed to play with little nigger children, but I really don't understand why not.

Not taking my eyes off Delia, I sidle over to stand beside Daddy, waiting to see what he will tell me to do. "Run tell Mama and Roy Jr. they're here," he says. "You folks go on in and see your new house." He directs this to Maggie as he and Silas start unloading the truck.

The barrettes on Delia's braids dance as she runs ahead of Maggie into the house, out of sight.

"Go on," Daddy says again. "Help Mama with the food she's bringing."

11

Mama has already made and hung curtains at the windows of the new house, using some of the old cotton feed sacks that she'd been saving, and now she's at home cooking extra food to bring down for Silas and Maggie's "Welcome" dinner—fried chicken and potato salad and the last of the collard greens from the winter garden. Daddy put a wood stove and an icebox in the kitchen so they could cook their own meals from here on, but those are the only furnishings in the house except for whatever they've brought with them in the truck.

By the time Mama gets all the food dished up and packed into Roy Jr.'s Radio Flyer wagon, and pulls it down to the new house, the truck has been unloaded and Daddy and Silas are leaning against it talking. I don't see Maggie or any of the children anywhere.

"Morning," Mama says to Silas, nodding at him while looking off to one side. "I brought y'all some dinner. I knew you wouldn't have time to get things unpacked and get anything cooked this morning."

"Yes, ma'am." Silas looks down at his feet like he always does when Mama speaks to him. "I'll get Maggie."

Maggie comes outside then, down the two steps at the front door, still holding the baby. The little boy has a handful of her skirt, and Delia is behind her, walking on her toes, almost dancing and smiling that wide, gap-toothed smile. Daddy makes introductions all around, and Maggie ducks her head, making her words hard to understand. "Pleased to meet you, Miss Julia." She moves the baby to her other arm and tugs the little boy forward, out of her skirt.

"Your children are so cute." Mama puts one hand on the head of the little boy, and I wish I could touch his head, too, to see what his hair feels like. It is kinked up into tight little knots of curls all over his head. But Mama is talking now, taking charge of the situation. "What are their names?"

"This here's Theo; he was two in December, and this is Jerome. He's seven months. And my oldest—over there—that's Delia."

Delia had jumped off the top step and has been slipping closer and closer to me so that we're standing side by side. I can see that she is almost exactly the same size as me, almost like twins. My chocolate twin. The idea is so funny that it makes me giggle, and Delia giggles with me, our eyes meeting and both of us covering our mouths in the same way, which makes us both giggle harder.

"You, Delia, get over here," Silas snaps at her.

12

When Delia doesn't move, Silas walks over and grabs her arm. I can see his fingers pressing into her skin. "You mind when I speak to you."

I feel myself being lifted into the air by Daddy and set astride his shoulders. I clutch a handful of coarse, curly hair and grin down at Delia, who is now sitting on the bottom step of the house, where her daddy has plopped her. She sticks out her lower lip in a defiant pout.

"We brought you some dinner." Mama indicates the dishes sitting in the wagon. "I know these children must be hungry."

"Yes, ma'am. Thank you, ma'am." Maggie flicks her eyes toward the wagon, then away.

After unloading the food, Mama puts Roy Jr. in the wagon and pulls him back up the lane, and I ride in the truck with Daddy as he drives it back to its usual parking place. After our own dinner, Daddy and Silas go off to the fields on the tractor, and I have to stay inside and play with Roy Jr. I beg Mama to let me go back to the new house and see Delia again, but she says no.

"You leave them alone," she says. "They got plenty to do today without you hanging around there. Besides, you remember what we told you; it ain't right for you to make friends with Delia. It's all right to speak to her when you see her and act nice, but remember you're white and she's colored. You have your place and she has hers."

I deliver a hard kick to Roy Jr.'s stack of blocks. "I want to play with Delia! I'm going there right now!"

"Stop that!" Mama orders, gathering up the squalling Roy Jr. to comfort him. "Throw a temper tantrum and see where that gets you."

I run crying to my room. I know that Delia isn't allowed to come inside my house or touch any of my things, but I'm not sure why that is. Mama doesn't allow Champ, our German shepherd, into the house either because he's dirty and smelly, but Delia looked clean enough to me. I play with Champ in the back yard all the time, and if I can play with a dog, then why can't I play with Delia, as long as we stay outside and don't bother anybody?

13

Chapter 3

Stepping back inside the gate, I latched it behind me and went to check on Mama. She was dozing in the recliner, the TV still blaring away. I hit the off button on the remote and stretched out on the sofa. Might as well get my own rest while I could. Sleeping at night was hard for Mama. With her shoulder immobilized, she couldn't turn onto her side or her stomach, and she would wake several times during the night and get up to pace the house, trying to tire herself out enough to go back to sleep. Her roaming would wake me, too, and I'd get up to check on her and open the safety cap on her bottle of pain pills.

Closing my eyes, I tried to sink into a deep state of relaxation, but my mind wouldn't shut down; instead, I found myself rehearsing a running commentary of that first meeting with Delia, justifying myself to some young person who had no idea of how different things had been back then. "At age four I had no idea that 'nigger' was a derogatory word," I imagined myself explaining. "It was simply descriptive: Silas and Maggie and Delia were niggers, just as apples were apples and oranges were oranges and the nuts I got in my Christmas stocking every year were nigger toes." The imaginary person I was addressing assumed the face of my daughter Erin, who had never heard this story before, had never even heard mention of Delia. "When I started school," I continued in my mind, "my girlfriends and I counted ourselves off with the rhyme, 'Eeny, meeny, miney, mo, catch a nigger by the toe; if he hollers, let him go.'"

I could picture Erin's horrified and unbelieving expression, her flinching at my matter-of-fact use of the "n" word. I couldn't remember how old I had been when I learned the correct spelling was "Negro," for no adult that I knew had ever used that pronunciation. Back then, if someone wanted to sound polite or refined, the term they used was "colored." Or sometimes "darkie."

"What?" I could imagine Erin saying back to me. "Darkie? That's so gross." Then she would flounce out of the room, uninterested in all that messy past history that had nothing to do with her.

I turned onto my side and pulled my legs up into a more comfortable position. It wasn't until I was in college in the '60s that "black" became the favored term, and now it was "African American." All those words made me feel old, as if I'd lived from Civil War times all the way up to the twenty-first century. If people could get past the words or ignore race altogether, the world would be a better place. Why couldn't we all just be Americans? Or, even better, all just people?

Delia had never let her color keep her from being a person. Silas and Maggie and the other children—Theo and Jerome and then the youngest girl, Rochelle—had all "known their place" as Daddy had put it, but not Delia. Never Delia. Delia was the sassy one, the feisty one, the one who was headed for trouble from the day she jumped down off that truck and stood facing me, braids dancing, eyes challenging, bare feet planted solidly on the ground. Delia had spunk. That's what caused those boys to decide to teach her a lesson—to take that sassy, feisty attitude out of her. If Delia had been like the other colored people back in those days, if she'd known and accepted her place in society, then nothing would have happened.

I thought I had put that evening out of my mind years ago, but being back here—seeing Delia at the bank—had slammed me back into that moment as if I were sixteen again. Delia hadn't known that I had overheard those boys call her names or promise to teach her a lesson she wouldn't forget, but even so, her ignorance of the fact didn't excuse my own failure to intervene, or even worse, my failure later to report to anyone what I had seen and heard. I opened my eyes, trying to get the memory of the snarl in those boys' voices out of my mind, but the scene kept replaying itself like a scratched record where the needle falls into the same groove over and over again.

I went to the refrigerator for a cold soda. Nearly four o'clock and Mama was still sleeping. Maybe I should wake her so that she would be able to sleep tonight—but then maybe she needed the sleep whenever and however she could get it. I was still undecided when the phone rang.

I headed for it, but Mama picked up the cordless phone from her lap and answered as perkily as if she'd been awake all along, as if she hadn't been softly snoring a minute ago.

"I'm doing as well as can be expected," I heard her saying into the phone. "And Katie's here taking care of me."

I tiptoed back to the kitchen, an unexpected lump in my throat at Mama's words. Russell wasn't happy about my spending my summer up here, but I'd promised Mama I'd stay as long as she needed me, and I'd keep my word. It was the least I could do. I opened the freezer and took out a package of chicken to defrost.

Had I really kicked over Roy's blocks because Mama wouldn't let me play with Delia? I didn't remember that part of the story, but years later that's what Mama had told me. "You had a real conniption fit," she had said in describing the scene. The only part of that first meeting that I could still remember clearly was the moment Delia landed in front of me off the tailgate of Daddy's truck, facing me toe-to-toe, arms akimbo, her head a carnival of colors, her lips parted in that gap-toothed, impish grin. I had been smitten—head over heels, falling down drunk infatuated—with that little chocolate girl who was the very same size as me.

I must have tried every ounce of Mama's patience those first few days, begging to see Delia again, refusing to take "No" for an answer. Another image came back to me—an afternoon in the back yard, Mama hanging wet clothes on the line.

* * *

I stay close to Mama for a while, handing her clothespins, but I soon get tired of that. I want to see Delia again, so I begin to see how far away I can get without Mama calling me back. I start tiptoeing quiet as a mouse toward the corncrib, but Mama's voice stops me. "Don't you go bothering them people. It's their house now. It ain't your playtoy no longer."

I freeze in my tracks, but just then a white sheet flaps into the air over the clothesline. Behind it I can see only Mama's legs and feet, which means that Mama can't see me. I chance a few more steps around the corner of the corncrib.

Champ, who has been dozing in the shade of the oak tree, suddenly jumps to his feet and races past me, hackles up, a growl rumbling in his throat.

I see Delia standing in the dirt lane in front of her house, wearing a red sweater that's too little for her over a thin dress that doesn't even cover her knees. Her bare legs and feet look cold in the March chill. I'm wearing a dress, too, but I have a corduroy jacket over it and socks and shoes to keep my toes warm. Delia is drawing in the sand with a long stick. Champ stops a few feet ahead of me, nose in the air, barking ferociously.

Delia, though, isn't afraid. When she sees me, she gives a wide smile and runs a few steps toward me.

I grab Champ by the scruff of the neck. "Stop it. That's just Delia. She lives there."

"Katherine Ann McCormick, what did I tell you?" Mama comes toward me, the threat of a persimmon branch switch in her voice, and I reluctantly turn and head back to the house, looking over my shoulder at Delia, who is still standing in the lane, moving the stick back and forth, making lines in the dirt.

"Come inside with me," Mama orders after she finishes hanging the clothes, scooping up Roy Jr. in one arm and motioning for me to follow. I know better than to push my luck, and so I try not to think about Delia, but the more I try not to, the more she's on my mind.

* * *

I sat at the kitchen table, sipping my diet soda and waiting for the microwave to beep. In the living room, Mama must have finished her phone conversation, for I heard the TV come back on. Another memory started to form, hazy at first. I searched further into the murky recesses of my mind.

* * *

I'm out back on the swing that Daddy hung for me from an oak tree branch. It's morning, almost noon, and Mama is in the kitchen. I have gotten the swing started all by myself and I'm keeping it going by "pumping," a new

18

trick Daddy has been trying to teach me for months. There's a crystal clear moment of exhilaration when I realize I've mastered the trick. "Look, Mama," I call through the open kitchen window. "Look at me!" I can hear the noise of the tractor somewhere in the distance, its motor getting louder as it comes toward me, then fading away as it turns and goes off in the opposite direction.

"That's great," Mama calls back. "I knew you could do it. Now run down to the gate and wave at Daddy next time he comes this way to let him know dinner's ready."

"Okay." I drag my feet to stop and head down the lane toward the gate that opens into the field. I like the important job of climbing up on the fence post beside the gate and waving both arms to let Daddy know it's dinnertime. As I trot off, Delia, for once, isn't even on my mind.

But as I get near Delia's house, Delia's head pops up in one of the front windows, and then her whole body appears in the open front door. "You want to play?" she asks me. "I got a doll."

Maggie comes up behind her. "Delia, get in here this minute."

"I got two dolls," I answer.

Before I can say any more, Maggie grabs Delia's arm, jerks her inside, and closes the door, but I can hear, through the open window, the scolding that Delia is getting. I feel my heart pounding inside me as I run the rest of the way to the gate, not looking behind me, and wait there for Daddy. When we pass Delia's house again, I don't see anybody, but the thrill of seeing Delia in that doorway stays with me for the rest of the day. Delia had talked to me, and I had answered her back.

* * *

I moved to the sink, looking out the back window at the spot where the swing had once hung. The thrill I'd felt at seeing Delia pop up so unexpectedly in that doorway still brought a tingle to my nerves. So many little snatches of time, moments that had no date or chronology, were coming back to me—things I hadn't thought about for decades. In spite of both our mothers' disapproval, Delia and I could not be kept apart. We were drawn to one another like moths to a flame. Whenever I was playing outside, my antennae were always alert for Delia, and Delia's for me. At some point—I had no idea how much time it had taken—Delia was slipping into my yard and we were playing together on the swing or building a playhouse at the edge of the woods, bringing our dolls outside and commiserating with one another, like we had heard the adults do, about the problems of tending babies.

Some rules, though, were strictly enforced. I was not to go into her house, and she was not, under any circumstances, to be invited into mine. "She's colored and you're white," Mama had kept reminding me, as if I couldn't see the difference.

There were also arguments at the supper table between my parents about my relationship with Delia, the same argument each time, always ending the same way.

* * *

"It ain't right." Daddy breaks off a piece of his biscuit and dips it into the puddle of cane syrup on his plate. "You're just asking for trouble, letting them play together. That little nigger's not old enough to know how to keep her place. Next thing you know she'll be in the house, sitting on the couch, thinking she's just as good as white folks."

"I talked to Katie about that." Mama gets up to pour more tea into Daddy's glass. "There's nobody else around for miles for her to play with. She gets so lonesome. Once she starts school, it'll be different. She'll get to know other little girls, but right now — "

* * *

Somehow, the arguments always ended with letting me continue to play with Delia, as long as I knew the rules and as long as I realized it was only temporary, only until I started school and made friends with some little white girls. Then Delia would be forgotten, discarded like a broken toy or an outgrown dress.

* * *

"And don't you let that little nigger girl boss you around," Daddy warns me. "You're the one who should be telling her what to do, not her telling you."

"I don't let her boss me." I stick out my chin and finish off the rest of my glass of milk.

* * *

The microwave buzzed, interrupting my thoughts. Of course, I hadn't admitted it to Daddy, but the truth was that Delia had always had the upper hand in all our games. I had been a follower, a pleaser, never one to rock the boat. That was why—

I resolutely shut out the image. I wasn't yet ready to dredge up the memory of that night in 1960, when I had failed Delia, my earliest childhood friend.

Chapter 4

Wednesday, July 12, 2006

The next morning, after helping Mama get a sponge bath and get dressed for the day in her last clean button-up shirt, I fixed breakfast for both of us and then washed the few dishes we'd used for our grits, eggs, and toast. Mama followed me around, putting things away with her one good arm, moving things around on the counters. "I feel so helpless," she said. "I'm not used to having somebody do for me."

"You go on and sit down," I answered. "Remember what the doctor said. You injure that shoulder again and you'll end up back in the hospital. You don't want that, do you?"

I was headed down the hall to gather up a load of laundry when the phone rang. Shiloh Methodist had activated its phone tree as soon as word got out about Mama's accident, and for the past week the phone had been ringing several times a day, everybody wanting to know how she was doing. I left Mama reciting all the details as I busied myself with starting the laundry, sweeping the kitchen floor, and then walking down to the garden to check for any vegetables that had ripened since yesterday.

When the mail came at ten o'clock, I welcomed the small diversion of walking outside to the mailbox and retrieving whatever letters and bills might have come. I felt cut off from the world up here, not being able to read my daily newspaper or check the Internet or even access my e-mail to see what was happening back at home. The only newspaper

Mama subscribed to was the *Pine Lake Gazette*, the local weekly, and she had no use whatsoever for one of those "new-fangled" computers.

"Is the *Gazette* there?" Mama asked when I came back inside.

"Right here." Leaving her reading the newspaper, I went onto the screened-in back porch, where one end had been enclosed to make a laundry room, and began folding clothes from the dryer. Through the screen I could see the lane that led past what had once been Delia's house. How many mornings had I raced down the back steps and across the yard, waiting and hoping for Delia to appear? When we were children, four and five years old, before Southern society imposed its rules on us, things had been so much simpler. Delia and I had created our own make-believe world that included just the two of us, had whispered secrets and giggled in childish conspiracy, delighted in one another's company. Each day had been an endless unreeling of new adventures. There had been the swing in the back yard and games of hide-and-seek and hopscotch and jump rope, but our primary preoccupation was our playhouses beneath the pine trees. We had built separate houses side by side, a fallen tree trunk forming the back boundary of both. Gathering up armfuls of pine straw, we had each lined off the other three walls, forming squares a few feet apart. Why two houses instead of one? Had we realized that we couldn't live together in the same house because of our color? Or was it simply that one house could have only one mother? I smiled at the memory, the crackly prickling of dry pine needles still ticklish against the insides of my arms after all these years.

Sometimes we would enlist Roy Jr. and Theo to be our children, but neither was very good at minding, so usually it was just the two of us and our dolls. After a few minutes of nighttime sleeping on their pine straw beds, the babies would wake simultaneously, and we would coo to them as we held them to our chests for their morning feeding. Then we would take turns "visiting" one another. I would walk over, knock in the air at the pretend door of Delia's house, and Delia would admit me and my baby, inviting me to sit on the fallen log, serving me pretend food and drink on the scraps of things we'd rescued from the trash—old lids from canning jars for plates, one coffee mug with its handle broken off, a syrup jug for a pitcher.

* * *

"How is Rebecca Jane this morning?" Delia uses her most elegant adult voice.

I lift Rebecca Jane to my shoulder and pat her on the back. "She's feeling better. She had a fever during the night. I need to go to the store and get some medicine. What about Nancy Jane?"

Delia unfolds the blanket from around Nancy Jane and cradles her in her lap. "She's sick, too. Let's go to the store and get some fever medicine."

* * *

Sometimes the babies were fine and happy, but usually it seemed they were sick or not sleeping or not eating. Had babies been that sickly back then? I had had the usual measles and mumps and chicken pox, along with the occasional cold, but I didn't remember my brothers or me being sick that much. Maybe pretend sickness created the drama that Delia and I felt we needed in our play and gave us the chance to tramp off to the pretend store somewhere down the lane.

Rebecca Jane, the first doll that I remembered having, had brown hair, like mine, that had matted, after years of play, into an unbrushable ugly lump, and bright blue eyes painted on her face. Her head and her arms and legs were hard rubber, but her body was made of huggable soft cloth. I can't remember now where the name Rebecca Jane had come from; had I named her that, or had that been Mama's suggestion?

Delia's doll, like mine, had a cloth body and a hard rubber head with painted-on facial features. Did it have rooted hair, or was the hair simply molded and painted on? I tried to bring up a mental picture, but I couldn't. It had definitely been a white doll, though, hadn't it? Did manufacturers make black baby dolls back then? The doll's name had been simply "Baby," until I persuaded Delia that she needed a more proper name.

* * *

"Nancy," I say. "You can name her Nancy."

"Nancy." Delia crinkles her forehead and nods in agreement. "Nancy Jane. Her and Rebecca Jane can be twins."

"They can't be twins," I counter. "Twins got to have the same mother. They got to be born together."

* * *

I carried the folded clothes inside. "Mama, you need anything?" I called as I walked past the living room.

"No, I'm fine. It's about time to start cooking dinner, though, isn't it? It's almost ten-thirty."

"We still have chicken and rice. I'll cook some beans from the garden and slice a tomato." I continued down the hall. For Mama and Daddy, dinner had always been the noon meal, the main meal of the day, and Mama always started planning it as soon as breakfast was finished. Me, I planned things I could throw together in an hour, tops.

I put away Mama's clothes and took my stack into my old bedroom, still thinking about Rebecca Jane. What had ever happened to her? There had been other dolls later, but none so loved or so tenderly cared for. I had probably worn her completely out with handling. Not like the new doll that never even got a name—the one with the blonde curls and organdy pinafore.

* * *

Christmas morning. A new doll is sitting under the tree, propped against a wrapped package. She's the most beautiful doll I've ever seen, with blonde curls, pink cheeks, and bright blue eyes. She is wearing a pink dress with puffy short sleeves and a full, gathered skirt. Over the dress is a white organdy pinafore with a sash that ties in back around her waist, like the picture in my book The Night Before Christmas. *I stand very still, simply gazing at her. She is too beautiful to believe.*

"Go ahead and pick her up," Mama says. "Santa picked her out just for you. He knew you would take good care of her."

I lift her very gently, both hands around her waist. Daddy is showing Roy Jr. his new dump truck, demonstrating how its bed can lift and dump things out.

"Look at her eyes," Mama says. "They can open and shut, just like yours."

I look. Instead of being painted on her face, her eyes are inset in sockets like real eyes, and they open when she's held upright and close when she's laid down to sleep. Fascinated, I move her up and down to watch them open and close.

"Careful," Daddy teases, looking up from his position on the floor by Roy Jr. "You'll wear her out the first day."

Roy Jr., who's already bored with his truck, tries to poke at her eyes with his fingers, and I hold her up high in the air away from him. "No. She's mine. Play with your own toys."

"Do you like her?" Mama asks.

I hug her tightly. "I love her. She's my favoritest doll ever."

"What are you going to name her?"

I hold the doll out at arm's length and look at her, thinking. Then it comes to me. "Delia Ann," I say. "Her name is Delia Ann."

Mama looks at Daddy, and he shakes his head, his festive Christmas mood suddenly turning sour.

"Um, Honey," Mama begins, "she doesn't really look like a Delia. Look at her yellow hair and her blue eyes. What about Linda? Or Susan. You know, I think she looks like a Susan. You could call her Suzie."

I see the wink she gives Daddy. "No." I hug the doll tightly against my chest. "Her name is Delia Ann."

Daddy stands then, his six-foot frame towering over me like a giant. His face goes dark and his eyes narrow. "No," he says. "You ain't naming no doll after a nigger!" He glares at Mama. "Now you see what I been telling you for months. This is what comes of letting her play with that little picaninny. I'm putting a stop to it, right now." He stomps outside onto the front porch.

I begin to cry.

"Here," Mama says, holding out her hands to take the doll. "Don't get Suzie all wet. It's okay." She pulls me down onto the sofa beside her, one arm around me, the other hand holding the doll. "Suzie is a nice name. Don't you think so, Suzie?" She moves the doll back and forth to look as if Suzie is nodding her head "yes."

"Suzie's lonely," Mama keeps saying the rest of that long, long day, picking up the doll and making a sad face. "She wants someone to play with her."

* * *

I put my clothes into my dresser drawers and then checked all the recesses of my old closet, but it was empty except for a few boxes of things that Mama had packed away. After college, when I'd moved away from home for good, I had cleaned out my room, taking everything that I wanted, and giving Mama permission to dispose of anything I'd left.

Had I ever played with that blonde doll? I couldn't remember. Certainly, she had never become the beloved baby that Rebecca Jane had been. Too nice to take outside and put on a bed of pine straw, she was soon relegated to a shelf, and I had never called her Suzie or any other name. Daddy wouldn't let me play with Delia for a long time after that, but finally, when my tears or Mama's coaxing, or probably a combination of the two, made him relent and we were permitted to see each other again, we had a special ceremony declaring Rebecca Jane and Nancy Jane twins for life, even though they had different mothers.

* * *

"They got separated at the hospital," I tell Delia. "But now they've found each other, and they'll never be apart again, ever."

"Yes," Delia agrees. "Nothing will ever separate them again." She holds Nancy Jane's arms out so that they hug Rebecca Jane.

"Never, never, never," I insist as I make Rebecca Jane return the hug, the two dolls face- to-face, hanging onto one another as if they are two halves of the same whole.

Chapter 5

That afternoon I wandered around the house, searching for something to occupy my mind. Mama had tuned in to her afternoon soaps, and in the week I'd already been here I'd read every magazine I could find around the house. The 6:30 evening news kept me aware of what was happening nationally, at least, but the local news was all about Tallahassee politics and social events, along with news about hog prices and corn production. I'd have to remember to ask Russell to save all the old copies of *Florida Today* and bring them the next time he came up so I could catch up on my hometown news from Titusville and Brevard County.

I picked up the local *Pine Lake Gazette* that had come that morning and flipped through it, but I had lived away from this area for so long that none of the names were familiar to me. I was about to put it aside when a photograph caught my eye. Below the photo in big black letters was printed, "Re-elect Mayor Lonnie P. Ramsey." Had I known that Lonnie P. was now the mayor of Pine Lake? Mama must have told me about it at some point, but if so, it hadn't made it into my long-term memory bank. I'd known the Ramseys all my life. They had a farm a few miles away, and Lonnie P.'s parents and mine had been friends. Lonnie P. had been two years ahead of me in school, so I had never been more than a blip on his radar screen, but I remembered him well. In high school everybody knew Lonnie P. Ramsey, one of the star players for the football team.

I studied the photo. In spite of the thinning hair, now smattered with gray, and the added weight—the fleshy jowls and double chin above the thick football-player neck—he was still recognizable as the Lonnie P. I remembered. Still unchanged were the bright blue eyes, smaller now in the doughy face, and the broad, "Like me!" politician's smile—the same smile that he'd used as a teenager whenever he wanted something from somebody, the smile that had charmed even the teachers into buying into his excuses. I scanned the information in the ad: married, two children, three grandchildren; businessman, mayor for the last four years, member of the Chamber of Commerce, the Elks' Club, chairman of the board for Pine Lake Academy, deacon at Hopewell Baptist Church.

I waited for a commercial. "Mama?"

Mama turned away from the TV.

"I didn't realize that Lonnie P. Ramsey was Pine Lake's mayor. I see he's running for re-election."

"Sure is," Mama said. "Who would have thought little Lonnie P. would be running Pine Lake? He come up hard, and now look at him. Goodness knows, his daddy never had two nickels to rub together, and his mama was always a little sickly after them twins was born—Jolene and Florene. She was Thelma Soames before she married Lonnie Ramsey, you know. All them Soames people was like that, with weak hearts." I studied the photo again while Mama continued talking. The P., I remembered, was for Patrick. He was a junior, the only boy in the family, so his parents had started calling him Lonnie P., to distinguish him from his father, Lonnie Senior.

Mama was still talking. "Lonnie P. married that Harris girl from town—Sherri Lynn. You remember her."

"Vaguely," I answered. "She was a year ahead of me."

"Jolene married one of the Hines boys from the south part of the county, and —"

I stopped listening. I knew Mama, once she got going, would recount the entire family history, going back several generations. The last time I'd seen Lonnie P. had to have been high school or a little after. At eighteen he had been at the top of his form—the football star who owned the halls and the "in" table in the cafeteria—the popular, charming ladies' man who had girls fighting for his attention, the loud, brash, utterly self-confident leader who had shown political promise even back then. And the one thing I couldn't forget—the one image that was burned into my mind forever—I was positive that he had also been the leader of the group of boys I had overheard in the movie theater lobby saying they were going to teach "that stuck-up nigger bitch" a lesson. The others I hadn't recognized, for I hadn't seen any of their faces, but I was sure of Lonnie P. because of the all-too-familiar swagger in his voice.

So now he was the mayor of Pine Lake, apparently quite the town leader. I wondered if he had changed any, or if he was still the Lonnie P. from high school, boastful and bigoted and obnoxious. I closed the paper and laid it down. Mama was still talking. "Florene married the Curtis boy. What was his name? Leon and Mavis's boy? You remember Mavis. She used to be a Johnson before she married a Curtis. I went to school with Mavis's sister Ruby."

I nodded and grunted "Um-m" every so often as Mama continued her litany of genealogies, but my mind was still back on that night. I didn't know the identities of the other boys, had never wanted to know. I'd always been afraid to probe my memory too deeply— afraid such probing might dredge up their names or faces. For years afterward I had even convinced myself that I hadn't recognized the voice of the leader, for not knowing any of their identities had justified my silence, but now it hit me hard with certainty that one of the voices I had heard that night—the voice that was egging on the other boys to act—belonged to none other than Lonnie P. Ramsey.

I stood and stretched, forcing the memory from my mind. "I'm going to get some more iced tea," I said to Mama. "You want anything?"

"No. I'm fine." Mama leaned back in her recliner. "I think I'll just rest my eyes for a little while."

In the kitchen, I refilled my glass of iced tea and reached for a cookie from the package on the counter. Being here again made me long for one of the big, thick sugar cookies that Mama used to bake—their centers soft and chewy as they came warm from the oven. I used to bake them myself for Erin and Travis when they were young, but with them grown now and on their own, I hadn't baked any for years. I stood looking out the window into the back yard.

* * *

Delia and I are at the swing. I'm twisting Delia around in a circle as tightly as I can so that when I let go, the swing will unwind so fast that Delia will get dizzy, and when she tries to stand, she'll stagger drunkenly across the yard and collapse in giggles on the new spring grass. The smell of homemade cookies drifts toward us, and I sniff the air in anticipation.

"They're ready." Mama steps onto the back porch, wiping her hands on her apron. "Wash your hands first, though."

I turn the swing loose and run toward the outside spigot, leaving Delia spinning. Inside, I take the plate on which Mama has placed four warm cookies — two for each of us — while Mama pours milk into the same two glasses that she uses each time, one with yellow and red stripes for me and the old plain one with the chip on its rim that is always reserved for Delia, the one that nobody in my family ever uses. Delia, of course, isn't allowed in the kitchen, but she can sit beside me on the back porch steps while we eat our midmorning snack.

I carefully carry out the plate of cookies while Mama follows with the two glasses of milk. "Don't spill it," she warns before going back in the kitchen, and Delia and I roll our eyes at each other. We're both nearly six now, too old to spill milk. Roy Jr. is only three-and-a-half, and he has to sit at the table under Mama's watchful eye while he holds his glass with both hands, tipping it up carefully to his mouth.

What Mama and Daddy don't know is that I've been inside Delia's kitchen, several times now. It wasn't like I'd planned on going inside, but one morning a few weeks ago, we were playing out under the pine trees with our dolls when Delia's mama called to tell us she had fresh-baked cookies. As she was bringing them out to us, a sudden gust of wind blew through the pines, and raindrops began to spatter the ground. Since Daddy still hadn't built any porches on Delia's house to shelter us from the drizzle, Maggie insisted that I come inside where it was dry and warm. I looked around to see if anybody was watching, but I didn't see anyone and didn't hear Mama calling for me, so I followed Delia inside, into a warm, dim, cozy kitchen where the smell of cookies baking in the oven overpowered any other odor and made me forget my fears.

Maggie poured us each a glass of milk, putting the glasses side by side on the oilcloth-covered kitchen table. Nothing unusual happened — by the time we finished our snack the rain was gone and the sun was shining again — and since neither Mama nor Daddy had said anything lately to warn me away from Delia, that little shower seemed to have broken something loose, to have relaxed the rules I'd always lived by. And so the next time Maggie baked cookies, I had naturally trooped with Delia into that warm, delicious-smelling kitchen — the two of us sitting side by side on the handmade bench at one side of the table with Theo and Jerome across from us, all of us eating the warm cookies fresh from the oven, swinging our legs and jabbering away.

The most glorious thing I've learned from being inside Delia's house, though, is that as Maggie works in the kitchen, she hums old spirituals, some of them the same ones I know from church but some different ones, too, and sometimes she bursts into a cascade of song that washes over me like a wave and sweeps me up in a happiness that makes me tingle all over. My favorite song of Maggie's is "Swing Low, Sweet Chariot," and sometimes when I'm alone, when no one is listening, I sing it under my breath, trying to capture Maggie's pronunciation and intonations.

* * *

In the living room, the TV was still on, but Mama's eyes were closed. The cordless phone was in her lap. I had promised to call Delia and make plans for getting together. Maybe one day next week I could meet her at a restaurant in town during her lunch break. Mama would be fine at home by herself for a couple of hours and would probably be glad to have her house all to herself for a while. Or she could go with me. It would be good for her to get out of the house, too, and be in someone else's company besides mine. But would Mama sit down at a restaurant table with me and Delia? Even though times had changed, and Mama felt comfortable enough talking to a black person on the street or in a store, I was pretty sure that in all her eighty-four years, Mama had never sat down to a meal with an African American.

I remembered an essay I had read in college, back in the sixties, by a man named Harry Golden. It was called something like "The Vertical

Negro," and its argument had stuck with me through the years because it was so true. The gist of the article was that white Southerners had no problem interacting with Negroes as long as both races were vertical. They could talk to one another on the street, work together in the fields, shop in the same stores, and share the same sidewalks. But when it came to sitting down—on a bus, at a movie theater, at a lunch counter, in a doctor's office—it was an entirely different story. The author concluded that the problem of integration could be easily solved if everything were done standing up. Remove the chairs from waiting rooms, the desks from schools, the stools from lunch counters, the seats from buses, and all the opposition to segregation would disappear. I chuckled again at the cleverness of the argument and reminded myself to check on the Internet when I got home and see if I could find a copy of it after all these years.

If Mama did consent to sitting down with Delia at a restaurant, how uncomfortable would it make her feel? Mama had always prided herself on her kindness to "the coloreds," as she called them, but for Mama, kindness was most certainly not the same thing as equality. To Maggie and Silas, Mama had always been "Miss Julia," the words uttered with bowed head, ready to take an order or a scolding, and I was sure both still called her "Miss Julia" to this day, at least to her face.

And I couldn't really expect Mama to be any different from what she was. She was a product of her time and place and upbringing, just as I had been. For the older generation, segregation had been so drilled into their brains that any other way of interacting was unthinkable.

* * *

It's summer, a Saturday afternoon. Daddy pushes back his dinner plate. "Hon," he says to Mama, "can you take Maggie into town for groceries? Me and Silas have to finish topping the tobacco." He fishes the truck keys out of his pocket and lays them on the table.

I'm bouncing with excitement. Usually we all go to town on Saturdays — Roy Jr. and me squeezed into the cab of the truck between Mama and Daddy, Silas and Maggie and the children in the back — but sometimes when Daddy and Silas are too busy with work, Mama drives us. Silas doesn't have his own truck yet, but he's saving up his money to buy one.

34

After the dishes are finished and Mama is finally ready to go, I claim the window seat, putting Roy Jr. in the middle. Mama drives down the lane and beeps her horn to let Maggie know we're here. Maggie's stomach is getting bigger every day, and I ask Mama why Maggie is getting so fat, but Mama doesn't answer. She just shushes me and tells me not to ask so many questions. Maggie puffs a little as she climbs into the back of the truck and settles herself on the floor behind the cab, pulling Jerome into her lap and Theo down beside her. Delia is dancing around the bed of the truck, refusing to sit down.

"This truck ain't moving till everybody sits," Mama says in a stern voice, frowning at Delia's antics. Maggie grabs Delia's arm and pulls her down.

As the truck crawls along the dirt road toward the highway, I hear a tapping on the glass behind me, and I turn to see Delia — not standing but up on her knees so that her head is even with the glass — her mouth curved in a wide smile, the gap between her two front teeth giving her a jack-o-lantern grin. I tap back.

"What's that noise?" Mama turns to look, catching Delia in the act of rapping again. "Ignore her," she tells me. "Face front and don't even look in her direction. Don't encourage such behavior."

I face front, but as soon as Mama turns her attention back to the road, I peek back at Delia, who now has both palms spread flat on the window glass. When Delia sees me looking, she sticks out her tongue and widens her eyes, and I have to stifle a laugh.

"Face front!" Mama warns again, and I reluctantly turn away.

Inside the Piggly Wiggly store, I have strict orders to stay with Mama and Roy Jr. and not even to let on that I know Delia. No silly faces or giggling or talking or goofing off of any kind. Maggie always hangs back and waits until Mama has pushed her buggy halfway down the first aisle before beginning her own shopping, and once we move on to the second aisle, we aren't likely to see Maggie again until we've paid for our groceries and Mama has loaded them into the bed of the truck. Roy Jr. and I are always safely seated with Mama in the cab before Maggie comes out with her buggy and loads her own groceries and children into the back for the ride home.

Today, though, Mama forgets the corn meal and sends me back an aisle to get it. Proud to be given such a grown-up task, I keep my eyes on the shelves, searching for the familiar white package with the partially husked ear of corn on the front, so concentrated on my search that I'm not paying attention to what's in front of me. Suddenly I find myself head-to-head with Delia, who has raced down the aisle toward me. To prevent bumping foreheads, I automatically put both hands in front of me and Delia does the same, resulting in the two of us smacking palms. The loud, sucking pop causes both of us to giggle, and Delia is about to say something to me when Maggie grabs her arm and pulls her roughly away from me, half-dragging her down the aisle and hissing under her breath like a stirred-up rattlesnake.

I've never seen Maggie this angry or this rough with Delia before, and I step back and beat a hasty retreat around the end of the aisle, back to Mama and Roy Jr.

"Where's the corn meal?" Mama asks me, and I hang my head. "I couldn't find it." Telling a fib is better than trying to explain how I'd just watched quiet, humble Maggie transform into a frightening stranger that I didn't know.

* * *

I quietly pushed open the front door and took my glass of tea to the front porch swing. From the beginning of my friendship with Delia, Daddy had constantly warned me that playing with "a little nigger girl" just wasn't right, and he had threatened almost daily to put an end to it soon, but, as a child, I had never understood his reasons. That day in the grocery store, though, when I had slunk back to Mama in shame, terrified that I had been at fault for something that I could not give a name to, some sin that was too horrible to mention, I'd had my first dawning awareness that the disapproval of my friendship with Delia went much deeper than Daddy's personal aversion to it. By age six, before I'd even started school, I had been thoroughly indoctrinated into white Southern society, and the lesson of that day remained with me all too well, a lesson that more than half a century later I was still trying to forget.

Chapter 6

I checked the time on my watch. Almost four. Delia wasn't likely to be home from work yet. I was looking forward to renewing our friendship, but, at the same time, I dreaded the encounter, my stomach clenching at the thought of confessing to Delia my terrible complicity in whatever had happened to her on that long-ago evening.

Of course, I could continue to leave the secret buried, as I'd been doing for forty-six years, but not telling would be a second betrayal, worse than the first, because I no longer had the excuse of youth or cultural pressure to conform. As children we had whispered secrets and collapsed in giggles over the silliest and slightest of confidences. When had that begun to change? The incident at Piggly Wiggly was a beginning, but the real demarcation point could be traced to the day we both started school, when my circle of friends opened up to include other little white girls like myself, girls who could come into my house and play with my toys, girls whose presence did not cause Daddy to glower at me and lecture me about the inappropriateness of our friendship. The summer of 1950 was our last real season of innocence, both for me and for Delia. School changed everything.

* * *

I'm six, finally, and ready for school. It's the middle of summer and I've been six since April 22, one month longer than Delia, who didn't turn six until May 19. Still, school seems an impossibly long time away. For weeks Delia and I have been preparing ourselves for first grade. Both of us can write our names in the sand with sticks; we have contests to see which of us can count the highest or say our ABCs all the way through; we talk endlessly to one another about what school will be like.

"How much longer?" I ask Mama that question every morning, trying to count the days on my fingers, keeping track to make sure Mama's answer is getting lower each day. I'm excited about school, but I'm also a little bit frightened about this new adventure. School is an unknown that I don't yet have any rules for. Mama and Daddy keep saying there will be lots of little girls in my class that will become my new friends, but I don't know any of them. I do know Delia. I wish Delia and I could go to school together. We would be best friends, would sit beside one another in class and play together at recess.

But Mama and Daddy say that Delia will be going to a different school, the school for nigger children. Niggers aren't allowed to sit in the same room as white children or to eat at the same table; they can't use the same bathrooms or drink from the same water fountains.

"Why not?" I want to know, but the only answer I get from Mama and Daddy is that's just the way it is. Niggers are different from white people, they say. They're not as clean, for one thing. And they don't want to associate with white people, just like white people don't want to associate with them except when they have to for work and things like that.

"Niggers have their own schools and their own churches," Daddy says. "They keep with their kind and we keep with ours. And remember what I told you: when you start school, this playing with Delia comes to an end, pure and simple. Them other little girls at school will make fun of you if they know you've been hanging around with a little nigger."

My eyes brim with tears, but I run away so Daddy can't see me crying. I want to go to school, but not if it means losing Delia. The trade-off doesn't seem fair to me, but Daddy's word is law in our house, especially when his face turns all splotchedy red like it's on fire and his voice hisses at me like cold water spitting on flames. When he gets that way, even Mama can't coax him into changing his mind.

In every minute that Mama can spare from the cooking and cleaning and the farm chores, she's been making five new school dresses for me, one for each day of the week. I picked out the prints I wanted from the cotton feed sacks that Daddy brings home every week full of chickenfeed and stacks in the crib.

Four new dresses are hanging in my room behind the curtain that Mama strung across one corner to make me a closet, and Mama is still working on the fifth one. She used the same dress pattern for all of them, but she changed the neckline and sleeves and used different trim and buttons for each one so that they don't all look alike. Every day I go to the corner and stand on my three-legged stool and tip the hangers off the rod that she made with an old broomstick, then hold the dresses up in front of me, admiring myself in the mirror. My favorite is a print of tiny yellow and purple flowers, its collar, sleeves, and hemline trimmed with yellow rickrack.

"Make one like this for Delia, too," I beg Mama, holding up the yellow and purple-flowered one, but Mama shakes her head.

"Matching dresses are only for twins. Or sisters, at the very least. Maybe I could make Delia a dress out of some of these old sacks I'm not going to use, though." Mama holds up a piece of cloth splashed with huge red and orange blooms. "Maggie probably never operated a sewing machine in her life, much less owned one, so I don't know what Delia will do for school clothes. And she's too close to your size for me to pass on your hand-me-downs." Mama smiles one of her Sunday shake-hands-with-the-preacher smiles. "You know, I will make Delia a dress. Remember, it's a surprise, though. Don't tell her."

The secret of the new dress is too delicious for me to keep to myself. "You have to act surprised," I tell Delia sternly as the two of us play hopscotch in the back yard. "Remember."

"Like this?" Delia stretches her eyebrows and eyelids up as high as they will go, opens her mouth in a perfect "O" of astonishment, and claps both hands against her cheeks.

I nod approvingly. "Just like that." Mama will never know that I told.

On the first day of school, I put on the favorite of all my new dresses, squirming with excitement as Mama carefully ties the sash and fusses with my hair.

"Me and Roy Jr. will walk you down to the road," Mama says, but I raise one hand. "You stay here." I make them wait at the front steps, secretly confident that Mama and Daddy are wrong about Delia going to a different school, certain in my mind that Delia will come skipping down the lane at any minute and get on the bus with me.

As I wait by the mailbox, I keep glancing anxiously toward Delia's house, as if by sheer will I can make Delia appear, but a few minutes later, when the school bus rounds the curve and rumbles to a stop, the lane is still empty and silent — no sign of Delia anywhere. The bus driver cranks the heavy door open right in front of me and booms a loud "Good morning!" and panic spreads through my body like cement, every part of me growing as tight and heavy as if all my muscles have turned to stone. I can't move; no part of my body will work — not my feet or my hands or my voice. Where is Delia? I want to go to school with Delia.

* * *

I stood and walked across the porch to the front door. It was strange that I had no memory of what happened next. Had the bus driver stepped down and guided me into a seat? Or had Mama run down the driveway to my rescue? My memory contained only that small fragment — that moment of sheer panic when the bus door swung open and Delia wasn't there.

Mama wasn't in the living room or kitchen. "Mama," I called down the hall. "You need something?"

"No. Go on with whatever you're doing. Don't mind me." Mama came out of her bedroom and disappeared into the bathroom, closing the door behind her.

"Call me if you need any help." The week after Mama's fall I'd gone into town and bought her some loose-fitting button-up shirts and some elastic-waist knit pants that she could get up and down with one hand, but sometimes she needed help getting them straight.

"I'm fine," Mama called back, so I stood in the hall, a few feet away from the door, waiting for her to emerge.

After she had remained in the bathroom a little longer than seemed appropriate to me, I knocked on the door. "Everything okay?"

My hand was still in mid-air when I heard a flush. I waited another minute and then cracked open the door. "You okay?" I asked. "You need any help?"

"No. I told you I'm fine. Just give me time, that's all. This hovering makes me nervous."

"Sorry." I closed the door and went back to the living room to wait, knowing how hard it was for Mama to admit to any loss of independence. I'd be the same way, I knew, if I were in her shoes. "What do you want for supper?" I asked.

Mama walked to the front window and looked outside. "Don't go to any trouble for me. I never eat much at night. Lots of times, since Daddy's been gone, I'll just fix myself a bowl of cereal or scramble me an egg for supper. One night Neil came by to see if he could borrow a car jack and caught me eating toast and egg and he told everybody in the county that I must be getting that Alzheimer's disease because I was eating breakfast at night." She laughed. "You know how Neil always was one for all kinds of foolishness. I still ain't lived that one down."

I didn't answer. Mama had told me that story about Uncle Neil at least a dozen times, at least once already on this most recent visit. I wondered if her short-term memory was really that bad, or if she just enjoyed telling the story so much that she assumed everybody wanted to hear it again and again. Or was telling that story on herself her way of apologizing for snapping at me earlier in the hallway?

As I headed for the kitchen to see what I could fix for supper, I was reminded of my earlier intention to call Delia. What would we talk about if we did get together? How comfortable would such an encounter be? For both of us, starting school had been the beginning of the end of our friendship, the gulf that had begun that August morning growing wider and wider until we became two strangers, eying one another with curiosity but occupying two completely different worlds.

* * *

"Harvey, go straighten your chair," Miss Hendricks admonishes. "And Quentin, pick up that pencil you knocked off Mary Jane's desk. You two will be at the end of the line today."

It's lunchtime, and the boys always get in such a mad rush to be first to the door that they run into one another or knock over their chairs and hold up the rest of the class. Miss Hendrick's rule is that nobody can leave until the room is set to rights.

41

I get in line between Louise and Gail. Harvey, in particular, is always misbehaving. As Quentin bends to pick up the pencil, Harvey shoves him in the back with the palm of one hand, sending him crashing into a chair.

"Hey!" Quentin stumbles to his feet and goes after Harvey, fists swinging.

"Stop it, both of you!" Miss Hendricks grabs one boy in each hand, holding them apart.

"He pushed me!" Quentin's lower lip juts out, his eyes glistening with tears beneath his uncombed mop of dirty-blonde hair.

"Harvey, you tell Quentin you're sorry for pushing him. That wasn't nice. I want you to shake his hand and apologize."

Harvey turns his head to flash a smile toward the other boys already in line. "I ain't touching his hand. He plays with niggers."

"Do not." Quentin's chin is quivering.

"Do so. Everybody knows it." He begins a singsong chant. "Quentin plays with niggers; Quentin plays with niggers."

Some of the other boys snicker, and Quentin's face turns a fierce red. I hang my head, eyes on the floor. What if Harvey (or someone else) knew that I had played with Delia? What if that person tattled on me? The room is growing hot. I need some air.

"That's enough!" Miss Hendricks releases Quentin and clasps both hands around Harvey's upper arms, turning him to face her. "I do not want to hear that word in my classroom ever again, you hear?"

What word? Had Harvey said a bad word? I had not heard him use a swear word, but maybe he uttered it under his breath. Miss Hendricks steers Harvey to the end of the line and then takes Quentin's hand and walks him to the door where she puts him at the front. Miss Hendricks is the only person in the classroom who is nice to Quentin. None of the other boys ever want to play with him at recess or sit beside him in the classroom. I had thought it was because his clothes are always dirty and he has a bad smell, but maybe it's because he plays with niggers. If the other girls knew I used to play with Delia, would they all avoid me like the boys avoid Quentin? I cringe and hang my head, and by the time Miss Hendricks finally opens the door and allows us to breathe some fresh outdoor air, I have firmly resolved in my mind that I will *never again play with Delia, not even if Delia begs and begs me. Nobody will ever catch me playing with a little nigger, never again.*

* * *

As I took a package of ground beef from the freezer and put it in the microwave to defrost, the thought hit me that the word Miss Hendricks had objected to was "nigger." Was this the first time in my life I had realized what she'd meant? Was Miss Hendricks somehow more enlightened than the other adults in the community? She had been young, just out of college, and had come to the community from somewhere else. I didn't know or recall where, but she wasn't a native of the area like the other teachers at the school, many of whom had taught Mama and Daddy when they were little. She had stayed only a year and then moved on, probably to some more progressive town without such a closed population, someplace where old habits and attitudes didn't get passed along so unrelentingly from one generation to the next.

I picked up the phone book, but I had no idea what Delia's last name was now. Mama had said she was living with a man, but they weren't married. But she had been married at one time, hadn't she? I was sure she had. I carried the book to the living room.

"Mama, do you know what Delia's last name is?"

Mama was still standing by the window. All this forced idleness was getting to her. Not being able to use her right arm meant that she couldn't do even simple household tasks such as sweeping the floor or folding clothes. She was getting better at using a fork and spoon with her left hand, but I had had to write and sign checks for her to pay her bills.

"Delia's last name? No. I don't know. Why?"

"She said yesterday to give her a call. I was thinking we could get together sometime, maybe over lunch."

"Lunch? You mean here?" Mama's eyebrows shot up. "I don't think—"

"No, not here. I thought maybe one day next week I could meet Delia at a restaurant in town during her lunch break from work. Or we could both go. It'd be something to do and would get us out of the house for a change of scenery. We could go to that barbeque place out by Winn-Dixie. You like barbeque."

Mama looked alarmed. "I don't know. I can't handle a fork that good with my left hand, and to go in a restaurant . . . Well, I don't think so." She pressed her lips together and shook her head.

"You could order a sandwich and French fries, and you wouldn't have to worry about it."

"I don't think so. You two go on and have lunch and visit all you want, and I'll stay home and eat something here."

I knew that what Mama really meant was that she wouldn't be comfortable sitting at the same table as Delia, but I didn't argue the point. The days of my teenage outrage at my parents' views on civil rights were best left buried in the past. For Mama and her generation, it was almost as if the last fifty years of progress had never happened.

"How can I call her if I don't know her last name?"

"Maggie's in the phone book. You could ask her."

I found the number for Silas Adkins and lifted the receiver.

"Hello?" The voice that answered was hoarse and wavery with age. How many decades had gone by since I had last seen and spoken to Maggie? Far too many.

"Maggie? It's Katie McCormick. I'm at my mother's. I guess you heard about her fall."

"Law sakes! I didn't know who that be calling me." Maggie's voice sounded younger now, higher pitched. "Delia told me she done seen you in town. How is your mama doing?"

"She's doing great. Better every day." Maggie and I talked for a while, exchanging news about Mama's and Silas's condition, and it was several minutes before I asked how I could get in touch with Delia.

"She be listed in the phone book as Delia Carmichael. That be her first husband, you know, the one that got killed. She took that name back after that second one ran off and left her. Her children all be Carmichaels, so I guess she wanted her name to match theirs. Sam adopted the first one, you know, so he be a Carmichael, too, just like the others." Maggie gave a little laugh of exasperation. "This latest man she ain't married to, but he treats her good, lots better than that Bo Thompson anyway."

"Thanks, Maggie. I'll give her a call. It was good talking to you, and I promise to get by to see you one day soon when Mama's better."

I opened the phone book again, turning to the C's. Delia's first husband had been killed? How? Had Mama told me about that? I did remember vaguely something about Delia having a child when she got married and how her husband treated it as if it was one of his own, a testament to his good nature and to Delia's good luck in finding somebody like that, after all she had been through. I hadn't really known what Mama had meant by "all Delia had been through," and I hadn't wanted to ask, too afraid of the answer I might get.

Delia answered on the second ring.

"Hello, Delia? It's Kate Riley, used to be Katie McCormick."

There was a slight pause on the other end while Delia processed the information; then Delia's voice, "Katie McCormick! Oh, my stars. It's good to hear from you."

"You said to give you a call. I didn't know your last name, so I called your mother to find out how to get hold of you."

"Wasn't that something—us running into each other at the bank like that after all these years? How you been doing?"

"Just fine. How about yourself?" We talked for a minute before I suggested getting together one day soon for lunch.

"M-m-m, that sounds good. You know I always did like to eat. It shows, too, don't it?" I could hear Delia's hearty laugh through the phone line. "I don't know how you managed to stay so skinny. You just say when and where."

"One day next week? Any day is good for me. Mama will be happy to have me out of her hair for a couple of hours, I'm sure."

"What about next Wednesday?" Delia asked. "I work half-days on Wednesdays. That way we can take our sweet old time eating and talking. I want to hear about everything you've been doing since you flew the coop and got out of this place."

"You moved away before I did," I reminded her.

"That I did," Delia agreed. "Law, I couldn't wait to be somewhere else, be somebody else, where folks didn't know me. I was going to invent a new me—be somebody, for sure."

"Did it work?"

Delia laughed. "It worked 'bout as well as a cow trying to grow wings and fly."

I laughed with her. "We never leave our childhoods behind, do we?"

We agreed to meet at the barbeque restaurant at noon on Wednesday and then talked for a few more minutes before saying goodbye. Good, comfortable talk. Like slipping off my high heels when I got home from work and leaning back in the recliner, stretching my toes and letting my calves relax against the leg rest. That kind of comfortable. Perhaps telling Delia my secret wouldn't be as bad as I'd been building it up to be. On the other hand, Delia's unfeigned delight in getting together and reminiscing about old times made me feel guiltier than ever; how could I spoil our reunion with news of my betrayal?

Chapter 7

Friday, July 14—Saturday, July 15, 2006

On Friday morning, I tried to get Mama to go to the grocery store with me and help with the weekly shopping, but she shooed me off to go by myself. "Buy whatever you want to cook," she said. "I'll eat whatever you fix."

So I headed into town alone, giving Mama strict instructions not to try to do any work while I was gone. Roy and Margaret were coming on Saturday, and Russell was driving up for the weekend, so I needed to stock up on provisions.

I was in Winn Dixie's produce section when I heard someone call my name.

"Kate? Is that you?"

I looked up to see Gail Nesbitt coming toward me—Gail Proctor she was now; had been since three weeks after high school graduation when I'd stood beside her as her maid of honor, holding the bridal bouquet while she and Gary Proctor exchanged wedding vows, for better or for worse, till death did them part. I'd known Gail since first grade.

I extended my arms for a hug. "Gail, how are you? You're looking good." I hadn't seen Gail since our fortieth high school class reunion a few years before, but we had been keeping in touch through the years by Christmas cards and, more recently, by e-mail.

"You, too." Gail returned my hug. "What are you doing here?"

I explained the situation that had brought me home. "I'll be here for another month, at least. I've been meaning to call you, but things have been busy. We'll have to get together for a long visit when Mama's better. How are things with you?"

"Great. Can you believe I have a granddaughter graduating from high school this year?" Gail pulled out her wallet and showed me her entire spread of photos—eight grandkids in all. I admired the pictures and then pulled out my own photos. "My daughter Erin has two now, a boy and a girl—six and four. Travis is still a bachelor, but he'll turn thirty this year, so I keep telling him it's time to settle down." I moved my cart out of the pathway, angling it into the space between the bin of yellow onions and a cardboard cutout of somebody wearing a NASCAR racing uniform. Gail did not have a cart or even a basket.

"I don't want to keep you," she said. "You go ahead and do your shopping. I just came in for some steaks. The church building committee is meeting tonight, and Gary had the bright idea to hold the meeting at our house and invite everybody to come for supper beforehand."

"Ouch. He should do the cooking then." I tore a plastic bag off the roll and pulled it open.

"Oh, he will. I bought him a new gas grill for his birthday, and he keeps creating occasions to use it." Gail chirped with excitement. "Don't you want to know what the meeting is about?"

"Sure." I dropped an onion into the bag. "Something important?"

"We're building a new sanctuary. Can you believe it?"

"Really? That's nice." Gail was a member at Hopewell Baptist; we had always attended Shiloh Methodist, where Mama was still a faithful member.

"We've outgrown the old building," Gail continued, "and it's getting in such bad shape anyway. A few months ago, we started a building fund, and Gary's on the building committee. Lonnie P. is chairing it. He's the one who made it all possible to begin with."

"Lonnie P. Ramsey?" Here was that name again, as if Lonnie P. himself were following me around, whispering in my ear, not letting me forget the most horrible night of my life.

48

"Yes. He's been so good for this town. Just think, he started off on a tobacco farm, same as you and me, and now he owns about half this county, seems like. If it hadn't been for him, we'd have never gotten off the ground with a new building. He started the fund with a check for fifty thousand dollars and said if anybody in church gave more, he'd match him, dollar for dollar."

"Fifty thousand? Wow. That's a lot of money."

"And that's not all he's done. He's very involved in community affairs. Anytime there's a fund drive for something, he's right there heading it up. The new addition to the hospital—I'm sure you know about that, right? He contributed most of the money for the new wing."

"Is that so? He must have done all right for himself over the years." How had Lonnie P. become so wealthy that he could be giving away that kind of money? I added another onion to my bag and knotted the top.

"Well, I gotta run." Gail took a couple of steps forward. "It was good seeing you. Tell your mother I wish her a speedy recovery. And give me a call soon. We'll have to get together for a long chat."

"I'll do that. And say 'Hi' to Gary for me." I raised one hand in farewell as Gail hurried away. Apparently Lonnie P. was now the exemplar of self-made success, the hometown boy who stayed home and helped out his own community, unlike those who forgot their roots once they moved off to the big city to make their fortunes. But his beneficence to Pine Lake didn't seem to square with my high school memories of him, especially the voice that kept echoing in my head, the voice in the movie theater lobby egging the other boys on to teach that "nigger bitch" a lesson. Which one was the real Lonnie P.?

On Saturday Roy and Margaret arrived first, around ten-thirty. Roy had spent two whole days building the wooden ramp up to the porch, but this was Margaret's first visit since Mama's fall.

"How's the shoulder feeling?" Roy asked. "Them pain pills working?"

"Lots better. The swelling's gone," Mama said. "I'm still not supposed to move it, but I go back to the doctor in two weeks, and I'm hoping he'll say I can take off this sling. I ain't used to letting somebody wait on me hand and foot."

"It's okay, Mama." I put one hand on her good shoulder. "You spent plenty of years doing for us, and now it's our turn to do for you."

Roy nodded. "You listen to the doctor, and do what he says. And you need anything, just let me know, okay?"

Russell arrived around eleven-thirty, and after all the greetings, I went out to help him unload the car. When I'd talked to him on the phone earlier in the week, I'd rattled off a long list of items for him to bring me—more of my tee-shirts and Capri pants, my other pair of sandals, and at least one dressy outfit—my blue-floral skirt with the sweater-knit top or maybe the black pants and the tan and black-checked short-sleeved jacket. When I'd gotten the call that Mama was in the hospital, I'd packed hurriedly, taking only a few days' worth of clothes, and now that I'd be staying longer, I realized all the things I'd left behind.

Russell had interrupted me halfway through my list. "Wait a minute. I'll have to write all this down."

I had waited for him to find a piece of paper and a pen and repeated my list. "And bring all the old newspapers that you haven't already thrown out, and any magazines that have come since I've been up here. I'm absolutely starved for news and some decent reading material."

As I looked into the back of his Ford Explorer, I could see that he had practically emptied out my closet and dresser drawers. I reached for the clothes still on hangers lying on top of the bags beneath. "Thanks for bringing these. And you brought newspapers, too!" I looked greedily at the stack of newspapers and magazines beneath the clothes. He must have brought every magazine in the living room, including the back issues I'd already read. "Finally some news from the outside world." We stashed everything in my old bedroom, and then Russell and Roy walked outside while Margaret helped me finish up dinner.

"Roy and I can come over on weekends and give you a break if you want to make a quick trip home or have some time for yourself,"

Margaret said as we dished up food for the table. "I wish we could do more, but with both of us working—"

"That's okay," I assured her. "Thanks, but we're doing fine."

Roy and Margaret left around four to drive home to Lake City, and by nine o'clock that evening Mama was tired and ready for bed.

"How's it going?" Russell asked once we were alone. "How much longer are you going to be up here?"

"I told you what the doctor said, but it all depends on how she does. So far, so good. I'll be home as soon as I can." I told him about running into Delia at the bank. "It was so strange. I didn't even know that she had moved back here."

"Who's Delia?" Russell asked.

"Delia Adkins. I told you about her. She's the daughter of the sharecropper who worked for Daddy when I was growing up. We used to play together when we were little. I hadn't seen her in years till the other day at the bank."

"How'd you know it was her?"

"I wouldn't have, except somebody else called her Delia. A young black man in line behind me at the ATM called out, 'Hey, Miss Delia.' Then she saw Mama in the car and walked over to talk to her. We're going to get together next Wednesday for lunch. That's why I wanted one of my dressier outfits."

"You going someplace fancy?"

"No, it's just that she works somewhere downtown, and since she'll be dressed for work, I didn't want to show up in a ratty old tee-shirt and shorts."

By ten p.m., Russell and I were ready for bed ourselves, but long after Russell was asleep, I lay awake beside him, my thoughts drifting once more to Delia, to how close we'd been at four and five, and how abruptly school had changed all that, had robbed me of my best friend in the world.

* * *

"Katie," Mama says. "It's cold outside. Put on your jacket before you go down to the crib." She comes in the back door with a basket of eggs. It's

Saturday, and my job is to fill up a bucket with chickenfeed and pour it into the wooden trough in the chicken yard. I swing my empty bucket in a circle around me as I walk, transferring it from hand to hand, seeing how fast I can make it swing.

As I approach the door of the crib, I see Delia out under the pine trees where we built our playhouses. She's wearing my old red coat that I outgrew last winter. It's too little for her, and the sleeves don't even reach her wrists. There's another little nigger girl with her, the two of them sitting on the fallen log, cradling their dolls and talking to one another, their voices a low hum of words that I can't make out from this distance. I feel a stab of jealousy, and I think about running down the lane and yelling at them to get away from my playhouse, but I don't. Instead, I fill my bucket with the chickenfeed, take it back to the chicken yard, and pour it in a steady stream down the length of the feeding trough. Daddy says I'm getting to be a good little helper, and he's so happy that I'm not playing with Delia any more.

And it's true; I'm not. Now when I get off the school bus in the afternoons, Mama and Roy Jr. are waiting for me on the front porch or in the yard, Mama ready to exclaim over the papers clutched in my hand and hear all about my day. Roy Jr. is always excited to see me, too, and he grabs me around the waist in a hug that sometimes knocks me down. I like school, but it's good to come home, too, knowing Mama and Roy Jr. are watching and waiting for me. I don't even look up the lane towards Delia's house any more. Ever since Harvey told everybody at school that Quentin played with niggers, I don't want anybody to see Delia and me together.

"I told you, didn't I," Daddy says, "that when you started school, you'd forget all this foolishness." He's already made it plain to Mama that now that I'm in school all day, there is to be no starting up with Roy Jr. playing with Theo and Jerome. "I won't have it," he says, putting his foot down. "He wants to play with somebody, he can walk up the road to Curt and Verna's place and play with their boys, or their boys can come over here." Our closest neighbors have two boys, Buster (who's really Curt Jr.) and Billy. Buster is just a little bit older than Roy Jr. and Billy a little younger, so Roy Jr. is luckier than I am with having somebody his age to play with. And then Theo and Jerome have each other, too, so it's not like Delia and me, with not another girl anywhere near our age within miles.

Now that I'm in school, though, I've made friends with other girls. Sometimes one of my new friends comes home with me on the school bus and plays until dark, when her mama or daddy drives over to pick her up. On those days we stay inside in my room, or, if we go outside, I keep a close lookout for Delia so I can run inside if I see her. But Delia seems to be keeping as much of a distance from me as I am from her. She never comes into my yard any more, asking if I want to play. Days go by that I don't even catch sight of her, not even on weekends.

* * *

Russell was snoring, so I gave a push to his shoulder, and then turned my back to him, curling the pillow around my ears, willing myself to drift off to sleep.

* * *

It's afternoon — a school day — and I run up the drive to the house, eager to be out of the cold winter wind. Mama is standing on the porch, rubbing her arms, and she waves to the bus driver before leading me inside to the warm fire where Roy Jr., in his overalls, is building a tower of blocks in front of the hearth.

"There's a new baby at Maggie's house," she tells me before she even looks at the papers I'm clutching in my hand. "I made her a gown." She holds up something small and white.

My eyes widen. A new baby? Where had a new baby come from? And why is there a new baby at Delia's house and not at my house?

"It's a girl," Mama adds, when I don't say anything. "You want to go see her?"

I'm shocked. Mama is asking if I want to go to Delia's house to see her new baby? Daddy said I wasn't ever to go there again. I don't want to see Delia. What if somebody sees me going to her house? Somebody from school?

I lower my head. "Daddy said. . ."

"Oh," Mama says, "I know, but this is special. Roy Jr. is going, too. We'll just look at the baby and give Maggie our present. Daddy won't mind us doing that."

Mama wraps the gown in a piece of white tissue paper, and leads the way down the lane. Roy Jr. follows, dragging a stick that makes a long line in the sand, and I think about Hansel and Gretel, marking the path so they can find their way home again. I bring up the rear, dawdling along slowly. I don't want to see Delia, don't want to go into that house, don't even want to see the new baby. Why can't we have a new baby instead of Delia?

Mama knocks on the door, and Delia peeks out the window. "It's Miss Julia," I hear her telling Maggie, but I don't hear Maggie's answer.

Delia opens the door, and Mama begins to talk in that high-pitched baby-talk way. "Why, hello, Delia. We've come to see your baby sister. Can we come in? We brought her a present."

Delia pulls the door open wider, and Mama steps inside. Roy Jr., who's never been inside Delia's house before, grabs hold of Mama's skirt, but I stand up tall and straight, not looking at Delia, just following Mama through the first room into the one behind it, where Maggie is in bed, propped up on some pillows. She's holding the baby, who looks tiny in her arms, a doll with a head full of black corkscrew curls, its eyes squinched tightly shut.

"Oh-h," Mama says, "she's beautiful. Can I hold her?"

Maggie lifts her up and Mama puts the package on the bed so that she can take the baby. Delia, Theo, and Jerome all crowd into the room against Maggie's bed, all of them beaming as if the new baby had been their own idea. I can't see the baby's face, with Mama holding her up so high, so I scuffle my feet and sneak a quick peek over at Delia, who still has a big smile on her face.

"Her name's Rochelle," Delia says.

"Oh, that's a pretty name. Hello, Rochelle." Mama croons to the baby and holds it out a little ways. "Katie, do you want to see the baby?" There's no place in the room to sit, except on the bed, so Mama remains standing but lowers the bundle so that I can see the baby closer. Her face is sorta tannish, not brown like Delia's,, and with her wide, flat nose and squinched-shut eyes, I can't see how Mama thinks she's beautiful, but I'm fascinated by all the curly black hair that covers her scalp. I reach one hand out and touch her hair just to see what it feels like, and then Roy Jr. has to copy me and touch her hair, too.

"Isn't she precious?" Mama says. "Katie, give Maggie the present we brought. It's not much," she says to Maggie, "just something I made myself."

I hand the package to Maggie, and everybody watches as she unwraps it and spreads out the gown. It's all white, except where Mama has smocked the yoke with pink and blue thread and embroidered some tiny flowers around the neckline.

"I been working on it a while," Mama says, "afternoons in front of the fire."

Maggie looks as far up as the bundle in Mama's hands, but she doesn't look directly at Mama's face. Both Silas and Maggie look down at the ground when talking to Mama or Daddy, making it hard to understand what they're saying sometimes. "I appreciate it," Maggie mumbles, "but this is too nice…"

"Pshaw," Mama says. "It's nothing much. Sewing's my hobby. I'm always working on something or other, especially in the wintertime. I just hope little Roselle gets as much pleasure out of wearing it as I did in making it."

"Rochelle," Delia says, and Maggie reaches out and grabs Delia's arm, shaking her head at her.

"It's just about too nice to wear," Maggie insists. "I do appreciate it, Miss Julia."

The baby stirs, and Mama hands the bundle back to Maggie. "Here, let me give her back to you before she starts to fuss. We have to get home, anyway. About time to start cooking some supper." She turns toward the door, with Roy Jr. and me following, and I'm thinking that I'm really glad to be leaving, but then she stops. "Is anybody cooking for you, Maggie?" she asks. "You can't cook supper."

"My mama be coming over soon as my daddy finish up his work and she can get a ride," Maggie says. "She be bringing supper."

"Oh," Mama says, relieved. "That's good. Well, you take care of yourself and little Roselle."

"Her name's Rochelle," Delia says again, louder this time, and Maggie's hand snakes out toward Delia's arm, grabbing it so tightly that I see Delia flinch with pain.

"Yes," Mama says. "Rochelle. Such a pretty name."

Delia smiles now through the pain, now that Mama has got it right.

* * *

The memory of Delia's face at that moment, a mixture of pain and triumph, made me smile. Silas and Maggie might have been cowed by white people, but not Delia. Even at age six, Delia had stood up for herself. She was no coward like me. I shifted into a more comfortable position, gave Russell another shove on the shoulder, and tried again to fall asleep.

55

Chapter 8

Sunday, July 16, 2006

On Sunday morning, Mama wanted to go to church. "The swelling's all gone," she said, "and everybody has been asking when I'd be back."

Russell begged off going with us, explaining that he hadn't brought any clothes other than what he was wearing at the moment—an old tee-shirt and stained jeans—but since he had obligingly brought nearly every dressy outfit I owned, I was fully outfitted. So after helping Mama wash up and get dressed in one of her new button-up blouses and her best pair of elastic-waist pants, we set off for Shiloh Methodist.

When we arrived, I parked near the handicapped entrance, with its sloping wooden ramp leading to a side door, to avoid the steep front steps, and we followed several other elderly people inside, entering the sanctuary near the choir loft. Once inside, Mama became the center of attention as her friends crowded around us, wanting to know how she was doing. Many of them had already talked to her on the phone during the week or had come by the house, popping in for short visits or dropping off a cake or a casserole, which meant we had both been eating well—too well, judging by the tightness of the waistline of my pants. With Mama used to having her main meal at noon and me with having mine in the evening, we'd ended up having big meals for both, and with my having inherited Mama's attitude toward not letting anything go to waste, we'd both felt compelled to eat up everything that had been provided. I'd have to go on a diet when I returned home.

As the opening music began, I followed Mama to her usual center pew, the third row from the front, and tried to give the service my full attention, but my mind was elsewhere, thinking about my upcoming lunch with Delia and about Gail's revelation of Lonnie P.'s generous gifts to Hopewell Baptist and to the hospital. A glance behind me during the opening hymn revealed Brian Simmons near the back of the church, over on the left-hand side, alone. Where was Edwina? I knew from years past that Edwina worked in Tallahassee and had an apartment over there during the week, but she came home on weekends. I'd found their living arrangement a little odd, but then if it worked for them, it was none of my business.

Brian and I had been in the same graduating class in high school, and I'd had a secret crush on him during my junior and senior years at Pine Lake High, though nothing had ever come of it. We'd never actually dated or anything like that. Back then, Brian had been rail-thin, with a red, acne-pocked face. He hadn't been one of the popular crowd—not an athlete or a class clown or a hot-rodding "good ole boy" with a souped-up Chevy—but more the studious type, the one with his nose always in a book, the one who made A's on all the tests, the one who beat me out for valedictorian of our graduating class.

I'd seen him occasionally over the years since graduation, mostly here at Shiloh Methodist when I'd attended with Mama, and he had grown more handsome as he aged, his skinny frame filling out into a nice build, his acne long since cleared up, and his hair lightening from its earlier drab brown to a distinguished silver-gray. Definitely an improvement, I noted as I kept glancing that way.

After the benediction, we again joined the contingent using the side door and the ramp, thereby missing the usual greeting with the minister at the entry. As we stopped near the front steps to talk to some more of Mama's friends, I heard someone call my name.

"Hey, Kate."

I turned, startled, to look behind me. "Hi, Brian. Where did you come from?"

He gestured toward the ramp. "I followed you. Didn't want you to get away without saying 'Hi.' I hear you're going to be up here for a while."

I took a few steps toward Brian, leaving Mama to her circle of friends.

"A few more weeks. Till Mama's better. How's Edwina?" Brian had started attending Shiloh Methodist only after he married Edwina Downing. That had been after I'd finished college and moved away, but whenever Russell and I came home for a visit and attended church with Mama and Daddy, we'd see them here, first the two of them, then with one tow-headed little boy, then with two, the oldest born the same year as Travis, our youngest.

Brian shrugged. "We're divorced. More than a year ago. You hadn't heard about that?"

"I don't think so." Had Mama told me that? I'm sure I would have remembered if she had. "I'm sorry."

"Don't be. It's better this way. She does what she wants, and I do what I want. You get used to being by yourself and doing as you please, and then pretty soon you don't want to have to answer to anybody, you know?"

"I guess." Would that happen to Russell and me? If I spent all summer up here with Mama, would Russell decide he was happier living without me? Or would I decide I was happier without him? It was a scary thought.

Everyone was beginning to disperse, and I lifted one hand in a goodbye wave to Brian as we headed for our car. "It was good seeing you again."

"You, too. See you next Sunday."

At home, after a hearty lunch of the previous night's leftovers, Mama went off to putter around in her bedroom, and Russell and I sat in the front porch swing.

"I need to get back on the road soon," Russell said.

"I know. Thanks for coming, and for bringing all the stuff." I laid one hand on his knee.

"So how much longer do you think it'll be?"

"I don't know. I wish I could convince her to come back home with me. But she won't hear of it."

"Don't give her a choice. Just tell her she's coming, like it or not."

"She's not up for a long car trip right now, even if I could convince her. And she goes back to the doctor next week. Maybe once the sling is off I can bring her down for a long weekend at least."

Russell put his arm around my shoulder, and we sat quietly, the only sound the slight creak of the swing's chains, until Russell broke the silence. "So," he said, "tell me about this lunch you're going to. The sharecropper's daughter. What's her name again?"

"Delia. We were best friends once, when we were four and five, before we learned that white people and black people weren't supposed to be friends with each other."

"Is that so?" Russell chuckled. "How come I never heard about that?"

I felt my muscles grow tense. "I'm sure I mentioned her. They lived in the little house that used to stand on the other side of the lane. Silas and Maggie were still living there when we got married. Remember?"

"I remember you saying it belonged to sharecroppers, but I don't recall you talking about having a little black playmate."

"Well, I did. What's wrong with that? It was only for a couple of years, until we both started school and got indoctrinated into 'Southern society.'" I made quote marks in the air. "Of course, Daddy had tried to put a stop to it all along, but Mama felt sorry for me not having anybody to play with, so she didn't try too hard to enforce Daddy's rules."

Russell, who had grown up in Ohio, in a typical suburban neighborhood where the houses and the people all looked pretty much the same, had no concept of what the South had been like during those years. "I guess you never knew any black kids when you were growing up."

"Nope. Can't say I ever even talked to a black person till I was grown. One of my friends had this black housekeeper and cook who was always in the kitchen when I went over there, but I can't say I knew her. And I remember a black man who put up our backyard chain link fence when I was about ten. I hung around in the yard watching him, but I didn't talk to him. I remember I kept wondering how long he could keep working out there without going to the bathroom. I didn't want to go inside because I was afraid I'd miss seeing him pee on the bushes in one corner of the yard."

"Did you?"

"Nah. Eventually I got hot and bored and went inside."

"You were a town kid. On the farms, black and white people worked together, side by side, but there were strict rules for behavior. Nobody broke the rules. And if they did, they paid for it." I crossed my arms, defending myself against attack for an action that Russell knew nothing about.

"So now you're going to apologize to her for all those years of good old Southern segregation? Lester Maddox, George Wallace, and the rest?"

"It's nothing to joke about. We're going to talk, that's all." I didn't want to get into any long discussion with Russell about Delia. I changed the subject. "I ran into Gail at the grocery store a few days ago. You remember Gail and Gary. We sat with them at my fortieth reunion. We're going to get together, too, as soon as Mama is a little better. And I talked to Brian Simmons this morning at church. You know him from years ago when we used to go to church with Mama and Daddy. Brian and Edwina and their two little boys?"

"Yeah, I remember. Anything new with him?"

"He and Edwina are divorced. Over a year ago. I just found out about it today."

"Too bad. What happened?"

"I don't know. Just grew apart, I guess. The boys grew up, and Edwina started spending all her time in Tallahassee. Brian was looking good, though."

"Is that so? You got a lunch date with him, too?" Russell tried to sound amused, but his voice betrayed a touch of jealousy.

"No. I talked to him for two minutes, if that." I reached for Russell's hand, interlacing my fingers with his. "I miss being home with you, and seeing the kids and grandkids. How is everybody? When I talked to Erin a couple of days ago, she said the kids had the sniffles."

"They're fine. Travis started a new job last week. The same type of work but with a different company. He says the pay is better and he won't be on the road so much."

"That's good, I guess, if it works out." I felt a pang of regret for all that I was missing out on at home, the Sunday evening suppers when Erin and Scott and their two children came over, Travis joining us, too, if he didn't have more exciting plans; the quiet evenings with Russell watching the news together on TV, sharing the newspaper, talking about our day. I missed my house, my colleagues at work, all the minutiae of my daily life.

"I'll be home as soon as I can. As soon as Mama can be left alone."

After Russell left for home, I skimmed through some of the newspapers that Russell had brought me. I couldn't decide if what I wanted most was to jump in my car and follow him back to my safe and comfortable life in Titusville or if I wanted to stay here and make amends with Delia, see if we could regain that closeness we'd once shared as children. And now there were two more items on my agenda. The first was to find out how Lonnie P. had made all his money. Was it on the up-and-up, or was there some nefarious secret behind his success? And secondly, why had Edwina walked out on such a nice, sweet guy as Brian Simmons?

I walked outside and dialed Gail's number on my cell phone, and after a few minutes of small talk I led into the real question that I wanted to ask. "I ran into Brian Simmons at church this morning, and he told me he and Edwina have been divorced for over a year now. How did that happen?"

"You didn't know about that?" Gail asked. "Gosh, girl, where have you been?"

"I don't live here," I reminded her. "What's the story? I always liked Brian."

"Liked him? That's the understatement of the year. You had a crush on him that wouldn't quit."

"So?" I laughed. "That was a long time ago. Anyway, what happened?"

"Well, you know that Edwina's been working in Tallahassee for ages, doing something in the Capitol building, don't you? You know about the apartment she got over there?"

"Yes, I knew about that, but last I heard, she was living over there during the week and coming home weekends."

"That was the arrangement for years, but even before that, when those little boys were no bigger than a minute, she was Miss Important Career Lady—leaving home before daylight and not getting back until eight or nine at night. Brian was holding down a full-time job plus doing all the cooking and cleaning and taking care of the two boys. Pretty soon she started acting all hoity-toity like she was above all us poor peons here in Pine Lake. Then, when she got the apartment, it was even worse. She'd show up at one of the boys' ball games on Saturday afternoons all dressed up in a suit and high heels, eyelashes slathered with mascara, and a fancy hat on to shield her face from the sun. We all figured with all that hobnobbing with senators and whatnot, something had to be going on."

"You mean cheating?"

"Well, what do you think? She sure didn't pay much attention to Brian, that's for sure. Everybody here was surprised they didn't divorce years ago."

"Sounds like he's better off without her, but still, it must be lonely not having anyone to share your life with, nobody to go out with to a movie or a restaurant, eating a frozen dinner in front of the TV night after night. Has he dated anybody since the divorce?"

"I think he's been out a few times with different women here and there, but there's not much of a pool for him to pick from in Pine Lake. He's too young to go after the widows and too old to be interested in the single crowd."

"There must be some women our age—divorcées, maybe?"

Gail laughed. "You trying to play matchmaker? Brian's old enough to make his own decisions in that department."

"I know, but he's such a sweet, both-feet-on-the-ground guy that he'd be a great catch for some lucky woman—somebody who'd treat him better than Edwina did."

"You still interested?"

"Me? I'm married, remember? But if I weren't…"

It was odd; I knew in my head that Gail and I were both past sixty, both long and happily married, both grandmothers, but being back here in this place where I hadn't lived full-time since I was eighteen, it was as if time had stood still all the years I'd been gone, and Gail and I were teenagers again, gossiping over the phone about boys. Was I actually getting excited about Brian's single state? All the men I'd met in my post-marriage life, either through work or in the neighborhood or at social gatherings, had been simply acquaintances, or, in some cases, friends, but I had never had any romantic fantasies about any of them—no quickening of the heartbeat, no racing of the blood, no thrill running through me at the mention of a name or the thought of seeing one of them again. But now, back here in Pine Lake, I felt caught in a time warp. Brian wasn't a sixty-two-year-old man; he was Brian from high school, before he had any commitments (a better looking and more suave Brian), and I was also my high-school self, but more experienced and more confident—no longer the tongue-tied, sweaty-palmed adolescent who'd been too shy and awkward to approach anyone of the opposite sex. Of course, in those days girls didn't do the approaching anyway, except for the brazen hussies; the rest of us suffered in silence while the "forward" girls stole all the good guys.

Gail was talking, and I had to pull my thoughts back to what she was saying. Something about getting together at her house. "One day this week?" she was asking. "What day would be good for you? We can gossip for hours."

"Any day works for me," I answered, "but I can stay only an hour or so. I don't like leaving Mama alone for too long at a time."

"I'm busy tomorrow, but how about Tuesday morning?" Gail asked. "I'll put on the coffee pot and make some blueberry muffins. Say around ten or so?"

"Tuesday sounds great." We ended our conversation without my having asked anything more about the source of Lonnie P.'s wealth, but I could pursue that topic in person.

Chapter 9

Tuesday, July 18, 2006

On Tuesday, after Mama and I had eaten breakfast and I had helped her get bathed and dressed for the day, I headed to Gail's, where we settled in her living room with our coffee and muffins.

Gail immediately resumed our previous conversation about Brian. "After I talked to you Sunday, I called up Brian and invited him over for supper this Friday. I told him you were coming, too. You are, aren't you?"

My thumb and forefinger smashed the muffin I was holding, and a big chunk of it dropped onto the carpet. I bent to pick it up. Gail was still talking.

"He sounded so excited about the dinner. Said he'd come before I could even finish my sentence. I could kick myself for not inviting him sooner, but things like that slip your mind. I guess I hadn't really thought about how lonesome it was, eating by yourself every night, until you brought it up. So now you have to come. I've already promised you'd be here."

I wrapped the chunk of muffin in my napkin. "A foursome? I don't know about that. What'll I tell Russell?"

"Who says you have to tell him anything? It's not a date, for goodness sake. We'll sit around and reminisce about high school. You'll come, won't you?"

"I'd love to, but—"

"But what?"

"I'll have to check with Mama. I guess I can make up a plate for her that she can heat in the microwave. Or maybe she can invite a friend over to have supper with her. I'll work it out."

Once that was established, I steered the conversation away from Brian, not wanting to set off Gail's radar on how stupidly nervous and excited the promise of dinner with Brian was making me feel. *Don't be foolish*, I lectured myself mentally. *It's nothing but dinner with three old classmates. Nothing to get all worked up about. Remember, you're a married woman, a happily married woman.*

I tried putting the shoe on the other foot, imagining Russell having dinner with some of his old high school buddies. What if one of them was an unattached female, a female whom Russell had been attracted to back in high school? Well, I trusted Russell, so it wouldn't bother me. Of course, I had to admit that I might feel just the teeniest bit threatened, but then, who wouldn't? Besides, I'd tell Russell about the dinner. We didn't keep secrets from one another. Should it be before or after? Before, for then I'd feel safer, feeling that Russell was watching over my shoulder the whole evening. But if I waited until after, I could tell him more about what was said, and how innocent it all was—four old fogies telling stories that would totally bore anyone who hadn't lived through them. Nothing that he would have enjoyed, for sure.

"How are the church building plans coming along?" I asked. "Did you decide on a design yet?"

"Not yet. We met with the architect and told him what we wanted, and he's going to draw up a plan to bring back for our approval. We're so thrilled that we're actually making progress. Our building fund is up to nearly two hundred thousand dollars!"

"All started by Lonnie P.," I said.

"Yes. If he hadn't made us believe we could do it, we'd still be sitting around on our hands complaining about our old building and doing nothing to improve our situation."

"Lonnie P. must be doing well, to be in the position to give so much money to the church and the hospital. What kind of business is he in, anyway?"

"Oh, he has an automobile dealership. Haven't you seen it? Ramsey Ford? Out on the highway past the community college?"

"I never go out that way, not past the Winn-Dixie plaza, anyway."

"It's huge. There's the main sales lot that sells new, and then a used car lot on the other side of the showroom."

"I wouldn't think Pine Lake would be big enough for him to sell that many cars."

"You'd be surprised. Of course, lots of them get repossessed, from what I hear." Gail laughed. "Then he sells them again."

"Business must be good if he's making enough money to keep giving it away."

"I guess so. That's not all he does, though. When he first moved back here, he bought up a bunch of woods and farmland just past the car lot and had it platted into homesites with lots of winding roads and cul-de-sacs. He even turned a cow pasture in the middle of the development into a golf course, and dredged out a mud hole and called it a lake. Called the place Rambling Acres. Nobody thought it would amount to anything, but it's about sold out. He built himself a big house right on the lake, and now it's become *the* place to live. "

"Moved back? From where? How long was he away?"

"Gosh, let me think. His kids must have been in high school. Maybe junior high. Trey (he's Lonnie the Third, but they call him Trey) played on the football team just like his daddy—and he got an athletic scholarship to some college out of state. I don't know where he is now, but the daughter, Allison, lives here. She married Hank Barnes' son. Remember Hank? They have two little girls. I hear she's pregnant again, and they're hoping for a boy."

So Lonnie P. had been back at least fifteen years, long enough for his kids to have grown up, married, and had kids of their own. "If he opened an auto sales lot and bought up land for a housing development right after he came back, that must mean he had already accumulated a lot of money somewhere else—wherever he had been living before."

"Well, the car dealership originally belonged to his father-in-law," Gail answered. "He took over when Mr. Harris retired. But he's certainly done a lot for this town. So many people who make good keep all their wealth for themselves, live high on the hog, but he isn't like that. He believes in giving back to the community."

We talked a while longer before I glanced at my watch. "Sorry, but I need to run. I promised Mama I wouldn't be gone too long." I carried my empty cup and saucer to the kitchen counter. "Thanks for the coffee, and the muffin was delicious. I'm looking forward to dinner on Friday. Want me to bring anything?"

"No, no. I'll take care of everything," Gail assured me. "See you at six."

I headed home, my curiosity about how Lonnie P. had made all his money quickly replaced with nervous excitement about Friday night's dinner and the anticipation of seeing Brian again. What would I wear? It was a good thing Russell had brought all those extra clothes from my closet.

Later that afternoon, as Mama watched her soap operas, I settled onto my bed, pillows propped behind my back and a handful of the magazines Russell had brought me from home fanned out beside me. I began to scan through them, reading the opening paragraphs of articles and looking for something to capture my interest, but my mind kept wandering to my lunch tomorrow with Delia. Would I be courageous enough to bring up the events of that long-ago summer night and tell her what I had seen and heard? How could I justify my failure to make my presence known and stand up for her against those boys? Perhaps the whole incident was best left buried in the past. If Delia had willingly come back to this place where Lonnie P. was mayor and she was okay with the situation, what was the point of opening up old wounds? Maybe we could skip over all that old ugly racial stuff and be two women reconnecting as equals, talking about children and grandchildren, husbands and jobs.

But even as I tried to convince myself that I could let it all go, I knew that I couldn't. I had to face up to my own complicity in the incident, or I would be no better than Lonnie P. and the others who were with him that night.

I slid down so that I was lying on my back and closed my eyes. Throughout my elementary years, I had remained an obedient child of the segregated South. With no television set in the house until 1957 and no newspaper except for the *Pine Lake Gazette*, which was mostly filled with social news — who'd been born or died, who'd gotten engaged or married or been sick or had out-of-town visitors over the weekend — I had led a remarkably sheltered life. I'd been in junior high school before I had any real awareness of events outside my home county, before the television brought news of what the rest of the country was like, before I even realized that black people were not happy with their second-class citizenship.

I'd read books, of course, my school readers, and then books from the school library, but there had been no Negro children in any of the stories I'd read; everyone was blonde and blue-eyed and lived in pretty, white houses with picket fences around them. There were sidewalks in front of the houses on which the children pulled their wagons and rode their tricycles and bicycles, and grassy lawns and next-door neighbors who talked over fences, and neighborhoods full of children who had one exciting adventure after another. None of it resembled my own life in the slightest, but I had found these stories fascinating, and I could not get enough of them.

As I continued to lie there with my eyes closed, I wondered for the first time in my life what books Delia had learned to read from or had checked out from her school library. Had the stories all been about lily-white kids living in suburban paradise, like my own early readers had been? How did those stories make the black kids feel, knowing they would never experience lives like that, knowing their own lives were not worth writing about? I felt ashamed that such questions had never occurred to me before, that I had never bothered, even as an adult, to put myself in Delia's shoes, to see life from her perspective.

During those early elementary years, Delia and I often saw one another whenever we were both playing outside, but the old ease was gone, replaced by a mutual wariness. I'd watch her playing at the edge of the woods with her brothers or with friends from her school, but if she stopped and looked directly at me, I'd glance away, unnerved by

71

her sullen stare. Then, out of the corner of my eye, I'd see her raise her chin and flounce off as if she had better things to do than whatever she had been doing. She no longer came into our back yard, and I no longer played under the pines beside her house, the spot where we'd built our playhouses.

Maggie and the children still rode into town on Saturday afternoons in the back of our truck, but on those occasions, Delia and I studiously avoided looking at each other. I sat in the cab facing straight ahead, terrified that one of my friends from school would see me riding in a truck with Negroes, and then I would be ostracized like Quentin. When Silas bought his own used pickup the summer I turned eight, using his share of the tobacco money, I'd felt an enormous relief, as if a huge burden had been lifted from me.

I took off my reading glasses, laid them aside, and rubbed my eyes. Were all children at that age so needy of their peers' approval, so concerned with how they appeared to others that they could see the world only from their own point of view? I had certainly been indoctrinated well into the culture around me. It would be a few more years before I developed any real empathy for Delia or for any of her race.

* * *

I'm ten, and Roy Jr. is eight. School is out for the summer, and Daddy decides it's time to teach us the value of work. I haven't been sent to the field before because I'm a girl, but now that Roy Jr. is old enough, there will be two of us working alongside Maggie and Delia and Theo, hoeing the weeds out of the rows of peanut plants. Late one afternoon after he's finished plowing, Daddy takes Roy Jr. and me to the field to demonstrate what we're to do and to make sure we clear out just the weeds and not the young peanut plants. Theo goes, too, since this will be his first time hoeing. Delia already knows how to hoe since she worked in the fields with Maggie last summer, while I helped Mama at home. I have another little brother now who is about to turn two years old. His name is Isaac, after our grandfather, who's really old, but we call him Zach. Mama tried to convince Daddy to let me stay home and take care of Zach while she does the cooking and cleaning and laundry, but Daddy says it's time for me and Roy Jr. to earn our keep.

So the next morning, after breakfast, I head for the field with Roy Jr., new straw hat on my head, a jug of cold water in one hand, and a newly sharpened hoe in the other, feeling solemn with my new responsibility. Maggie and the children are waiting for us at the gate. Maggie, Delia, and Theo all have hoes, and Maggie has a gallon jug of water. Three-year-old Rochelle is carrying a doll that looks awfully familiar (Is that Delia's Nancy Jane?), and six-year-old Jerome has an empty coffee can and a big kitchen spoon. As we approach them, I say "Good morning" very formally, as I've heard Mama and Daddy do, and Roy Jr. doesn't say anything, but he puts one hand up to the brim of his cap and nods his head slightly. "Morning," Maggie replies, looking off toward the field. Delia doesn't look away; she stares me straight in the eyes but doesn't speak.

I unhook the chain from the nail driven into the post and open the gate, and everyone follows me into the field. "Going to be a hot one," I say, looking up at the sun, which is still low in the east, and Maggie mumbles agreement. We set our water jugs down in the shade of the single oak tree, mine and Roy Jr.'s a suitable distance away from Maggie's, and Maggie directs Jerome and Rochelle to sit beneath the tree and stay put. Then Roy Jr. and I head off to the far side of the field as Daddy has told us to do, leaving Maggie, Delia, and Theo the rows closest to the gate so Maggie can keep an eye on her two youngest. Mama doesn't have to work in the fields; she has enough work to do in the house, including taking care of Zach.

Pretty soon, we've settled into a steady pace of hoeing, with me keeping tabs on Roy Jr. to make sure he's hoeing out the weeds and not the peanut plants. Then I hear Maggie's voice across the field, just a low mutter at first and then getting louder and clearer as she gains momentum, singing one of the gospel hymns I had listened to years before in her kitchen. "Swing Low, Sweet Chariot" is coming across the field, as if the wind is lifting and carrying the words to me, and I sing along under my breath, not loud enough to be heard by Maggie or Delia or even by Roy Jr., one row over. My hoe moves automatically down the row, my mind disassociated from my hand motions. In my mind I'm back in Maggie's kitchen with Delia, sitting on the wooden bench, biting into a cookie fresh and warm from the oven. Maggie moves on to "When the Saints Go Marching In" and then to "Down by the Riverside," and I'm back with Delia in our playhouses under the pine trees, crooning lullabies to our dolls.

73

I lift my eyes from the row and look across the field at Delia, but her back is to me, and even from this great distance I can see that her hoe is chopping furiously at the weeds as if she has some personal rage against them. Some sort of anger has been building in her for a while now; I've noticed it in the direct, challenging stare she gives me whenever we encounter one another outside, as if she's daring me to say or do something that will provoke a fight. Daddy calls it sass, and Maggie and Silas both have tried to take that sass out of her, but they're not having much success. I don't understand what she has to be so angry about, but her look scares me a little, and I steer clear of her as much as I can. Those days of playing together seem to have happened a long time ago in a dim, distant past.

* * *

I opened my eyes and looked at the clock on my nightstand. Almost three. I could hear the low noise of the TV from the living room, but nothing else. I closed my eyes again. A few more minutes of rest and then I'd check on Mama. At least Delia hadn't still had that sullen, angry stare when I'd run into her at the bank. She had seemed genuinely glad to see me, as I was to see her. At some point she must have managed to put aside the bitterness that she'd felt growing up in that little house, being groomed to accept her designated place in the segregated society of the South. Why hadn't the black people gotten together and murdered every white person they knew? The fact that so many of them could remain so submissive in the face of such injustice was a great mystery to me.

I was thirteen when Daddy brought home our first TV set in late summer of 1957, purchased with the proceeds of that year's tobacco crop, and I was introduced to the daily national news, where the inequities of Southern segregation were laid bare before me in all their seething turmoil. Over the next few years, as I finished up junior high and moved on to the big consolidated high school in town, I watched the bloody but determined march of the Civil Rights movement across the Deep South. Backed into a corner, the Southern establishment was fighting tooth and nail against every advance, scared to death that any change in the relations between blacks and whites would so rock the world as they knew it that the earth would be thrown out of its normal orbit and go spinning off somewhere into outer space.

I learned (belatedly) about the murder of Emmett Till in Mississippi in 1955, then about Rosa Parks refusing to give up her seat on a bus to a white man. I watched in horror as black students were taunted and pelted with eggs and rotten fruit as they tried to integrate colleges and high schools in Mississippi and Alabama and Arkansas. The livid, twisted faces of Orval Faubus, George Wallace, and Lester Maddox filled the screen as they vowed to stand in schoolhouse doors with ax handles to keep their schools lily-white. And that wasn't the worst of it: I witnessed, close up, black people being savagely beaten by white policemen for marching for their rights and for trying to register to vote, people being dragged off to jail for doing nothing more than sitting down in a Woolworth's cafeteria. I was sickened by the violence, ashamed to be a Southerner.

* * *

"Our niggers here ain't like them uppity city niggers," Daddy says for the umpteenth time as we watch the evening news from the dinner table. "You don't see any of them behaving like that. They don't want this integration business any more than white folks do."

I'm almost sixteen now, in tenth grade, old enough to have developed a sense of justice, and I've seen and heard enough to know that Daddy is wrong, that he and his generation want to convince themselves that segregation is the Negro's own choice to justify its continued existence. With all my teenage zeal, I try to make him see that things have to change.

I heave a huge sigh. "Sure they do," I say. "They're just too scared to speak up. What if the tables were reversed and white people were on the bottom? Would you be happy being a second-class citizen?"

Daddy continues as if I hadn't spoken. He has his little speech all rehearsed and memorized by now. It's the same each time, repeated back to him by all the neighbors, their voices like the church choir when they do one of those songs where the deep voices echo the higher ones. "The trouble is caused by all them outside agitators," he insists. "Northern town niggers and white nigger-lovers who don't know how good we folks in the South treat our colored people. Southern niggers know where their bread is buttered."

75

"They're people, Daddy," I argue, "just like you and me. And the word is Negro — N-E-G-R-O, not that word you said." I have begun to cringe whenever Mama and Daddy use the word "nigger." Roy Jr. uses it, too, and so does Zach, who is still too young to understand that it's a bad word. "They just want to be treated like people, have the same rights as everybody else."

"They got rights," Daddy answers. "They got their own schools and churches, ain't they? And their money is as good in any store as a white man's, ain't it?"

"They can't eat in a restaurant, can't drink from a public water fountain or even use a public bathroom, Daddy. That's not right."

"Then let them build their own restaurants and bathrooms. You want to sit on a toilet a nigger's been sitting on?"

That line brings snickers from Roy Jr. and he jumps into the conversation. "You go on talking like that, and everybody at school will be calling you a nigger lover," he says. "That what you want?"

I glower at him, but I blush at the same time, remembering some of the comments I've heard at school, especially from the boys. I don't have the necessary courage to be a martyr, but if the people who feel as I do (and I know I'm not the only one), don't speak up, then people like Daddy will continue to spew out those dumb platitudes.

Daddy continues his spiel. "Everything had been going fine just the way it was till a few Yankee agitators decided to stir things up. They're the ones causing all the trouble. Look at Silas and Maggie. I provide them with a roof over their heads, a good job, and a milk cow. I buy the seeds and fertilizer for their vegetable garden every year, and Silas uses my tractor and plow to plant it. You hear them complaining?"

None of my arguments have any effect, and I get no support from Mama or from Roy Jr., both of whom agree with Daddy that any change from the established social order is too dangerous to contemplate. The only person I have any hope of changing is seven-year-old Zach, but he is too young to understand what the fuss is about.

* * *

My hand brushed against a magazine, and I startled, jerking my hand away and opening my eyes. Had I fallen asleep? Had I been dreaming about arguing with Daddy about integration? He had gone to his grave still convinced that God meant for the races to be segregated. I guess he figured that Heaven would be segregated, too, each race in its delegated section.

When I walked into the living room, Mama was still leaned back in her recliner, eyes closed, so I pushed open the front door and stepped onto the porch. Coming back to this place had dredged up a lot of old memories, but none so painful as the one I'd been avoiding up to now. The details of that summer night had been buried so deeply in my subconscious that bringing them out into the light of day would be difficult, but it was something I had to deal with before facing Delia.

It had been a Saturday. That much I knew for sure. I had turned sixteen a few weeks before and had a brand new driver's license in my wallet. That evening I had picked up two girlfriends and headed into town for the movies, my first grownup solo driving experience. I had felt so excited that night, so newly independent and mature, filled to the brim with the promise that a new stage of my life was about to begin.

I'd had no inkling whatsoever as to how that night would end.

Chapter 10

An early afternoon shower had cooled things off, and a slight breeze stirred the trees in the front yard. I sat on the front porch swing, idly pushing myself back and forth, and forced myself to go back to that night, to recapture everything I could remember about it.

In 1960, the only vehicles we owned, besides the tractor, were the beat-up blue pickup that Daddy had had as far back as I could remember, and the black 1950 Ford sedan that had belonged to my grandfather. Since my grandmother had never learned to drive, Daddy had inherited it in 1955 when my grandfather died, and that was what I had used to take my driving test. The car was old and ugly, but it was my only ticket to town.

* * *

"Hey, look!" I wave my new driver's license at Bobbie Sue in the desk across from me and at Louise behind her. "Want to go to the movies Saturday night?" None of us knows what movie will be showing on Saturday, but its title doesn't matter anyway; there is only one choice per week, so everybody sees the same feature. The experience is what counts. I don't ask Gail to go with us, for she will be there with Gary Proctor; she is the only one of us who has a steady boyfriend — the only one who has a boyfriend, period.

We get to the theater early, in plenty of time to buy our tickets and visit the concession stand in the lobby before the movie begins.

"Ugh. Another Western," Louise groans. "That's all this old place ever shows."

"Hey, don't complain. That's what the guys like," Bobbie Sue counters. "So you know what that means." As if on cue, a group of teenage boys push through the door, barging their way up to the concession stand. We're clumped in the middle of the lobby, studying the wall menu from afar, still deciding what we want before going up to the counter to place our orders.

I recognize two of the boys, both ninth graders, a year behind us in school. Too young to be driving. A parent must have dropped them off. Bobbie Sue and Louise, also noticing that the boys are beneath our attention, walk over to look at the life-size cardboard cutout of John Wayne, off to one side of the lobby. Brian Simmons is behind the counter at the concession stand, and when I notice him looking at me, I duck my head and join Bobbie Sue and Louise in sizing up the cutout. Brian is in my biology class at Pine Lake High. He's on the skinny side, and his face is red with acne, but I have sort of a secret crush on him that I haven't told anybody about. Nobody except Gail, that is, and I made her promise to keep it our secret. "Ugh," they'd say if they knew. "How could you? All those pimples!" And I wonder myself. I don't know if I'd really go out with him, even if he asked me (which he hasn't), but if his face didn't look so fiery and inflamed and just plain horrible, he'd be pretty cute. And he's smart, which means a lot to me.

"I'm going to slip in here a minute." I point to the door of the women's restroom. "Save me a seat, and I'll find you inside."

"We can wait for you," Louise said.

"No, go ahead." I clutch at my stomach, which has begun to twist into a cramp. "I think I just started my period."

As I come out of the bathroom, the lobby is empty except for Brian behind the counter. "A large Coca-Cola," I say, hoping I'm not blushing.

"You ready for the biology final?" Brian asks as he takes down a cup and pours my drink.

"I hope so. I've been studying enough. How about you?" I reach into my purse for my wallet, and as I'm pulling out the right change, one of my pennies falls to the floor and I bend to pick it up.

"I wouldn't worry," Brian answers. "Her tests are always pretty easy," and just then the theater manager comes racing down the stairs from the projection room, his face a purplish bruise of bulging blood vessels.

"Hey!" His voice echoes in the high-ceilinged lobby. "You two! Get out of here. Now!" His watery blue eyes are about to burst from their sockets and he chops at the air with one hand, motioning frantically at someone behind me. I glance around and see two teenage Negro girls coming in the door. Negroes are not allowed inside the theater's lobby area or the restrooms. They buy their tickets at the outside window; then they have to go up a rickety set of outdoor steps to a door that opens into the upstairs balcony. Except for the noise coming from upstairs, the white patrons wouldn't even know they're there.

Now, though, with all the civil rights demonstrations on TV every night, rumors have been swirling around Pine Lake about how we are going to be put to the test, sooner or later, and there's been lots of private tough talk about what would happen if any Northern agitators come into Pine Lake and try to start something.

"Most of our niggers here don't want no trouble," my father keeps pronouncing to anybody who will listen. "They know their place. But there's a few of the younger ones — "

"All they're asking for is equal treatment," I tell him. Just last week I'd brought up the fact that black people weren't allowed to buy anything to eat or drink while they watched the movie, and how unfair that was.

"If they let niggers buy all the popcorn and soda pop they wanted, then you know what would happen?" Daddy answered. "Pretty soon they'd be demanding to go to the restroom, and then where would you be? You want a nigger coming in while you're doing your business? Sitting her bare bottom on the same toilet seat you sit on? You better watch your mouth, young lady," he had warned. "Talk like that will get you into trouble. You say things like that in public and see what happens to you."

"I don't care," I had slung back at him. "They deserve the same rights as white people. They work just as hard for their money as whites do — maybe harder. They should be able to spend it wherever they want to."

Last week at home I had stood my ground, but now, caught between the girls and the manager, with Brian looking on, I chicken out. I slip behind the cutout of John Wayne, so that nobody can see me. I can't see the two Negro girls, but I know they're still there. One of the girls is Delia. I had hardly glanced at them, but a glance was all it took. Now it's Delia's voice I hear speaking to Brian. "We want some popcorn. And some Co-Colas."

"You know you're not supposed to come in here," the manager yells back, now down the stairs and waving both arms, flapping them up and down like a bird about to take flight. "You better get out now while the getting's good. We don't sell no food or drink to niggers. That's our rule."

"Don't serve them anything," he barks at Brian before turning back to the girls. "I'm calling the sheriff right now. If you ain't out of here in two seconds, you'll be spending your asses in jail tonight."

Behind the cutout, I draw in my stomach, to make of myself as small a package as I can. There's nowhere to escape to without being seen. I'm not sure if Delia noticed me in the moment before the manager burst down the stairs. My back was to her, and I was bent over picking up my penny, so perhaps, even if she saw me, she hadn't recognized me. Surely she hadn't, for if she had, she would have given some indication of my presence. Or was she waiting for me to speak first, to stand up for what was just and right?

"Now," I tell myself," now is the time to step up and let my actions match my words. Now is my chance to defend Delia — my first and fiercest childhood ally — against this blustering, red-faced rooster of a man."

But instead of stepping forward, I find myself cowering behind the cutout, desperate for a way out of the situation. Before I can think any further, I hear the front doors open, bringing in a burst of male rowdiness and laughter.

"Step back, boys," the manager says. "These gir…, these niggers are on their way out. Git, now."

I can't see the boys' faces, but I can hear their laughter turn to snickers of derision. "Hey, you coons looking for somebody?" one of them says. "You coons want some action? That why you come in here?" A general snort of laughter goes up, and I hear Delia's voice again, low and hissing with rage. "We sure don't want nothing from the likes of you trash!" Then the front door opens and closes.

"Sorry about that, boys," the manager says. "I don't think they'll be back." A faint click sounds as if he is tapping his fingernail against his watch. "Movie's starting, but if they come back I'm getting the sheriff out here." He hurries up the stairs.

"Uppity nigger bitches," somebody mutters. I stay in my hiding place, listening to the voices. I'm not sure how many boys there are, but there must be three or four at least from the sounds of the laughs and snorts. Behind the *counter, Brian has set down my drink and is busily making up for lost time, scooping popcorn into boxes, leaning them up in a row inside the machine.*

"Somebody needs to teach them nigger bitches a lesson," one voice says.

"We could go after 'em right now," somebody else adds. "Show 'em what they got coming for trying to sashay in here like white people."

"Nah. We don't want to miss the movie. We'll get 'em later. Have us some fun later on tonight."

"But how'll we find 'em then?" another protests. "Who can tell one coon from another?"

"I know one of 'em." This voice seems to be the leader of the group, the one who approves or vetoes all the decisions. The voice sounds familiar to me, but I can't quite place it. And I don't dare peek out from my hiding place to find out. "One of them's that nigger girl who lives on the McCormick place. I don't know the other one."

The boys are approaching the concession stand. And one of them knows Delia, knows who she is, at least, knows where she lives. Now is my chance to step out and make my presence known. But I'm alone, and there must be at least three or four boys in the group. If I step out and defend Delia, what will they do to me? Now I'm really scared. I slide further around the stand, keeping it between myself and them until they finish their purchases and take them into the theater. Only then do I dare leave my hiding place.

My hands are shaking as I pay Brian for my soda. "You think they meant it, those boys?" I whisper.

Brian shrugs. "I doubt it. Just trying to look tough."

"Yeah," I agree. "They'll forget it by the time the movie's over."

"You okay?" Louise whispers as I slide into the seat beside her. "We were getting worried."

"You were gone a long time," Bobbie Sue says.

"Sorry," I whisper back. The movie has already started, so I don't tell them about the scene in the lobby. A man on horseback is riding through a narrow canyon somewhere out West, red cliffs rising on either side. I watch numbly, with no idea who the man is or where he's headed. All I can think about is Delia. Surely by the time the movie ends the boys will have forgotten about their boastful threats. I try to relax, try to follow the plot of the movie, but my hands

clench my paper cup of soda so tightly that when the lights come up, I can barely spread my fingers.

It's sometime after eleven, and the house is dark and quiet. Everyone is asleep except for me. I'm lying awake, my bedroom window open, listening for the slightest noise from the direction of Delia's house. I can't stop thinking about what the boys said at the movie theater about teaching her a lesson. I wish I could tell somebody what I'd heard, ask somebody for advice about what I should do. Talking to Daddy would be useless, though, even if he were awake; to tell him what the boys had said, I'd also have to tell him what Delia had done, how she'd come into the theater lobby and tried to order popcorn and Co-Cola, and then Daddy would get so mad that he'd be ready to kick the whole family out of their house, not wanting it said around the county that he was harboring belligerent Negroes in his own back yard. He certainly wouldn't let me go out at midnight knocking on Silas and Maggie's door, waking them up at this ungodly hour. "Forget it," he would say. "Them boys was just talking, like boys will. And if they do scare her a little, it's for her own good." Daddy has already mentioned a couple of times that Silas is worried about Delia, about how angry and rebellious she's been acting lately and how he's afraid that one of these days she's gonna get herself into bad trouble.

I think about waking up Mama and telling her what I heard, but Mama doesn't like to think bad of anybody. "Sh-h," she would say. "Delia's home safe in bed by now, and nobody's gonna try breaking into their house without waking up Silas or one of the boys. You're just getting all worked up over nothing."

My stomach is cramping now in earnest, and I curl onto my side and bring my knees up against my chest. All is quiet, and eventually I fall into a fitful sleep.

A noise outside startles me awake — a car coming up the road, its headlights shining in my window as it rounds the curve, stopping at the mailbox. I hear car doors opening and closing, a radio playing, and then the car's engine growing fainter as it continues down the road. I cross the room and kneel below my window, pulling the curtain aside. An almost full moon lights up Delia's features as she walks down the lane toward her house. She is alone, I *note with relief. I look at my bedside clock. Almost one a.m. Is Delia just coming home at this hour? I marvel at her daring, her brazenness. What could she have been doing that would have kept her out so late?*

I watch her glide silently up the lane, past the tobacco barn, and am about to return to bed when I see some other figures — three, at least, maybe four — step out from the far side of the tobacco barn and surround her. My heart begins to pound as the figures merge with Delia's — two of them grabbing an arm from either side, throwing her off balance. One must have clasped his hand over her mouth, for all is eerily silent as they drag her behind the barn and out of sight.

Every nerve in my body twitches in horror. In my mind, I am running out the front door in my pajamas and racing barefoot down the lane, screaming at the boys to leave Delia alone, tearing at their arms to loosen their grips, to help Delia escape, calling at the top of my lungs for Silas and Maggie to wake up, to come to Delia's rescue.

But my muscles remain frozen as I crouch beneath my bedroom window, unable to move, unable to form a whisper, much less a scream.

Too late. Too late to warn Delia of the danger awaiting her. Too late to be the person I had so self-righteously proclaimed myself to be in all those arguments with my father. Too late to come to Delia's rescue. Much, much, much too late. Too late. Too late. I crumple to the floor, bent double, head on my knees, shaking and sobbing.

I do not sleep for the rest of that night, my only thought a fervent prayer, repeated over and over and over, for the sun to come up, for the night to be over, for the boys to be gone and for Delia to be okay, to be the same Delia that she was yesterday.

Chapter 11

Tuesday, July 18—Wednesday, July 19, 2006

My heart pounded even now, forty-six years later, at the memory. Why hadn't I done something? Why hadn't I awakened Daddy and told him what I'd seen? He could have grabbed his shotgun and scared those boys off, and then nothing would have happened to Delia. I had been so terrified that I hadn't been thinking clearly. Instead, I had cowered beneath the window, letting those boys drag Delia into the woods, letting them do whatever it was they had done.

And I still had no idea of what exactly had happened. Had they raped her? At sixteen, I had no conception of how devastating rape could be, of what long-term consequences it could have. And Daddy and Mama had both been so adamant about us not touching anything that a black person touched, not drinking from the same glass or eating from the same plate — the whole culture so obsessed with blacks and whites not using the same water fountains or the same bathrooms — that I suppose I had assumed that the boys would recoil from touching Delia's body in any intimate way. I guess I had expected them to scare her with insults and taunts, to let her know that she'd better not try anything again like coming into the theater lobby.

Later, when it became clear that something had happened to Delia, something that nobody talked about — not Silas or Maggie or Delia herself — something so bad that she missed the last week of the school year, I still didn't tell anybody what I had seen. No charges were ever filed. Silas had no more desire to stir up trouble than most of the other older black people in the community. He didn't want his daughter to be known as a troublemaker, and he certainly didn't want to lose his livelihood.

After the theater incident (the word "incident" whitewashing that horrible memory into something I could stick into a back corner of my mind), I had not seen Delia again, at least not close enough to speak to her, and a few weeks later she was gone. Silas told Daddy that she had gone to Georgia to take care of a sick grandmother, and that was all the information we knew.

My reaction to Delia's disappearance had been mostly relief. How terrible it made me feel to admit that now, but it was true. What I had heard and seen that night had become a daily cross that I had borne in guilty silence, but Delia's absence had lifted the burden somewhat and the passing years had lightened its load—until last week, when seeing Delia again had brought all those memories crashing back. Now, after all these years, would I finally be able to break that silence and ask Delia's forgiveness? And would Delia give it?

The next morning I fixed a plate of food for Mama to heat in the microwave before leaving for my lunch in town with Delia.

"Take your time," Mama insisted. "Callie's coming over for a visit right after dinner, and we'll just be sitting here gabbing."

Ms. Callie Upshaw, one of Mama's oldest friends, had already been over a couple of times since Mama's fall, bringing something each time—first a sour cream cake and then a peach cobbler hot from her oven—so I wondered what it would be today. Something delicious, for sure.

"Okay, that's good. Delia said she works only half days on Wednesdays, so we can have a nice leisurely lunch and catch up on each other's lives."

I arrived at the barbeque restaurant a little before twelve. Delia didn't get off work until noon, so I had a few minutes to wait. I was still idling my engine, keeping the air conditioning running, and trying to decide whether to wait in the car or go inside and get a table when someone tapped on the window right beside my face.

Startled, I looked up to see Delia's smile. I turned off my engine and exited the car.

"Hi. I wasn't expecting you so soon."

"What, girl, you figured I'd be late for dinner?"

"No." I gave Delia a hug, truly glad to see her again. "I just thought you didn't get off work until twelve, and with the drive here and all . . ."

"Shucks, girl, I'm not more than two minutes away, and I may have sneaked out a minute or two early today, seeing as how I had this appointment here to keep." Delia's eyes twinkled, and I remembered the first time I saw her, jumping down off the back of Daddy's pickup, landing smack dab in front of me—those big brown eyes and all that riot of plaits and barrettes.

I laughed and grabbed her arm. "Let's go get us a table. I'm starved."

The place was crowded, it being one of the few eating places in town, and I was pleased to see that there was a good mix of white and black customers, mostly men, taking their lunch hour from work. We were seated promptly in a side booth by a young blonde waitress who handed us menus and took our drink orders, saying she'd be right back. Mama had been uneasy about me eating at a restaurant with Delia, certain our lunch would become grist for gossip from anybody who recognized me, but the waitress had shown no discomfort or surprise at the two of us together. Mama was just out of touch with how much things had changed for the younger generations, even here in Pine Lake.

Delia settled back into her seat after our iced tea had been served and we had both ordered the pork barbeque sandwich special, "So tell me all about yourself, who you married, your children, what you've been doing for the last forty-some years."

"Nothing too earth-shattering," I answered. "I guess you know I'm a librarian, right?"

"That's what your mama said. Said you lived down near that place where they launch the rockets. What's it called?"

"Kennedy Space Center. I live right across the river in Titusville. In the sixties when I graduated from college the area was exploding with the space program taking off. That's when the push was on to land a man on the moon, you remember, so I figured it would be an exciting place to live. Plus the papers were saying that's where all the young men were headed, every engineer in the country wanting to work at the space center."

"And you wanted one of 'em?" Delia's eyes twinkled.

"Well, I figured it was better than coming back here and marrying some farmer." I laughed along with Delia, our chuckles causing people at a nearby table to look over at us. "It worked, too. That's where I met Russell, my husband. He's originally from Ohio, but somebody from NASA came to his college doing interviews, and he applied for a job at the space center and was hired right out of college. We have two children, Erin and Travis. Erin is married and has a boy and a girl. I have pictures." I reached for my wallet and opened it as I continued talking. "Travis is still a bachelor. He turns thirty this year, so I tell him he needs to find a wife and settle down, but he's in no hurry, I guess." I handed Delia the pictures.

"Hum-m" Delia said. "The little girl—she looks a lot like you. How old is she now?"

"That's Megan. She's almost four. And Caleb is six."

"Look at that grin. I bet he's a handful."

"He is," I agreed. "What about you? When you left here, where did you go? What have you been up to all these years?"

"Oh, nothing much. Up in Georgia, mostly. We got lots of kinfolks up there. I stayed with my grandma for a while till I met this boy…" Delia's voice trailed off. "You know how that is. I was sixteen and he was eighteen. Soon as he found out I was in the family way, he took off, and do you know, to this day I haven't heard a peep out of him. My grandma just about raised my first boy while I got a job to support us.

"Then along come George Fisher and took me off to Atlanta. Flashy car, nice clothes. Told me he was a lawyer working for the civil rights movement, and I fell for his story—hook, line, and sinker. Well, come to find out, all his money was coming from drugs. Drugs was new back then, you know, so I didn't have a clue what was going on, not until he got caught and sent off to jail. I was going to meetings on civil rights day and night and marching in the streets, and instead of him being in a courtroom defending demonstrators like he told me, he was off dealing heroin and such. He didn't like children, so my oldest, David, was still staying with my grandma back in Macon."

We were interrupted by the server bringing our sandwich plates.

"M-m-m," Delia said. "Don't this look good?"

After we'd both taken the edge off our hunger with a few minutes of eating, Delia picked up the thread of her story. "So after he was arrested, here I was in the big city with no job and nobody to support me, and a two-year-old back at my grandma's. I was determined to take care of myself and get David back with me. I told myself right then that no man was ever again going to come ahead of my child."

"Good for you," I said. "So what did you do then?"

"First thing I did was go back for David. I didn't want to keep imposing on my grandma, and I had a little bit of money saved up — George had been generous while he was raking in the drug money — so I got David, took him back to Atlanta with me, got a job there, and stayed away from men for a few years. Just me and David. Then I met Sam Carmichael. Best man on the face of the earth." Delia's eyes began to mist over, and she wiped at them with her napkin. I remembered something Maggie had told me over the phone — "She stills goes by the name Carmichael. That was her first husband, and all her children are Carmichaels except the oldest one." So that meant she wasn't married to the first two. What else had Maggie said about this husband? Something about him dying, and then Delia marrying someone else who wasn't good to her? I couldn't remember exactly.

I reached across the table and laid my hand over Delia's. "I'm sorry. Want to tell me what happened?"

Delia shook her head. "We had some happy years together. He treated David like his own, and then we had three more together — two girls and then another boy. He was a policeman in Atlanta — one of the first black men they ever hired — and I worried about him all the time."

"Oh, no. He died in the line of duty?"

Delia nodded. "He was only thirty-four. Sam Jr. was hardly more than a baby — five years old. That was a bad time." She dabbed at her eyes with the fingers of both hands. "Let's talk about something else."

"Your daughters. What are their names? Where do they live now?"

Delia brightened. "Well, first there's Nancy. Nancy Jane. She's still up in Georgia, just outside Atlanta. Married with three children of her own."

"Nancy Jane?" The name sounded familiar, but I couldn't place it at first. "Now where have I heard that name?'

Delia took another bite of her sandwich, and something in her expression jogged my memory.

"Our dolls. Rebecca Jane and Nancy Jane. You named your baby after your doll?"

Delia grinned. "I liked the name. You mean you didn't name your girl Rebecca Jane?"

"No. Wouldn't that have been something if I had? Imagine introducing our daughters to one another. Rebecca Jane, meet Nancy Jane. Your twin." I looked at Delia, and she giggled, prompting me to break into a spasm of laughter. Each time one of us would stop and compose ourselves, the other would let another giggle escape, until we were like two schoolgirls, hands over our mouths, eyes watering with laughter. Everyone in the restaurant was looking at us, smiling indulgently. They must have been wondering what two women of our age could find so funny.

We were still trying to return to our sober selves and finish our meal when the front door of the restaurant burst open and a large man swaggered in as if he owned the place, bellowing out a hearty hello to the girl behind the checkout counter and then striding noisily over to a table of businessmen in the center of the room. At first I thought he was going to join them, but he didn't sit. Instead, he went around the circle, clapping each one on the shoulder and then extending his hand for a handshake, his voice carrying into every corner of the restaurant. "Hello, Bill. Hey, Chuck, how's it going? Tom, you old coot, what you up to?"

He was wearing a short-sleeved white dress shirt and dark dress pants, and I could see that something, a badge or ID of some sort, was pinned to his shirt pocket, but he was too far away for me to read what it said.

Delia was sitting across from me with her back to the door, but when she looked around to see what was causing all the commotion, an immediate change came over her face. The laughter in her eyes drained away in an instant, replaced with a cold hatred that made me shiver.

"What is it?" I managed to ask.

Delia slid to the edge of the booth and stood. "I have to go." Her voice trembled somewhere between fury and fright, and before I could ask any more questions, she rushed out the front door. I didn't know what to do. I couldn't follow her out without paying the bill, but I couldn't just let her leave without an explanation.

The man had moved on to the next table of customers, where he was doing the same thing—greeting each one individually—and it suddenly dawned on me who he was and what he was doing. I looked carefully at his face—the ruddy complexion, the full jowls headed toward a double chin, the once wavy brown hair now thinning on top and streaked with gray. Lonnie P. Ramsey, campaigning for re-election.

So that was why Delia had left so quickly. Maybe she would wait for me in the parking lot. I looked around for our server so that I could request our bill, but before I could get her attention, Lonnie P. had finished his spiel at the second table and was headed straight for me, a big smile plastered on his face, hand already outstretched in my direction.

"Hello," he boomed, stretching his hand across the table. "I'm Lonnie P. Ramsey."

Instead of shaking his hand, I held up my glass of tea, pretending wariness, as if I didn't know this stranger who was approaching me. "Hello."

"I'd appreciate your vote for mayor," he boomed heartily. "We have some big things planned for Pine Lake."

"I'm just visiting. I don't live here." After all these years, he wasn't likely to recognize me, was he? And where was Delia? Had she driven off already? Would we not be able to continue our conversation?

"Oh. Where you from?"

"Central Florida. Just passing through." Why wasn't he moving on? I obviously wasn't a constituent.

"Here with the hubby, huh?" He glanced down at Delia's plate, her unfinished sandwich, the pile of French fries still on her plate. Had he seen her hasty exit? Was this some sort of test?

"Um, no, just a friend." Where was our waitress? "We were on our way out. I have to catch up with her." I put my napkin on the table and opened my wallet, pulling out a few dollar bills for a tip.

"Well, glad to have you drop by," Lonnie P. said. "Come again, any time. Pine Lake's a nice, friendly little town."

"Thanks." I'd ask for the bill at the checkout station. My urgent priority was to find Delia. Where had she gone?

Chapter 12

Outside, I scanned the parking lot. What had Delia been driving? I had no idea; she had suddenly appeared at my car window, and we had gone into the restaurant without my having seen what vehicle she had exited. Not seeing her anywhere, I unlocked my car and got inside. Delia's reaction to Lonnie P. confirmed what I had always known: Lonnie P. *was* one of the boys that night, the one whose voice was so familiar to me, the one who knew who Delia was and where she lived. I had to talk to her, but how? I had my cell phone with me, but I didn't have a cell phone number for her and I didn't know where she worked or lived, so I had no way of contacting her.

I sat for a minute, engine running, deciding what to do next. There was no hurry to get home, for Miss Callie would be arriving at Mama's right about now for her visit, and Mama had told me to take my time. I had assumed that Delia and I would linger over lunch, catching up on one another's lives. Maybe I'd drive to the library. I could look up Delia's number in the local phone book and if she had gone home, I could try reaching her there.

As I headed downtown, I noticed a red car behind me, making the same right turn that I made onto Main Street and then following me through three traffic lights, so when I pulled into the left turn lane at Willow Street and the red car did the same, I felt a moment of irrational panic before a glance in my rear view mirror revealed that it was Delia. She followed me into the library parking lot, and as I opened my door, she hurried over, open wallet in hand.

"I'm sorry about bailing out on you like that," she apologized. "How much do I owe you for lunch?"

I waved off her money. "My treat, remember? Are you okay?"

She nodded. "I had to get out of there."

"Come around and get in my car," I said. "We need to talk." Once we were both inside, I turned the ignition key so that the air conditioning came on. "Lonnie P. Ramsey," I said. "I didn't recognize him at first. He came over to me after you left, asking for my vote to re-elect him mayor, but I told him I didn't live here. He didn't have a clue who I was."

Delia's face hardened and her hands clenched into fists. "I want to kill him," she said. "Still, to this day, I want to kill them all."

I didn't need to ask why. "Lonnie P. was there that night you and your friend came into the movie theater, wasn't he?"

Delia looked at me, surprised. "How do you know about that?"

It took me a while to get out my answer. "I was there. I heard the whole thing."

"You were? Where?"

"I was at the concession stand, paying for a soda when the manager came running down the stairs yelling and foaming at the mouth, saying all those ugly things to you. I stepped behind a big cardboard cutout of John Wayne that was off to the side so nobody could see me. My friends had already gone into the movie, and I was all alone out there. I plain panicked. Then that crowd of boys came in the door and started in on you, and I couldn't move. One of them was Lonnie P., wasn't it? I couldn't see them, but I thought I recognized his voice."

Delia didn't answer, but I could tell from her expression that I was right.

"Who else?" I asked. "Did you know any of the others?"

She shook her head. "No, only Lonnie P." She spit out his name.

"I thought they were just talking tough. I never dreamed…"

Delia turned her head away so that I couldn't see her eyes.

"What happened that night?" I asked as gently as I could. "You don't have to tell me if you don't want to."

Delia looked at me then, my earlier words sinking in. "You were there? You heard what they called us?"

"I'm sorry." I clenched the steering wheel with white-knuckled hands. "I never thought they'd carry out their threats. But, later, when I heard you'd moved to Georgia, and then when you never came back, not even for a visit . . . it was them, wasn't it? Lonnie P. and that gang came after you?"

When Delia didn't answer, I continued, begging Delia now to forgive me. "I should have stepped out and said something to let them know I heard. I wanted to. You don't know how badly I wanted to."

Delia shook her head, as if in disbelief.

"I was sixteen. I was scared. You know what life was like back then. I wanted to defend you, but..."

"I gotta go." Delia exited my car, got into her own, and drove away, all without a backward glance.

I leaned forward, my forehead touching the steering wheel. I hadn't even told her the worst part, that hours later, from my bedroom window, I had seen her walking home, had seen those boys grab her and drag her behind the tobacco barn into the woods. That later scene, I knew now, I could never reveal. I could only hope that my failure to step forward at the movie theater would be something she could come to understand and forgive, but my inaction later that night was unforgivable.

I sat for another minute or two, my hands trembling, trying to calm myself. Would Delia ever speak to me again, or had I lost her for good? Maybe I shouldn't have told her; maybe I should have kept all that guilt locked up inside me. But it was too late now to take back what I had said. I straightened, pressed my back into the car seat, and unclenched my hands from the steering wheel. What now? I was determined to do whatever it took to get back in Delia's good graces. And the only way to do that was to make sure Lonnie P. was held accountable, even at this late date, for what he had done. But how? I had no idea, but I had to do something.

I exited my car and walked into the library. Gail's comments yesterday had aroused my curiosity about how Lonnie P. had made all the money he'd been handing out left and right around Pine Lake, and knowing now with certainty that he had been one of Delia's attackers made me want to find something else nefarious in his past, something I could offer up to Delia as an atonement of sorts for failing to take action at the movie theater. The library would have computers with Internet access, and maybe I could find something about his business background that would give me some clues.

After spending a few minutes checking my e-mail, which I hadn't accessed since I'd been up here, a search for the name Lonnie P. Ramsey rewarded me with several hits. The first one listed took me to a website for Ramsey Ford. Flashy and impressive with a slide show of photos and streaming text, it had obviously been created by a professional.

A click on a heading labeled "About the Owner" brought up the same photo of Lonnie P. that I'd seen in the *Pine Lake Gazette*—the small beady eyes in the doughy face, the jowls and double chin, the streaks of gray in the hair. I skimmed the text beneath: his humble beginnings on a farm, his high school athletic feats, his football scholarship to the University of Florida, then the military and combat in Vietnam. In 1966, he had returned home, married his high school sweetheart, Sherri Lynn Harris, and taken a sales job at his father-in-law's local Ford dealership. I had only a vague memory of Sherri Lynn from high school. A cheerleader? I seemed to remember bouncy blonde hair, but nothing else came to mind.

Then there had been more Ford dealerships in various locations along Florida's East Coast, first in Jacksonville and then Daytona Beach, Vero Beach, and Fort Lauderdale, a steady migration south. At least there hadn't been a stop along the way in Brevard County, so I'd had no occasion to hear the name Ramsey Ford. By the time they reached Miami, Lonnie P. had become interested in the real estate market. Being a farm boy, he knew how valuable land was, for as his father had always told him, "God's not making any more of it," so he began to buy up property and develop it into residential communities.

By this time two children had come along, a son and a daughter, and as the children reached their teen years, Lonnie P. and Sherri Lynn had returned to Pine Lake to take over her father's Ford dealership upon his retirement, thus completing the circle back to where they had begun. Lonnie P. had also bought several large tracts of farmland just outside town, replatting the former cornfields and cow pastures into individual one to three-acre home sites, naming it Rambling Acres and building a home for his family right in the middle of it. A click on a live link to Rambling Acres took me to another web site with the same streaming text and a slide show of custom-built homes on expansive lots, shots of emerald green golf fairways and a clear blue lake with white geese swimming along the edge.

I went back to the first site to finish reading the last couple of paragraphs of the profile. Had Lonnie P. written this himself, or had he hired someone to write it for him? Anyone reading it would have been swept up in the rags-to-riches story—the struggling farm-boy who had morphed into popular athlete, then into patriotic war veteran, and finally into inheritor of the American entrepreneurial spirit. I could almost see the flag waving in the background, an eagle soaring across the sky, a band striking up the national anthem.

Back at home, not only had Lonnie P. parlayed both Ramsey Ford and Rambling Acres into wildly successful businesses, but he had also jumped right into offering his services to the town: volunteering for various projects and donating money to charitable causes, thus leading to seats on the boards of several of the local businesses (all duly listed, along with his awards) and finally his election as mayor of Pine Lake.

I went back to the list of hits and clicked on the other websites—one for the city of Pine Lake, with a Welcome page from its mayor, then a couple of local civic organizations, and finally the Rambling Acres site again. Maybe Gail's enthusiasm about Lonnie P.'s philanthropy to the town was well-deserved; it was certainly reasonable to assume that Lonnie P. had matured since high school into a loving and responsible husband and father, an astute businessman who had made wise or at least lucky financial choices and now wanted to share his good fortune with the town.

Certainly the fact that he had been elected mayor showed that people in Pine Lake liked and respected him, and with the population within the city limits likely more than fifty-percent African American, he would have had to court the black vote. Had that long-ago summer night when he'd boasted to his friends that they would teach Delia a lesson been an impulsive incident that he had lived to regret?

Delia, understandably, hated him, wanted to kill him, but an hour ago, when she got out of my car in the parking lot, she had hated me, too, for hiding like a coward, for not stepping out and defending her against that crowd of boys. Was Lonnie P., like me, living under a burden of guilt that he was now trying to assuage with all his good works and service to the community? Who was I to cast a stone?

I didn't know what to think or believe. Maybe the dinner at Gail's house would help me get a truer picture of who the adult Lonnie P. was. Until then I'd have to reserve my judgment.

Chapter 13

Friday, July 21, 2006

By Friday, I had worked myself up into such a state of anxiety about the dinner at Gail's house that evening that I kept debating with myself about whether to go or to call Gail and cancel. I'd been looking forward to it since Tuesday, but the disastrous ending to my lunch with Delia on Wednesday had left me feeling unworthy of enjoying the evening. My hair was also overdue for a trim and a color treatment, but since I didn't know any stylists up here, I'd done nothing about it. I'd have to make do with a shampoo and a blow dry and hope it would look halfway decent — split ends, gray strands, and all.

I had told Russell over the phone about Gail's invitation, but remembering his rather sarcastic question when I'd mentioned Brian and Edwina's divorce — "Do you have a lunch date with him, too?" — I hadn't told him that the dinner would be a foursome. Russell knew that Brian and I had been classmates, but I'd never let on that he was anyone special , so Russell had no knowledge of my high school crush on him. And there was no need for him ever to know that little detail. Besides, I had wanted to keep the anticipation to myself, treasure it as my small treat rather than subject it to Russell's scrutiny and derision.

Part of my reason for wanting to see Brian was to ask him about that night at the movie theater. From behind the concession stand, he had seen the boys who had burst through the door. He would have known them. Could he still recall who they were? Of course, he had no way of knowing what happened later that night, so the event wouldn't have been something that he had relived over and over in his mind as I had. It was a long shot that he remembered anything about that evening at all, but it wouldn't hurt to ask.

The problem would be finding a way to question him without involving Gail and Gary. With them being fellow church members and friends with Lonnie P., I couldn't let them into my confidence. Probably best to forget the whole idea. If Russell had any inkling of what was going through my mind, he'd come and drag me home to Titusville, impress on me the danger of inserting myself into a situation that was best left alone.

"You sure you'll be okay by yourself?" I asked Mama before I left. "I don't have to go, you know. I can call Gail and cancel."

"I'll be perfectly fine," Mama assured me. "Go on and see your friends and don't worry about me. I feel bad about you having to be up here in the first place, away from your own family."

"You're part of my family." I gave her a hug on her good side as I left. "I'll try to get home early."

I arrived at Gail's before Brian. "Sorry I'm early," I said to Gail as she answered the door. "I'm used to heavier traffic, I guess."

"No problem," Gail answered. "Come on in. You look great. I like your outfit."

"Thanks." Partly to compensate for my lackluster hair, I had dressed in my best pants outfit and had even applied eyeliner and mascara in addition to my usual makeup routine of foundation, powder, and lipstick. Looking at Gail now in her casual Capri pants and pullover top, I was beginning to feel a little foolish. "I like yours, too," I told Gail. "That color looks good on you. I wasn't sure how to dress."

"Oh, any old thing is fine. We're not formal around here. You know that." Gail led me into the living room where I greeted Gary and took a seat on the sofa. Gail perched briefly on the edge of a chair and then excused herself to go back into the kitchen.

I hurried after her, feeling as nervous and jittery as a teenager on her first date. Not only had I let myself be partnered with Brian for the evening without my husband's knowledge, but I'd left Mama on her own again for the third time this week—first on Tuesday morning when I'd come here for coffee, then on Wednesday for my lunch with Delia, and now again tonight. How well did that reflect on my priorities? If I made it through the evening without being completely crushed by the truckload of guilt that was hanging over my head, I'd be lucky.

"Can I help you with anything?"

"No, not really." Gail took glasses down from a cupboard. "The rolls are in the oven, and everything else is keeping warm on the stove. We're just waiting for Brian."

It seemed an eternity before the doorbell rang.

"I'll get it," Gail called, but Gary had already started for the door, so Gail and I followed along behind him, an entire welcoming committee.

"Hello," I said after Gail and Gary had welcomed Brian inside. "You're looking good." I extended one hand for a handshake, but he put both arms around my shoulders and pulled me toward him for a hug.

"Hi, Kate. You, too. Wow, something smells good."

"Gary grilled the chicken," Gail answered. "I hope you like it."

The food was good, and we all stuffed ourselves to the point that nobody had room for dessert. "We'll have it later," Gail said. "You're not leaving here, though, until you've had my special coconut cream pie."

Gary and Brian disappeared out the back door while Gail and I cleared the table, put the leftover food away, and loaded the dishwasher. "Gary's showing off his new gas grill. He's so proud of that thing you'd think he built it himself." Gail rolled her eyes at me. "So, this is fun tonight, isn't it? I don't see Brian all that often any more, hardly at all, really. He's turned into quite the hunk, hasn't he?"

"His looks have certainly improved since high school," I agreed. "Too bad about his marriage. I can't imagine anyone leaving such a nice guy."

Gail smiled at me. "You know what that proves, don't you?"

"What?"

"That you're happily married. Other folks would say, 'Wow, the single life must be great. I wish I were single again.' I'm with you, though. I can't imagine life without Gary. We've been together since we were sixteen, married since we were eighteen, and we're still crazy about each other. You just know when it's right, don't you?"

"Um-m," I agreed, but I really wasn't interested in discussing mine and Russell's marriage. The truth was that I hadn't given much thought to it lately. Sure, the thrill had worn off after thirty-seven years, but we were still together, weren't we? Since the kids had grown up and moved out, we didn't seem to have that much in common any more. But wasn't that true of most long-married couples? I'd never thought of our marriage as being "in trouble," but if it was still as solid as I'd always considered it, then why was I getting so excited at being around Brian?

When we joined the men in the living room, Gary had claimed his leather recliner and Brian had taken a seat at one end of the sofa. Gail took the armchair near Gary, leaving me to join Brian on the sofa. I took the other end cushion, the middle sofa cushion empty between us. Brian, like me, had somewhat dressed up for the occasion, in a pair of khaki trousers and a button-up shirt, loose at the neck so that I could see chest hair beneath.

"So," I said, turning to face him. "I guess you're still teaching at the community college. Or have you retired?"

"Still there," Brian answered. "I have two more years to go before they force me out. I don't know what I'll do all day once I stop teaching."

After discussing everyone's work, we moved on to remembering high school days. As the only one of the foursome who had left the area, I had lost touch with most of our classmates and was soon lost in the complications of who was doing what. Somehow the conversation got around to Vietnam and who in our class had served over there. Brian, who had gone to the University of Florida after high school, had escaped the draft, but Gary had spent four years in the Air Force, choosing to join up rather than wait for his Army draft notice to arrive in the mail.

"I didn't get to Vietnam, though," he said. "They promised to show me the world, and guess where I ended up? Canada. Nearly froze my butt off. Then, the next year they sent me to Louisiana. You think it's humid in Florida? We didn't see no place that we'd want to go back to, did we, Hon?"

"No," Gail agreed. "Of course, Gary didn't want Vietnam, but he did hope they'd send him overseas, at least, to France or someplace like that. We were lucky that he got out when he did—in '66—before things really heated up in 'Nam. Nobody in our class died over there, but if you look at the classes after ours, all those lost some Pine Lake boys. Their names are engraved on a memorial on the court house lawn."

Gail began to mention some names, helped by Gary and Brian, and I was astounded at the number they came up with for such a small place as Pine Lake.

"Did Lonnie P. put up the money for the memorial?" I asked. I hadn't seen it, so I didn't know what sort of memorial they were discussing.

Gail looked at Gary. "I don't think so. He wasn't even here when it was erected, was he?"

Gary shrugged. "I think it was one of the clubs. The Jaycees? Or maybe it was the VFW group. I'm not sure."

"I just wondered," I said, "seeing he spent a tour of duty in Vietnam himself. I thought maybe he had a part in it."

Gary laughed. "So you've been reading his campaign literature, I take it. I'll bet money Lonnie P. got about as close to Vietnam as I did."

"But he says—"

"That's he's a Vietnam vet? Well, he was in the army, far as I know, and it was during the Vietnam years. Maybe he was there. I don't know. Heck, get in a group of men my age and three-fourths of them were in 'Nam, fighting off the Commies, getting jungle rot, leaving babies over there they'll never see."

"But you just said you weren't there, so you don't lie about your experience."

"I'm not running for public office." Gary laughed. "If I was, I'd probably exaggerate a little, too. Everybody does."

"But what if he wasn't there, and somebody does some research and finds out he's lying?" I asked. "Wouldn't that hurt his chances of re-election?"

Gary waved off my concern. "He's done enough for this town that nobody's gonna care about a little thing like that."

Gail spoke up. "It's so wonderful all the things he's done for Pine Lake." She turned to Brian. "Did you hear about the new sanctuary at Hopewell Baptist he started the drive for? I already told Kate about it."

Brian hadn't heard, so Gail and Gary filled him in on the details, and the conversation moved on to other topics. By the time I decided to check my watch, it was past eight-thirty.

"I hate to leave good company," I said, "but I left Mama home alone, and I promised not to be out too late."

Gail wouldn't let me go without a piece of pie, so by the time we'd all had dessert and I stood to say goodbye, it was five minutes till nine.

"I'd better be going, too," Brian said, standing along with me as we both thanked Gail and Gary again for dinner.

As we reached my car, Brian threw one arm around my shoulder as he reached with his other hand to open my driver's side door, bringing my face close to his neck and to the musky, masculine scent of aftershave. "This was fun. We should get together like this more often."

"Yes, it was." I ducked into my car, away from the warmth of his hand, my blood pulsing with the long-forgotten tingling of first love.

"See you Sunday. And say 'Hi' to your mom for me."

"Okay. See you," I promised, knowing that I would not tell Mama that Brian had said "Hi." Mama had not known that Brian was going to be at Gail's for dinner, and I had no intention of telling her. Not that I had anything illicit to hide from her or from Russell, but there was no need to arouse suspicion when there was nothing going on to warrant it—nothing at all.

Chapter 14

Sunday, July 23, 2006

On Sunday morning, after church was over, Mama and I again used the side ramp to exit, and as we merged with the crowd descending the front steps, I looked around for Brian. I had seen him inside earlier and had turned to smile and mouth a "Hi" from my seat up front beside Mama, but we hadn't yet had a chance to speak.

Several of Mama's friends gathered around us, while others headed to their cars or clumped into small knots beneath the shade of the oak trees, talking about the sermon or more likely, the hot, dry weather. I noticed several people scanning the sky, looking for possible rain clouds. Brian, deep in conversation with a man I didn't know, was one of the last people out of the building, but upon looking up and seeing me, he waved and headed in my direction, causing me to feel a little giddy inside, as if I had some power of attraction that had long lain dormant and was being awakened again after years of hibernation.

I took a few steps forward to meet him, moving away from the circle of Mama and her friends. "Hi. How are you?"

"Great. And how about yourself?" Brian smiled, and I felt my cheeks and forehead grow warm.

"Fine. Mama's doing well." I nodded in her direction. "She should get the sling off this week."

"So you'll be leaving us soon?" Brian asked. "It seems you just got here."

"Oh, not that soon. Mama will need a few weeks of therapy to get strength and range of motion back in her shoulder, so I'll be here through mid-August or so."

"I bet your husband is ready for you to get back home."

"I guess so. He drove up last weekend, and he wants me to persuade Mama to come stay with us. But she'll never do that. So I'm here as long as she needs me." The minister, now finished with shaking hands, was heading toward Mama. I turned my attention back to Brian.

"That's good to hear." Brian smiled again. "Friday night was fun. Hey, you want to go to dinner sometime this week and finish catching up on all the things we didn't get a chance to talk about on Friday? There's this new restaurant in town that's rumored to be pretty good, and I don't like eating out alone. You want to give it a try?"

"Um-m, I don't know." Was Brian asking me out on a date? He had just mentioned my husband, so it wasn't a "date" date. There was nothing wrong with two friends having a meal together, was there? And it would give me a chance to ask him about that night at the movie theater, to see if he remembered anything.

"You pick the evening. I'm free anytime."

"Okay, dinner sounds good. What about Tuesday?" Having decided on the spur of the moment to accept Brian's invitation, I didn't want to wait another whole week. Saying "Tomorrow," though, would have sounded too eager, too forward.

"What about Tuesday?" Mama was at my elbow, the minister having finished his greeting and headed for his car to escape the hot July sun.

"Kate and I were talking about trying this new restaurant in town, the one out by the college," Brian said. "I've been wanting to go there, but I was telling Kate I hate to eat out alone. You want to come with us?"

I felt like crawling into a hole. Here I was pretending in my deluded fancy that Brian was asking me out on a date, and now he was including my mother?

"Me? Oh, no," Mama said. "Not with this contraption on my arm. I heard that's a steak place, anyway. Only way I like steak is pounded down until it's tender and then pan-fried. None of this grilled steak for me that's still pink in the middle. I don't eat no raw meat."

Brian laughed. "You don't care then if Kate and I try it out?"

"You go right ahead. I'll eat my steak at home."

I breathed a huge sigh of relief. Now that Mama knew about our dinner and thought nothing of it, I could put aside this uneasy feeling that I was hiding something from her and Russell. The reality was that Brian and I were old friends and classmates—nothing more—and I had to remember that fact and keep things in perspective.

By mid-afternoon I had carried on half a dozen different conversations with Brian in my head about that night at the movie theater, and I was itching with impatience to find out how much he remembered. Now that we had re-established our friendship, why did I need to wait until our dinner on Tuesday to ask him about it? I looked up his phone number, programmed it into my cell phone, and walked outside to call him.

"Hi, it's Kate," I said when he answered. "I hope I'm not interrupting anything."

"No, not at all. What's up?"

"I had a question I wanted to ask you, and I didn't get a chance this morning or Friday night."

"Oh, what's that?"

"It concerns something that happened a long time ago. You probably don't remember it. We were in our sophomore year of high school."

"That far back, huh?"

"There's no reason for it to have stuck in your mind, I guess, but one Saturday night at the end of our sophomore year, I was at the movie theater with a couple of friends, and I was buying a soda from you at the concession stand when two black girls walked into the lobby. The manager ran down the stairs yelling and screaming at them to leave or he was going to call the sheriff. Do you remember that?"

Brian hesitated, as if he were thinking. "Yeah, I remember. They wanted to buy something, and Old Man Drexler told me not to sell them anything. Then they left, didn't they? Nothing happened."

"Some boys came in the front door and starting calling them names and making derogatory comments. There was this big cardboard cutout in the lobby. I think it was John Wayne—anyway, somebody dressed in cowboy getup—and when the manager started yelling, I stepped behind it so nobody could see me. I could hear the boys, but I couldn't see them, so I don't know who they were. The girls sassed back to them and then left, and afterward the boys talked about catching up to the girls and doing something to teach them a lesson. You remember that?"

Brian paused again. "Um, I vaguely remember some other people being there. And I remember that cutout. It *was* John Wayne, and it stayed in that lobby forever, it seems. I wouldn't be surprised if it's still there, somewhere. Weren't you there with some other girls? All of you buying sodas?"

"Yes, but I had to go to the bathroom, so I told them to go on and save me a seat. I was alone out there when the two black girls came in. You were asking me something about the biology final—if I was ready for it, I guess."

"Boy, you've got a good memory," Brian said. "I have a hazy recollection of that night. Why are you remembering it now?"

"I knew one of the black girls. Her father sharecropped for my father, and they lived on our place. We'd known each other since we were four years old. She moved away soon after that night, but she's back up here again. I ran into her in town, and the two of us had lunch one day last week."

"So she brought it up over lunch?" Brian asked. "The two of you discussed it?"

"Well, it came up is the best way to put it, I guess. I feel so ashamed that I hid behind that cutout and didn't defend Delia against those boys."

"That was a long time ago."

"I know, but seeing and talking to Delia brought it all back, and I can't stop thinking about it. You were there. Do you remember the boys coming in? Do you recall who they were? Any of them?"

"Gosh, I don't remember anything about any boys. I just remember the two girls coming in and Old Man Drexler telling me not to sell them anything."

"One of the boys was Lonnie P. Ramsey. He's the one who knew who Delia was and where she lived. She didn't know any of the others, but she recognized Lonnie P."

"So the boys called them some names? And she's still upset about it now?"

"It wasn't what happened in the theater, but what happened later that night. Those boys carried out their threats — to Delia, at least. I don't know about the other girl. And Lonnie P. was the ringleader. He led them to her."

"How do you know that?"

"Delia told me." There was no way I could tell Brian over the phone about my own complicity in what had happened — in what I had seen from my bedroom window. "I don't know the details, but it was plenty bad. You didn't hear any talk afterward, any bragging?"

"Me? You know me. I wasn't a part of Lonnie P.'s crowd — no way, shape, or fashion. If something did happen, I'd be the last to know."

"Delia told me she wants to kill Lonnie P. She wants to kill them all."

"Kill them? Are you serious? You think she's going to do something to Lonnie P.?"

"No. That was just her way of expressing how upset she still is. I'm not worried about that. You sure you don't know who else was there that night?"

"I really have no idea. All I remember is a big commotion. I was scared the sheriff was going to come and there'd be a big stink in the paper and I'd be in the middle of it. I remember you being there, but I don't remember much else. Maybe if I thought about it a while..."

"Think about it, okay? Try to remember Lonnie P., at least."

111

"What's this all about? Your friend can't press charges now, can she, after all these years?"

"Oh, I'm sure she doesn't want to do anything like that, but something really bad happened to her, and those boys got off scot-free. And the worst part of it is I was standing right there and I didn't do anything to help her."

"What could you have done?"

"I don't know. Maybe if I hadn't hidden, if they'd seen me there at the counter, they wouldn't have made those threats. Lonnie P. knew that Delia lived on our place, and maybe his seeing me there would have made him think twice before leading those boys into doing whatever it was they did."

"Hey, ease up on yourself." Brian's voice was comforting and supportive. "Whatever happened wasn't your fault. If we were sophomores, this was back in what—spring of 1960? Think about what was going on then all over the South. Even if your friend had reported it, nothing would have happened to those white boys for roughing up a Negro girl, especially after she broke the law by coming into the theater. If anybody had been thrown in jail, it would have been the girls."

"I know you're right, and that upsets me even more. Now that I know for sure Lonnie P. was one of those boys, I can't sit on my hands and stay quiet while everybody praises him for all the good he's done for Pine Lake."

"Hey, Katie, I'm sorry about your friend, I truly am, but you're talking about something that happened when we were teenagers. There's nothing you can do about it now."

"Maybe. Maybe not. All I know is I have to do something to clear my conscience and make it up to Delia. She hates me now, and you don't know how bad that makes me feel."

"Hates you? Why? You said the two of you had lunch together."

"We did, but when I told her I was at the theater, that I was hiding behind the cutout and heard what the boys said, and did nothing to defend her, she ran off without a word. So now I have to make it up to her, whatever it takes."

"Seriously, Kate, listen to me. You need to think about what you're saying. This is crazy. And dangerous. You're talking about stirring up a hornet's nest of trouble here. Lonnie P. is probably the most powerful person in the county right now."

"I know that, but the way I see it, I don't have any choice if I want to keep living with myself. I'm not asking anything of you. I just wondered if you remembered who the boys were that night. And you said you didn't, so forget it."

"Forget it? You tell me how you want to call Pine Lake's mayor to account for something that happened nearly half a century ago, drag him through the dirt somehow and stir up a whole mess of trouble Pine Lake doesn't need, and then I'm supposed to forget it?"

"I simply asked you a question, that's all. It's not like I'm going to chase him down and throw a rope around his neck or anything. Forget I asked."

"Katie, I understand how you feel. I really do." Brian's voice was calmer. "But believe me, the best thing you can do for your friend is to put it in the past and move on. You bring this out in the open, and you'll both regret it. I promise."

"You're right, I'm sure." Brian was the voice of reason. What could I do now nearly fifty years after the fact, except try again to apologize to Delia for my inaction? "Thanks for listening, anyway. I guess I'll see you on Tuesday."

"Wait," Brian said. "Before you go, you want to hear something really stupid? The reason I wasn't paying attention to the boys that night is because I was focused on you. I had a real crush on you in high school, you know."

"You did? You never asked me out."

"Remember what I was like in high school? I was a first-class nerd, and my face was a mess. You wouldn't have gone out with me. But when you ordered that soda, all I could think about was how I could make my hand touch yours when I handed it to you. There we were, the two of us alone in the lobby, and I couldn't say anything to you except something stupid about school. I remember thinking that if the sheriff did come, I was going to be your protector, do something grand and heroic that would make you fall head over heels in love with me."

"That's sweet," I said. "I had a crush on you, too. You were so smart and so serious. I would have gone out with you if you'd asked me."

"Thanks." Brian laughed to make light of the direction our discussion had taken. "I don't believe it, but it's nice of you to say so, even if it is about forty-five years too late."

"Sorry about that."

"Well, better late than never, as they always say."

"Better late?" I put one hand on my throat, feeling a flush creeping up my neck, and as we said goodbye, I felt sixteen again, my heart knocking against my chest. I should never have agreed to go out to dinner with Brian. What was I getting myself into?

Chapter 15

Tuesday, July 25, 2006

"So, you've got two good arms again," I told Mama as we got into the car after her doctor's appointment on Tuesday morning, marking three weeks since she had fallen. "How does it feel to be out of that sling?"

"A little strange," Mama answered. "It still feels like the sling is there, you know?" She was sitting with her elbow crooked, holding onto her right arm with her left hand.

"You'll have to get used to moving it again. We'll do the exercises as soon as we get home so you can start getting the muscles back in shape." The doctor had given her a sheet with illustrations and instructions, simple lifts of the arm out in front of her and to the side but not yet over her head. The nurse had also set her up for therapy sessions on Tuesday and Friday mornings for the next couple of weeks to help her regain full range of motion. "Want to get some lunch in town before we go home? You can eat with your right hand again."

"Whatever you want to do. The first thing I want when we get home is to take a real shower. That's the thing I've missed the most."

"I can imagine." For the past three weeks I had been helping Mama with hand baths with a washcloth, helping her get undressed, being ever so careful not to move her shoulder, and then washing her back and other areas that she couldn't reach with her left hand, and the procedure had been uncomfortable for both of us. Thank goodness those days were over now. "Let's get something quick, and then we'll get you home and into the shower."

By four-thirty it was time for me to start getting ready for my dinner with Brian, a dinner about which I'd been having second thoughts. "I don't have to go," I told Mama. "I can call Brian and cancel if you'd rather I stay here with you."

"Go. Go." Mama insisted. "Now that the sling's off, I can take care of myself perfectly well. Remember, I've been living by myself for over a year now since Daddy passed on, and I've been doing just fine."

"I don't want you to feel like I'm neglecting or deserting you. Is there anything you want me to do for you before I go?"

"Nothing," Mama answered. "I can take care of my own supper. Go on and let me enjoy the peace and quiet for a change."

"Okay, if you're sure." I went into my bedroom and closed the door. Mama's dependence on me over the past three weeks had reversed our normal roles, but now with the sling removed, we'd be on a more equal basis, and I could feel a little less guilty about leaving her.

As I turned into the parking lot at the restaurant, five minutes before six, I noticed Brian's silver Isuzu was already there. I pulled in beside it.

"Wow, good timing," he said as we both exited our cars. "I just got here. I hope you're hungry."

"Starved." For the last few weeks, I'd been cooking the way Mama wanted things cooked, and I'd been craving a grilled steak, baked potato, and fresh green salad all day.

We were seated at a booth near the back, next to a window overlooking the college campus. Brian pointed out the science building and his upstairs office beside the chemistry lab, and then we studied the menus and made small talk as we waited for our server to return.

Once we'd placed our orders, however, and the menus were taken away, I was left facing Brian across the table with nothing between us for distraction. I sipped my iced tea and looked around at the restaurant décor, not wanting to meet Brian's eyes. What was I doing here, a married woman, having dinner with another man? A man to whom I felt a strong physical attraction? Russell had no idea of what I was doing. And what if Gail and Gary walked in and caught us together? Gail hadn't known what she was setting in motion by inviting us both to her house for dinner, and if she saw me alone with Brian tonight, her Baptist apron strings would surely be tied into knots. My heart began to race, and I wiped my sweaty palms against my napkin. How did people actually carry out affairs without their blood pressure exploding?

"Hey," Brian said, startling me. "Something wrong?"

"No, just hungry. Shouldn't our salads be here by now?"

When our salads and basket of rolls arrived a moment later, I dug in greedily, grateful for the diversion. I'd accepted the invitation on Sunday morning partly because it would provide a good opportunity to question Brian about the scene at the movie theater and find out what he remembered about the boys, but now we'd already discussed the subject over the phone and he'd more or less told me to drop the matter. So what was left to talk about?

We both concentrated on our salads until the arrival of our meals and the simultaneous jingle of my cell phone inside my purse broke the uneasy silence. "I'd better get this," I said to Brian. "I told Mama to call if she needed me." But when I pulled out my phone and looked at the caller ID, I saw that it was my own home phone number. Just my luck for Russell to pick this time to call.

"Hi," Russell said in response to my hello. "How's your steak meal?" He chuckled into the phone.

"How did you know?" I put one hand to the side of my face, aware of Brian's questioning eyes on me. I felt like sliding under the table.

"I talked to your mother. She said you had gone into town to some steak place for dinner. So I was wondering how it was."

"Oh." What exactly had Mama told him? Surely Russell would know that I hadn't driven into town to eat dinner at a restaurant all by myself. "Is everything all right at home?"

"Fine," Russell said. "I just finished a bowl of soup and some crackers."

If he was trying to make me feel guilty, it was certainly working. Brian was sitting patiently, waiting for me to finish my conversation before starting to eat.

"Our meal just came," I told Russell. "Can I call you back later tonight?"

"Sure," Russell said. "Enjoy your dinner. You can tell me all about it later. I'll be sitting around here doing nothing."

So Mama must have told him that I was having dinner with Brian. And then he, of course, had called to let me know he was keeping tabs on my actions. My guilt switched to irritation. I wasn't his property or some underage child who couldn't be trusted to use good judgment or be home by a certain curfew. "I'll call you later," I said and disconnected without waiting for his goodbye.

"That was Russell," I said to Brian. "He had tried calling me at Mama's number, and she told him I was out having dinner in town. So naturally he had to check up on me. Let's eat." I picked up my fork and knife, and Brian followed suit.

"He the jealous type?" Brian asked. "I didn't mean to get you in trouble."

"No, it's nothing. He's lonely at home all by himself, and he wants me to feel sorry for him. Let's enjoy our meal."

We spent a few minutes eating in silence before I brought up Lonnie P.'s name. All Brian needed was a little more convincing—more time to get used to the idea that Lonnie P. had done something really bad to Delia—and then he'd be on my side, I knew. How could he not? In high school, he'd had as much disdain for the "cool jocks" crowd that Lonnie P. hung with as I'd had.

"You have any idea how Lonnie P. made all the money he's giving away to Pine Lake?" I asked Brian. "He sure seems to have deep pockets."

Brian shrugged. "All I know is he's got that Ford dealership that belonged to his father-in-law and he bought up that farmland for next to nothing and started a housing development. Both of them have done well, from what I hear."

"I wish Mama had a computer. If I could get on the Internet, I'll bet I could do some digging into his past."

"I thought you were going to drop this vendetta against Lonnie P." Brian leaned forward and lowered his voice. "You're heading into treacherous territory here. As for something that happened way back in high school, whatever it was, it's best left alone. Lots of folks did things in high school they'd just as soon forget, probably you included."

"Me? I never hurt anybody. And you didn't either. I'd bet my life on that. Only person you hurt was me when you won valedictorian for our graduating class." I smiled to show I was only teasing. "I assume you have a computer at home?"

"Of course." Brian smiled back, "Sorry about the valedictorian thing. But I'm warning you for the last time. You can't go digging up dirt on Lonnie P. or anybody else. I live here, remember, and I've got a good job I want to keep for a couple more years till I'm eligible for retirement."

"Warning taken. I sure miss my computer, though. Since I've been up here I haven't even been able to check my e-mail to see what's going on back at home. I checked it once at the library, and that was a week ago."

"If that's all you want, you're welcome to use my computer anytime. In fact, you can follow me home when we're finished here and check it tonight."

"You mean it?" I looked at Brian, grateful for the offer. He was giving me a foot in the door, at least. "Thanks. I'll take you up on that. And I'll be quick. I promised Mama I wouldn't be gone long."

After we finished eating, I followed Brian to his house, giving Mama a call along the way to let her know I was going by Brian's for a little while to use his computer and promising to be home before dark. I didn't ask her what she'd told Russell over the phone, but I could find that out later.

Brian invited me inside and led me down the hall to a bedroom that had been converted into a comfortable home office, with an L-shaped walnut desk that filled one corner. Another wall contained floor-to-ceiling bookshelves. "Here you are." He jiggled the mouse to bring the computer back to full power. "All yours."

"Thanks." I sat and pulled up my e-mail account while Brian went back toward the living room, probably to do some tidying up since he hadn't been expecting company. After checking through my e-mails, deleting most of them and typing short responses to a few others, I went back to the Ramsey Ford website I'd found at the library. "Okay if I print something?" I called down the hall.

"Sure." Brian called back. "Long as it's not a book."

"It's only a couple of pages from Lonnie P.'s website for the Ford dealership. Pretty interesting stuff. Have you seen it?"

"Hey!" Brian's voice was closer. "I thought you weren't..." and then he was at the door of the room.

I clicked on "Print" and motioned for him to come inside. "Don't worry. It's nothing incriminating. Take a look."

Brian took the pages from the printer and scanned the paragraphs, his curiosity pulling him into the spirit of my quest in spite of his misgivings.

"Pretty self-congratulatory, wouldn't you say? You think he wrote this himself? Or hired a PR person to write it for him?"

Brian looked up from his reading. "Doesn't sound much like ole Lonnie P., does it? Listen to this. '*After a victorious debut season with the Florida Gators, I felt compelled to forfeit my dream of a promising professional career in football to serve my country.*' I bet old Lonnie P. never used words like 'debut' and 'forfeit' in his life."

I scrolled down to read the same sentence on the computer screen. "Victorious debut season. That means he played football for only one year? You think he dropped out to follow the call of country? Flunked out is more like it, I bet."

"He probably didn't play his freshman year. Got paid a full scholarship to warm the bench, most likely. But maybe his sophomore year. Anyway, he didn't finish, obviously. Something happened."

I could see that the article had aroused Brian's curiosity, and now I had to capitalize on that interest. "I wish I knew what it was. You remember any talk about Lonnie P. back then, after he went off to

Gainesville? He would have come home for holidays and such." Brian had run the concession stand at the movie theater throughout his high school years, so he might have seen Lonnie P. there or at least heard some gossip about him.

"I remember the whole town bragging about him getting that football scholarship, big write-ups in the newspaper and all that, but I don't recall hearing anything about him dropping out of college or leaving the football team. I didn't follow football myself, so I didn't pay any attention to who was or wasn't on the team."

"Hey, you were a Gator, too. I wasn't thinking about that." I had gone to Florida State University in Tallahassee, but Brian would have been starting at UF at the beginning of Lonnie P.'s junior year. "You don't remember if he was on the football team when you were a freshman?"

"I don't have a clue. Back then I was a skinny little nerd with my nose so high up in the air it collected raindrops. College wasn't about football; it was about academics. And not just academics, but Science— with a capital S." He laughed. "You just made me remember something, though. Fall of my freshman year, some big game was coming up and a bunch of students were holding a pep rally right outside the science building. They were so noisy they were disturbing our chemistry lab session, and my lab partner started telling me about a big cheating scandal the year before among some members of the football team. Some of them had been given answers to one of their final exams, and they'd been suspended from the team or maybe from school. He was telling me the story to prove a point about how dumb football jocks were and how all us little squinty-eyed geeks squirreled away in the chemistry lab with our test tubes and Bunsen burners were so superior to them, after all."

"You don't look like a squinty-eyed geek to me." I swiveled my chair around to look at Brian. "You turned out pretty well, actually." Our eyes met for a moment before he looked back down at the pages he was holding from the printer, and I turned my chair back toward the computer. Being here alone with Brian maybe hadn't been such a good idea.

I focused my attention on the computer screen. "Maybe one of the suspended players was Lonnie P."

Brian had taken a step back. "Could be."

"I wish we could find out. What about somebody older than us who went to Florida? You know anybody who would have been there the year the scandal occurred?"

"I'm sure we know someone. I've got some old yearbooks up on one of these top shelves." Brian pulled a two-step wooden stepstool out from a corner and used it to reach the top shelf of the bookcase. "Here we are—1959-60, our sophomore year." He handed the yearbook to me and then pulled the stepstool up beside my chair and sat as I opened it to the senior class. We both bent forward, examining the faces, Brian filling me in on the present lives of those who were still in town. His stool was not quite as high as my chair, putting our heads even, so close together that I could hear him breathing. I kept my eyes on the yearbook, avoiding looking at him. What was it we were looking for? For a moment I couldn't remember.

"Here," Brian said. "Millicent Owens. Millie Flanders now. She teaches with me at the college, and I know she's a Florida grad. I don't know if she followed football, but I know her husband's a big Gator fan. Got Gator stickers and signs on his car. Remember Ken Flanders?"

"Um-m. Not really. Was he related to Phyllis Flanders in our class?"

"Yeah, her older brother. Millie teaches English classes, so she's in a different building from me, but I see her at faculty meetings and such."

Millicent Owens. I remembered her as a tall, thin girl with glasses. Quiet and studious—editor of the school newspaper her senior year, the year I'd been a sophomore reporter. Not the type to be a big football fan. But she'd remember the scandal, especially if Lonnie P. was involved. "Hey, that's great. Is she teaching summer term? Can you ask her if Lonnie P. was one of the players in the scandal?"

Brian stood, flipping the yearbook closed and taking a couple of steps backward. "Hey, I thought we had an agreement. You were going to drop this whole investigation into Lonnie P.'s past. What if he *was* involved in the scandal? What does that prove? He already got punished for it by losing his football career." Brian carried the yearbook and the stepstool over to the bookcase. "You gotta forget this whole notion of pinning something on Lonnie P. It's dangerous, and the only person who'll get hurt by it is you. I thought you wanted to check your e-mail."

"I already did when I first got here. Everybody knows by now I'm out of town, so I didn't have that much. Mostly junk." I quickly exited the Ramsey Ford website. Brian obviously wasn't going to talk to Millie Flanders, and it wouldn't do to press him any further. But why was he so afraid of Lonnie P.? What power did Lonnie P. exert over him? I stood and exited the room, Brian following. "Thanks for the use of your computer. I really appreciate it, but I'd better run. I promised Mama I'd be home by dark."

Brian walked me outside to my car and opened the driver's side door for me.

"And thanks again for dinner. It was great. The evening was great—all of it." I laid one hand on Brian's arm as I slid quickly into the car before there could be an awkward decision of whether to hug or not to hug goodbye.

"Thank *you* for saving me from another TV dinner. And remember what I said about playing with fire. Whatever happened in the past, it's best left there. Okay?"

"Okay. I hear you." *But I'm not making any promises*, I told myself as Brian closed my car door.

After I'd backed into the street and shifted into "Drive," Brian was still standing in his driveway. I waved, and he waved back, looking forlorn as I drove away. I should have hugged him goodbye, I told myself. It was the least I could have done after he bought me dinner and let me use his computer. And ungrateful wretch that I was, I hadn't even given him a hug.

But a hug would have been too suggestive of a real date, and I didn't want to give him the wrong idea. All the way home, I kept picturing Brian standing in that driveway looking so lonely and wistful that I almost wanted to turn around and go back. What if he *had* asked me out in high school? What if I had accepted? Would my life have turned out differently? What would he have been like as a husband? As a lover? Dangerous thinking, I knew, but I couldn't stop my mind from pondering the question.

Chapter 16

Wednesday, July 26, 2006

I woke the next morning to the sounds of Mama stirring around in the kitchen — the rattling of pots and pans, water running in the sink.

Reluctantly, I rolled out of bed and with eyes still half-shut tried to make out the time on the clock. Six-fifteen. I walked sleepily down the hall in time to see Mama setting an iron skillet onto the stove burner. "What are you doing?"

"I'm going to scramble some eggs."

"Whoa. Don't go overboard now that you've got your arm back. You don't want to injure your shoulder again." I took the carton of eggs out of the refrigerator and reached into a cabinet for a bowl. "How many eggs you want?"

"I'll do it." Mama opened the carton and took out an egg. "You've been doing for me long enough." She cracked the egg against the edge of the counter, dumped its contents into the bowl, and reached for another as I stepped out of her way. "You can go on home now to your own house and husband. Long as I can make my coffee and cook my eggs and grits, I can get by."

I could smell the coffee beginning to drip into the pot. "That's good to know. But the doctor didn't give you permission to drive yet, and we've still got those therapy sessions for the next couple of weeks. That means you're stuck with me for a while longer."

After breakfast, Mama and I walked to the small backyard garden to gather the ripe vegetables, and once we were back in the house I washed the green beans and gave them to Mama to snap while I washed and cut up the squash to prepare for the freezer.

"It was so great to get on Brian's computer last night," I told her as we worked. "You should get one. Then we could e-mail each other and you could look up all sorts of things—medical information, new recipes, news, whatever you wanted to learn about."

"I don't need none of them new-fangled electronics." Mama snapped a bean into neat fourths. "Thelma Ramsey's got a computer now, and she's got no use for it whatsoever. Lonnie P. bought it for her and showed her how to use it, but the first time she turned it on right there by herself, she forgot everything he'd told her and couldn't make heads or tails out of how to do anything. She turned it off and ain't turned it back on since."

"Computers aren't that hard to use once you learn a few basics. I could show her if you want to go over there for a visit later this afternoon. Then you could see how it worked, too, and see if you want me to get you one. Why don't you give her a call and ask? A visit would be good for both of you." It would also be the perfect opportunity for me to congratulate Mrs. Ramsey on Lonnie P.'s success in the world and ask a few discreet questions.

"I guess I could call her," Mama said. "We haven't visited in a while, and she enjoys company, especially since Lonnie passed on."

I walked outside to get the mail while Mama made the call. The new issue of the *Pine Lake Gazette* was in the box, so I laid the other mail on the table and thumbed through it while Mama continued her phone conversation. A special four-page insert of political ads for the upcoming fall election was tucked inside, and I looked through it to see if I recognized any of the candidates. Lonnie P.'s ad for re-election as mayor was displayed prominently on the front, along with one for Kip Hardwick, who was running for re-election as sheriff. The name "Hardwick" was familiar to me; Otto Hardwick had been sheriff when I was growing up here in the '50s and early '60s, so apparently the job had stayed in the family. Inside the section were more ads—an earnest-looking, round-faced young man running for mayor against Lonnie P. and a young black deputy running for sheriff. I studied the photos. Both were too young, too inexperienced, to make much headway against the establishment. But I admired them for trying. There were more ads for other local positions, but nobody that I knew. I laid the paper aside.

After lunch, we headed over to the Ramsey place a couple of miles away. Mrs. Ramsey came out onto the front porch as I pulled up.

"Thelma, you remember Katie," Mama said as we walked toward the front steps.

"Of course she does." I gave Mrs. Ramsey a hug. "It's nice to see you again. I'm so sorry about Mr. Ramsey. Mama told me about his passing, but I couldn't make it up for the funeral."

"That's all right. I got the nice card you sent. And it's so good of you to bring your mama for a visit." Mrs. Ramsey ushered us inside. "There used to be a time when all the young-uns was little that I wished for nothing more than peace and quiet, just some time to be all by my lonesome, but sometimes now the peace and quiet gets to weighing on me something awful. But you know how that is, Julia."

Mama nodded. "Sometimes I still think Roy's in the next room or out in the field plowing, and he'll be inside in a minute for dinner. Night's the worst, though. I never thought I'd miss his snoring, but I do."

Mrs. Ramsey and Mama kept up the commiserating and comparing as we went inside—all the little things they missed, the times that were the hardest to get through—and I got a catch in my throat. I missed Daddy, too, but it wasn't the same for me as it was for Mama.

"Things ain't as neat as I used to keep 'em," Mrs. Ramsey apologized, "but I'll declare, I just ain't got the energy to do all the things I used to do."

We all sat and Mrs. Ramsey and Mama continued their conversation, discussing their latest medical news, what was going on in the community, the hot weather and the lack of rain, and so on.

"I see Lonnie P. is mayor now of Pine Lake," I inserted during a lull. "I guess he's done all right for himself."

"I'd say so." Mrs. Ramsey beamed. "There was a spell there during his wild teenage years when we didn't know what would become of him, but he tamed down considerably once he got in the military."

I leaned forward. "What branch was he in?"

"Army," Mrs. Ramsey said proudly. "He surprised us, just up and joining like he did. Hadn't told us a thing about it."

"So he joined up? He wasn't drafted?"

"No, him and a couple of his friends signed up together. We didn't even know he'd been thinking about it."

"When was that?" I asked. "I thought he won a football scholarship to college. University of Florida, wasn't it?"

Mama looked over at me, her eyes questioning why I was pursuing this line of conversation when she wanted to get back to her dislocated shoulder and Mrs. Ramsey's arthritis. But I wasn't giving up my advantage.

"He did play football a year or two for the Gators, but he didn't get along with the coach too well. He was still in his rebellious streak then." Mrs. Ramsey waved her hands in frustration. "We wanted him to stay there, keep playing, and get his education, but he didn't feel like the coach treated him right, didn't give him enough playing time or something, and he just dropped out, off the team. Come home for Christmas one year and refused to go back."

"That's when he enlisted in the Army?"

"Not right away. He helped Lonnie plant the crops that spring, started hanging out with his old friends from high school, falling back into his old ways. He didn't know what he wanted to do with his future. Said he didn't want to be a farmer all his life. Sometime that summer was when he joined up with the Army. I remember it was June because it was right after all that civil rights mess started with that colored preacher that come into town and got folks stirred up."

"Wasn't there some sort of celebration with fireworks?" I asked. "And a house caught fire?" I had to dig deep into my memory for the details. It had been early summer, a week or so after my high school graduation, and the *Gazette* had run a front-page story about it. "Whose house was it?"

"Some colored preacher from up North was renting it. He'd come down South to register the Negroes to vote, and he'd organized some big to-do at the colored church. What was it they called it, Julia?"

"I can't remember," Mama answered. "Something with 'June' in it."

"Juneteenth," I answered. "I remember now. Juneteenth celebrates the day Lincoln freed the slaves."

"I guess that was it," Mrs. Ramsey continued. "Anyways, them colored people started shooting off fireworks, and one of them set that preacher's house afire. Burned it clear to the ground, with his wife and two babies inside. He was still out with the crowd, celebrating, but she had gone home and put the babies to bed."

"Oh, gosh, I hadn't thought about that in ages." I put one hand to my mouth. How could I have forgotten about that mother and her two children? "How horrible."

"Sheriff Hardwick had called all his deputies out on duty that night," Mama added. "In case there was violence, you know, but nothing much happened, from what we heard. All that preacher did was lead a parade through town, all of them colored folks dressed up fit to kill, and ending up with a big dinner on the grounds at the colored church."

"I remember Daddy saying we weren't going anywhere near town that day." I looked at Mama. "Did Silas and Maggie go to the parade?"

"No. Your daddy put his foot down to Silas, made sure he didn't get in the middle of trouble, but we found out later that Theo and Jerome sneaked off sometime that evening and hitchhiked their way into town. They was teenagers then and wanted to see what was going on."

"Hey, that's right. I'd forgotten about that. Daddy lectured me and Roy Jr. about what would have happened to us if we'd sneaked off like Theo and Jerome did." I could see Daddy's face across the supper table and hear his voice in my head. "Then I remember reading in the paper a few days later about the fire. Were they sure it was fireworks that caused it?"

"That's all they could figure out," Mrs. Ramsey said. "You know how the colored people are when they're partying. They don't have the sense God gave a goose."

"I wonder what ever happened to that preacher," Mama said. "I never heard no more about him."

"Me neither," Mrs. Ramsey agreed. "Anyways, I remember it was right after that fire that Lonnie P. enlisted in the Army. Him and Cole Tanner and that Stutts boy—I forget his name—all joined up together."

"Jesse," I said, and Mrs. Ramsey nodded in confirmation. Jesse Stutts hadn't been a jock or even popular in high school, but he'd been slavishly devoted to Lonnie P., one of his admiring minions. "So that would have been the summer of 1962. Did Lonnie P. get sent to Vietnam?"

"No, thank the Lord." Mrs. Ramsey sighed. "About half his unit went there after their training, but the other half got pulled out and sent somewheres else. Me and Lonnie was so thankful he didn't go, but later on, he kept talking about how he wished he'd been in the group that'd gone, like he'd missed out on something. 'Course that was after he'd served his time and was out of the military altogether." Mrs. Ramsey laughed. "He did learn a lot from the Army, though, I can say that. We could see it when he come home, how he held himself, how he behaved." Mrs. Ramsey stood. "Goodness gracious. I didn't even offer you a drink. You want some iced tea? I made some fresh this morning."

"Yes, thanks, that would be great." So Gary's hunch had been right; Lonnie P. hadn't gone to Vietnam, which meant he had exaggerated his military exploits on his website and in his campaign literature. But like Gary had pointed out, those things happened with every war and every generation. That one little falsehood wasn't that big a blot on his character, but I could see a pattern developing. If he had dropped out of college in December of 1961, then he almost certainly was one of the players involved in the cheating scandal. He wouldn't have told his parents the real reason, or even if they knew the truth, they wouldn't have advertised it to the community. It would have been kept out of the local paper, and Lonnie P. would have invented a plausible story to explain why he was no longer a Gator.

I sipped my tea slowly, and listened to Mama and Mrs. Ramsey talk. If Lonnie P. had stretched the truth about his football career and his military service, what else had he exaggerated? The money he'd made had been real, or else he couldn't have given so much back to the town, but how had he come by his success? Over the years he'd either become a smart and savvy businessman or he'd been incredibly lucky in his business dealings. Or the third and more likely alternative—there was something underhanded in his background that nobody had yet discovered.

Finally, when no one else mentioned it, I asked about the computer, and we all trooped into one of the spare bedrooms to look at it. I turned it on and brought up the Internet, but Mrs. Ramsey didn't show any interest in searching for anything—not in looking up a new recipe or finding information about arthritis treatments or checking current news events. Even Lonnie P.'s Ramsey Ford website, when I brought it up, didn't arouse her enthusiasm.

"He showed me that already when he brought the computer over here." Mrs. Ramsey took a step closer and peered at the screen. "He showed me how to click on certain words, but I forgot what all he said, so I ain't been back to it."

"It's easy," I assured her. "All you do is move the mouse so that this little arrow is over a word and then click." I moved the cursor to the highlighted term "Rambling Acres" and clicked on it to illustrate. We went to a glowing description of the neighborhood, complete with photos of the lake and golf course. "You want to try it?"

Mrs. Ramsey shook her head. "Not right now. Maybe another time."

I went back to the Ramsey Ford website and clicked on the profile that I had already printed out at Brian's, but she had already seen that, too, as well as all the other links. Lonnie P. must have bought her the computer just so he could show her around his web site and demonstrate to her how successful he was, and her lack of interest must have been a big disappointment to him. I soon gave up, and Mama and I headed home.

"I can't imagine having that computer sitting there and not using it," I said to Mama in the car.

"Don't you go buying one for me now," Mama answered. "I'd be just like Thelma. I get all the news I need from the paper and the TV."

"Okay, if you say so. But you don't know what you're missing. Computers are becoming as necessary as a phone. Or a car."

Mama didn't respond, and we fell into silence. Mrs. Ramsey's mention of the fire and the deaths of that young mother and her two children weighed on my mind. I hadn't thought about that tragedy in years, and I didn't want to think about it now. I tried to focus on something else, but I couldn't get the flames and smoke out of my mind—imagining that baby and toddler asleep in a bedroom, the firework whizzing through an open window, the mother rushing into the room and grabbing the children in her arms, only to be blocked by a wall of fire.

At the time it happened, it had hardly registered with me. Flushed with my new status as a high school graduate, still basking in the glow of those last few whirlwind weeks of school and caught up in the excitement of planning for college, the story and picture of the burned-out house had been one of those "Oh, what a horrible accident" stories that I'd reacted to briefly and then forgotten. After all, I hadn't known the victims, and I'd heard no follow-up talk about the fire from my parents or anyone else.

Why had Mrs. Ramsey brought it up today? That fire had happened in 1962—forty-four years ago. I couldn't even remember how it had come into the conversation. What were we talking about? Something about Lonnie P. joining the army. She remembered it had been in June because it was right after that Juneteenth celebration that Lonnie P. and his friends Cole Tanner and Jesse Stutts had all run off together and joined up without even telling their families beforehand what they were doing.

An explosion seemed to go off in my head. What if that fire hadn't been an accident? What if...? No, there couldn't have been any connection. The thought was too terrible to contemplate. But what if there was?

132

Chapter 17

I didn't say anything to Mama about my suspicions, but the possibility that Lonnie P. and his friends could have had something to do with that fire so unnerved me that I gripped the steering wheel with white-knuckle intensity. How could I find out more about what happened that night? *The Pine Lake Gazette* had made the fire front page news in its next issue, so maybe I could start there. The newspaper office would have kept copies of all their past issues—if not actual paper copies, then at least on microfilm or microfiche. I'd drop Mama off at home and go there right now to see what I could find out. I glanced at my car clock; almost four, and the office should be open until at least five.

Mama, tired from our afternoon excursion, settled into her recliner as soon as we arrived home, but I was too pumped up with adrenalin and too consumed with my suspicions to sit down. "Mama, I'm going to run into town for a few minutes. I won't be gone long. You'll be okay by yourself, won't you?"

"Into town? Now?" Mama looked at me suspiciously.

"Just for a minute. I'll be right back." I rushed off before she could ask me any more questions.

Once in the car, I went back to planning my investigation. Assuming that I found the newspaper article, I doubted it would be much help. Given the tension of the times and the terror the whites had back then of any change in the status quo between the races, the newspaper account would almost certainly be a whitewashing of the facts.

What else? The fire department would have conducted an official investigation into the cause of the fire, wouldn't it? That report should be a matter of public record, but, again, how honest would it be? From what I could remember, the fire had been reported as a tragic accident caused by an exploding firework—and as far as I knew, Mama and Daddy, along with all the other adults I saw regularly, had accepted the story as fact. If there had been doubters, none of them had made their suspicions known, and if there had been talk in the black community, I would not have heard it. The preacher, the grieving husband and father who'd lost his entire family at one fell swoop, apparently had left town almost immediately, and things had quickly gotten back to normal, the blacks returning to their old patterns of bowed heads and "Yassuh, Yassum" mumbles and nods. Schools had not been integrated in the county for another five years, at least, and by that time I had graduated from college and moved more than two hundred miles away to Central Florida.

I was so hyped up by my suspicions that I had to share them with someone, but I couldn't tell Mama, and I hadn't tried to talk to Delia since our conversation in the library parking lot. Besides, I didn't want to go to her until I had something specific to offer in return for my failure all those years ago. The only person left was Brian. True, he had warned me to stay away from any investigation of Lonnie P.—for my own safety and to "avoid stirring up trouble that Pine Lake didn't need," as he had put it—but once I told him what I suspected about the fire, his attitude would change, and he'd be as curious as I was to find the truth. Maybe he was right about nobody caring if a teenage Lonnie P. and his friends attacked a black girl whom everyone would have agreed "had it coming," but murder was another thing entirely— especially the murder of two innocent children. I was positive that Brian would share my anger and outrage and would agree that if Lonnie P. had had anything to do with that fire he had to be brought to account. Maybe I couldn't have the satisfaction of seeing Lonnie P. punished for what he had done to Delia, but I could still make amends to her by getting to the bottom of what happened the night of the Juneteenth celebration.

I pulled my cell phone from my purse and called Brian's number. "Guess what," I said as soon as he answered and continued talking without waiting for a reply. "Mama and I visited Lonnie P.'s mother this afternoon, and I learned some pretty interesting information. Lonnie P. quit the football team at Christmas time of his sophomore year because he didn't get along with the coach. At least that's the story he told his parents. And he was in the Army, but he never went to Vietnam. But that's only the beginning."

"Whoa, hold on," Brian interrupted. "You went over to grill Lonnie P.'s mother? Kate, you're getting way out of bounds here. I told you last night—"

"To forget it. I know. I wasn't grilling her. She and Mama are old friends. Mrs. Ramsey has a computer that she's afraid to use, one that Lonnie P. gave her, and we went over so I could show her how to operate it."

"So while you were showing her, you just casually asked her if Lonnie P. cheated on a final and got kicked off the football team and if he ever served in Vietnam? That just came up naturally in the conversation?"

I didn't like Brian's supercilious tone. "For your information, yes, it did. I didn't say anything about a cheating scandal; she voluntarily told me that he quit the team and dropped out of school over a disagreement with the coach about playing time. That's probably what he told his parents, and they believed him. But that's not even important. That's not the big thing I called to tell you."

"And what's that?" I could hear Brian's sigh over the phone. "I can't imagine his mother telling you her son's a criminal, that he made all his money by cheating people out of their life's savings or whatever it is you think he did."

"It's much worse than that. I don't have any proof yet, but believe me—"

"Worse? Kate, what in the hell are you talking about?" Brian's tone changed from mocking to angry. "You need to stop this right now.

Lonnie P.'s got a lot of influence in this town, so whatever you think he did, it's not worth putting yourself in danger. Forget it, take care of your mother, and then go home. That's an order."

"An order? And who are you to be telling me what I can or can't do?"

"A friend, okay? Someone who cares about what happens to you."

"Fine. Forget I told you anything at all. I'll handle things on my own."

"Handle what things? What are you talking about?"

"I can't tell you yet, not until I do some more checking. I'm on my way into town right now to check some old issues of the *Gazette*."

"What's this about?" Brian asked again. "What are you looking for in old issues of the newspaper?"

"Never mind. You don't want to hear it anyway."

"Kate, this is crazy. Maybe you'd better tell me what's going on."

"If you really want to know, meet me at the newspaper office in fifteen minutes. I'll tell you then." I disconnected, leaving Brian hanging. Maybe he'd meet me and maybe he wouldn't. Either way, I was not going to be deterred. If he didn't want to be involved, I'd handle things on my own.

When I pulled into the newspaper office parking lot at four-thirty, Brian was already there. He met me at my driver's side door, opening it for me before I even shut off the ignition.

"What's going on?" he demanded. "What are we doing here?"

"You'll see." I wasn't about to tell him anything if he was going to be like this. I walked toward the building, leaving him no choice but to follow.

Only one person was in the front office, a young blonde who looked to be college-age. She looked up from her seat behind a computer and smiled. "Can I help you? Oh, hi, Dr. Simmons. Are you enjoying your summer?'

"Hi, Emily. Yes, I am. How are you?" Brian looked around at the walls, avoiding Emily's eyes.

"Yes," I said, bringing the conversation back to the initial question. "At least I hope so. Do you keep copies of old issues here? Issues from say, the early sixties? I'm doing some research and need to look up something that happened in June of 1962."

"Family genealogy?" Emily stood and came toward us, looking from me to Brian. Did she take me for his wife? I was wearing my wedding rings, so it would have been a logical assumption, but if she knew that he wasn't currently married, (and in a small town like this his marital status was probably well established) then what? Maybe a sister or a family member? She kept her polite smile. "We get those requests all the time. We keep paper copies here in a back storage room, but we usually tell people to go to the library. All the back issues are stored on microfiche, and the library has a complete record. It's really easy to use, and you can make copies right from the machine."

Asking Brian to follow me to the library was a stretch. He'd probably accuse me of leading him on a wild goose chase. "Do you let people access the paper copies? I'll be really careful. The library closes at five, and we're sort of pressed for time." I wasn't at all sure that the library closed at five, but in a town this size, it was a pretty safe assumption.

"Well..." Emily hesitated. "My boss isn't here right now, but I guess it'd be all right since I know Dr. Simmons. They're right back here." Emily led us down a corridor and ushered us into a small room where shelves held long rows of identical white boxes. "You said 1962?" She took down a box labeled January—June 1962 and set it on a small table in the center of the room. "Is this the right time frame?"

"Yes. That's it. June 1962. Thanks."

"If you want to make copies, they're ten cents a page." She pointed to the copier on the other side of the room "Anything else I can help you with?"

"Thanks, but we can take it from here. I'm a librarian, up here visiting with family." I nodded my head toward Brian as if to indicate he was the "family" I was visiting. "I'll be sure to put everything back in correct order."

"Oh, well then. I'll get back to my desk. Call me if you need any help."

"Thanks. We will."

I started with the issue dated Wednesday, June 7, 1962. The Juneteenth parade would probably have been held either that Saturday, June 10th or the following one, June 17th, so this issue was almost certainly printed before the fire, but it might have an announcement about the upcoming celebration or news about the preacher's attempts to register black voters.

I pulled up a chair and quickly scanned the front page headlines. "Congratulations, Class of 1962," read the main header, and almost the entire page was taken up with news of our graduation. "Hey, here's a photo of you," I said to Brian, "giving the valedictory speech."

"You brought me here to look at pictures of our graduation?" Brian asked. "Why? I thought this had something to do with Lonnie P." Nevertheless, he pulled up a chair beside me and examined the photograph. "Boy, that was a long time ago."

"Yes, it was. You gave a good speech."

"Thanks. I was so nervous I don't even know what I said."

I looked from the photo of the skinny eighteen-year-old kid to the mature Brian beside me. "I was jealous because it wasn't me up there, but I was proud of you, too. And your speech was much better than any I could have composed."

Brian tried to hide the smile my compliment had triggered. "You're just saying that. Yours would have been better, I'm sure." Our faces were inches apart, and for a moment I imagined us both at eighteen again, giddy with the excitement of setting out into the world as adults. For an instant, I had the distinct feeling that Brian was going to kiss me and that I was going to let it happen, was even wishing for it to happen, but then he looked away and broke the spell.

I turned the pages. More pictures of graduation, an automobile accident, the list of hospital admissions and discharges, more community news. On page six was a brief two-sentence announcement about the Juneteenth celebration planned for the following Saturday, led by the Reverend George C. Harper. So I was right about the date, only one week after our high school graduation. The rest of the paper held nothing of interest, so I folded it carefully and laid it aside.

"That's it?" Brian had been sitting silently, watching me scan the pages, not knowing what I was looking for. "You ready to go now?"

"No. The next issue is the one I want." I picked up the following week's paper, dated Wednesday, June 14, 1962. Pay dirt. The front page had a huge headline, "Juneteenth Celebration Ends in Tragic Fire," and a picture of the burned-out house, nothing remaining but a few blackened wall studs. I quickly skimmed the first paragraph of the article, which confirmed the account that Mrs. Ramsey and Mama had told of an errant firework starting the blaze.

"Remember this?" I moved the paper over in front of Brian. "The fire that killed that black preacher's wife and two children? One week after our graduation."

Brian looked at the picture and headline. "What about it?"

"It was labeled an accident," I said, lowering my voice to a whisper. "A firework went through an open window and exploded. But what if that's not the real story? That black preacher was an outsider who had come into Pine Lake to stir up trouble, to persuade the black people to register to vote. Everybody was scared out of their minds about what might happen. What if somebody deliberately set that house on fire to get rid of him?"

Brian stood, walked to the door, and closed it. He came back to me, hissing in a fierce whisper. "Kate, this is crazy talk. People in Pine Lake didn't do that kind of stuff. We never had any Klan here."

"Are you sure?" I answered. "We may not have made the evening news, but that doesn't mean things didn't happen. We had our share of racists just like everywhere else all over the South. Look at what happened to Delia that night she came in the movie theater. You didn't know about that, did you?"

"So what are you implying?" Brian was still whispering. "And keep your voice down, for goodness sake. Now you're trying to tie Lonnie P. to this fire, too? What on earth gave you that idea?"

"Right after that fire, Lonnie P. and two of his friends, Jesse Stutts and Cole Tanner, left town together and joined the Army without telling their families they were going."

"And how do you know that?"

"His mother told me. She said she remembered when Lonnie P. joined the Army because it was right after the fire. She didn't make any connection, but I did."

"So, what does that prove? It could have been coincidence."

"Sure. It could have. But it's a pretty strange coincidence, don't you think?"

"So now you're suggesting that Lonnie P. is a murderer?" Brian shook his head in disbelief. "You seriously think he set that fire and then came back here and ran for mayor? That makes no sense. Let's get out of here right now." He took a step toward the door.

"Go ahead. I want to make copies of everything about the fire."

"I'm not going without you." Brian followed me to the copier and stood behind me while I copied all the photos and text about the fire, shifting his feet with impatience and talking over my shoulder. "This has gone far enough. Emily knows me, for heaven's sake. She was one of my students. I don't want to be any part of this. Come on." He reached for my arm, but I backed up a step.

"In a minute. I have to check the next week's paper, too." The June 21st issue had a small story, an update on the official cause of the fire. The fire department had ruled it accidental, just as the previous week's paper had reported. I copied that article, too, before returning both issues to the box and replacing the lid.

A knock sounded on the closed door, followed by Emily's voice outside. "You find what you needed?"

I rushed to open the door. What would she think we were doing in here behind closed doors? "Yes, thanks. I copied six pages." I held them up, rolling them into a loose tube so that none of the pictures or text was visible. Any further searching I could do at the library on the microfiche machine. "And I returned the papers to the box in good order." I started to remove the lid so that she could check.

"I'm glad we could be of help." She smiled brightly to show that she trusted me.

I reached into my purse for my wallet and pulled out a dollar. "Keep the change."

"Okay. Thanks." She followed us out and back to the front lobby.

"Bye, Dr. Simmons."

"Bye, Emily." Brian had finally found his voice again. "Have a good summer."

Outside, he followed me to my car. "You're so set on pinning something on Lonnie P. that you're pulling things out of thin air. All of this is just conjecture, you know. The fire was investigated years ago, and it was an accident, plain and simple."

"I could be wrong," I admitted. "I hope I am. But what if I'm not? I'm not publicly accusing Lonnie P. or anyone else of anything right now. I'm just following a hunch. I thought you'd be on my side, but obviously you're not. So just go home and forget it." I was puzzled and angry at Brian's reaction. The Brian I remembered from high school would have been eager to listen to my theory, willing to consider the possibility that the fire might not have been what it seemed, enthusiastic about piecing together the evidence and coming up with a hypothesis that would account for all the known facts. What had turned him into this jittery, frightened "Don't rock the boat" stranger? Had he lived in this place for so long that he'd become like the rest of the establishment, terrified of anything that might upset his comfortable insulated world?

"I'm warning you for the last time to forget this craziness," Brian demanded. "Whatever happened or didn't happen is so far in the past that digging it up now does nobody any good. All it does is stir up a hornet's nest of trouble. You're going to be gone from here in a few weeks, but some of us live here, have families here, have a lot invested in this town, and we don't need anybody coming in and making accusations and insinuations about something they know nothing about. That fire was an accident, and all the evidence proved it. End of story."

"That's what everybody wanted the evidence to show," I countered. "And they would have covered up any evidence that didn't fit that convenient explanation. Why do you think those boys were rushed out of town so quickly? Somebody told them to leave. That's what I think. There have to be eyewitnesses who know what really happened. Those people wouldn't have been interviewed back then, but times are different now. We just have to find somebody willing to reopen a cold case."

"We?"

"Well, me, then. I have to find somebody." I opened my car door and started the ignition, leaving Brian standing in the parking lot. I'd made a big mistake by thinking I could count on him for support. I'd already alienated Delia, and now Brian, so from here on out I was completely on my own.

Chapter 18

Thursday, June 27—Friday, June 28, 2006

All day Thursday as I went about the daily chores of cooking and cleaning and gathering vegetables from the garden, I kept thinking about the fire. According to the *Gazette*, the blaze had been blamed on an exploding bottle rocket that had sailed through an open window of the house, setting the bedding on fire in a back bedroom where the children were sleeping. From there it had spread rapidly to the rest of the house, and by the time the fire trucks arrived, nothing was left to save. It seemed strange to me that a bottle rocket could do that much damage in such a short time, but I was no fireworks expert.

I tried to recreate the scene in my mind, putting all the facts in proper order. The parade through town had ended at the Mt. Zion AME church, where a big picnic had been planned on the church grounds, followed by fireworks as soon as the sky grew dark. Sometime after the picnic and before the fireworks began, the preacher's wife had slipped away from the celebration to take the children home and put them to bed. The house, once a parsonage, was right across the street, so it was a short walk for her. No one was sure where she was at the time the fire started, whether she was in her own bedroom or in the living room watching the festivities out her front window. Perhaps she had stepped outside onto the front porch to better view what was happening across the street.

I wasn't familiar with the area being described, but if the fireworks had been set off in the churchyard and the house was right across the street, lots of people would have been milling around, not only the blacks who were celebrating but also some white law officers. Nothing was mentioned in the article about deputies keeping watch on the proceedings, but knowing Sheriff Hardwick and the tension of the times, I was certain that some had been ringing the churchyard, ready to stop any trouble before it started. That meant lots of people would have seen the fire before the house was completely engulfed and before the firefighters arrived—people who would have been afraid to talk then but might be willing to speak up now. Had anyone seen or heard something that would suggest the fire was not an accident as officially reported?

Retreating to the privacy of my bedroom on Thursday afternoon while Mama watched her daily soaps, I reread my copies of the newspaper articles, looking for clues. The article in the following week's paper had given a few more details from the fire department's official investigation. The house, old and in disrepair, had sat vacant for some time before the preacher and his family rented it, so old, frayed electrical wiring and overloaded circuits had contributed to the quickness and intensity of the blaze. But their conclusion of the fire's origin was the same as their original explanation—an exploding bottle rocket, found at the scene in the children's bedroom. That scenario sounded too convenient for me. What if the fire had another cause and the bottle rocket had been a red herring, tossed in to provide a facile explanation for the gullible public?

On Friday morning, as I drove Mama into town for her first therapy session, my mind was still on the fire. The question that kept coming back to me was why there was no investigation into who threw the bottle rocket. The fire was simply labeled an accident and left at that. The more I thought about it, the more strange that seemed to me. It would have been fairly easy to interview those attending the celebration to see if anyone saw the bottle rocket being thrown toward the house. Perhaps the witnesses wouldn't have cooperated, not wanting to incriminate one of their own, but for no interviews to even be conducted? If it had really been an accident, I could see Sheriff Hardwick picking out a scapegoat—the person he most wanted to teach a lesson—and hauling him into jail to be charged with a crime.

The only scenario that made sense was that Sheriff Hardwick knew who started that fire, someone whom he didn't want to arrest. Maybe he had even been the one to see that the three boys left town immediately before talk started, knowing that he couldn't very well arrest them if they were nowhere to be found.

And the most intriguing question of all—how had a bottle rocket thrown from the church grounds gone across the street, around the house, and into the window of a back bedroom? I was convinced that I was onto something.

Once Mama's name was called for her therapy session, I walked outside. She'd be busy for the next hour, so I had some free time to begin my investigation. Thinking ahead, I had already made a call to Maggie on my cell phone earlier in the morning, asking if it would be convenient for me to drop by for a few minutes while Mama was in therapy. Silas and Maggie hadn't gone to the celebration, but if there had been talk in the black community afterward about the fire, Maggie would know about it. I could also ask her a few questions about Theo and Jerome—where they were now and what they were doing. Did either of them still live in the area? Perhaps they had seen something that night that would shed new light on what had happened.

Maggie had been happy to hear from me. "Come on by," she'd said. "I ain't doing a thing but sitting here and getting older by the minute."

Following the driving directions she had given me over the phone, I was soon turning onto Martin Luther King Boulevard, looking for Washington Street. As a child I'd always known there was a section of town where the colored people lived, but I'd never driven into it, so I felt like an explorer heading into uncharted territory. All was quiet: a few children were outside riding bikes or playing in the yards, but no adults were in sight. I made a left onto Washington as Maggie had instructed and drove slowly, looking for Carver Road on my right.

In my focus on street names, the sign in front of a church on my left didn't register in my brain until I was already past. "Mt. Zion African Methodist Episcopal Church." Wasn't that where the Juneteenth celebration had been held back in 1962? Forty-four years ago. Was the church still being used for worship?

I checked the road behind me, backed up, and pulled into the gravel parking lot beside the church, giving myself time to survey my surroundings. The building was old, but in good condition, a fresh coat of white paint having been applied fairly recently. A wide expanse of lawn in front of the church was shaded by several old moss-draped live oaks. Was that where the tables and chairs had been set up for the picnic? Where had they set off the fireworks? In the street? Here in the parking lot? I made a U-turn to head back onto the street, half-expecting to see an empty charred lot where the house that had burned had once stood, but I saw only a pair of matching duplexes. They weren't new; they looked as if they'd been there for decades, as if they'd always stood in that spot—their pastel green paint dingy with age, yards overtaken with weeds, a tricycle in one driveway, a rusty basketball hoop attached to a pole in another. I felt disoriented, as if I were maybe in the wrong place. Maybe this wasn't the right church, after all.

But the newspaper had said Mt. Zion AME Church, so it had to be the same one. I blinked my eyes rapidly a few times, feeling time compressing and expanding around me. Delia and I were four again, twisting ourselves on the swings until we were so dizzy that when we tried to stand our feet would not hold us up—the world a blur of colors and sensations, our giggles spurting out like hiccups as we flung ourselves on the ground and watched the world spin around us.

I gave my head a slight shake to regain equilibrium and pulled back onto Washington Avenue. How could I expect evidence of the fire to remain forty-four years later? Was I crazy? What hope did I have of proving something that happened more than four decades ago, something that had been covered up at the time by all the people then in charge of investigating such things? No one would have saved incriminating evidence; no honest accounts would have been written; no one would have admitted any wrongdoing. The task I had set for myself seemed hopeless. Maybe Brian was right. Maybe I should just forget the whole mad idea, concentrate on taking care of Mama, and then go quietly home to my own husband and my own concerns.

I found Carver Road at the very end of Washington Avenue, a narrow asphalt lane that soon gave way to dirt as it led away from town. The houses here were more spread out, with watermelon-red crepe myrtles and tall oak trees shading deep front yards. Number 55 had a neat patch of lawn in front with colorful flower beds below the front windows of the house. As I pulled into the driveway, I could see corn stalks and rows of okra and tomatoes off to one side in the back yard. I was glad to see that although Silas and Maggie had moved closer into town, Maggie still had her flowers and garden to tend.

Maggie opened the front door before I had time to knock. "Law sakes. Little Katie McCormick. Is that really you?"

"It's really me." I stepped forward to hug her. Her hair was white now, and her step slower, but she was still the same Maggie I remembered. "Gosh, it's been a long time."

Maggie laughed. "My goodness, chile, I ain't seen you since forever, I guess. Come on in. I'll fix us some cool drinks." She headed to the kitchen and returned with glasses of iced tea.

"Thanks." I took a big gulp, the thick sweetness coating my tongue. "How is Silas? Mama tells me he's in a center now during the day. That must make things a lot easier on you."

We talked for a minute about Silas's condition and about Mama's shoulder before I thanked her again for giving me Delia's new name and phone number. "Did Delia tell you I called her and we had lunch together last week?"

"Sure did. She said you hadn't changed much over the years." Maggie nodded. "She was right, too. You're looking good."

"Thanks. So are you." Maggie had not shown any discomfort at my question, so obviously Delia hadn't told her about my confession at the library. I was pretty sure Delia had also never told her parents about how she and her friend had sauntered into the lobby of the Pine Lake theater and tried to buy something at the concession stand, so there was no way she could tell Maggie about my cowardice that night without giving away her own secret.

"I can only stay a minute," I told Maggie. "I need to be back at the hospital by eleven to pick up Mama. But tell me about all the kids. Where are they now? I see you've got lots of pictures."

Maggie pointed at one photo on the wall. "There's Rochelle with her family. Two girls and a boy. She's way off in Virginia. And this is Theo with his wife and three boys. 'Course the children—they all grown up now. This was took when they was still little. Here's Jerome and his second wife. I took down the picture of him with his first wife and children, but I got it here someplace. A boy and a girl." She stood, and I thought she was going to look for the picture of Jerome, but instead she handed me a framed photo from beside the TV. "Here's Delia and the man she's with now, John Franklin. I guess you didn't meet him yet."

"No, I didn't." I studied the photo. Unlike the ones on the wall, it had been taken recently, for Delia looked just as she did now. The man was big, with broad shoulders and muscular arms, but his face looked gentle, a smile lighting up his features, his short curly hair beginning to gray at the temples.

"He looks very distinguished," I said. "Very handsome."

"He's a good man." Maggie nodded with satisfaction. "Delia finally done all right for herself."

"You said Rochelle was in Virginia. What about Theo and Jerome? Are they close by? Do you see them often?"

"Theo's close. He's got his own little mechanic's shop in town, does good business. He's over here most every week, checking on me and his daddy. Jerome's one of these wanderers, never satisfied. He was in the army for a long time, and now he can't put down roots nowhere. Him and his wife just moved again, from Chicago to someplace out west."

"Where does Delia live?" I asked her. "Is it near here?"

"They staying at one of them duplexes on Washington Street across from the church," Maggie said. "They just renting for now. Delia keeps talking 'bout moving to Tallahassee near where her oldest boy David lives. Says he's got a big house there that's fixed up real nice."

"Tallahassee's a pretty town. I lived there when I went to college."

"I've been telling her to go ahead and do whatever she wants. I don't want me and Silas to be a burden on nobody, and Theo's right here, anyway, but she feels like she's gotta make up for something, for being away for all them years, I guess, and hardly coming back at all. I tell her she don't owe us nothing, but that ain't the way she sees it." Maggie sighed. "I wish things could have been different, but, like I tell Delia, there ain't no point in crying about what's over and done. It's time for her to live her own life and stop worrying about us."

I nodded, not trusting myself to speak. Delia would have had to tell her parents about the attack. I had no idea how she had explained what happened, but whatever Silas and Maggie had been told, it was enough to convince Silas not to go to the sheriff, demanding justice. Instead, they had sent Delia away to stay with her grandmother, and she, like me, had not returned to live in this area until her father's condition brought her home. And she had come back knowing that the boys who had attacked her were most likely still here, living their lives as if that night had never happened. "She only got what was coming to her," they would have said then and would probably say now if confronted with their actions. How much courage had it taken for Delia to come back home after all this time? Had the intervening years dimmed her memory of that horrible night? Not likely, not from Delia's reaction when Lonnie P. came into the restaurant where we were having lunch.

"What about you?" Maggie asked. "You back here now to stay?"

"Um, no. I'll be here as long as Mama needs me, but my family and work are back home in Titusville." I felt guilty. Was Delia a better daughter than I was? If I had been in her shoes, could I have willingly moved back to this environment that held so much trauma and humiliation? I didn't think so.

"You said Delia was living in one of those duplexes across from the church," I said, taking advantage of the opening Maggie had provided me. "I came past those on my way here. Is that the church where the Juneteenth celebration was held? Where the house across the street caught fire and burned? I don't remember the particulars, but I remember how tragic it was—that poor family." I pretended to be dragging up bits from memory, vague on the details. "Where was the house? It had to be near where the duplexes are now, I guess."

"That house sat right on that very spot. I didn't want Delia moving in there, but she's in the end one on the left if you're facing 'em. Promised me she wouldn't live in that other one to the right that sits smack dab where that house used to be. Folks is living there now, but word is there's ghosts still on the place." Maggie shivered a little. "You want more tea? I got plenty."

"No, thanks. I need to be going. It's almost eleven." I put my glass on the table and stood. It was like Maggie to believe in ghosts. I wouldn't want to live on that spot either, knowing its history.

"Do you know what happened?" I asked as I moved toward the front door. "I remember the newspaper said it was an accident. A firework or something?"

"I don't know nothing 'bout that fire. We was working that day, all day." Maggie followed me to the front door. "We weren't nowhere near town when that house burned." All the liveliness seemed to go out of Maggie's face, and her tone was defensive, a clear shut-down of any further questions. The fire was obviously not something she wanted to talk about, not to me anyway. Even if I was little Katie who had sat in her kitchen and eaten her cookies, I was still a white person, someone not to be trusted. I was surer than ever that there had been talk among the black community about the cause of that fire and that Maggie knew more than she was letting on. But if she wouldn't talk to me, who would? I wouldn't push. Now that I knew Theo was still in town, I had another pathway to pursue.

I reached for the doorknob. "Thanks for the tea. It was good seeing you again, and say hello to Silas for me."

Maggie, clearly relieved that I had let the subject of the fire drop, became her old self again, thanking me for coming, and urging me to came back anytime. I drove away with not much more knowledge than I had come with, but Maggie's obvious discomfort in talking about the fire had reinforced my suspicions and made me more determined than ever to continue my search for answers.

Chapter 19

Friday, July 28, 2006

"How was it?" I asked as Mama and I walked to the car after her therapy session.

"Not bad. The therapist says I'm doing good."

On the way home, after listening to Mama describe all the exercises the therapist had put her through, my mind began to wander back to the Juneteenth fire. I was sure that I was onto something with my theory about Lonnie P.'s connection to it, but even if I was right, what would I do with the information? I had been counting on Brian's support, but when I'd told him about my suspicions, he had clearly become frightened of what I might discover. Considering that he had lived here all his life and had burrowed himself into a nice little nest at the community college—a nest he didn't want to see disturbed—I could understand and even sympathize a little with his attitude, but in retrospect, it was just as well that my teenage daydreams hadn't come true—that he hadn't asked me out in high school. If I'd married Brian, that would have meant settling for the provincial life of Pine Lake, my entire world view encompassing a fifty-mile radius, attached like a pencil on a compass that could only revolve around the fixed center of my birthplace.

If Brian wouldn't help me, then whom could I count on? I didn't know if Delia would even talk to me again after my confession at the library, and I hadn't tried contacting her. Every time I'd taken out my phone to call her, I'd ended up putting it back in my pocket, not knowing how to begin to make her understand how terrible I felt about my failure to come to her aid on that long-ago evening.

All through our lunch of sandwiches and the kitchen clean-up afterward, I kept pondering the situation, and when Mama turned on her soaps, I walked into the back yard and out the left side gate that led to the grove of pecan trees. Beyond them, on the lowest point of the property, a wooded, swampy area enclosed a small natural pond, a private spot surrounded by water oaks and cypresses. As a teenager I'd often gone there whenever I wanted to be alone with my thoughts, and I headed for it now.

Finding a level, grassy spot, I sat and stared into the water. What could I say to Delia to make up for all the years of distance between us? In spite of the closeness we'd shared as four and five-year-olds, everything had changed the instant we started school. From first grade on, we had grown further and further apart, our communication limited to polite nods and "Hello's" whenever we worked next to one another in the fields and at the tobacco barn or encountered one another as we went about our daily chores and wanderings. Both of us had kept our emotional distance, exchanging nothing more than the most cursory comments about the weather or about the work we were doing. I'd had no idea what her favorite subject in school was or what she dreamed about doing with her future, and she'd known nothing of my thoughts and dreams.

It wasn't until I reached high school in the late 1950s that I began to regret that the distance between us had deepened into a chasm. Contrary to the assurances that had been drilled into me by my father and other white adults, I was beginning to see daily on our small black-and- white TV that Negroes all over the South were not the perfectly content simpletons that white Southerners had portrayed them to be, who wanted nothing more than to keep to their own kind and not upset the status quo. Certainly by the time I turned sixteen in the spring of 1960, I had a well-developed sense of justice and compassion, and that awareness had made me re-evaluate my relationship to Delia. How had we been so close as five-year-olds and then grown so far apart as teenagers? It became my secret mission to make Delia my friend again, to show her that not all Southerners were like George Wallace and Orval Faubus and all those red-faced, hate-spewing bigots on TV.

I had known that reconnecting with Delia wouldn't be easy. During our primary grade years, Delia had remained a happy-go-lucky child, overflowing with ideas, making up games with her little sister Rochelle, showing her how to bundle her baby doll into a blanket and tuck it into a bed of pine needles in the same spot where the two of us had once played house, teaching her how to play hopscotch and jump rope. But whenever she would catch me watching enviously from my back yard, she'd turn her back and whisper to Rochelle, and soon the two of them would disappear into their house, leaving me feeling exposed as an interloper.

By the time we both reached puberty, though, Delia's attitude and behavior had grown more sullen and rebellious. The civil rights movement had awakened her too, just as it had me, and she had reacted by becoming defiant. I knew that Maggie and Silas were worried sick about her, afraid that she'd say or do something that would get her in real trouble. By high school, she had deserted Rochelle for older friends, seeking excitement she couldn't get on the farm. A long purple and white Pontiac with fins on front and back had begun driving up to her house on weekend evenings, a black teenage boy at the wheel— sometimes alone, sometimes with a carload of black teenagers—and soon I'd see the car drive off again with Delia in the front passenger seat. Mama and Daddy noticed it, too, and the car's frequent appearance and the ear-splitting, heart-pounding volume of its radio gave Daddy one more reason to lecture me about keeping my distance and having as little to do with Delia as possible.

But with us living in such close proximity, I couldn't avoid her altogether. Quite often I would encounter her alone, walking down the lane to retrieve letters from their mailbox, picking beans or tomatoes in the garden for supper, or just sitting down here at the pond in my own favorite spot for thinking.

Normally, whenever I'd headed for this spot and found Delia here before me, I'd always made a quick, silent retreat, but as my sixteenth birthday approached, I had resolved that the next time the opportunity arose, I would not tiptoe away but would walk right up and engage her in conversation, just as we'd done when we were four and five, before society had thrust us into different camps. I had been determined to regain that old closeness we had once shared—to show her I wasn't like all those other white people she viewed as the enemy.

* * *

Delia is at the bank of the pond, sitting with knees drawn up in front of her, arms around them, lost in contemplation. I walk up behind her. "Hello," I say cheerily, not the usual guarded greeting I've learned from years of observing my elders. "Are you as ready as me for school to be out?"

Startled at the sound of my voice, Delia looks up and back at me, her expression telling me I'm disturbing her solitude. "Hello." Her voice shows no emotion, and she waits warily to see what I'm up to.

I drop down beside her, assuming the same position she's in. She's barefoot, and I kick off my sandals and dig my toes into the dirt, looking not at her but out at the pond and the reflection of upside down trees and clouds. I search for something more to say. I've been building myself up to this moment for weeks, and now I'm in it and I'm so nervous that I've forgotten all my carefully planned lines. What if someone sees me sitting here on the bank of the pond beside Delia? I glance behind me to make sure there's no one else around. "What's your favorite subject in school?" I ask, something I've wondered about for years.

She looks at me as if I'm a secret agent sent to pry information out of her for the sheriff or some government agency. She shrugs and doesn't answer.

"Mine's English," I volunteer. "Literature, in particular. I'm thinking about becoming a librarian."

"Ugh." She makes a face and I giggle at her. She giggles back, and it feels like old times again.

"You got a boyfriend?" I ask. I know she does, and I want to know more about the driver of the purple and white Pontiac.

She looks out across the water. "Maybe." A smile plays across her face. "You?"

"No. Not really." I pick up a stick and throw it into the pond. "There's this one boy I kinda like, but he's never asked me out or anything."

We sit in silence for a moment. "What's his name?" I ask.

"Who?"

"Your boyfriend. The one in the big car I see driving up the lane every Saturday night."

Delia ducks her head, but I can see the smile she tries to hide. "You don't know him. He lives in town."

"Is he cute?"

Delia laughs. "You think I go out with ugly boys?"

"Just asking." There's an uncomfortable silence again. I'm beginning to feel awkward sitting here, growing more nervous by the minute that somebody will see the two of us together. "I'm sorry about all that's going on," I say, getting to my point quickly before I lose courage. "All the things on TV. Some of those people make me ashamed to be a Southerner. The color of a person's skin shouldn't make any difference at all in where he goes to school or what restaurant he eats at or anything like that." There, I've said it, and if anybody has overheard me, then I'll stand behind my words, come what may.

Delia doesn't say anything. Too little, too late, she's probably thinking. I wish I could read her mind, but it's a blank to me. How can I know what she thinks or feels about being black in a world that sees every black face as inferior?

I stand, wiggle my toes back into my sandals, and brush off the seat of my shorts. "I just wanted to tell you that," I say. "I wish things could be different, that it could be like it was when we were little, when we used to play together. I'm really sorry; that's what I came to say." I don't look at Delia as I walk away.

I've gone maybe ten steps, headed back to the house when I hear her voice. "Donnie," she calls.

"What?" I half turn, looking back.

"Donnie. That's his name."

"Oh." I can hear the little trill of excitement in her voice when she says the name, and I'm envious. Donnie doesn't sound dangerous; he sounds young and funny and cute and all the things I'd like to have in a boyfriend. I hurry away before anyone sees me.

* * *

I stood, shook the stiffness out of my arms and legs, and walked back toward the house. I couldn't remember exactly when that conversation had taken place, but it had been springtime—warm enough for me to be wearing shorts and sandals — so it couldn't have been too long before the incident at the movie theater. A few weeks? A month?

I'd thought myself so brave for saying what I'd said to Delia, and then, only a short time later, when I'd had the chance to put my words into action, I'd hidden like a coward, deserted Delia when she needed me most. And then within another week or two, Delia was gone completely out of my life, sent to care for a sick grandmother in Georgia, and there had been no opportunity for a confession or an apology. I had not seen or spoken to Delia again until our encounter at the bank two-and-a-half weeks ago.

That night after supper I walked outside and called Delia on my cell phone. "Delia?" I said at her hello, "This is Kate. Please don't hang up on me. I have to talk to you. Please."

"Mama said you came to see her this morning." Delia's voice was flat, noncommittal.

"Yes, Yes, I did. We had a nice visit. Got caught up on a lot of family news."

Delia didn't answer.

"Delia, I'm sorry about being such a coward all those years ago. You don't know how much that has weighed on my mind. I know saying 'Sorry' isn't nearly enough, but I want us to be friends again. I want us to start over. Can we do that? I have something important to tell you, and I want to do it in person. Can we get together again? Soon?"

"Something to tell me? About what?" Delia's voice was tinged with suspicion. Had Maggie told her that I had asked about the fire?

"Can we talk in person?" I asked. "Tomorrow afternoon? Roy and his wife are coming over to visit, and Margaret keeps telling me to go off and do something while they're here, to take a break from being cooped up in the house with Mama. I can meet you whenever and wherever you say. Please?"

"Okay." Delia's voice softened. "You want to come to my house?"

"Your house sounds great. But I was hoping we could be alone — just the two of us."

"We will be. John works Saturdays at Theo's shop to help out."

"Then that's great. Around three? I'll call when I'm on my way," As we said goodbye, I felt a new optimism building. I would finally be able to redeem myself in some small measure by telling Delia what I had discovered and divulging my theory of what happened the night of the fire. More than anything, I wanted Delia's friendship and forgiveness, and I'd do whatever I had to do to earn it back. I'd grovel on my knees, if that was what it took.

Chapter 20

Saturday, July 29, 2006

By the time I arrived at Delia's on Saturday afternoon my hands were clammy with perspiration, and I wiped them against my pants as I walked toward her door. Delia had good reason to hate me, and I had to make her understand that I hated myself as much as she did for my failure to act that night.

The flutter in Delia's hands as she invited me in and waved me toward the sofa indicated she was as nervous as I was about the meeting.

"I like your house," I said to lighten the tension as I took a seat. "The coziness of it. Sometimes I wish my house was smaller, now that the kids are grown and gone. Less to take care of, you know." The living area was small, sharing space with a metal dinette table and chairs to the right, and a compact kitchen behind the dining area.

"We're just renting for the time being, till we decide what we want to do." Delia sat in a chair across from me, a small glass-topped coffee table between us. "We're looking at buying us a place in Tallahassee."

"Near your son. Your mother told me." I twisted my still damp hands in my lap as I apologized again for my long-ago inaction, repeating the phrases I'd been rehearsing in my head. "I know it's forty-six years too late to be saying this now," I concluded, "but it's really important to me for us to be friends again. When I saw you at the bank, it brought back so many good memories. When we were little and playing together with our dolls. Remember those playhouses we built with pine straw walls?"

Delia had leaned back in her chair as I was delivering my litany of apologies, nodding occasionally at something I said. Her broad smile flooded me with relief. "I remember. Gosh, the two of us was like this." She held up two fingers tightly together.

"Why did it have to change? Why did people have to act the way they did back then? My father used to get so upset about us playing together. He would forbid me to play with you. Then when he was out in the field somewhere, you'd come around and I'd beg and wheedle Mama until she gave in and let me go out and play."

"Law, don't I remember them days." Delia chuckled, the old chuckle I remembered from childhood. "My daddy was the same way. Scared to death I'd get him in big trouble and lose him his job. But we didn't let 'em stop us, did we?"

"No, we didn't." Maybe we could work past this, get back to that place we'd started from, when we'd both been too young to worry about the color of somebody else's skin. "If I could go back to that night," I said. "I'd do things differently, for sure."

Delia shrugged. "Ain't nobody yet figured out a way to change the past. All anybody can do now is make the best of whatever time we got left."

"I guess so. I hope we can start fresh and get reacquainted all over again."

Delia nodded. "I guess I didn't react none too well either. See, my nerves was already on edge from seeing Lonnie P. come in that barbeque place like he owned it, and then when you told me about being at the movie theater and overhearing them boys, it took me plumb by surprise. So I guess I owe you an apology, too, for taking off like that and not letting you explain."

I leaned forward, intense with belated anger. "If I'd had any idea that those boys would come after you later, I'd have jumped out from behind that stand and scratched Lonnie P.'s eyes out!" But even as the words left my mouth, I knew they weren't true. I couldn't hide from the real secret I was keeping from Delia, the memory of what I'd seen from my window later that night when, again, I'd done nothing but sit frozen in fear.

"You couldn't have known. Nobody could." Delia stood. "You want something cold to drink? I got tea and soda."

"Sure. Iced tea sounds good."

I waited until Delia was seated again and we'd both taken sips of our drinks before I brought up the subject I'd come to discuss. "What I really came to talk about is something that happened in 1962, two years after you moved away. I know you weren't around then, but I guess you heard about the fire that destroyed the house that once stood right here, the house where that minister's wife and two children died?"

"Right over there where that other duplex is." Delia pointed. "Mama didn't want us moving in here. Said their ghosts were still around."

Did Delia, like Maggie, believe in ghosts? I didn't, but even so, I felt a shiver between my shoulder blades. It would be hard to live in the spot where such a tragedy had occurred.

"Well, you know about the fire, right? You know it was ruled accidental? A firework sailed in an open window and exploded?"

Delia nodded. "Mama told me about it when we started looking around for somewheres to stay, and I saw the ad for this place. I guess I'd heard about it before, but I'd forgot till she reminded me."

"Well, I have reason to believe the fire wasn't an accident, that the story reported at the time is not what really happened that night." I told her about my visit with Mrs. Ramsey and her revelation about Lonnie P. and two of his friends leaving the next morning to join the Army. Then I recounted my trip to the newspaper office to find the original reports and all the questions that had been raised in my mind regarding the fire's origins.

Delia set down her glass of iced tea. "Mama said that everybody round here knows that fire didn't happen the way the sheriff said it did. Nobody knows for sure what started it, but it sure weren't no firecracker."

"A bottle rocket is what the newspaper said." So I was right. Maggie had been defensive on Thursday because she did know something, or at least suspect something, about that fire that it wouldn't do to share with white people. "You think somebody saw something? Somebody who was too afraid to talk then but might talk about it now?"

"Maybe. Maybe not." Delia's voice was noncommittal. "Even if what you say is right, if Lonnie P. did set that house afire, that was a long time ago. There ain't nothing to be accomplished bringing it up now."

"If that fire was deliberately set, it doesn't matter how long ago it was. People can be tried years, even decades, later for murder. Like the Emmett Till case in Mississippi. Even if the sheriff and his cronies are dead by now, Lonnie P. is still around. And so are the other boys, I bet."

Delia shook her head doubtfully. "You forgetting one little thing. You ain't got no evidence. All you got right now is suspicions. And black folks know better than anybody that suspicions don't get you nothing. There ain't no way, all these years later, to prove them boys set that fire."

"We'll find the evidence—you and me. If there's talk in the neighborhood, then that means there were eyewitnesses, people who saw something but were powerless back then to do anything about it. The churchyard was full of people. We have to find them and persuade them to tell what they saw." I was getting excited. "We'll make sure Lonnie P. gets what's coming to him—see that he pays for what he did to you."

Delia's hands trembled as she lifted them from her lap. "I don't want nobody bringing that up. I got children to think about. All that's best left in the past."

"Oh, I didn't mean that," I said quickly. "I understand completely. We'll just investigate the fire, that's all. If those boys set it, somebody had to see them in the neighborhood that night—lurking around the house or running away or something."

"You talking 'bout going up against somebody with a lot of power in this town. You don't know what might happen."

"I know it could be dangerous, but I've been tossing this around in my mind for a few days now, and it just seems to me that something ought to be done. It makes me sick to see Lonnie P. strutting around town, being looked up to by everybody, throwing money around like he could buy himself out of anything, even murder."

Delia sat up straighter, and I could see the fearless teenager reawakening, an avenging spirit gathering in her eyes. "You wouldn't say nothing 'bout what happened to me?"

"No. I promise."

"Then I'll talk to Mama and some of the other old people that was around back then. See what I can find out."

"You want me to come with you? Tell what I know?"

Delia shook her head. "No. No offense, but folks around here is more likely to talk to me alone than if I was with you. I'll let you know what I find out."

"Thanks. That's great. With you and me working together, I'm sure we can build a case against Lonnie P. and those other two boys."

"Who they?" Delia asked. "The other two?"

"Jesse Stutts and Cole Tanner. They were friends of Lonnie P. from town. I never knew either of them that well."

Delia shook her head. "Names don't mean nothing to me."

Delia and I talked a while longer about children and grandchildren before I stood to say goodbye. "Gotta get back. I told Roy and Margaret I'd be home by five."

Delia walked with me to the front door. "I'm glad you come, and we had this little talk, no matter what may or may not come of it."

"Me, too." I hugged Delia goodbye. "I'm really glad, too. And while you're talking to people in this neighborhood, I'm going to see what I can find out about Cole and Jesse. Maybe one of them will talk to me." I had no idea how I could come up with a plausible reason to contact either of them or how I'd get them to talk, but that had to be my next step. Right now, like Delia said, I had nothing to go on except a hunch, coincidences that seemed too convenient to be accidental, but nothing concrete enough to take to a prosecutor. I'd have to find a way to get Cole or Jesse to tell me things without realizing what they were revealing or without my making it appear that I was trying to get them in trouble with the law.

In high school I hadn't known either of them except by sight; both had hung around with Lonnie P., but I knew little else about them. Cole had been tall and skinny, with a mop of dark hair that was always falling in his eyes, eyes that were jade green with long, black eyelashes. He'd had a motorcycle and a leather jacket, and his reputation was such that any girl who wanted to go out with him had to sneak out a bedroom window in the middle of the night to avoid her daddy finding out about it. Jesse was shorter, with such a close-cropped crew cut that his sand-colored hair almost disappeared, giving him a bald look that contrasted with his freckled nose and cheeks. He was not a jock or a bad boy, so how he came to be in Lonnie P.'s group of friends and hangers-on was not too clear, but he followed Lonnie P. around like a puppy, carrying his books, doing his homework for him, and following his orders. We knew next to nothing in high school about homosexuality, but everybody joked about how Jesse was in love with Lonnie P. Instead of the joking making Lonnie P. angry, though, Lonnie P. laughed it off and took full advantage of Jesse's infatuation.

If Cole had taken part in setting the fire, he'd probably have seen it as living up to his wild reputation and proving his courage to the girls, but if Jesse had done it, his only objective would have been to please Lonnie P. After Lonnie P. left for college and later married Sherri Lynn, where did that leave Jesse? And what had happened to him since?

I'd give Gail a call. We hadn't talked since the dinner at her house, so maybe now that Mama's arm was out of the sling and she was getting close to independence again, Gail and I could meet somewhere for a long, leisurely lunch. I'd work the conversation around to old high school classmates, and ask her what ever happened to Cole Tanner and Jesse Stutts. She would be sure to know all the dirt on both of them.

Chapter 21

Sunday, July 30—Wednesday, August 2, 2006

The next morning, Brian was at church in his usual left-hand pew, but we didn't speak after the service was over. His insistence that I forget about investigating Lonnie P. had made things uncomfortable between us, so I devoted my attention to the friends that spoke to Mama without even glancing around to see where he was, and by the time we reached my car, I didn't see him or his silver Isuzu anywhere. The rift between us made me feel a little guilty, but I told myself it was just as well that it had occurred. At least now I could forget all those silly teenage fantasies I'd been harboring, and I wouldn't have to feel that I was hiding something from Russell.

Later that afternoon, I called Gail, thanking her again for dinner at her house and apologizing for not calling earlier. "Let me take you to lunch one day this week. My treat. We still have so much to talk about, and now that Mama's got her arm out of the sling, she's getting tired of having me around all the time."

Gail sounded happy to hear from me. "I'd been wondering if you were still here or if you'd gone back home. Lunch sounds great, but let me check my calendar." There was a pause and then she was back on the line. "What about Wednesday? I have a hair appointment tomorrow and the Women's Club meets on Tuesday. I could do it Wednesday or Thursday."

"Wednesday works for me. You pick the place since you know what's good around here."

"There's this new steak place out by the college." Gail named the restaurant that Brian had taken me to. In a town the size of Pine Lake, there obviously weren't many choices. "They have a great lunch menu. And their cheese steak sandwich is divine."

We agreed to meet there at noon on Wednesday, and in our conversation about old times, I'd find a way to bring up Jesse Stutts and Cole Tanner and ask what they were doing now.

"Well, Mama," I said as I hung up the phone. "I guess you heard that I'm having lunch with Gail on Wednesday, if that's okay with you. I can drop you off at a friend's house, if you'd like, or maybe you can invite someone over here while I'm gone."

"No, thanks," Mama said. "I don't want to go anywhere, and I don't need company. I just need to have my house back to myself. I'll be fine here all by my lonesome."

"Okay, if you say so. But I don't want you to think I'm neglecting you." Now that Mama was doing more and more for herself, she'd been insisting every day that I could go home anytime I wanted, and I knew the time would be coming soon when I'd have to go back to work and leave her alone again. But I couldn't go yet, not without finding out what actually happened the night of the fire.

I spent Monday cleaning house, doing laundry, and planning menus for the weekend, when Russell was coming up again, along with Erin and Scott and the kids, and on Tuesday, after Mama's therapy session, we did the weekly grocery shopping, but still the time seemed to pass at a snail's pace, with me not able to make any progress on my search. I checked the phone book for both Jesse Stutts and Cole Tanner, but neither was listed. I'd have to wait until my lunch with Gail to learn anything new. There was a listing for Theo's garage, but I'd leave Theo for Delia to approach. He would tell her more than he'd tell me.

On Wednesday, Gail was already at the restaurant when I arrived, and after our greeting, as I followed the hostess to our seat, Gail lagged behind, waving and mouthing "Hi" to everyone we passed, sometimes zigzagging over to clasp someone's hand or pat a shoulder. "Isn't this nice?" she said when she finally slid into the booth across from me. "We've been needing a place like this for a long time—something besides barbeque and fried chicken and hamburgers." She motioned toward the window. "It's a nice setting, too. Lots of folks from the college walk over for lunch."

"Um-m." I nodded, studying the menu. I hoped Brian would not be among those people walking over today. Besides creating an awkward moment, Brian's presence would mean that I could not bring Cole Tanner or Jesse Stutts into our conversation, no matter how innocently the names might appear to be brought up. Now that Brian had made it abundantly clear that I was to drop all thoughts of investigating Lonnie P.'s role in the fire, I could not let him suspect that I was ignoring his warning.

Following Gail's suggestion, we both ordered salad and the cheese steak sandwich, and as we waited for our food to arrive, I remarked to Gail about how many people she had spoken to on the way to our seat.

"When you live in a little town like this, you know everybody," she said. "And their parents and grandparents and first cousins and grandkids. Everybody's related, more or less, so you have to be extra careful what you say in any group of people." She smiled and put one finger to her lips. I looked around, but nobody was paying attention to our conversation. The restaurant was less than one-third full, this being a weekday and the middle of summer when not many college classes were running.

I looked toward a table where three women about our age were conversing, a table that Gail had zigzagged over to earlier to say hello. "Those women over there," I whispered. "Anyone I should know?"

Gail gave it some thought. "Oh, yes, you know Linda. Used to be Linda Curtis. She was a grade behind us. I don't think you know Marcia or Joanne. Marcia moved here from somewhere down in south Florida a few years ago. Joanne's from here, but she's quite a few years younger than us—Joanne Stutts, she used to be. You may remember her older brother, Jesse. He was a couple of grades ahead of us."

Surprised, I took a deep gulp of air that sounded like a hiccough. Here was Jesse's name right out in the open, and I hadn't even had to bring it up. And sitting only a few yards away was his sister.

"I remember Linda." I glanced over and immediately knew which one she was. Although older, of course, she hadn't changed that much since high school. I considered going over to say hello, but the three women were already well into their meals, and while I was debating, our salads came. I turned back to Gail. "What is Linda doing now?" All three women were dressed professionally in business attire and high heels, obviously taking their lunch break from work.

"She works at the college. She's assistant to the president, and Marcia works in Financial Aid, I think. Something like that."

"What about Joanne?"

"Oh, didn't you know? She's the president. Has been for the last three or four years. She worked her way up through the ranks, and everybody thinks the world of her."

"I didn't know that. Or if I did, I didn't make the connection. I'm sure her last name is something different now, isn't it?"

"She's Dr. Joanne Jameson now. Her husband isn't from around here. They met in college. If you didn't know the family connection, you'd never guess she was related to Jesse. He was such a. . ." She made quotation marks in the air, "'you know what' in high school."

I ignored her insinuation. "I didn't really know him. All I remember is that people used to talk about how he was always hanging around Lonnie P. What's he doing now? Is he still around?" I kept my voice low so as not to be overheard, but the women at the table were deep in their own conversation, not even glancing our way.

Gail shook her head sadly, speaking in a whisper with one hand up to the side of her mouth. "It's pitiful. It really is. From what I hear, he doesn't do much of anything except stay drunk all the time. He lived by himself in an old trailer for years, but when his daddy died, he moved back in with his mama, and he's been there ever since, drinking up her Social Security checks. Nobody mentions him around Joanne."

The women were now preparing to leave, pushing back their plates and pulling out wallets and credit cards to pay their bills. I glanced that way again, focusing my attention on the one Gail had identified as Joanne. She had some of the same physical features as Jesse—the fair hair and skin—but on her they were very attractive. Nothing about her appearance or bearing even slightly resembled what I remembered about Jesse's fawning adoration of Lonnie P.

"What part of the county do the Stutts live in?" I asked after they left. "I never knew any of the family except Jesse, and I didn't really know him."

"I'm not sure just where," Gail said, "but it's somewhere south of town, off one of those dirt roads around the old turpentine camp. When Joanne became president of the college, there was a big write-up in the paper, all about her childhood and how she'd won all these scholarships to college, and it mentioned how she grew up on a farm down around Rock Creek. She and Mike live in town now, but Jesse's still in the old house with his mother. Somebody told me they saw him at the Double Oak truck stop not long ago, and he was drunk as a skunk."

"The Double Oak? I can't believe that place is still open. I'd have thought it would have fallen down years ago."

"It's still there, but it's nothing but an eyesore. One of the oaks is even gone. Got hit by lightning a few years ago. Nobody goes there any more except to get drunk and cause trouble." Gail wrinkled her nose in disgust.

The waitress brought our sandwiches, and I took a bite while I absorbed this new information. I'd wanted to know about Jesse and Cole without arousing Gail's suspicions, and I couldn't believe how easy it had been to get the lowdown on Jesse without anything seeming the least bit contrived. The only problem was how was I going to manage to talk to the town drunk? I couldn't very well go down to the truck stop some Saturday night—a woman alone—and ask around about Jesse Stutts. Maybe if I went to his house on the pretense of seeing his mother? But I had no reason to go see his mother. I had never met her and had no idea where she lived. Besides, if Jesse was always drunk, even if I did manage to find him, would I even want to try to talk to him in that condition? He'd need to be sober to be able to carry on an intelligent conversation. Or would he? Maybe he'd be more inclined to talk after the alcohol had loosened him up. Or maybe he had turned to alcohol to shut out the memories of that night and what he had done. The possibility made me gasp with excitement.

"What?" Gail asked. "You okay?"

I coughed to cover myself and took a sip of tea. "Oh, sorry. Something went down wrong for a second there. I'm okay. Hey, this sandwich is great. Thanks for recommending it."

"See. I told you." Gail smiled triumphantly. "Pine Lake is coming up in the world."

"Speaking of Jesse, there was that other kid that was always hanging around with Lonnie P.," I said. "Cole Tanner. What ever happened to him?"

Gail laughed. "The James Dean motorcycle guy. God, every girl in high school had a crush on him. You know, I have no idea where Cole is now. I haven't heard anything about him in ages."

"So he's not around here any more?"

"Oh, no. Last I heard he was out in California somewhere. Maybe he was trying to be a movie star."

"Did he ever marry and settle down?"

"About a dozen times." Gail shook her head. "Nah, I'm exaggerating. But maybe three or four. I lost count after a while."

"Anybody from around here?"

"First he was married to that Clarke girl. Bitsi? Mitsi? Something like that. She was lots younger than him. That was right after he came back from the army. Folks said her daddy made him marry her after he got her in the family way. After the baby came along, they divorced and he married Tonya Stuart."

"Tonya?" I tried to place her.

"Her family lives here in town. She's a lot younger than us, too. Used to be real pretty, but after she had the twins she let herself go something awful. Anyway, that marriage lasted only a couple of years, and then he took off for parts unknown. I know he's been married another time or two since he left. Folks say every time he comes back for a visit, he's got a different wife, younger each time."

"Sounds like he hasn't changed much since high school," I said. "Does he still look the same? I remember those green eyes and his long eyelashes."

"I haven't seen him in ages, but somebody told me he came to his fortieth class reunion a few years ago wearing his leather jacket and boots like he was still eighteen."

If Cole was in California, talking to him wasn't an option, not for me anyway. I'd have to focus on Jesse for right now.

"Wasn't Jesse in the military for a while?" I asked Gail. "Maybe he got sent to Vietnam and that's what got him started drinking."

"I think he tried to join up. Or maybe he got a draft notice. I'm not sure. Anyway, he went to basic training, but he flunked out, so I heard, and they sent him home. Or maybe it was for something else." Gail gave me a knowing look. "You know how he behaved in high school, around Lonnie P."

"Oh, you mean for being gay?"

"Right-o. If you ask me, that's what caused all his trouble. When people go against nature and God, that's what happens."

I tied to keep my voice calm and not call attention to our conversation. "If he *is* gay, then he was born that way. He didn't have any choice in the matter."

"Homosexuality is a sin. The Bible says so," Gail answered.

"How can a person sin for being what God made him? That's like saying it's a sin to have blue eyes or to be more than six feet tall."

"A sin is an action," Gail argued. "I'm talking about his behavior around Lonnie P. back in high school. And his drunkenness now. He has control over his behavior. Just because a person has a hot temper doesn't mean he's allowed to go out and murder anybody he gets mad at, does it?"

"Of course not, but you're missing the point." All throughout school, from elementary to high school, Gail and I had been best friends. Now I felt uncomfortable around her, as if we had nothing in common any more. Apparently Gail's Southern Baptist God had created everybody "normal," and then some of them decided just for a lark or out of pure devilment to go against all their normal instincts and be attracted to people of the same sex. There was no point in getting into a huge argument with her right now. Mama would soon be fully recovered and I'd be going home, leaving Gail back in her insular world in which right and wrong were clearly defined and passed down from generation to generation, unchanged and unchallenged. I picked up the check. "I'd love to talk longer, but I really need to go. I promised Mama I wouldn't be gone too long."

As we said goodbye, Gail said something about how we'd have to do this again before I left town and I mumbled agreement, but I knew that we probably wouldn't. Another few minutes with Gail right now, and I'd be lecturing her about the problem with so many Christians was that they didn't know or care much about what Jesus actually taught about loving your neighbor and doing unto others. So what if Jesse was gay? To grow up gay in Pine Lake had to have been brutal, so no wonder Jesse had become an alcoholic. I'd have to find a way to talk to him and gain his trust. But how?

Chapter 22

After leaving the restaurant, I checked my watch. Only one-fifteen. Mama, I knew, was enjoying her quiet house and time to herself, so instead of heading north, I turned east onto the highway and drove out past the Double Oak truck stop to see how much it had changed since my high school days. Back then the restaurant's huge juicy cheeseburgers on sesame seed rolls and thick crinkle-cut French fries, along with the jukebox up front that provided all the latest rock and roll hits, had made it a favorite teen hangout on Friday and Saturday nights.

The jukebox would be long gone by now, but if Jesse spent his evenings there drinking, that meant the restaurant must still be open, unless he was buying six-packs from the convenience store cooler and drinking outside in the unlighted gravel lot where the big trucks parked. Back in the '50s and '60s we'd known that unsavory things happened in that parking lot after dark, but we weren't quite sure what they were. I'd been to the restaurant a few times for a burger and fries with girlfriends after a movie, but I'd never been there with a date. As a teen I had fantasized over and over about sitting across from Brian in a cozy back booth, sipping cherry Colas, our hands touching across the table as Paul Anka's voice crooned from the jukebox — "Put your head on my shoulder, whisper in my ear..."

But those fantasies quickly deflated as I rounded the curve and saw the place. In the summer glare of early afternoon, the passage of time was all too evident. The restaurant was still there — its paint faded and peeling, the sign missing half its letters, one lone pickup parked out front. The gravel lot off to the side where the big rigs used to park was completely empty, weeds having broken through the gravel and overtaken it. When the interstate was put through south of town, all the big gas companies moved out there, and the little stations on Highway 90 got left behind. It didn't look like a place I'd want to go in the daytime, much less in the evening. I drove on past, turned around, and headed back into town.

Still not ready to go home, I turned toward the library. When I'd looked for Jesse in Mama's phone book, I hadn't found him, but there had been two other listings for Stutts. I copied the names and addresses from the library phone book—Elmer Stutts at 124 Sycamore Street and Harriet Stutts at 166 Sycamore. Harriet must be Jesse's mother and Elmer perhaps her brother-in-law or a nephew. Or maybe another son? Had Jesse had a brother? I didn't know. All of the computers were in use, but the reference librarian had a county map. Sycamore was right where Gail had thought, south of town, near the little community of Rock Creek.

I drew a quick rough sketch of the area on the back of an old grocery list. Now that all the roads in the county had names and road signs to help emergency workers find their way around, I'd have no difficulty following the map. When I'd been growing up here, none of the dirt roads had been named, and giving directions depended upon describing such landmarks as "the dead pine tree" or "the white house with the covered front porch" when there were dead pine trees and white houses with covered front porches everywhere.

Upon leaving the library, I checked my watch again. A little after one-thirty. Mama would be right in the middle of her first soap of the afternoon. I got in my car and pulled out my cell phone.

"Mama? Just checking. Everything okay?"

"Fine," Mama answered. "Take your time. I'm watching TV."

"Okay. I'm going to run a couple of errands while I'm here. I'll be home in an hour or so."

Ten minutes later I had turned onto Sycamore Street. With the spell of hot, dry weather we'd been having, the road was dusty, with washboard bumps where the wind had settled the soil into ridges, so to avoid knocking my wheels out of alignment and shaking myself to pieces, I had to slow down to about ten miles an hour, barely above walking speed. The first house on the road (a house trailer, really, one of the old single-wide styles) had the number 124 on the mailbox. So that was Elmer's place. I was looking for Harriet at 166. A little further up, around a bend, were a couple of newer looking double-wides, and across from them, an older house, all with numbers in the 140s. Then woods and fields again for a while, and then another old house on the right, behind a cluster of shade trees, twenty or thirty yards off the road. The leaning mailbox had the number 166 painted on the side.

There was no sign of life anywhere around. At one-thirty on an August afternoon, everyone would be inside — resting for a spell after their noon dinner and waiting for the worst heat of the day to disperse a little before venturing back outdoors. I drove on past the house and continued down the road a little ways until it forked off to the right. Then I turned around and headed back the way I'd come, slowing almost to a stop as I approached the house again, this time on my left.

A dark pickup truck coming toward me made me swing to the right as far as I could so that the truck could pass. As I continued past the house, the man behind the wheel raised his hand as we met and tipped the brim of his cap, and I nodded and lifted one hand in return, remembering the old country habit of greeting everyone you meet, known or unknown. Behind me, in my rear view mirror, I watched the truck turn into the driveway of Harriet Stutts. Was that Jesse? I hadn't gotten a good look at the man, only noticed that the driver was male, a ruddy face beneath a farmer's cap, friendly-looking, nothing to set it apart from the dozens of other faces I'd passed on other country roads during the weeks I'd been up here.

I could feel my heart begin to hammer in my chest. If that was Jesse, I could stop, back up, and maybe catch him getting out of his truck before he disappeared inside the house. But what would I say to him? I had no idea. We had not known one another in high school; he would have no idea who I was. I had gone to elementary/junior high at Green Glen, while he would have gone to a different elementary down at Rock Creek. Though we'd both been at the consolidated high school in Pine

Lake at the same time, he had been two grades ahead of me, and there was nothing about me to make him remember my face or name. The only reason I remembered him was that his infatuation with Lonnie P. was the talk of the school, the subject of endless behind-the-hand snickers and whispers.

I stopped in the road and put my car into reverse. No other vehicles were visible in either direction. If that was Jesse, this was a perfect time to become reacquainted before I lost my nerve. I wouldn't have to bring up the fire right away, not even today. I could introduce myself and say I'd been talking to a friend about old classmates, and I'd driven down this way on impulse, looking for what? Whom? Whom did I know who came from this part of the county? Surely there was someone in my class I could ask about. I would save my real questions for a later time.

Luck was with me. Jesse, if that was indeed Jesse, had pulled into the drive and was walking back toward the road while popping open a can of beer. As I backed up level with the driveway, I saw him open his mailbox and take out a handful of mail. Rolling down my window, I called to him. "Are you Jesse Stutts?"

"That's me." He glanced at my car, apparently not recognizing it as one that belonged on this road, and then at me. "You lookin' for someone?"

"Yes, as a matter of fact." I searched my brain for a name, any name, but nothing. One of the hazards of getting old. Too much information in there, and sometimes retrieving a particular bit took a while.

"The old turpentine camp," I said, the only thing that came to mind. "I was having lunch with a friend, and we got to talking about the old turpentine camp that used to be back in here somewhere. I remember going there on a field trip from school when I was in third grade, and I wanted to see if anything was left of it." I was babbling. I'd had no intention of looking for the turpentine camp, but that was the only excuse I could think of for being here.

"I can tell you where the camp used to be, but there ain't nothing left of it now. My daddy used to tell us tales of goings-on there when he was young."

"Really? Can you give me directions to it? I'd appreciate it. And I'd love to hear your stories. I'm planning to write down my childhood memories of how things used to be for my grandchildren. And I thought I'd go around and take pictures to include, too." Too late, I realized I didn't have a camera with me, not even back at Mama's. My digital camera was at home in Titusville in my bedroom closet. I crossed my fingers, hoping Jesse wouldn't notice the obvious.

"You from around here?" he asked.

"Used to be. I'm Kate Riley. I used to be Katie McCormick, from the north part of the county, the Green Glen area. I'm a couple of years younger than you."

He took off his cap and scratched his head. "Can't place you," he said finally. "Sorry. I don't remember no McCormicks in school."

"That's okay. I didn't expect you would. I'm the oldest, so you wouldn't have known my brothers either." His not remembering me was a plus, as far as I was concerned. He wouldn't connect me with any of his tormentors in high school, so we could establish ourselves in the present as two people becoming acquainted for the first time. "How far away from here was the camp?"

He came closer to my car window. His eyes looked clear, no redness or enlarged pupils, and there was no saturated alcoholic odor emanating from him. Maybe Gail was exaggerating his condition. I wouldn't put it past her, since to Gail's way of thinking one beer put you on a straight path to hell.

"Not too far. You just keep going down this road to the fork and then bear left." He pointed. "Then go 'bout half a mile and you'll come to the old Richards place. Right past there you take the first right and go till you see a dead pine tree, and then—"

"Hey, wait a minute. What's the name of the road I turn onto from here?"

Jesse took off his cap again and ran his hand through his hair. "I don't pay attention to road names. I'm used to the old directions. Just bear left at the fork and keep going till you come to the Richards place."

"I don't know what the Richards place looks like."

"Oh, sorry. Heck, it's a big old white house with a covered porch, sitting right in the curve of the road. Then after you pass it, take the first right, and—"

"Sorry. I need to write this down." I reached into my purse for a pen and paper.

"Heck, I'll show you. It won't take but a minute. Let me put this mail inside and tell my mama where I'm going."

"Thanks. I'd appreciate it. I'll wait right here."

While Jesse walked to his house and went inside, I pulled into his driveway and then backed up into the road headed back toward the fork where I'd turned around earlier. What was I thinking, following a strange man whom I knew next-to-nothing about into an abandoned turpentine camp somewhere deep in the woods? When, furthermore, the only thing I did know was Gail's assertion that he was a chronic drunk who spent his mother's Social Security checks on alcohol? Strangely enough, I felt no fear, only curiosity—curiosity at myself for doing something so out of character for me and curiosity at what I would find out from Jesse Stutts.

As I followed Jesse's truck, I took note of the street signs as we bore left at the fork. Soon I saw the big white house he was describing, but there were two or three more turns before he pulled off the road onto a narrow overgrown lane and stopped. I pulled off behind him and watched him emerge with his beer can still in his hand. The same beer he'd opened earlier or a new one? I couldn't tell. "This is 'bout as far as your car can make it," he said, coming up to my window, which I'd rolled partway down. "We'll have to walk the rest of the way."

"Is it far?"

"No. Just a couple hundred yards thattaway." He pointed down the path. "Want a cold beer? I got more in the truck."

"No, thanks. I'm fine." I rolled up my window and got out of the car, locking my purse inside. My keys and cell phone were in my pocket, in case I needed to make a quick escape.

As we reached Jesse's truck, Jesse drained the last of the beer in his can, tossed it in the bed of the truck and then reached through an open window into the cab to twist another one from the six-pack on the seat. "So you're writing your autobiography, huh?"

"Not really. Just a little something for my grandkids. I moved away from here right after high school, nearly forty-five years ago, and I'm up for the summer taking care of my mother. She fell and dislocated her shoulder, and I'm staying with her till she gets full use of her arm again. While I'm here I thought it would be a good way to stay busy and do something useful at the same time. Now that she's getting better, we're starting to get on one another's nerves a little bit, so I've begun getting out of the house for short stretches, driving around to all the old places I remember, snapping photos and thinking about how different life used to be."

"Time in a bottle." Jesse chuckled, and I laughed with him.

"That means we're getting old, doesn't it, when instead of looking to the future, we keep trying to recapture the past?"

Jesse shrugged. "Nothing special about the past," he said. "Except it's long gone, and that's a good thing, far as I'm concerned."

I followed Jesse down the overgrown path, stepping over dead tree branches and peering into the tall grass for snakes. What if Russell could see me now, walking into the woods with a strange man—beer can in hand? Another incident I'd have to put on my list of secrets that I was keeping from him.

Chapter 23

After about a hundred yards, the path opened up to a clearing in the woods. Jesse stepped onto a square wooden platform that was raised about two feet off the ground. Posts at each corner had apparently once held up some kind of roof. "We used to pretend this was a fort to protect us from the Indians," Jesse said. "There was a tin roof when I was a kid, but it's gone now."

"What was it used for?" I stepped up onto the platform alongside him.

"Watch your step," Jesse warned. "Some of the boards are rotted."

"Oops." I felt a board give beneath one foot and moved sideways to a more secure spot.

"Here's where they kept the barrels for the turpentine. They cooked the pine sap in a big copper kettle right over there." He pointed to the right. "Then, after it cooled, it was poured into barrels. I guess this was to protect 'em from the elements and make it easier to load onto a truck to take them someplace to sell. This was a pretty small operation, not like the big camps they had some places."

"Cooked? How did they cook it?"

Jesse stepped down from the platform and walked to a sloping depression in the ground. I followed. "Used to be a big old copper kettle right here," he said. "It's gone now, but you can still see where it used to sit."

I looked down at the rounded pit, mostly filled now with dead leaves and pine needles. If Jesse hadn't pointed it out, I would have assumed it was a natural part of the landscape, but now I could imagine a blazing fire beneath a pot, the flames curling around the sides of the kettle. "Like cooking cane for syrup," I said. "My grandfather used to do that."

"Sorta, I guess," Jesse said. "Cept there wasn't no mule walking around in a circle for turpentine." He grinned and I smiled with him.

Scuffing one foot at the edge of the depression, Jesse moved aside the leaves to show more of its depth. "I remember seeing the kettle when I was a kid, but I don't know exactly how it worked. This place has been shut down since before I was born." He drained the last drops of beer from his can and dropped the can onto the ground; then, apparently thinking better of it, picked it up and crushed it with his fingers. "I don't know what happened to the kettle or the other equipment. Not much to take pictures of any more. Some of the turpentine camps had housing for the workers, even a commissary. But this one was never like that. Once the owners got all the money they could out of the trees in the vicinity, they shut down and moved on."

"Darn," I said, as if I had just realized it. "I don't have my camera with me. I'll have to come back another time. Do any of the trees still have the cups on them for catching the sap?"

"Nah. I doubt it. The trees used for turpentine are likely all dead now. What you see around you is new growth." He waved one hand toward the trees around us.

I looked at the encircling woods and listened to the quietness, broken only by the call of an unseen bird somewhere in the pines. I searched my mind for images from that long-ago third-grade field trip. I remembered walking into the woods, seeing the slashes cut into the trees, being told about how the sap drained down into cups and then was poured into buckets. Gosh, if I'd been eight at the time, that had been fifty-four years ago. Over half a century.

"When I was a kid, I remember hearing talk about this place. The grownups made it sound so sinister. Was it really that dangerous?"

"My daddy said a man got killed here once," Jesse said. "Knifed over a woman."

The comment made me shudder. "When?" Here I was, alone in the woods with a man I hardly knew, a man with a crushed beer can in his hand, out of sight of my car or of any other people. Nobody would even hear me if I screamed. And he was talking about a murder. I started walking away in the direction of the path leading back to my car.

"Long time ago. Maybe in the '30s. Before I was born." Jesse followed me toward the path.

I continued walking, intent on getting back to the safety of my car. I didn't want to let Jesse know he'd scared me, though, so I turned my head to talk behind me.

"I need to get back. I left my mother home alone, and she'll be getting worried about where I am." By that time I could see the car, still parked where I had left it. I slowed down, relaxing now, lecturing myself about my unfounded fears. I waited for Jesse to catch up. "Thanks for showing me the place, even if there isn't much left of it."

"No problem. Sorry I don't know more about how everything was done—the cooking and all. I could introduce you to some folks who could tell you a lot more than I can, if you want to talk to them."

"Thanks. I'll have to come back later with my camera and take some photos."

I followed Jesse's truck back to Sycamore Street, and gave Jesse a final wave as he pulled into his own driveway. In retrospect, he had seemed perfectly polite and friendly—a genuine good-old-boy with no pretensions—just like most of the boys I had grown up with. He certainly didn't seem the type to have committed murder. Did I really want to send someone like him to prison for the rest of his life? Someone whose sister was the president of the community college where Brian worked? And not only Jesse but Cole, too, whom, again, I knew next to nothing about, who for all I knew was an upstanding and respectable citizen out in California or wherever he lived. If I continued my pursuit into what happened the night of the fire, they would be caught up in the net along with Lonnie P.

For that matter, was Lonnie P. still the same person he had been as a teenager? His mother had talked about his "wild, rebellious period," but according to Gail's glowing account, he seemed to have turned his life around as an adult and devoted himself to giving back to his hometown. Maybe I should heed Brian's advice. The fire had happened such a long time ago, when we were all kids, and none of us were the same people we were back then. Besides, I'd be going home soon, away from Pine Lake and all its ugly racial history, and it was none of my business, anyway. That's what Russell would tell me if I told him what I was planning. Let bygones be bygones; let sleeping dogs lie; bury the hatchet; don't stir up a hornet's nest.

But that would also mean letting Delia's attacker go unpunished— letting Lonnie P. be re-elected mayor, letting him revel in the glory and the power he had amassed in Pine Lake, letting him continue to walk the streets and proclaim himself the great savior of his beloved home town—its most generous benefactor and its most illustrious citizen. It would mean Delia would continue to run, not walk, out of any building he entered, would tremble with fear and anger at the knowledge that he was still here, walking around, making jokes, probably still feeling smug about the wildness of his youth, all the "crazy" things he had done back then to put the blacks in their place, to show them that Pine Lake wasn't going to put up with any of that civil rights mess. Backing out now would mean that I'd be aligning myself with all those segregationists back in the fifties and sixties who didn't consider blacks to be real people, not in the same sense as whites, anyway—those people who'd rationalized the attack on Delia and the murder of that mother and her children as simply showing a "nigger" who was boss in these parts.

* * *

Maggie and Rochelle are picking beans in the garden, their backs to me as they make their way down the rows, bending nearly double to find the beans hiding among the green leaves. I'm in the back yard getting corn from the crib to throw out for the chickens, and I take my time filling the bucket, watching for Delia to come outside, but she is nowhere in sight. I haven't seen her all week, not since the night of the attack. Her boyfriend has driven up the lane a couple of times this week in his purple and white Chevy, but in a minute or two he's gone again, nobody in the passenger seat. I slowly scatter the corn on the ground for the chickens and wash out their water bowls and refill them from the hose, worrying all the while about exactly what those boys had done to Delia. I can't ask any questions without giving away what I know and confessing that I was a witness who did nothing to stop the attack or to help Delia.

No police cars have come to their house that I'm aware of, and I'm sure I would have heard about it if they had. That means Silas and Maggie have not reported the assault. I wonder if Delia told her parents about going into the movie theater lobby where she wasn't allowed and they're afraid to say anything to avoid getting her in more trouble. I think about all the violence I've seen on TV — blacks being set upon by dogs and fire hoses and then dragged off to jail. Maybe it's just that Silas and Maggie both know that reporting the attack to Sheriff Hardwick and his redneck deputies would be a waste of time.

The entire past week has been a fog in my mind. The school term ended two days ago, so summer vacation has begun, but I'm worried about how I did on my final exams. All week I hadn't been able to eat or sleep or study because of worrying about Delia and wondering if she was okay. At school I'd been constantly on guard, listening for any mention of what happened at the movie theater or later that night. Every time I'd seen a group of kids in a cluster, talking among themselves, I'd imagined that was what they were discussing, but I'd heard nothing except talk about teachers and exams and summer plans.

Maggie and Rochelle have finished picking beans and gone inside. I return the empty bucket to the crib and latch the door, but I don't go into my own house just yet. I sit on the crib step, alone with my guilt and dread and fear. If I tell anyone what I heard at the theater or saw later out my bedroom window, I'll have to admit my own inaction, and I may get Delia and her friend into even more trouble for coming into the theater lobby and demanding to be served. And I don't know who the boys were who grabbed Delia and pulled her into the woods. It was dark, and I didn't see any faces, didn't hear any voices. I couldn't even say how many there were.

I'm full of rationalizations for remaining silent. Wait and see, I keep telling myself. Things will be all right. The boys just wanted to scare her, that's all. They wouldn't have done anything too horrible. I'll make new efforts during the summer to become friends with Delia again, try to regain some of the closeness we shared as kids. I'll find out more about Donnie, and maybe I'll even tell her about my crush on Brian, the super smart guy in my chemistry class whom I've been daydreaming about for months.

It's another week — two weeks? — before I hear Delia's name mentioned again, and it comes from my father. "Hey, Katie," he says to me at the supper table. "We need another stringer for the tobacco barn this summer. You know anybody who needs a job?"

I think about it. "Maybe Becky. She worked for the Bensons last summer. Why do we need somebody else?" For the last several summers we've had three people stringing tobacco at the barn — Delia, Maggie, and me, with the younger kids as handers — but now that Daddy has decided that Roy Jr. and Theo are old enough to be in the field cropping tobacco this summer instead of at the barn with the women and children, maybe he is going to add a fourth one.

"Delia's not going to be here this summer," Daddy says. "Her grandmother's not getting along so well, and she's going to Georgia to help out. So we need somebody to take her place."

Delia going away? This is the first I've heard of it. "When is she going?" I ask.

"Tomorrow. Silas is driving her up there. I think the whole family is going for the weekend, maybe."

I'm crestfallen. Now I won't get a chance to carry out my plan to renew our friendship. But if she's going to help her grandmother, then she must be okay. Maybe getting away for the summer will be good for her — allow her to put what happened out of her mind. When school starts again, she'll be back, and we can talk then.

* * *

But when school started in the fall, Delia didn't return, and I had never gotten my chance to atone. Our lives had taken separate paths, and the next time I'd seen her had been less than a month ago when I'd stood in line behind her at the bank's ATM. Forty-six years had passed in the interim, but that chance encounter at the bank had brought all the events of that night rushing back with a vengeance, as if they had happened just last week. How could I walk away again and say nothing, do nothing?

I couldn't. That was all there was to it. I couldn't walk away and continue to live with my conscience. I had to right a wrong that I should have stopped forty-six years ago. If I had run out in my pajamas and screamed or grabbed my father's shotgun from the rack, I could have scared those boys away. But I hadn't. At the time, I hadn't had the maturity or the presence of mind to act, but now I had no excuses to fall back on.

The living room clock read two forty-five when I arrived home. "Sorry I'm later than I planned," I apologized to Mama. "Time got away from me. Did everything go okay?"

Mama hardly took her attention from the TV. "Of course it did. You can stop all this fussing over me and go home anytime you want, back to your own house and husband where you belong."

I walked over and laid one hand on her good shoulder. "That time will come soon enough. When your doctor gives the okay. But you're gonna miss me when I'm gone."

For answer, Mama placed one of her hands on top of my own, and I felt my throat close up. In the past month I'd spent more time with Mama than at any point over the past forty years, and my leaving was going to be hard for both of us. I remained there for a moment before walking into my bedroom to return my purse to its accustomed spot on the dresser. Now that Mama was better and Delia was speaking to me again, my mind was a little lighter, but that only left more room for me to obsess over proving that Lonnie P. set that fire. I'd have to remember to call Russell tonight and ask him to bring my digital camera when he came for the weekend. I needed an excuse to visit Jesse again.

Chapter 24

Saturday, August 5, 2006

On Saturday morning I was in the kitchen peeling potatoes when I heard Russell's car pull into the drive. I hurried out the front door and down the steps. "Hi. You made it." As he exited the car, I put one hand up to touch his shoulder and gave him a quick peck on the lips.

"Yep. Made pretty good time." He put one arm around my shoulder. "You doing okay?"

"Fine. Mama's eager to show everybody how well she's doing. She still can't lift anything heavy, but she can eat with her right hand again. And take a real shower. Come on in." I stepped back while he reached into the car for his overnight bag and for my camera. "Oh, thanks. You remembered. Now I can take pictures of everything up here." I walked with him into the house. "Erin called from her cell phone. They'll be here in about half an hour."

Russell said hello to Mama and remained in the living room, making small talk with her while I returned to the kitchen. I should have been looking forward to the weekend—to having Russell up here and seeing Erin and Scott and the grandkids after weeks of being away—but what I really felt was more complicated. I was happy and excited to see everyone, but at the same time having them around was thrusting me back into the old role of dutiful wife and mother, putting on hold the search I'd begun into the truth of what happened the night of the fire. I found myself already making plans for Monday morning, when they would all be gone and I could get back to pursuing my suspicions.

Russell walked into the kitchen and leaned against the counter. "Your mother told me you could come home any time you wanted. She said you didn't need to stay away from your own family to take care of her."

"That's what she thinks, but she still has a ways to go to have full use of her arm again. She can't drive yet, and I have to take her to therapy twice a week."

"So you're planning on staying up here indefinitely?"

I looked up from the potatoes I was cutting into cubes. "A couple more weeks. Until she finishes her therapy sessions and the doctor says she can stay alone."

Russell shrugged. "I'm going outside. Look around for a while."

"Okay. I'm pretty busy here right now."

He walked out the back door and I returned to my work. What did he expect? Was I supposed to stop cooking dinner, fall into his arms, and tell him how much I'd missed him? Pack my bags and go home with him tomorrow? Watching through the window over the sink, I felt a twinge of guilt as I saw his slumped shoulders heading away from the house toward the lane. Maybe the passion and romance had cooled over the years, but we were still happy, weren't we? After thirty-seven years together, we'd accepted each other's shortcomings. I should have offered him a warmer welcome—a longer hug, some words of reassurance about missing him—but I hadn't. A caring and loving wife would lay down her knife and walk outside to give him a few minutes of personal attention. I finished cutting the last potato and looked out the window again, but he had walked out of my sight line. I added the potato to the pot of water and turned on the stove burner. I'd make time for Russell later, I told myself. I had too much work to do right now.

I was mixing the potato salad when Erin and Scott arrived half an hour later. I hurriedly rinsed my hands and dried them on my apron as I rushed outside.

Six-year-old Caleb was first out of the car. "My goodness, you're getting so big." I managed a quick hug before he squirmed away and ran for the sloping porch ramp, new since his last visit up here. Megan, who would be turning four in a couple of weeks, ducked her head and pretended shyness at first, but then she wound her arms around my neck as I scooped her up and held her tight. "And here's my pretty girl." I continued to hold her as I greeted Erin and then Scott.

"Come on in," I said. "Grandma's inside."

After we had all stuffed ourselves with a big noon country dinner, Erin helped me clear the table and put the food away while Russell and Scott took the children off into the yard to give Mama a break from the noise and activity.

"There's a ton of food left over for tonight," Erin said. "I'll heat up the leftovers for Grandma and for me and Scott and the kids. Why don't you and Dad go out somewhere for the evening? You haven't seen each other for weeks now, and I know how much he's missed you. Go out and have a good dinner, maybe a movie or something. You deserve an evening off. I can take care of Grandma."

"Oh, honey, thanks, but I don't know. I haven't seen you and Scott and the kids for weeks, either, and I want to spend time with everybody."

"You'll have all afternoon with us. By then you'll be ready to get away someplace where it's quiet. I guarantee it."

"You mentioned this to Dad?" I asked.

"No. I think you should tell him. Let it be your idea."

Had Russell been complaining to Erin about my absence? Well, he did deserve more than I was giving him. "Okay," I told her. "Thanks. I'm sure Dad would like that."

After a couple of hours spent catching up on family news and my marveling over all the changes in the kids since I had last seen them a month ago, Scott and Russell decided to take the kids for a ride in the back of Daddy's old pickup, down the lane to the pasture, even though there were no longer any cows in it. I left Erin visiting with Mama and went to take a shower and get dressed for my evening "date" with Russell. I hadn't had any occasion to go out at night since I'd been here except for the evening at Gail's house and then dinner with Brian at the new steak restaurant. Both those evenings seemed ages ago, and I hadn't talked to Brian for nearly two weeks, not since he'd gotten angry with me at the newspaper office and practically ordered me to stop my poking and prodding into the events surrounding the fire. Last Sunday at church, our eyes had met across the aisle before the service, but we hadn't spoken afterward, and I'd sensed that he was deliberately avoiding me.

As I shampooed and conditioned my hair, I found myself humming in the shower. When I had told Russell earlier in the afternoon what Erin had said, he had acted nonplussed, saying, "Sure. That's okay with me if you want," and I knew that he and Erin had already discussed it, planned it out between them. Even so, I had let myself get excited about the prospect of an evening out, away from the house and my caregiver duties to Mama. Where would we go for dinner? Should I take Russell to the new steak place out by the college? I'd been there twice already, first with Brian and then lunch with Gail two days ago, but it was the only classy place in town. Russell liked the barbeque restaurant in front of Winn-Dixie, but there was no point in dressing up for barbeque. It would have to be the new place.

"This is it," I told Russell as we walked inside. "Pretty swanky for Pine Lake, isn't it?" Dressed in the most feminine outfit I owned—a gauzy floral skirt and soft, sweater-knit top—I felt different from usual, more aware of my body and more in control of how the evening would go. I, not Russell, would be taking the lead tonight. Would I be sympathetic and apologetic for having spent so long away from home? Or would I be flirty and sexy—the enchantress proving that I still had that power? Or maybe I would be cool and distant, showing Russell how much I was enjoying being on my own, how maybe I'd decided I liked my new status as an independent woman. I held all the chips, and the power gave me a rush of confidence.

Russell had dressed up, too, or at least dressed up for him, in a blue and tan pullover with a collar over dress pants instead of his usual T-shirt and jeans. Another clue that he and Erin had been in cahoots before the trip. Lately whenever the two of us had come up for a weekend, before Mama's accident, he had brought only everyday clothes; no dress clothes always gave him a good excuse for not going to church with Mama and me on Sunday morning.

We were seated in a booth by a window and handed menus. "I hear the New York strip is really good." I had told him about having lunch here with Gail a couple of days ago but hadn't mentioned the dinner with Brian.

"So you're the expert already." Russell's voice sounded peevish. "Your mother must not need you too much if you're going out to lunch and yakking it up with Gail."

"Going out for a couple of hours is a lot different from just taking off and going home. Mama still can't do much around the house yet, not until she gets full strength and range of motion back in her arm. That's what the therapy is for."

"Where are Roy and Margaret? They can come and stay with her for a while, give you a break."

"They both work full-time, remember? They've been driving over every weekend to see her, and Zach calls. I'm not doing anything this summer—not until school starts up again—so I'm available. This is my mother, and I haven't exactly spent much time with her over the last thirty-seven years, you know. And now she needs me. What am I supposed to do? Put her in a nursing home?" This evening was getting off to a bad start. Russell's neediness was becoming irritating. "Actually, I'm enjoying being up here again, getting reacquainted with people I haven't seen in a coon's age, as folks up here would say."

Russell frowned and was about to speak when a young blonde waitress appeared to take our order. Once she was gone, I changed the subject. "Tell me about things at home. What's happening down there? How's your work going?"

Russell started a long explanation of what was happening at the space center. Atlantis was being prepared for a late August launch, and he began telling me about the work his group had been doing— something about a gas line that needed replacing—when a couple walked past our booth, the man with his hand possessively and confidently placed on the small of the woman's back. I tried not to gasp, but something in my face made Russell stop in the middle of a sentence.

"What?" he asked. "What is it?" He looked concerned. Had my reaction been that visceral?

My eyes followed the couple as they were seated a few booths away. The man sat with his back to me, but I had a good view of the woman as she faced me. She was about my age, maybe a few years younger, and it was clear that she had once been very attractive. She still was, for that matter. Her hair had obviously been colored and permed, and she had on too much lipstick for my taste, but she had maintained a trim, youthful figure, as evidenced by her low-cut blouse and form-fitting pants.

"Kate?" Russell was still talking to me. "Is something wrong?"

"No, no." I took my eyes off the woman to look at Russell. "I thought I saw someone I used to know. But probably not. It just startled me for a minute, that's all."

If I leaned a little to the right, I could see the back of the man's head. It was Brian, all right. But who was the woman he was with? And why did I care? After all, I was here with a man—not just a man but the man I'd been married to for thirty-seven years. Brian had every right to be out with any woman he chose.

"Anyway, as I was saying, the gas wasn't getting through the line, so stupid ole Bernie decided…" Russell was back to his work story, and I tried my best to concentrate on what he was saying. He was proud of his work at the space center, and one question about it could lead to an hour-long discourse that quickly lost my interest. As I listened to him drone on about the gas line, the excitement of the evening began to drain away. After all the time I'd spent on my hair and make-up, Russell had said nothing about how I looked. All he had talked about was work.

The steaks, when they arrived, lived up to all the promises I'd made to Russell, and I was determined to enjoy the meal, regardless of the circumstances. A few booths down, I could see that Brian and the woman were having an animated conversation. Although I couldn't catch any of their words in the general hubbub of the restaurant, the woman was smiling and her eyes shone with merriment at whatever

Brian was telling her. Every so often she would lift one hand in the air and wave it toward him as if to say "Pshaw! No kidding?" Whenever she lifted her napkin to dab at her mouth, her eyes lowered sexily and she patted her lips daintily so as not rub off any of the lipstick. I found myself filled with envy. Brian was obviously having the time of his life, and here I was stewing in my misery. At that moment I'd have given anything to trade places. She could have Russell, and I'd find out what was so entertaining about Brian.

"The steak's good," Russell said. "Pine Lake is moving up in the world."

"Um-m." I nodded agreement, brought back to the mundane conversation that Russell and I were having. "Gail says it's doing really well. Being here by the college is great for lunch business, I imagine."

"You want to go somewhere afterward?" Russell asked. "A movie or something?"

"There's only one movie screen in town," I told him. "I doubt it's something we want to see."

"What do folks do here for entertainment?"

I shrugged. "Beats me. Back when I was in high school, after the movie, everybody went out to the Double Oak truck stop to eat cheeseburgers and listen to the juke box. But that was the teenagers and twenty-somethings. Back then adults stayed home. I guess they still do." Mentioning the truck stop made me think of what Gail had said about Jesse going out there on weekend nights and getting drunk, and I wondered if he was there tonight.

"You said earlier you'd been reconnecting with old friends. Maybe an old boyfriend or two from high school?"

Was Russell jealous? Had he been worrying about what I'd been doing away from him? I laughed. "Of course not." Some of the power I'd felt at the beginning of the evening was coming back. "Who would I go out with up here? Besides, I'm a married woman."

"Just checking," Russell said. "I've been sitting at home, too, in case you're wondering."

"I haven't been wondering. I trust you." And it was true: picturing Russell going out with another woman was beyond my imagination. He was not a romantic at all; if he did go out with someone, he would bore her to death in the first hour.

Russell looked a little disappointed. Did he want me to see him as this dashing, handsome lady killer whom the women couldn't resist? The thought was laughable. I was stuck with him, for better or for worse.

We had finished our dinner and were still sipping the refills of our iced tea when Brian and his date slid out of their booth and came down the aisle straight towards us. As Brian's eyes met mine, I could see them widen with surprise. He quickly looked up and away as if deciding to walk on by as if he didn't see me.

But I wasn't going to let him get away with it. Still caught up in the afterglow of Russell's question about old boyfriends, I smiled and fluttered my eyelashes, atypically heavy with mascara. "Hello, Brian. How are you? Isn't this a nice surprise?"

Chapter 25

"Hullo," Brian muttered, glancing at me and then away, as if looking for an escape route. The woman with him continued her forward momentum for another step or two, a bright, impatient smile on her lips. We were just a minor blip on her radar, nothing to detain her from whatever future plans she and Brian had made.

"You know my husband Russell." I gestured across the table. "Russell, you remember Brian Simmons."

Russell extended his hand. "Hi, Brian. Nice to see you again."

Brian returned the handshake, somewhat reluctantly, it seemed to me. "Same here." He shifted his weight from one foot to the other, clearly eager to be gone, but I was relishing the moment.

"Hello," I said to the woman, giving her my friendliest smile. "I don't think we've met, but I'm Kate. Kate Riley. Brian and I go way back. We were classmates at Pine Lake High."

"Hi. Nice to meet you." She waved one hand toward me and Russell and took another step forward, already past our booth. Was she not going to introduce herself? And why was she in such a hurry to be gone? What was she looking forward to after dinner?

"I don't think I caught your name," I said.

"Shauna," Brian answered. "This is Shauna. Sorry to run, but we really have to be going." He looked at his watch.

"Okay, bye. Nice meeting you, Shauna." Why was Brian so nervous? I couldn't resist calling after them as they hurried away, "See you tomorrow, Brian."

"Tomorrow?" Russell asked after they were gone. "What do you mean, you're seeing him tomorrow?"

"At church," I explained. "Brian goes to Shiloh Methodist, as you know. I've been taking Mama every Sunday."

"So," Russell said. "I suppose Brian is one of the people you were talking about getting reacquainted with up here? One of the old high school boyfriends?"

"Brian?" I tried for a dismissive laugh, but it came out as a nervous giggle. I'd never mentioned anything about my crush on Brian to Russell, had I? I was sure I hadn't. But I had to admit it felt good to see him express a little bit of jealousy. The evening was getting more interesting. But I still felt a weird letdown at seeing Brian with another woman. Even though intellectually I knew I had no rights in the matter, something in me felt cheated on.

"Let's go," I told Russell, suddenly eager to be on the move—to be doing something, anything except sitting in this booth. We could put the car windows down and cruise through town, pretending we were teenagers again, on the prowl for friends and fun. Or we could check out the movie marquee or drive out past the old truck stop to see what was going on there.

We were on our way out the front door when it was pulled open from the outside, and Lonnie P. Ramsey filled the doorway, accompanied by a petite blonde woman whom I assumed was Sherri Lynn, his wife. "Evening, folks," he boomed as he held the door for us to exit. "Nice night, isn't it?"

I muttered agreement and hurried out, head down, hoping that Lonnie P. wouldn't recognize me. He hadn't shown any recognition at the barbeque restaurant when I'd had lunch with Delia, but since then I'd been to his mother's house and had asked her all sorts of questions about him. By now word had surely gotten around that I was in town, and if he had an opportunity to look at me closely, it wouldn't be that hard for him to realize who I was.

Just as I thought I'd made my escape, Lonnie P. came after me. "Hey, aren't you little Katie McCormick?"

I considered shaking my head "No" and continuing to the car, but Russell had stopped. I could see his face darken a bit as he looked Lonnie P. over. Two men out of my past in one night. It was too much for him to absorb.

"Yes," I acknowledged. "That's me."

"Bet'cha don't know who I am, do you? I've put on a few pounds since high school." Lonnie P. grinned and rubbed his ample stomach, apparently not connecting me to our previous encounter at the barbeque place.

"I know you. I saw your picture in *The Pine Lake Gazette.* Congratulations on being mayor."

"Thanks. I hear you and your mama paid a visit to my mama a week or so ago."

"Yes, we did. Your mother's looking good. Same as always." I tried to walk away, but Lonnie P. was in a talkative mood, waving Sherri Lynn over to join the conversation.

"Hon, you remember Katie McCormick, don't you? Weren't you two in the same graduating class?"

Sherri Lynn gave me a blank look. I didn't really remember her, either. She had been one of the "town girls" and had been a grade ahead of me in school, so we hadn't moved in the same social circles. Nevertheless, she stuck out her hand. "Hi. It's good to see you again," and I returned the greeting.

"This is my husband Russell," I said. "Russell, Lonnie P. Ramsey and his wife Sherri Lynn. Lonnie P. is Pine Lake's mayor."

"Pleased to meet you." Lonnie P. shook Russell's hand vigorously. "Checking up on the little lady, are you? I hear she's been up here over a month now taking care of her mama. You let her out of the house for that long?"

Russell frowned and didn't answer. I reached for his hand. "We really need to be going. Nice seeing both of you again."

"What's your hurry?" Lonnie P. winked at Russell. "Got big plans for the night, do you? I remember Katie when she was only knee high to a grasshopper." He turned to me. "Always with pigtails and your nose in a book. On the school bus you never talked to anybody, just kept reading. I never could figure out what you found so interesting in all them books."

"You'd be surprised all the things you can learn by reading." I smiled and hurried Russell away. Now that Lonnie P. knew that I was in town and had recognized me, I'd have to be more careful in what I said and to whom. I had no idea what the alliances were between Lonnie P. and others—who might be a friend or an enemy. The only person I knew for sure was in my camp was Delia; other than that, I couldn't trust anyone, not even Brian.

"Who was that?" Russell asked as we got into the car. "He another one of your high school boyfriends?"

"Lonnie P.? Heavens, no!" I shuddered at the thought. "He was a neighbor. I never liked him. Back in high school, he thought he was cock of the walk, and he hasn't changed a bit. His mother and my mother are friends; that's all. I took Mama over to visit with Mrs. Ramsey a while back. I was going to show her how to use her new computer, but she wasn't interested."

Russell turned the ignition key. "So, where to now? Where else do you think we can run into some more guys you knew in high school?"

"Sorry," I said. "When you live in a town this small, you know everybody. When I went to lunch with Gail on Wednesday, I swear she spoke to everybody in the restaurant. I don't think there was a person in there she didn't know. And you should have seen Mama at the grocery store yesterday. We went to Winn-Dixie after her therapy session, and she had to stop and talk to everybody in there—ask all about their children and their grandchildren and their brothers and sisters, and who knows what all. Believe me, nobody can keep a secret in these parts." I directed Russell to turn left at the next light. "We could check out the movie title. It might be something interesting."

In directing Russell to the movie theater, I had him turn down the street that Brian lived on. "A short cut," I explained, but Brian's house windows were dark and there was no car in the drive. Maybe he and Shauna had gone to the movie. As we neared the downtown theater, I kept an eye out for his silver Isuzu, but I didn't see it anywhere. The movie, with showings at 7:15 and 9:15, according to the lighted marquee, was *Ocean's 13* with George Clooney and Brad Pitt.

"Another one?" I said. "How many of these have there been now?" We had seen *Ocean's 11*, but had skipped *Ocean's 12*, assuming it was another bad sequel. I didn't even know that another one was being made.

"Want to see it?" Russell asked. "Might be fun."

I shrugged. "Might as well. There's nothing else to do." I wasn't particularly interested, but George Clooney was always worth watching. Besides, Brian and his date might be here, and perhaps I could spy on them without them knowing they were being watched.

Russell bought two tickets and we walked inside. It wasn't quite seven, so people were just beginning to arrive. A clump of teenagers had gathered at the concession stand, talking loudly and jostling one another as they placed their orders. Popcorn kernels danced inside the glass of the popcorn machine, making a noise like a kid shooting a cap gun, and popcorn aroma permeated the lobby. Above the row of levers for the fountain drinks hung a red metal rectangle with the words "Drink Coca-Cola" embossed in curvy white script. The same black and white tile squares that I remembered from high school still covered the floor, long tubes of fluorescent lights still flickered in the high ceiling, the same dark carpeted stairs led up to the projection room. I looked around for the life-size cardboard cutout of John Wayne standing off to the side, but it, at least, was gone.

"This place hasn't changed a bit since I was a teenager," I said to Russell. "Look at it."

Russell took in the surroundings. "Yep," he agreed. "Like a museum or something."

"Exactly." I felt as if I'd stepped into a time warp, half-expecting Rock Hudson and Doris Day to be on the screen when we went inside.

"Want some popcorn?"

"No, thanks. I'm stuffed from dinner."

"Can't enjoy a movie without popcorn and a soda." Russell stepped into line at the concession stand. I remained in the center of the lobby, taking in the scene around me. Behind me the outside doors opened and a black couple walked past me and on into the theater without stopping at the concession stand. At least some things had changed over the last forty-some years. Had Delia attended the movies here since she had moved back to Pine Lake? Had she and John walked triumphantly into this lobby, heads held high, daring anyone to question their right to be here? Or had she been so traumatized all those years ago that she could not revisit the scene of that night? Feeling suddenly a little light-headed, I took a few steps back to the wall and leaned against it.

Still no sign of Brian and his date. If they hadn't come to the movie and hadn't gone back to his house, where were they? Maybe her place? Or was there some other night spot that I didn't know about? Maybe the members-only country club? Did Lonnie P. and Brian run in the same social circle now, rubbing elbows at the country club, tossing off mixed drinks while telling off-color jokes and discussing local politics?

"All set." Russell joined me, one arm circled around a big bucket of popcorn, the other clutching a large paper cup.

As the previews ran and then the movie began, Russell chomped on his popcorn and laughed at the on-screen antics, but my mind was racing ahead to next week when I could get back to my search for more answers. Had Delia found out anything of interest? How could I gain Jesse's trust and get him to talk to me about what happened the night of the Juneteenth celebration? And what was going on between Brian and Shauna? Where were they now? And why had Brian been so nervous at the restaurant? Had our discussion about our mutual high school crush made him feel the same possessiveness toward me that I was feeling toward him?

Once the movie ended and we were outside, Russell stretched his arms and gave a big yawn. "Ready to go home? Bout my bedtime."

"Pretty soon," I said. "First, though, drive back out to the highway. I'll show you where all the action used to be, way back when I was in high school."

Russell grinned. "I can't believe this little town ever had any action. Folks got excited just watching the traffic light change colors, I bet."

I didn't dignify his comment with a response but directed him to turn east onto the highway.

"Where are we headed?"

"Out past the old Double Oak truck stop. It was where everybody went in the sixties." The place had looked sad and abandoned when I had driven past on Wednesday afternoon, so I didn't have high hopes. "Slow down," I told Russell. "It's just ahead on the left." I pointed and was surprised to see a dozen or so cars and pickups in the parking lot in front of the restaurant. Probably a bunch of boozers, like Gail had said—oldsters trying to relive the fantasies of their youth or, more likely, drown their failed dreams in the comfort of an alcoholic stupor. "It doesn't look like much now," I told Russell, "but that's where everybody used to go. They had a big jukebox with all the latest songs."

"Creepy," Russell observed as we drove past. He pulled into the next left turn opening in the median. "You want to stop and check it out?"

"No. No. I don't think so. It looks pretty run-down."

Russell slowed again as we approached, this time with the building on my right. I looked for Jesse's pickup. That dark one over there looked like it, but I couldn't be sure. As we drew even with the restaurant, a man stumbled out the front door, almost falling as he tripped over the door sill. He had what appeared to be a beer bottle in one hand, and as he regained his balance, legs wide apart, he tilted the bottle up for another swig. I looked back as Russell kept driving. I couldn't see the man's face in the darkness, but he looked too tall and thin to be Jesse. I shivered and crossed my arms in front of me. I hoped Gail was wrong about Jesse hanging out here every weekend and drinking up his mother's Social Security check. The man I'd talked to on Wednesday certainly hadn't seemed the type, but then, who really knew a person from one encounter?

"Home?" Russell asked, and I nodded. "Yes, let's go home. I'm pretty tired."

Russell put his right hand on my shoulder and squeezed it, then moved his hand to the back of my neck, and I leaned toward him, resting my left hand on his leg. The security of his presence felt good, and as his fingers massaged my neck, I let myself relax in the moment, putting all the previous events of the evening out of my mind, determined to concentrate on Russell. I wouldn't give any more thought to where Brian was or what he was doing with Shauna. I'd missed my chance with him forty-some years ago, and it was too late now for regrets and teenage fantasies.

But later that night as Russell and I made love in my childhood bed, our actions hampered by the need to be as quiet as possible so as not to wake any of the others—as I returned Russell's kisses and whispered endearments, it was Brian's lips, Brian's hands, Brian's voice that I kept picturing in my mind.

Chapter 26

Sunday, August 6, 2006

The next morning, when Russell got up, instead of putting on his usual jeans and t-shirt, he pulled on the dress pants and collared pullover he had worn to the restaurant the night before.

"What's with the dress clothes?" I asked. "I thought you'd be taking the grandkids for a truck ride again to see the farm."

"Not much to see anymore. With the cows and hogs gone, it's just empty pasture. Anyway, I thought everybody was going to church."

"Well, I guess I'll take Mama if she wants to go. I don't know about Erin and Scott and the kids, though. We'll see what they want to do." I had already heard the kids' voices coming from the living room long before I was ready to get up and Erin shushing them, telling them to let Grandma and Grandpa sleep.

I swung my feet out of bed and sat on the edge. "I can't believe you're going with me to church just because Brian will be there." Did this have something to do with the phone call at the restaurant when I was out with Brian? I never had asked Mama what she had told Russell about who I was having dinner with that night. Had she told him that I was out with Brian? I couldn't ask Russell, for if she hadn't told him and I told him now so long after the fact, I'd look like I was hiding something. "Brian's been going to Shiloh Methodist ever since he married Edwina Downing. You know that. We used to talk to them whenever we went to church with Mama, back when the kids were little, remember?"

"Yeah, I remember. It must be awkward now, both of them going to the same church when they're divorced."

"Oh, Edwina hasn't gone to Shiloh Methodist in ages. She lives full-time in Tallahassee now. From all accounts, she's become much too gentrified to attend a little country church."

"Is that so? Brian tell you that? You're his counselor or confessor or something?"

"No. Brian hasn't said a word to me about Edwina. Gail told me the whole story—how snobby Edwina became after she started working in the Capitol building, how she was too good to associate with anybody in Pine Lake, how badly she treated Brian for so long."

Russell sat on the bed beside me to pull on his socks. "He must not have been too unhappy if he put up with it for all that time. Anyways, it looks like he's doing all right for himself now, judging from what we saw last night."

"I guess." I stood and pulled my nightgown down, straightening it around my knees. My heart was beating faster in anticipation of seeing Brian at church, at the prospect of inquiring teasingly about this Shauna he was squiring around last night.

After breakfast, everybody decided to go to church with Mama and then eat lunch at the barbeque restaurant in town instead of eating more leftovers at home. Delighted to show off her visiting granddaughter and her family, Mama insisted that everybody sit with her, up front and center, kids included, so we all dutifully trooped in after her. As we took our seats, I checked out the left hand pew where Brian always sat, about halfway up the aisle, but I didn't see him. Being so near the front prevented me from seeing newcomers as they entered, and I was determined not to show any obvious signs that I was watching for Brian, but I didn't have to. Every so often Russell, beside me, would swivel around and scrutinize the crowd, each time coming up empty.

Where was Brian? It wasn't like him to be late. As we stood for the opening hymn, I could no longer resist the temptation to check for myself. A quick half-turn to the left still revealed no sign of him. Was he not coming? Had he overslept? What had happened last night between him and Shauna to keep him from attending church? Had he stayed home to avoid seeing me? And if so, why?

As the service continued with more hymns and prayers and responsive readings, Caleb and Megan grew restless and squirmy. During the offertory, just before the sermon was to begin, Scott whispered to Erin that he was going to take the kids outside, and Russell quickly volunteered to go with him, leaving me, Erin, and Mama inside to listen to the preacher's message. I turned to watch them make their way down the aisle in the opposite direction of the men carrying the collection plates. Brian always handled the collection for the left hand pews, but someone else was filling in for him today.

One part of me wanted to laugh. Here Russell had come with me to church—a place he typically found an excuse to avoid—specifically to check out my relationship with Brian, and Brian hadn't even shown up. But another part of me roiled with anxiety. Would Brian's absence raise Russell's suspicions? After all, I had insisted that Brian would be here, that he was *always* here, that we were old friends, nothing more, and his not showing up might suggest otherwise.

Besides, I'd wanted Brian to be here for me. I'd wanted assurance that no matter what had happened between him and Shauna last night, by this morning he would have returned to being "my" Brian again— that he would have gotten over his anger at me for poking and prodding into the past and would once again make me feel special by seeking me out after the service just to say hello, that he'd go back to being my old friend with whom I shared so many high school memories. The fact that he wasn't here must mean that those high school feelings we'd both kept secret were still smoldering for him just as they were for me—long-dormant embers that we could not allow ourselves to stoke into flames.

By the time the sermon ended, I had determined that Brian had been right to stay away this morning. Both of us had our own separate lives, and neither of us wanted to put temptation in our path. The only viable solution was to simply avoid, or at least ignore, each other for the remaining weeks of my visit.

When we returned from the restaurant, Roy and Margaret were at the house. Roy had used his house key, and they were sitting inside in the air conditioning.

"Why didn't you call?" I asked. "We ate lunch in town. You could have joined us."

"We had sandwiches at home," Margaret answered. "We knew you'd be in church, so we didn't want you thinking you had to prepare a big meal for us."

After Roy and Margaret greeted Mama and exclaimed over how much Caleb and Megan had grown since Christmas time when they'd last seen them, everyone settled down for a family visit to catch up on the news. "Let's call Zach while we're all here together," someone suggested, and we got Zach on the phone, passing it around the room so that everyone could say hello.

By five o'clock, however, everyone had left for home, even Roy and Margaret declining to stay for supper, and Mama and I were alone again. After all the noise and activity of the weekend, the sudden emptiness was unsettling. I hadn't felt lonely or homesick up to now, but everyone's abrupt departure left me feeling a little deserted. Was this what Russell had been feeling in my absence? Tonight he'd walk back into an empty house, wake up alone tomorrow, drink his coffee alone and then go off to work with nobody to come home to, nobody to tell about his day. For a moment, I felt such empathy for him that I wanted to cry. I wasn't being fair to him by staying up here all summer with Mama, but what other choice did I have? I couldn't leave her alone, at least not until she was better able to take care of herself, not until the doctor gave her the okay to resume her normal activities and to drive again.

Besides, I had unfinished business up here to take care of. I had to talk to Delia to see what she had found out, had to arrange somehow to meet with Jesse again, had to figure out what I was going to do with the information I was accumulating. Two more weeks, I'd promised Russell. Two more weeks up here, and then I'd come home.

After Mama and I ate supper and cleaned up the kitchen, I walked outside into the summer dusk. The sun had dropped below the horizon, leaving the western sky streaked with a wash of pink and purple-tinged clouds, but with no lessening of the day's heat and humidity. Perspiration soon beaded on my forehead and dampened the small of my back. Between Mama's therapy sessions and my preparations for the weekend of company, Delia and I hadn't talked since my visit to her house a week ago, and I was eager to know if she had learned anything more about the night of the fire. After forty-four years, would people finally be willing to talk, or were they still too frightened or complacent to want to see justice done?

I walked across the back yard to the lane that led to where Delia's house had once stood and had just opened my cell phone when I heard a car coming up the lane behind me. Who on earth could be driving up here? This lane was private property, leading nowhere except to the gate that opened into the pasture. Russell had driven it yesterday when he and Scott took the kids for a ride around the farm, but nobody except family ever used it. I felt a moment of panic before I recognized the car as Delia's.

I snapped my phone shut and held it up as Delia stopped beside me and rolled down her window. "I was just about to call you to see if you'd found out anything."

"I was thinking about calling you, and then I thought I'd just drive out here and see you and say "Hey" to Miss Julia. I haven't been back to this place in forever. . ." Delia's voice trailed off and her face took on a haunted look. Directly across the lane was the tobacco barn, large sheets of tin missing from its roof, its door sagging on rusty hinges, but still standing. Delia had stopped her car at almost the exact spot in the road where I had seen the boys suddenly emerge out of the darkness and grab her.

I shook off the memory, wanting to distract Delia and keep her from reliving that night, wanting to put it out of my mind, too. If I could only go back in time and change things, I would, but that was impossible. "Remember those gingerbread cookies your mother used to make?" I asked. "The thick, chewy ones? And how she used to sing all those gospel songs? 'Swing Low, Sweet Chariot.' That was her favorite."

Delia opened her door and got out. "She still sings. Drives me crazy, sometimes." Delia herself burst into the first verse of "Swing Low, Sweet Chariot," and her voice was rich and throaty, fuller than Maggie's, but without Maggie's pure, sweet timbre.

Delia crossed the lane in front of the car with me following. "Right there," she said, pointing. "It was ten steps from the lane to the front door."

"Daddy used it for storage for a long time after your family moved out. Then one summer a windstorm ripped off half the roof and ruined most of his tobacco crop he had stored in there, so instead of repairing the damage, he built a new storage building. Over there." I pointed. "The little house here got left to the weather, and eventually he tore it down."

"It's just as well that it's gone." Delia gave her head a shake as if to dispel any lingering memories. "I don't want to go back to those days. No sir-ree."

"You talk to anybody yet?" I asked.

"Several folks saw some white boys running away from the preacher's house just as it went up in flames. Two of 'em, they say, but nobody knows who they were. At least nobody is naming names."

"You think they don't know? Or they just don't want to say?"

"Lonnie P. Ramsey's mighty powerful right now, being the mayor and all, and donating money for the new hospital wing and such. Him and the sheriff is like that." Delia held up two fingers touching one another. "All he's got to do is tell Kip Hardwick he wants somebody arrested, and Harwick's out there with some trumped-up charge."

"Kip Hardwick? Is he related to Otto Hardwick, who was sheriff when we were kids?"

"Grandson," Delia answered. "And just as mean a snake as his grandpa, from all I've heard."

"Is Grandpa Hardwick still alive?"

"I don't know. And don't care." Delia's eyebrows lowered in a scowl. "I hope he's dead and rotted in the ground."

"Don't you mean burning in hell?" I asked, laughing a little to lighten the mood. The Sheriff Hardwick that I remembered from high school—heavy, jowly, scowling from the sidelines of football games, had to have been at least in his fifties back then, so it wasn't likely he was still around.

"That, too." Delia nodded with satisfaction.

"It's the twenty-first century. You'd think there's been enough change even in Pine Lake to drag it out of the dark ages. Surely the young people at least must be ready to stand up for justice."

Delia's face lit up in a smile. "We'll soon see, I guess. Marcus Boyd is running for sheriff this year against Kip Hardwick."

"The young black deputy? I saw his ad in the *Gazette.* You think he has a chance?"

"Depends. He's honest and fair, got the respect of whites as well as his own people. But he's young—only been a deputy for 'bout ten years now. He's done a lot to wipe out the meanness going on in the neighborhood—guns and drugs and such. But he's promising to clean up the sheriff's department, and that's scaring a lot of folks. Lonnie P.'s been pouring a bucket of money into Hardwick's campaign."

"But if we can prove Lonnie P. set that house on fire, then that'll give him a real advantage, right? What's his name again?"

"Marcus Boyd."

Marcus Boyd. That's a name I'd have to remember. He might be somebody I'd want to have on my side.

Chapter 27

Monday, August 7, 2006

I spent Monday morning at home with Mama, changing the bed linens, doing laundry, and generally getting the house back in order after the weekend of visitors, but by two o'clock in the afternoon, I was itching to talk to Jesse again. Last week's visit to the site of the old turpentine camp had gone well, but I hadn't brought up the subject of the fire. Now that I had my camera, I could go back and take some pictures of the area. And Jesse had promised to give me the names of some people who knew more about the operation of the camp, so that would provide me with a good excuse to pay him another visit and feign interest in learning more about the manufacture of turpentine. I'd just have to find a way this time to work the Juneteenth celebration into our conversation.

I got my purse and camera from my bedroom. "Mama, I'm going out for a while. I want to take pictures of some places around the county—my old school at Green Glen and the old high school in Pine Lake and such. Since I've been up here, I've been thinking a lot about my childhood, and I want to write down some of my memories for the kids and grandkids. You think you'll be okay alone for a couple of hours?"

"I'll be fine. I won't be doing nothing but enjoying my quiet house. Go on and do whatever you want, and don't worry about me."

"Okay. I'll be home in time to fix supper."

I left Mama watching her soaps and headed into town. When I'd mentioned to Jesse my plan of making a scrapbook for the grandkids, it had come off the top of my head, but since then I'd been giving the idea serious thought. As far as I knew, we didn't have a photo anywhere of the little sharecropper's house, and now it was too late. I wanted to capture the crib and the tobacco barn and Daddy's old tractor and all the other farm implements before they, too, disappeared. But I could get those photos later. Right now my priority was to talk to Jesse again.

After running into the drugstore to buy a small spiral notebook, along with a cold six-pack of beer and a couple of bottles of water, I checked my watch. Almost three o'clock. Would Jesse be at home? The polite thing to do would be to give him a call, but I didn't have his number, and I'd rather the visit seem more impromptu, like the last one. Maybe I'd catch him outside again and tell him I was headed back to the turpentine camp to take some pictures and he'd volunteer to go along for the ride.

As I slowed to a crawl on approaching his mailbox, I could see his truck parked beside the house, but no sign of him. Last week there had been an older-model, light-colored car parked beside the truck, but today it was gone, so that meant Jesse was home alone. This was a bad idea: my driving out here to see a man I hardly knew, bringing him beer, no less. What would Russell think if he knew what I was doing? But Jesse had told me to come back any time, hadn't he? And right now he was my best lead in finding answers to what happened the night of the fire. I resolutely pulled into the driveway and stopped behind Jesse's pickup, steeling myself for a moment before opening the car door to walk the few yards to the wooden steps, flanked on one side by a lush wisteria vine buzzing with bees.

Jesse opened the front door before I reached it. "Hey, it's you again. Kate. See, I even remembered your name. Kate McCormick. I ain't talked to nobody yet about the camp, but I can give you some names and tell you where they live. Old man Tipton, up the road, he used to work there, but he don't remember much of anything these days. Got that old timers' disease."

He invited me inside, but I declined. "I thought I'd just drive back out there and take some pictures. I remembered my camera this time. Want to come along?"

"Sure. Ain't got nothing pressing to do here." He wiped his forehead with his palm. "Hot as blazes, ain't it? Want to take my truck? Wouldn't want your car to get scratched up or stuck in the sand."

I hadn't considered that possibility. The truck could get closer to the site, meaning we wouldn't have to walk so far, but if I left my car here, I'd be totally dependent on Jesse to get me back. Then there was the six-pack of beer in the bag on my back seat, meant to relax him and hopefully make him more talkative. I hadn't planned to introduce it quite so soon.

"Thanks, but my camera and other stuff are in my car. Besides, I wouldn't want your mother to come home and find your truck gone, a strange car parked beside the house, and nobody here. She'd be calling the sheriff."

"Hadn't thought of that." Jesse ran one hand through his hair. "She went into town to refill some prescription or other, but she'll be back soon. I'll be out in just a minute."

Jesse went inside and returned with a cap clamped over his head and an open beer in one hand. The fingers of his other hand curled around one of the empty plastic rings of a six pack still containing three beers. "Want a cold beer?"

"No, thanks. I have some bottled water in the car." Obviously he was on at least his third beer of the afternoon, so those plus the six-pack I'd brought along should be enough to loosen his inhibitions. I'd have to watch him carefully, though. I wanted him relaxed but not downright drunk.

Jesse headed for his truck, but I motioned to my car parked right behind him. "Why don't you ride with me instead of taking two vehicles?"

"Okay. Sure. If my truck's here, Mama will figure I'm somewhere on the place."

Jesse got in my passenger seat, and I stopped at the same spot where we had parked on Thursday and reached for my notebook and camera. As I lifted out the plastic bag containing the drinks, Jesse tossed his empty beer can into the woods and took the bag out of my hand. "Hey, let me get that. Wow, that's a lot of water, ain't it?" He hefted the bag and then peeked inside.

"Just a little something to thank you for all your help." I looked away. "I didn't know you were going to bring your own."

"You didn't need to do that. No payment required." But Jesse was grinning at the sight of the six-pack. "But since you did, it won't go to waste, I promise." He stuck his three remaining beers in the bag on top of the others and led the way down the overgrown path.

After setting the bag on the raised platform, Jesse popped open another beer and we wandered around the place for a while, me asking questions, writing a few lines in my spiral notebook, and snapping photos of the area before returning to the wooden platform. I took out a bottle of water as we both sat for a rest and wiped the sweat from our faces.

"It's been so long since I lived up here. I miss the woods, the silence." I lifted my head and listened. "No people. No traffic. Just quiet. You lived here your whole life?"

"Most of it." Jesse looked off into the distance. The clearing was surrounded by pine trees, closing us into our own private world. "I was away for a while, a few years, but I didn't like it. Wasn't home. So I came back. Worked at the paper mill till it closed down. Now I putter around and do a little farming. Just enough to get by."

"You were two grades ahead of me," I said, "so I didn't really know you back in high school. Only thing I remember is that you used to hang around with Lonnie P. Ramsey. Everybody knew him."

Jesse laughed bitterly and drained the last of the beer in his can. "Hang around with? Not hardly. Lonnie P. didn't know I was alive unless he wanted something from me."

"Really? I thought the two of you were friends."

"Nah." Jesse shook his head. "We was never friends." He reached into the bag for another beer and popped it open.

"Oh, sorry. I guess I'm mistaken then." What now? If Jesse didn't want to admit to ever hanging around with Lonnie P., that was his prerogative. Where could I go from here? I remained quiet for a moment before trying again. "Looks like Lonnie P.'s done all right for himself, getting elected mayor. Folks say he's donated a lot of money to the town, too."

"Harrumph." Jesse cleared his throat. "Don't know where he got it, but I can betcha it wasn't legal. Lonnie P. never knew a law he couldn't get around, one way or another."

I looked up, surprised. "You really don't like him, do you? Everybody else I talk to seems to think he's Mr. Wonderful."

Jesse didn't answer, so I continued. "He grew up just down the road from me, so I knew his whole family. Lonnie P. always thought he could use his charm to get out of anything, and he usually did. Never was too bright, though. I'd really like to know how he made all that money he's been giving away. These last few weeks that I've been up here staying with Mama, it seems that every time I turn around, there's something else he's got his hand in."

"Lots of folks are wondering that same thing, but they like his money too much to ask questions."

I could feel my heart begin to beat faster. "I'm so glad to hear you say that. I thought I was the only one with suspicions about him. But if folks are wondering, why did they elect him mayor?"

"A town this poor—nobody cares how dirty his hands are, long as they're holding out money." Jesse's voice was bitter with sarcasm.

"I've been away for so long I don't really know anything about the politics up here, but it sounds like you know more than you're saying." I'd have to tread cautiously here, for I didn't want to push too hard and shut Jesse down, but I felt exhilarated with the progress I'd already made, as if Jesse had been waiting for years to air his grievances about Lonnie P. to a sympathetic listener.

Jesse paced back and forth in front of me, pausing only for swigs of beer from his can. "It ain't just since he come back waving his money around either. It goes back a lot further than that."

I took another sip of water. "Further back? You mean to high school? Before he moved away from here?"

"Oh, you don't want to know about all that." Jesse waved one hand in dismissal. "How'd we get off onto the subject of Lonnie P. anyhow? I thought we were talking about turpentine."

Oops. Had I pushed too hard? I'd have to back off and try another tactic. "I mentioned high school, I guess. And Lonnie P. was on my mind. I ran into him Saturday night when my husband and I went out to eat at the new steak place in town. He acted all friendly-like, the charm just oozing out of him, but he was so condescending at the same time, you know? It just reminded me how much I disliked him."

"That's him all right. Makes you think you're his friend and then, bang, uses you and throws you away like a dirty dishrag." Jesse's tone was no longer just sarcastic and disgusted; it was raw pain exposed to air after long hiding.

I looked at the back of his neck and his slumped shoulders, wanting to say something to take away that pain. "It wasn't just you," I said. "He used everybody—anybody he could get away with using. He was a star athlete and was good-looking and had charisma to spare. He even had the teachers buying into his flimsy excuses. He asked me once to write an essay for him for English class, and dumb twerp that I was, I did it for him." I took another sip of water and waited. The story about writing the paper for Lonnie P. wasn't true, but it could have been if I hadn't been two years younger than he was; it was common knowledge around school that Millicent Owens had written all his essays. Everyone supposed she had a giant crush on him, but all she'd ever gotten for her hard work was a few minutes of wheedling flattery each time he had a new assignment for her, not even a thanks afterward. Someone else— was it Jesse?—had done his math homework.

"I can't believe I let him boss me around like I did." Jesse took another swig of his beer. "Back then I thought if I did his bidding, he'd like me, but it didn't work out that way. It only got me laughed at."

I glanced at my watch. Already a little after four. I needed to get to my point. "I heard him threaten some black girls once," I said. "Back when civil rights was all over the TV. Two girls came into the movie theater lobby, and Lonnie P. and some of his friends called them terrible names and threatened to teach them a lesson they wouldn't soon

218

forget." *Forgive me, Delia,* I said silently. *I won't use your name or give away your identity, but I need some reason to bring up the fire.*

"Sounds like him," Jesse agreed. "He was gung ho back then on keeping blacks in their place. Even talked about joining the Klan."

"Was there a Klan? In this county?"

Jesse shrugged. "Probably. And if there was, I could name plenty of folks who were likely part of it."

"My father believed blacks and whites should remain separate, but he would never have joined the Klan. He would never have hurt a black person."

Jesse was quiet, and I wondered about his father, what he had been like. I summoned up my courage. "Remember the black preacher's house that got burned?" There, I'd finally said it. Jesse didn't answer, so I plunged ahead. "The newspaper called it an accident, but I don't think it was. I think somebody set fire to it. Somebody who wanted to scare that preacher out of town. And I'll bet anything Lonnie P. had something to do with it."

Jesse crumpled his empty beer and dropped it on the ground, then kicked it hard, sending it careening across the clearing.

"What do you think?" I asked. "You think it's possible?"

"I don't think. I know." Jesse gazed into the distance, his eyes not meeting mine.

"You know? You know he did?" I held my breath for his reply.

"Heck, I ought to. I'm the one who bought the can of gas."

"The gas?" I looked at Jesse, at the agonized expression on his face. Did I really want to hear this, even if Jesse was willing to tell me the entire story? But this was what I had come for, wasn't it? "Want to tell me what happened?"

Jesse opened another beer and took a long, deep gulp. He wiped the back of his hand across his mouth and made a guttural sound halfway between a sob and a laugh. "Forget I said that. Time to get out of here before my mama and yours starts worrying about where we are. You ready to go?" He picked up the plastic bag in his free hand and started to walk away, his steps a little unsteady.

"Wait," I called. "Wait a minute." How could I get him to come back? To keep talking? I had to know more.

Chapter 28

I talked to Jesse's back. "The newspaper said a bottle rocket went through a bedroom window. You're saying it was gasoline?"

Jesse stopped walking but didn't come back to where I was still seated on the platform. At least he had stopped, though. One point in my favor. I didn't move. As long as I was the one driving, I was in control.

"Hey, what I just said. That was a bad joke, okay? You finished with what you came here for?"

I remained seated. "You don't have to worry about me telling anybody. I'll be going home in a couple of weeks, soon as Mama gets permission to drive again. Anything you say is in strictest confidence." Now I'd locked myself into a box, but that was okay. If I could learn the truth, I'd be satisfied, I told myself. For now, anyway. I wanted Jesse to keep talking, to tell me what happened. "You bought the gas and then gave it to Lonnie P.? I'll bet he didn't tell you what it was for, did he?"

Jesse took a couple of steps back toward the platform. "I swear on a stack of Bibles I had no idea. Lonnie P. called me at home and said he needed gas for a lawn mower. Said he had a job to finish up and had run out of gas."

"When was that?" I asked.

"That Friday. 'Bout five o'clock. Wanted me to meet him on some little dirt road outside of town."

"The day before the fire?"

"Yep." Jesse came back to the platform, took another beer out of the bag, and popped it open, taking a few swallows before speaking. "He acted all buddy-buddy on the phone, asking for this one little favor. Told me he'd pay me for it soon as he got paid for the job. I filled up a little old two-gallon can and dropped it off to him, just like he said."

"And then what?"

"I didn't see no lawn mower anywhere around, so I asked him where he was mowing and he laughed and said him and Cole was gonna have themselves a little bonfire Saturday night and asked me did I want to come along." Jesse paused for another swig of beer. "I should'a known he was up to something then, but dumb me, I was just happy to be invited, you know?"

I nodded. "Sure. Anybody would have been."

"First time he'd ever asked me to one of his night-time shindigs. I thought it was gonna be a party out in the woods somewheres, with everybody sitting around drinking and talking and having a good time."

"I remember hearing boys talk about night-time drinking parties in the woods, but I never went to one. My daddy would have skinned me alive for even thinking about such a thing." I took another swallow of water. "So what happened the next night? Did he pick you up for the party, or did you meet him somewhere?"

Jesse sat on the edge of the platform, the plastic bag of beer and water between us. "He wanted me to meet him at the same spot as before, on a dirt-road turnoff outside of town. I didn't know nothing about what was gonna happen, I swear. He drove up in his daddy's pickup, just him and Cole. I was in my daddy's big ole Ford Fairlane, and they wanted me to drive since I had a back seat. Lonnie P. drove his pickup off the road behind some trees, and then him and Cole got in my car. Lonnie P. got in the back seat with the can of gas on the floor in front of him. He had a paper sack, too, from the grocery store. I thought it was stuff for the party. I had a bottle of Jim Beam somebody had got for me from across the county line, and Cole sat up front with me, holding onto his own bottle, so I figured we was all ready to party. Then we drove around for a while, just checking things out. Wasn't dark yet, so we was just killing time."

I could imagine how important Jesse must have felt that night with Lonnie P. and Cole, the two most popular boys in high school, riding around in his car—the promise of a party in the woods still ahead. "What happened then?"

"We was still driving around, waiting for dark, and Lonnie P. wanted to go into nigger, um, colored town." Jesse stopped and looked at me. "Sorry, but that's what we called it back then."

"I know. Everybody did. Go on." I nodded encouragement for him to continue. "So you drove past the church where everybody was gathered?"

"I didn't want to, but Lonnie P. was itching to see what was going on." Jesse stood, took a couple of swallows from his can, and began pacing again. "I swear I didn't know nothing 'bout his plans, about what happened later, but I knew I didn't want to be in the middle of no trouble, so I tried to talk him out of it. But nothing would do him except to drive through there and see what was happening. Him and Cole started calling me a scaredy cat and such for not wanting to go, and of course back then I wanted to impress Lonnie P. in the worst way, and this was the closest I'd ever got." Jesse stopped his pacing to wipe one hand across his forehead. "If I would'a known, I would never..." He shuddered and then sat again on the platform, elbows propped on his knees, his face covered with both hands.

"So he tricked you," I said. "That sounds like Lonnie P., all right. He could use people and make 'em feel like *he* was the one doing *them* a favor. How do people do that?"

Jesse shook his head. "Beats me."

"You drove past the black church," I urged, getting Jesse back to the story. "What was going on there?"

"Nothing much. Everybody was eating. They had set up tables and chairs in the church yard. and folks was just sitting around with plates full of food. I was driving, so I kept my eyes on the road, but I was bracing myself, waiting for Lonnie P. to stick his head out the window and yell something—get somebody riled up. He didn't, though, and that was the first time I got this funny feeling that something wasn't right. You know, when you feel like something's crawling up the back of your neck?"

I shivered myself as Jesse mentioned it, hunching my shoulders, lifting my chin, and giving my head a little shake. "I know what you mean. What was Lonnie P. doing? Did you look around at him?"

"Yeah, I looked back a time or two, and he was sorta slunk down in his seat. He was wearing a cap, and he had it pulled down low over his face. Cole was slumped down, too, looking out his window across the street, not even paying attention to what was happening in the church yard. "See, nothing's going on," I remember saying. "Let's get out 'a here." I asked Lonnie P. again about why we weren't going out to build the bonfire. 'Ain't dark yet,' he told me. 'Have to wait for good dark.' By that time I was getting really spooked. I didn't care no more 'bout no bonfire. All I wanted to do was drive Lonnie P. and Cole back to the truck and then go home."

"But they wouldn't let you." I kept my voice low and, I hoped, sympathetic.

Jesse took off his cap, ran one hand through his hair, and put his cap back on, carefully adjusting the brim. He took another long drink from his beer, staying quiet for so long that I was afraid he wouldn't tell me the rest of the story.

"There was no party in the woods," I said. "The only bonfire was the preacher's house. And Lonnie P. lit it." Jesse had told me enough that I could figure out what happened next.

Jesse stared off into the pines, not looking at me. "Nobody was supposed to be home. Everybody was supposed to be across the street at the church. Hell, nobody expected kids to be there." He choked back a sob.

My throat felt so knotted up that I couldn't swallow. I took another sip of water. I wanted Jesse to go on, but I couldn't get any words out. My imagination conjured up the scene of those two babies screaming, the mother frantically trying to get to them through the flames.

"Did you see him do it?" I asked finally. "Were you there?"

Jesse took another long swallow of beer and shook his head emphatically. "I had nothing to do with that fire. Nothing." His voice took on an edge of anger. "It was all Lonnie P. and Cole's doing. We parked out behind the junkyard, still waiting for good dark, and had some nips from our bottles that we'd brought along. Then Lonnie P. wanted to sneak back on foot to the church where everybody was gathered. Said he wanted to scare some niggers is the way he put it. I said I was having nothing to do with whatever he was planning, and he just laughed and said I already did, seeing as how I was the one that bought the gas and seeing as how we was all in my daddy's car, and everybody had seen me driving past the church earlier, scoping things out. Only way he wouldn't tell on me and get me into really big trouble was for me to do just what he said. We all had a few drinks in us by that time, see, and we was all getting a little tipsy." Jesse stood and stretched. "Whew. I'm gonna have to walk off into the woods for a little bit, if you'll excuse me."

"Sure. Go right ahead." Having watched Jesse drink for the last hour, I'd been wondering how much liquid his bladder could hold. As he disappeared into the woods, I pulled my cell phone from my pocket and called Mama. "Everything okay?" At her assurance that it was, I continued. "I ran into a friend in town, and I'm still here. We've been talking about old times. I'll be home by six, but if you get hungry before I get there, go ahead and eat without me." The refrigerator was still full of leftovers from my weekend cooking-for-company spree, plus Mama was capable by now of heating up a meal for herself. My duties here were nearly at an end.

Mama didn't ask who the "friend" was, a lack of curiosity that didn't register with me until after I'd closed my cell phone and returned it to my pocket. Had she just assumed it was Gail? But in that case, I would have said, "I ran into Gail." I wouldn't have said "a friend." And Delia had come inside for a minute last night to say "Hi" to Mama after we'd talked in the lane, so Mama would know it wasn't Delia again. I hoped she wouldn't get it into her mind that I was meeting Brian on the sly and didn't want her to know. I'd have to make up a story to tell her when I got home to cover my tracks.

Jesse returned from the woods looking relieved. I sat back down, but he remained standing, gazing around the clearing and avoiding meeting my eyes. "I guess you need to get home," he said. "We been out here a long time."

"No, I'm fine. In fact, I called my mother while you were gone to let her know I wouldn't be home for a while yet. Unless you need to get back? Do you think your mother's worried about where you are? You can use my phone to call if you want." I pulled it out of my pocket.

"Nah." Jesse waved off my offer. "I come and go as I please. She don't keep tabs on me." As if to emphasize his independence, he took another beer from the bag, opened it, and took a long drink.

Noticing that his legs were a little unsteady beneath him as he tipped his head back, I felt a flash of uneasiness, but I couldn't stop now. I was too close to learning what actually happened that night. "So Lonnie P. and Cole were in cahoots to frame you. Were they going to blame you for the whole thing? That doesn't seem possible."

Jesse focused his attention on the can of beer in his hand. "I think they just wanted to make sure I didn't talk to nobody 'bout what happened. If I was in on it, I'd have to keep my mouth shut."

"But why you? Why not somebody else who'd have been more willing to play along? Or why not just the two of them?"

Jesse shrugged. "I was Lonnie P.'s go-to stooge, I guess. Whenever he wanted a favor, I was the first one he came to. He knew I'd do anything he asked, just to be around him." He dropped his head, but I could see a redness creep up his neck and brighten his ears beneath his cap.

I didn't say anything. Should I acknowledge Jesse's crush on Lonnie P. or avoid the subject? I didn't want to embarrass him any further, but maybe I should let him know I understood.

Jesse decided for me. "Enough of that. You ready to go? Must be getting 'bout suppertime."

I glanced again at my watch. Five-fifteen. "In a minute." I took my time screwing the top back on my nearly empty water bottle and gathering up my notebook and camera, trying to delay departure until

I'd heard the rest of the story. "So Lonnie P. and Cole went back on foot to the preacher's house? You didn't go with them?"

"Heck, no. I told Lonnie P. I was having nothing to do with whatever he had planned, so he told me to stay in the car and wait for him and Cole to come back. This was after they started shooting off fireworks over at the church. We could see and hear 'em from the junkyard where we was parked."

"You could have gone home then and left them there."

"Yeah, I could have. You don't know how many times I wished I had'a done just that." Jesse reached for the plastic bag, which was nearly empty by now. "If I'd a known about them kids, that Lonnie P. was gonna set fire to that house with kids inside, I would'a stopped him somehow. Run into that churchyard and warned somebody. But I didn't know. I had no idea what he was gonna do with that gas—only I knew it couldn't be nothing good. But if I'd drove off and left 'em there, I would'a suffered for it, you can bet. Lonnie P. would'a come after me." Jesse started to walk away toward the path leading back to the car.

I followed, talking to his retreating back. "But you could have gone to the sheriff, and Lonnie P. and Cole would have been locked up, charged with arson and murder."

"Ha!" Jesse shook his head in disgust, talking over his shoulder. "Shows what you know about it. Heck, Otto Hardwick is the one that planned the whole thing. He was the one recruited Lonnie P. for the job, told him what to do and how to make it look like an accident."

"You can't be serious. The sheriff was in on it?" I hurried to catch up with Jesse. I should have guessed as much before, but I hadn't. Had we been such a racist and lawless county in 1962 that our sheriff condoned the murder of black babies?

Jesse continued walking. "Course he wasn't expecting nobody to be at home neither. When he found out there was babies in the house, he's the one arranged for us all to leave town the next day and go to the army recruiting place. I sure as heck didn't have no plans to join the army, but the sheriff said I had to—said I was an accessory even when I didn't even know what Lonnie P. and Cole had done. I only found out about it the next day on the drive out of town."

"What about Lonnie P. and Cole? Did they see the babies before they set the fire?"

Jesse stopped and looked up at the sky as if seeking the answer there. He was quiet a long time before speaking, his words barely audible. "They said they didn't, but I don't know. Honest to God, I don't know to this day the answer to that." He crushed the beer can in his hand and flung it as hard as he could into the woods, stumbling as he did so, and then regaining his balance. "Ever since that day, I been hating Lonnie P. and hating myself for how I let him take advantage of me all them times. I'd kill him if I wasn't such a coward."

I remained a few paces behind Jesse. The car was just ahead. "It's time, finally, to lay down this burden you've been carrying around, to let justice be done. All you have to do is tell somebody else what you just told me, and then let the legal system take it from there. Can you do that?"

Jesse shook his head. "Nope. Can't do it."

"Why not? Times have changed, even here in Pine Lake. You said yourself lots of people hate Lonnie P. but they're all too chicken to say so. Once they know about this, he'll be exposed for what he really is, and his money won't be able to save him any more. Don't you want to see him punished for what he did?"

"I know what he's like," Jesse said. "He'll lie like hell and try to pin it all on me. Not that it matters so much to me, but I can't do that to my mama and my sister. My sister's president of the college now."

"I heard about that. That's great. Hey, I'm not a lawyer, but I don't think there's anything for you to worry about. You weren't an accessory like the sheriff said; you were duped. If you testify against Lonnie P. and Cole, you'll be given immunity, I'm sure. We can talk to a lawyer first, if you know somebody you trust, to make sure. I'll go with you if you want."

"No lawyer." Jesse shook his head. His words were slowing down and beginning to slur. "My family don't know nothing 'bout this, and I don't want 'em to know. This is strictly between me and you. I don't know why I told you 'cept you seem like a nice person and you're the first one who's ever asked me about that night, but you can't go telling nobody else. My mama and my sister can't know about this. It would nearbout kill 'em." The plea in Jesse's voice was almost a sob.

We had reached the car by now. "Hey, don't worry," I assured him. "Your story is safe with me. I promised I wouldn't tell, and you can trust me on that. But if you ever change your mind, you'll let me know, okay?"

"What's all this to you?" Jesse asked. "You said you didn't even live here any more."

"That's true. I don't. But believe me, I have my own reasons for wanting Lonnie P. to get what he deserves." I opened my driver's side door. "Now let's get us both home where we belong."

Chapter 29

Monday, August 7—Tuesday, August 8, 2006

I drove home feeling an odd mixture of horror and elation at what Jesse had told me. My suspicions had been right all along, and Lonnie P. was an arsonist and a murderer as well as Delia's lead attacker. Had he seen those two babies in the bedroom and still poured the gas and set the fire? And, if so, had he, in all the years since, ever felt a smidgeon of remorse for what he had done? How, I wondered, could he walk into Hopewell Baptist every Sunday with his head held high and proclaim himself to be a Christian? Were all his church and community donations attempts to somehow buy his way back into God's good graces?

Jesse's confession had been given in strictest confidence, so I had to respect his wishes, but if he had been willing to tell *me*, someone he really didn't know at all except as a sympathetic listener, then I could only hope that after some more soul-searching, he would come to realize that he didn't have to carry the entire weight of his secret alone — that others would understand and forgive once the truth came out — and that it was his duty to expose Lonnie P. for the monster he truly was.

I had no doubt that what Jesse had said about Lonnie P. trying to deflect the blame for the whole thing onto him was a real fear, but I also felt it highly unlikely that Jesse would face any legal consequences regarding the fire. He would almost certainly be granted immunity in exchange for his testimony, and if he were to go on the witness stand and tell his story just the way he had told it to me, I could imagine

231

everyone in the room having the same sympathetic reaction that I had felt. So why not let the truth come out? But then the person on the witness stand became not Jesse, but me, telling the jury what I'd heard in the movie theater and what I'd seen later that night, cowering beside my bedroom window while Lonnie P. and those other boys dragged Delia into the woods. Would I want to have to tell that story publicly, revealing my failure not only to Delia but to the whole county, even if it meant putting Lonnie P. behind bars for the rest of his life? No, I had to admit that I wouldn't want my family to know those details — no more than Jesse wanted to reveal his trail of humiliation at the hands of Lonnie P. Was I asking Jesse to do something that I was not willing to do myself? My excuse was that Delia didn't want the attack on her to become public knowledge, but what if that excuse didn't exist? Would I do it then? I didn't know.

I turned north toward Mama's, puzzling over the quandary I'd placed myself in. I'd promised Jesse not to reveal any of what he'd told me, and I'd keep my promise, but with Delia already making inquiries of her own, it was too late to stop the sequence of events that had been set into motion. Even if I told Delia now to forget it, the hornet's nest I'd stirred up was already buzzing with activity, and there was no way to silence all the hornets or shepherd them back into their nest.

And if the black community knew something was wrong with the story that was told about the Juneteenth fire, that meant other people in town also knew more about what happened that night than had ever been made public. If the sheriff had planned the whole thing and the newspaper account was a whitewash, who's to say the fire department wasn't in on the cover-up, too? If they had conducted any sort of investigation, they would have discovered the presence of gasoline. There had to be someone from the fire department, someone long retired but still alive, who knew what the investigators really found at the scene, even if it hadn't made it into the written report. Why had that information never come to light over the last forty-four years? Was it fear or just complacency?

Delia had said that the current sheriff, Kip Hardwick, grandson of Otto Hardwick, was cut from the same cloth as his grandfather, but still, how could people remain silent and knowingly allow a murderer to be elected as their mayor? Did Lonnie P. have that much power over the town? Maybe everybody around here thought so, but his money and status meant nothing to me. I owed it to Delia—and to those two little children and their mother, whom I'd never met and whose names I didn't know—to see that justice was done. How to go about it was getting more complicated by the minute, but I couldn't abandon my pursuit.

When I arrived back home, Mama had set the table for supper and was warming up the leftovers from the refrigerator. "Sorry I'm so late," I apologized. "I took a few snapshots around town." I waved the camera as proof.

Mama dropped ice cubes into the two glasses she'd already set on the counter. "Must be more than a few if it took you all that time."

"I told you I ran into a friend from high school and we got to talking. You didn't have to wait supper for me."

"Five more minutes and I would have been eating without you."

I glanced at the clock on the microwave. "I said over the phone I'd be home by six, and it's five-fifty-four, so I made it with six minutes to spare."

"Who did you run into in town?" Mama asked as she carried the glasses to the table.

"Oh, nobody you'd know." I washed my hands at the kitchen sink and got the tea pitcher from the refrigerator. "Just someone I knew in high school."

"Try me." Mama said. "You might be surprised who all I know from town. I always made a point of getting to know your friends. Take Brian Simmons, for example. He's from town, and I been knowing him ever since he married Edwina Downing and started going to Shiloh Methodist. That's a lot of years now."

"It wasn't Brian, okay?" Did Mama think that because Brian and I had talked to each other at church a few times and had gone out to eat one meal together weeks ago (a meal to which she was invited, by the way) that I was sneaking around and seeing him behind her back? The microwave beeped, and I took out one bowl and put in another. "For your information, I haven't seen Brian since — well, since Saturday night. When Russell and I went into town to eat, we ran into him at the steakhouse. He was with a woman, somebody named Shauna. He introduced us, but I don't think she's from around here, not originally, anyway." There, that ought to allay any suspicions she might have been harboring about Brian and me.

"So Brian's got a new girlfriend? I'm glad to hear it. What did you say her name was?"

"Shauna is all I know."

"Don't know anybody by that name. But who was it you ran into today? I might know them."

"For heaven's sake, Mama." I filled the tea glasses and set the pitcher on the table a little harder than necessary. "That's the trouble with living up here. Everybody knows everybody else's business. It drives me crazy. I deserve a little privacy, you know."

"Well, if you don't want to tell me, then fine. I just thought..." Mama huffed a little to show that I had offended her, but she didn't finish her sentence.

We watched the news silently while we ate and after I'd cleaned up the kitchen, I walked outside, still irritated with Mama's nosiness into my business. Had she suspected that I had been with Brian? Admittedly, I had gone back to his house after our dinner at the steak restaurant to use his computer, but I had told Mama all about that. And we hadn't seen each other since that night, except at church, which hardly counted, and the time he'd met me at the newspaper office. Since his lecture to me that day — his order, actually, to abandon my inquiries into the cause of the fire — I had not talked to him about Lonnie P. or about anything else of importance. So why had seeing him at the restaurant with another woman had such an unsettling effect on me?

For the last forty years, I'd been seeing him occasionally during my brief visits back home, mostly at church when I went with Mama, him accompanied by Edwina and his growing family (the two tow-headed little boys) and me with Russell and our own two kids when they were little, but later on, both of us oftener without our spouses as the kids grew up and moved on with their lives. On those occasions (maybe two or three times a year), Brian and I had always exchanged a few polite comments, and that had been that. Even at our fortieth class reunion four years ago, which both of us had attended — Brian alone (explaining that Edwina wasn't interested in coming) and I with Russell — we'd done nothing more than trade greetings and small talk about the weather and the occasion.

So why should anything be different now? True, Brian was no longer married, but I was. So why this new sexual tension between us? I'd been feeling it ever since the dinner at Gail's house, and I knew that Brian was feeling it, too. Was it because we'd both finally gotten around to confessing our teenage feelings about one another? Was it that my extended visit had gradually lulled me back into a world that I thought I had moved beyond — had made me forget the wife and mother I'd been for the last thirty-seven years and turned me into someone else entirely — someone younger and more impulsive and newly recharged with the pangs of first love?

Brian's nervous behavior at the restaurant on Saturday night and his failure to show up at church on Sunday morning obviously meant that my seeing him with Shauna had put him on the defensive. But why would he think I cared if he was out with another woman? Even if Brian's feelings for me had reawakened during these last few weeks, he would never act on them unless he was getting a signal from me that those feelings were reciprocated. Was I giving off such signals?

Time to clear the air, to let Brian know that his dating Shauna was perfectly fine with me, and for the two of us to get back to being nothing more than old friends. I'd hate to be responsible for his missing church again, and it was up to me to return our relationship to its previous status.

When Mama went into the bathroom at nine o'clock for her shower, I dialed Brian's home number. "Hi," I said brightly when he answered. "I hope I'm not calling too late."

"Kate?" His voice sounded a little wary. "No, it's not late. Everything okay?"

"Fine. How are you? We missed you at church yesterday."

"Yeah, that." Brian coughed and cleared his throat. "I guess I overslept."

"That's okay. We're all allowed a skip day every once in a while." I wanted to put Brian at ease, but I didn't know what to say. "Um-m. Shauna seemed nice."

"Yeah. She's a friend. We're not dating or anything."

"Oh. Well, it was good running into you, anyway." Something in my chest did a little flip. So Brian and Shauna were not dating. But why did that make me feel triumphant, as if I had just won some sort of competition? I went blank, trying to think of something to say.

"I guess your husband's gone back home by now." Brian seemed as much at a loss for words as I was.

"Yes, he went home yesterday afternoon." Silence filled the air again. I couldn't tell Brian what Jesse had told me, and besides, Brian wanted me to drop the whole idea of investigating the fire. So what else was there to talk about? "It's pretty quiet around here, and I'm getting a little bit stir crazy," I said. "I guess I just needed to talk to somebody besides Mama."

Brian chuckled. "That so? Well, I'm listening."

"I feel so closed off from everything up here. Without my daily newspaper and my computer, I don't even know what's happening in the world. I wish Mama would join the modern age and get a computer, but she won't hear of it."

"Hey, if all you want to do is check your e-mail or catch up on the news, you know you can use my computer anytime. Standing invitation."

"No, that's okay. Thanks, but I don't want to impose on you. Mama has another therapy session tomorrow, so while she's there I can run by the library and keep my fingers crossed there's a computer available."

"Hey, no need for that. Mine's available anytime. How about tomorrow? I have a class in the morning and a lab from one to three, but I'll be home after that."

"Thanks for the invitation, but—"

"I'm not taking 'No' for an answer. I'll see you tomorrow at four, okay? And how about we go out for supper afterwards? I'd invite you to eat here, but I'm not a cook, not unless you want a bowl of soup and crackers or a TV dinner. Any excuse I get to go out for a real meal, I don't pass up. What do you say?"

"Well, I guess that would be okay." I'd be doing Brian a favor by going out to eat with him rather than him eating alone in front of the TV. "I get tired of my own cooking, so I don't pass up offers to eat out, either."

"There's this little country restaurant south of town by the interstate—Grandma's Kitchen. Great chicken and dumplings. Unless you'd rather have steak again. Or barbeque."

"No. I love chicken and dumplings. Let's go there."

"Your mother won't mind?"

"Oh, Mama will be happy to get me out of the house for a while. We're starting to get on each other's nerves."

By the time I hung up, I hardly knew what had happened. When I'd picked up the phone to call Brian, I'd meant only to have a brief, casual conversation to reestablish our friendship status, and now it had turned into a visit to his house and an invitation to dinner. But going out to eat with him again didn't signify anything illicit, did it? Grandma's Kitchen, after all, wasn't exactly some swanky, romantic place with candles and linen tablecloths and napkins. Then why was I feeling so goosebumpy with anticipation? I'd have to calm down and review my plans carefully. Nothing would happen except that Brian and I would talk about old classmates and mutual friends. I'd ask about his two boys and show him pictures of my grandchildren. Nothing romantic or titillating about that, was there?

I procrastinated all the next day, debating with myself about whether to tell Mama the truth about going over to Brian's. Finally, at three o'clock I had to say something before going into my bedroom to change clothes and freshen my makeup. "Mama, I'm going to run into town again for a couple of hours. I need to get on a computer to check my e-mail. It's getting close to time for the new school term to start, and I'm sure I have a ton of messages to answer about work. And I may run by and see Gail while I'm there, so don't worry if I'm gone for a while. I'll call if I'm not back by seven or so."

"You don't need to drive all the way into town to use a computer," Mama reasoned. "You could go over to Thelma's and use hers any time you wanted. She says it's just sitting there, a waste of Lonnie P.'s good money as far as she's concerned."

"That's okay. I haven't seen Gail in a while now. And I need to get the oil changed in my car. Maybe I'll run by Theo's garage and make an appointment for later in the week."

"What about your supper?"

"I'll get something in town. Want me to bring you a cheeseburger and fries? Or a fried chicken dinner?"

Mama shook her head. "I got plenty to eat here. Besides, I ain't never been one for all this drive-thru food. Don't people cook any more?"

"Lots of people don't, I guess. Too busy with wives working full-time nowadays. I don't have to go. If you'd rather I stayed here with you—"

"No. No. You go ahead and do whatever you need to do." Mama waved me off. "I can fix my own supper here. Don't forget, I been living by myself for the last year, and I'll be all by my lonesome again soon as you go back home. You don't need to fuss over me."

"Well, I don't want you to feel like I'm neglecting you." Was Mama trying to make me feel guilty for going off and leaving her so much lately, or was she asserting her independence? I couldn't tell.

Chapter 30

I arrived at Brian's promptly at four. He answered the door dressed in a blue and white pinstriped shirt, open at the collar, and navy slacks. His work clothes? Or had he showered and changed? Ignoring the warning voice in my head, I had worn my black dress slacks and the same low-cut, clingy sweater-knit top that I had worn the previous Saturday night when I'd gone out with Russell.

"Hi. You look good." Brian stood back as I entered.

"You, too." I walked inside, clutching my purse in front of me with both hands. What was I doing here, all vamped up, to go to a restaurant called Grandma's Kitchen? Brian hadn't made a move to touch me, but I could sense the electricity arcing in the air between us. *"Come into my parlor, said the spider to the fly,"* ran through my mind. By accepting Brian's invitation into his lair, had I implicitly agreed to something left unsaid over the phone? I didn't know, but I was here now, and it was too late to back out. The scene at the restaurant on Saturday night, that other woman laughing and flirting with Brian, hanging on his every word, had awakened something in me—a fuzzy, dormant memory of how love used to be, of how it *should* be, new and exciting and romantic and charged with desire and curiosity and neediness and fulfillment.

"The computer is on and ready to go." Brian waved down the hall. "All yours."

"Thanks. I really appreciate this."

Brian didn't follow me to the office. "Anything you need, just call. I'll be right out here."

"Thanks." I logged on and quickly opened my e-mail. Not too many new messages, but there was one from my principal at school, welcoming everyone back for the new school year, accompanied by a schedule of meetings and activities planned for the first week back before students returned and a list of assigned work hours for student registration on Wednesday and Thursday of that week. Only one-and-a-half more weeks before I had to go back to work. Where had the summer gone? "Okay if I use your printer?" I called to Brian.

"Go right ahead. Ten cents a page," Brian called back jokingly from the direction of the living room. What was he doing out there? Just sitting and waiting for me to finish? Pacing the floor? I clicked on "Print" and then on "Reply," but as I typed a chatty message back about looking forward to a new school year, I kept listening for sounds of Brian's whereabouts, and a paragraph that should have taken five minutes to compose and type ended up taking nearly fifteen.

As I finally clicked on "Send," I could hear noises coming from a back part of the house. A refrigerator door opening and closing? Ice clinking in a glass? Brian must be in the kitchen, fixing himself a drink. Then I could hear his footsteps on a hard surface.

"Want a drink?" Brian's voice sounded so close by that I looked up, startled, but I didn't see him.

"No, thanks," I called back. "I'm almost finished."

"No rush. Take your time. I have some school work to do, anyway. Lab reports to check. I'll be at the dining table." The voice wasn't as close as it had first sounded. I let out the breath I'd been holding and turned my attention back to my other e-mails.

I hit "Delete" for most of the other messages—a few "You have to see this!" stories and jokes forwarded from friends and acquaintances, and lots of advertisements from websites where I had purchased something in the past—but only a couple of personal messages required an answer. I dashed off quick replies and then looked at the computer clock. Five-eighteen already. Where had the time gone? I exited, pushed back my chair, and went to find Brian, who was still sitting at the dining table, papers strewn across it.

"Sorry I took so long. You ready to go eat?"

"Done already?" Brian smiled up at me. "You didn't need to hurry. I'm ready whenever you are. These papers will still be here when I get back."

On the way to the restaurant, I kept the conversation going with small talk about the weather and questions about Brian's summer classes, which were ending this week. Then he had two weeks off before the fall term began.

"That reminds me," I said, "how little time I have left up here. One more week after this one, and then I have to go back to work, too. It's hard to believe summer is almost over."

"Seems like you just got here," Brian agreed. "You sure you have to leave so soon?"

"Work calls. And I'm looking forward to getting back. One of my e-mails was from my principal. Welcome to another great year! You know the type." We reached our destination without my bringing up the topic of Lonnie P. or the fire. Tonight I was going to relax and put aside all my obsessions about Lonnie P. I wanted to make this dinner with Brian nothing more than a nice visit between old friends—no ulterior motives or hidden agendas.

Both of us opted for iced tea and the chicken and dumplings special, and while we were waiting for our food to arrive, I brought up what was really on my mind. "So, tell me about this mysterious Shauna. Who is she?"

"Oh, just someone I work with at the college." Brian looked into the air above my head and then past me down the corridor between the tables, not meeting my eyes.

"Another teacher?"

"Not exactly."

The subject clearly was making Brian uncomfortable, but why? If not a teacher, then someone in one of the administrative offices? A secretary or student advisor? Why such secrecy? Surely she couldn't be one of his students, could she? I wasn't ready to let the subject go. "She's very attractive. And she seemed to like you—a lot."

"We're friends. That's all." Brian waved one hand dismissively. "So tell me more about your work. You like it?"

"Sure. What's not to like? I'm surrounded by books all day. And I don't have to deal with one classroom after another of hormone-addled adolescents. They come in; I help them find what they're looking for, offer suggestions for what to read, and they actually come back and thank me. I don't know why more people aren't librarians."

"A lot of the work looks tedious to me—all that cataloging, shelving, keeping records."

"That's why we have student assistants. I assign them all the tedious stuff." I was beginning to relax and enjoy my camaraderie with Brian. This was more like it—two friends talking about work, being comfortable in one another's presence, nothing simmering beneath the surface.

"Maybe it's the stereotype people have of librarians. You know, the stern old maid with glasses on her nose and hair in a bun, going around shushing everyone."

I ran my fingers through my windblown hair, growing longer now than I usually wore it since I hadn't yet made time to get it cut, batted my eyes at Brian, and gave him my best flirtatious smile. "Maybe that's it. But I don't fit that stereotype, do I?"

"No, not at all."

Brian's eyes lit on me then, the first time he had looked directly at me all evening, and I returned his gaze—my teasing flirtation turning to nervous anxiety as I saw what was in his expression. This was all wrong. How could I have thought that we could just be friends? One of my hands rested on the table, and Brian covered it with one of his own. What now? Should I pull away? That seemed too abrupt, too dismissive. Brian's fingers rubbed back and forth, caressing the back of my hand. Had he taken for granted that my marriage to Russell was as unhappy and as much of a fraud as his marriage to Edwina had been? I hadn't given him any indication of that, but I hadn't said anything to the contrary either. And here I was dressed in my most alluring outfit, trying to outshine Shauna, whoever she might be and whatever she might mean to Brian. I drew my hand back, confused and frightened, knocking my fork off the table in the process.

As I leaned down to pick it up, Brian did the same, and our fingers brushed again as we fumbled for it beneath the table. Feeling his touch, I jerked away, and he brought the fork up triumphantly, laying it aside at the far end of the table. "I'll ask the waitress for another one when she brings the food."

"Thanks," I mumbled, my face burning under his gaze. On Saturday night, having Russell with me, I could safely envy Brian's date from afar, safely fantasize about it being me sitting across from him, flirting across the table, looking forward to whatever later events the evening might bring, but now that it *was* me, and Russell was hundreds of miles away, my nerves were going haywire. What would happen when we got back to Brian's house? Would I simply get into my car in the driveway and leave? That didn't seem very polite after Brian had let me use his computer and had paid for my dinner. But would he even invite me inside? I had no idea—and no idea of what I'd do if he did. Did I want something to happen between us? More to the point, was I going to let something happen?

The arrival of the food somewhat distracted both of us from the awkward moment, and I tried my best to enjoy my meal and make more friendly small talk with Brian, but by the time we finished eating and the waitress brought the bill, I was in agony, torn between wanting to fulfill all those teenage fantasies of me and Brian—fantasies fueled by the popular songs of our high school days—and the strict, adult voice in my head warning me of the dangers I was exposing myself to, all that I would be risking if I allowed myself to act on those fantasies.

On the drive back to Brian's house, we both sat in nervous silence, Brian concentrating on his driving, eyes ahead on the road. Neither of us said a word until we pulled into his driveway.

"Well, here we are." Brian turned off the ignition. "Want to come inside for a few minutes? I have some pretty good red wine I've been saving for a while—waiting for a special occasion."

I looked at my watch. "I don't know. It's getting late, and I promised Mama—"

"Come on. It's not even dark yet. Just one glass? Wine is meant to be shared. It's no fun drinking alone."

243

Instead of answering, I opened my door and stepped out. I should leave right now before there was the remotest possibility of anything happening. Brian got out his door, and we met in front of the car. "I'd really like to, but—"

"So what's keeping you? The night is young."

Brian's lips were smiling, but I could see the mute appeal in his eyes, remembered the forlorn look on his face as I had driven away after our first restaurant meal. If one glass of wine would make him feel better about the evening, I couldn't refuse. I owed him that much, at least. "I'll have a small drink, but I can't stay long, really."

"That's more like it." Brian put one hand on my back as we walked to the front door, dropping it only when he had to reach into his pocket for his key. "Have a seat," he said as I entered ahead of him. "I'll be right back with the wine."

I sat on the sofa as Brian disappeared into the kitchen, soon returning with two glasses of wine. I took a small sip, holding the wine on my tongue for a moment before swallowing, hoping to calm my nerves. Another sip, and I felt an almost immediate flush of warmth in my throat, in my chest, spreading throughout my body. "Good wine."

"Thanks." Brian sank down beside me on the sofa, not touching, but still too close for comfort.

I swiveled away, looking around the room for an opportunity to change the subject. On the side table were several frames, all holding photos of what seemed to be the same family: one group portrait of a young couple with three children—two toddlers and a baby—and other individual and group photos of the children alone. Two of them looked like school pictures—a grinning, gap-toothed boy of about seven or eight and a smiling, dimple-cheeked girl maybe kindergarten age.

After taking another sip of wine to further settle my nerves, I set my glass on the coffee table and picked up the group portrait. "Nice looking family. You're a grandpa now?"

"That's Wayne and his family. You remember Wayne, don't you?"

"I remember two little tow-headed boys, but it's been years since I saw either of them. Wayne's the older one, right? Wayne and Dennis. Gosh, how are they? Are they both still living close by?"

"Wayne is. He married a local girl." He took the portrait from me. "This was taken a few years ago. The kids are older now. Jake here on the left—he's eight now. And Jenna is six." He reached across me to return the picture to the table. "That's last year's school pictures. And here's Jared. He's almost three." He turned one of the frames so that it was facing me.

"Cute kids. All of them. They call you Grandpa? Or Granddaddy?" Somehow I hadn't thought of Brian as a grandfather before. Did that change my fantasy?

"Pa-Pa." Brian grinned as he took another sip of his wine. "You have two, you said?"

"Yes, Caleb and Megan. Caleb is six and Megan is almost four." I pulled the folder of photos out of my purse. "Did I show you their pictures?"

Brian set down his wine, scooted closer to me, and took the two wallet photos I handed him. "The girl looks like you," he said. "Your eyes and hair."

"You think?" Brian was so close that our shoulders were touching. I leaned forward, picked up my wine glass, and took another sip, willing myself to stay calm. I needed to bring this evening to a close.

"Definitely," Brian answered. "Don't you think so?" He turned his eyes from the picture to me, his face inches away.

How many times as a teenager had I fantasized this moment— Brian beside me, gazing into my eyes, me lifting my face to his, our lips meeting? My wine glass tilted in my unsteady hand, and Brian laid the two photos on the coffee table, took the wine glass from me, and set it down.

I remained in place, held by an invisible magnet, knowing what was coming but powerless to do anything about it. Brian reached for my hands and held them in both of his own, his hands completely covering mine. "You still look just like you did in high school," he said. "Your lips parted like that. Like you know the right answer; it's right on the tip of your tongue, but you're afraid to say it."

"The answer?" I began, but Brian laughed and stood, pulling me up with him. I didn't resist, no more capable at that point of saying "No" than a rag doll. Then I was enveloped in his arms, my body against his, his lips brushing my cheek, searching for and then finding my mouth. I let him kiss me, felt myself responding to him until his mouth began to travel down my neck. The hardness at his groin was pressing into me, and panic was fighting with desire. This wasn't right. I was a married woman. I had a husband waiting at home for me—waiting for me to come back to him.

I pushed at Brian's chest and stumbled away. "No. I have to go. Right now."

Brian, confused, stepped back. "Wait. You can't …"

"No, I have to go. Russell is going to be calling any minute now." I looked at my watch. "He always calls around this time."

"But your wine. You hardly even tasted…"

"Thanks, but I have to go, really." I reached for my purse. "Thanks for dinner. For everything." I headed for the front door without looking at Brian, intent only on getting out of there.

Brian was talking behind me, but I didn't listen. Letting myself out the door, I practically ran to my car and locked myself inside. This evening—this visit—had been all wrong, and it was entirely my fault. I'd instigated this whole catastrophe, accepting Brian's invitation and teasing him along, flirting with him at the restaurant and then going inside for a glass of wine, even letting him kiss me and kissing him back—and now I'd ditched him, most likely sending him right back into the willing arms of the lovely, bleached-blonde Shauna. Well, lucky Shauna.

It wasn't until I was back at Mama's that I realized my wallet photos of Caleb and Megan were still lying on Brian's coffee table.

Chapter 31

Tuesday, August 8—Wednesday, August 9, 2006

I arrived back at Mama's at a quarter to eight. On the way home, I had called Russell from my cell phone, but our conversation had been brief, neither of us having any news of import—none, at least on my part, that I was willing to share—and it hadn't calmed me down any. Was Russell keeping any secrets from me? My own list was getting so high that the stack might topple at any minute, burying me beneath the rubble.

Mama was watching *Jeopardy* on TV, and not yet ready to face her questions about where I'd been or whom I'd seen, I mumbled a greeting and walked on past the dining room into the kitchen where I poured myself a glass of iced tea, tilting the cold glass up to my lips, which still felt hot from Brian's kisses. As I carried the glass back to my bedroom and returned my purse to its accustomed place on the dresser, I stopped to glance at the face staring back at me in the mirror. I didn't look any different than usual, nothing that Mama would be able to decipher, anyway, but as I leaned forward to examine myself more closely, the dry, crepey skin above my low-cut sweater puckered into a tiny washboard of wrinkles. What had I been thinking? I wasn't seventeen anymore, and neither was Brian. We were both grandparents, for heaven's sake.

Still carrying my glass of tea, I walked back through the living room and out onto the front porch. The first stars were visible in the twilight sky, and a mosquito buzzed around my face. I slapped at the mosquito,

sky, and a mosquito buzzed around my face. I slapped at the mosquito, smashing it against my cheek, still trying to process what had happened. How had I let things progress to the point that they had, with Brian clearly expecting more to follow? That certainly had not been my intention. When I'd called him on the phone, my only motive had been to restore our relationship to its previous friendship status. But if that were the case, then why had I gone to his house dressed this way? Why had I batted my eyes and flirted with him in the restaurant? Why had I gone inside for a glass of wine? I had only myself to blame.

So what now? It was too late to go back and undo what had happened. All I could do at this point was apologize to Brian for my horrible lapse in judgment. I'd have to let him know in no uncertain terms that I was a happily married woman and that I took my marriage vows seriously, regardless of whatever my hormones were screaming. That would mean another phone call, but I was too shaky to do it right now. It would have to wait until I'd had time to calm down and plan out what I wanted to say. I'd also have to make arrangements to get back my photos of Caleb and Megan. And since I couldn't risk another encounter alone with him, the best solution all round was to ask him to bring the photos to me at church on Sunday, where I could thank him and say my final goodbye before heading home to Titusville.

By the time the mosquitoes drove me inside, *Jeopardy* had ended and Mama had turned off the TV. "You get your computer business taken care of?"

"Yes, I'm all caught up. I had an e-mail from my principal about the new school year. I have to be back to work by August 21st. You think you'll be ready to be on your own by next week?"

"I'm ready anytime you need to go." Mama picked up a magazine from the side table. "There's plenty of people can get me to town and back for groceries and such till I'm ready to drive again. You want something to eat? I made myself an egg sandwich for supper."

"No. I had something in town." I didn't volunteer any more information, and Mama, apparently still muzzled from my earlier outburst, didn't ask any more questions.

The next morning I picked the vegetables from the garden and gave Mama the beans to snap while I washed, cut up, and blanched the squash for the freezer.

"Mail's here," Mama called at a little after ten, and I walked out to get the accumulation of bills and circulars. I flipped through the stack— nothing of importance except for the weekly *Pine Lake Gazette*, which always arrived on Wednesdays. I handed the newspaper to Mama and laid the rest of the mail on the dining table before returning to the kitchen.

"Oh, my goodness," Mama exclaimed, loudly enough that I could hear her from her recliner. "Thelma's going to be upset over this."

"What is it?" I walked back to the living room. "What happened?"

"Somebody's making up stuff about Lonnie P.," Mama answered. "All this political mess and name-calling. I just know Thelma's gotta be upset with all this meanness going on."

My stomach lurched into my throat. Had someone else been investigating Lonnie P.? What had they found? "What are they saying?"

"Listen to this." Mama read from the paper. "'Pine Lake Mayor Lonnie P. Ramsey Caught in Lie about Vietnam Service.' That's the headline."

"Who caught him?"

Mama was silent for a while, reading through the article. "Somebody named Hal Crawford. He's running against Lonnie P. for mayor. Must be one of them Crawfords from over in the western part of the county. I never knew none of them 'cept for Maysie Crawford that married the Shadrick boy. What was his name? Anyway, he says Lonnie P. never set foot in Vietnam."

"But he didn't. Remember when we were over at his mother's house a couple of weeks ago, and she said Lonnie P.'s biggest disappointment about being in the army was never getting to Vietnam?"

"Then I don't understand what the big stink is about." Mama fluttered the paper and went back to reading. "Says here that Lonnie P. is claiming he was in Vietnam on his campaign literature, and this Hal Crawford says he wasn't. Says he has proof of his military records."

"Is that so?" After our visit to Mrs. Ramsey's house, I'd thought briefly about researching Lonnie P.'s military records myself, but then all my energy had gotten focused on the fire instead. Everything else, including how he made all his money, I'd let slide. "Anything else? Any other skeletons in his closet?"

I held my breath while Mama skimmed down the column. "Nothing else that I see. It's all about Vietnam."

"Well, it serves him right for lying about it, don't you think?"

"Lonnie P. was always a little too big for his britches," Mama conceded, "but you can't blame it entirely on him. Everybody knows that Thelma and Lonnie spoiled him something awful, him being the baby and the only boy after that whole passel of girls. The whole family did—all them girls, too. They all thought the sun rose and set in him. But he turned out all right in the end, and look at all the good he's done in town. Folks will still support him, no matter what anybody says."

I left Mama to the rest of the newspaper and returned to the kitchen. How would she feel if I told her what I knew about Lonnie P.? She and Mrs. Ramsey were long-time friends, and here I was digging up enough dirt on Lonnie P. to expose him as a murderer. Would Mama regard me as a traitor? Would she disown me? Never speak to me again? And what would bringing charges against Lonnie P. for a forty-four-year-old crime do to his mother and to the rest of his family—his older sisters and their families, his wife and children and grandchildren? Did any of them know or suspect the truth about him? Would putting Lonnie P. behind bars for the rest of his life finally bring justice, or in seeking closure for myself and Delia, would I only succeed in bringing anguish to his many family members, all well-known and well-respected in the community?

The magnitude of what I was about to unleash was becoming more and more clear to me. It was like an octopus, tentacles churning every direction I turned. I continued moving about the kitchen, from stove to counter to table, hardly aware of what my hands were doing, my mind entirely on this new public revelation about Lonnie P. The facts themselves didn't surprise me, for I already knew, as did probably half the county, that Lonnie P. had never been to Vietnam, but what did startle me was that someone in Pine Lake had dared to challenge Lonnie P.'s assertion, and even more revealing, that the editor of the local paper had had the gumption to print the story.

Nothing in Pine Lake was more "establishment" than *The Pine Lake Gazette*, a paper that was almost as old as the county itself, so for its editor to take on someone as powerful as Lonnie P. indicated a seismic shift in the town's structure. This editor, whoever he was, along with Hal Crawford, had managed to open a small chink, at least, in Lonnie P.'s armor, reason enough to give me hope that even in this little rural county a new generation was taking charge, a generation that wasn't intimidated by Lonnie P.'s money or his bluster.

After lunch I picked up the *Gazette* to read the story about Lonnie P. for myself. Sure enough, Harold (Hal) Crawford, the other candidate for mayor, had obtained a complete list of Lonnie P.'s army postings — none of them remotely near Vietnam. When contacted for a quote before the story broke, Lonnie P. had given the usual disclaimer. He was a military veteran who served *during* the Vietnam War years; any suggestion that he had served *in* Vietnam was a misinterpretation of what he had claimed, and he was sorry for the misunderstanding.

Hal Crawford, a young man who could not have even been alive during the Vietnam era, if his photo was an accurate representation of his age, had been put on to his search by a conversation with an unnamed local couple at a recent candidate's rally. The husband and wife had both been high school classmates of Lonnie P. and in conversation had casually related to Hal Crawford that years before, at a twenty-year class reunion at Pine Lake Country Club, Lonnie P. had regaled several old classmates with stories of his army experiences, including a vivid description of his last post, in the winter and spring of 1965-66, at a little out-of-the-way army base in Turkey, near the Russian border. Lonnie P. had nearly frozen to death, according to his own account, and had declared that, looking back on it, he'd rather have been sent to Vietnam than to all the Podunk little places he'd been. That chance conversation had started Hal Crawford on his search, and he'd soon turned up the official military records, proving that the story was correct.

The local couple wasn't identified in the article, but how many husband/wife combinations had both been in the 1960 graduating class? *And* still lived in Pine Lake? *And* would be attending a rally for Lonnie P.'s opponent? The number had to be pretty small. Keeping the paper open on my lap, I tried to think who it might be. When Brian and I were looking through the 1960 yearbook at his house, to see if Brian could identify anyone who might have been at the University of Florida during the football scandal of Lonnie P.'s sophomore year, Brian had made comments about different people — who still lived in town, who had married whom. He had pointed out Millicent Owens in particular, saying that she was now an English professor at the college, one of his colleagues, and he knew that both she and her husband had gone to UF because they were big Gator fans.

But whom did he say she married? The name had been vaguely familiar to me. I hadn't known him, but he'd had a sister in our class. Who was it? Then it came to me. Flanders. Ken Flanders. Brother to Phyllis Flanders. Had Ken Flanders also been in Lonnie P.'s class? Could they have been the couple at the rally? When Brian had pointed out Millicent's photo in the yearbook, I had recalled a tall, thin, quiet girl with glasses, editor of the school newspaper when I'd been the sophomore reporter, but it wasn't until my conversation with Jesse that I'd remembered the rumor going around high school — that Millicent Owens had had a giant crush on Lonnie P. and that she had written all his senior English essays. She certainly had good reason to resent Lonnie P. for his treatment of her in high school. Or had the conversation been initiated by her husband, still seething with resentment at Lonnie P. for the way he had used and humiliated the girl who was later to become his wife?

I went to the kitchen and thumbed through the local phone book, looking for the last name Flanders. There he was, Kenneth Flanders, Attorney at Law, with a business address and phone number, followed by Kenneth and Millicent Flanders with a home address and phone. So Ken Flanders was a lawyer? Brian hadn't mentioned that. The more I thought about it, the more certain I was that they were the couple that Hal Crawford had talked to at the rally. Exhilarated, I returned the phone book to its shelf and went back to the article, rereading it for more clues. Now I had at least half a dozen people whom I could count on for support if it came down to the town taking sides. I had Delia, of course, and Jesse, both of whom hated Lonnie P. enough to wish him dead, and now the unnamed couple, whom I was willing to bet money was Ken and Millie Flanders, along with Hal Crawford, plus the reporter who had dared to write the story and the editor who had let it run.

I looked at the reporter's byline, but the name meant nothing to me. The name of the editor would be much more likely to sound familiar. When I was growing up, the paper had been owned by the Bascom family, and from what I remembered, it had been in that family since it had been founded sometime in the 1800s by William C. Bascom. His great-grandson, or maybe great, great grandson, William C. Bascom, IV, was editor during my school years, and his son, William Charles Bascom, V, had been in my class in school. Charles, a good-natured but not very academically inclined student, had made it clear to anyone who would listen that he had no interest in the newspaper business. Had he, at his father's death or retirement, finally sold the paper to someone else? I couldn't imagine it going out of Bascom family hands.

I turned to the masthead to look for the editor's name, and there it was: Charlie Bascom Sims. So it was still in the family in some fashion. But who was Charlie? I knew from Gail and from class reunions over the years that Charles had married Diana Stevens and that they'd had only girls—no boy to become William Charles Bascom, VI, a severe blow not so much to Charles himself, but to his father, William C. Bascom, IV. I also knew that Charles had an older sister. Perhaps she had married a Sims, and this Charlie was her son, keeping the Bascom name and heritage alive but lightening it up with a "Charlie" as opposed to another "William" or "Charles," signifying a new era for a staid old publication. Good for him! This new editor sounded like someone I'd like to know.

I thumbed through the rest of the newspaper and laid it aside. It was still too early to reach Delia at home to see if she had discovered anything new or to call Brian and explain about last night. I went to my bedroom, lay back on my bed, and started planning my next move. Millie and Ken Flanders sounded like a couple I'd like to have on my side, but I really didn't know either of them, and they didn't know me. Ken Flanders was a lawyer, but what kind? Did he handle criminal cases, or did he only do wills and such? In a town this size lawyers must have to do a little bit of everything.

And if Ken had been in Lonnie P.'s graduating class, then he and Jesse had also been classmates. They weren't likely to have any current contact since they wouldn't move in the same social circles, but would Ken be someone Jesse could trust? Everybody in the county, of every social status, read *The Pine Lake Gazette*, so Jesse would have seen by now the exposé of Lonnie P.'s fabrication of serving in Vietnam. Would this beginning crack in Lonnie P.'s armor make Jesse more willing to trust someone else with what he knew about the night of the fire? Someone like Ken Flanders? I had no idea. Having lived away for so long, I wasn't in the know about all the tangles and burrs in the relationships of those who'd burrowed into the community for life.

Then there was the official fire investigation. How would I go about finding the names of firemen in 1962? Would the fire department keep a roster going back that far? Mama and I both had hair appointments for tomorrow morning—I'd decided I couldn't wait any longer to get my hair trimmed, and Mama wanted a new permanent wave—so maybe I'd get an opportunity to slip away while Mama was under the dryer and make a quick trip to the fire station. But what excuse would I use for wanting such information, even if it was easily available?

I was planning out what I'd say at the fire department when a knock sounded on the front door. Probably someone dropping by to say hello to Mama. Folks up here often did that—just dropped in with no preliminary phone call—bringing some extra vegetables from their garden, half of a cake they'd baked, or just themselves.

I slipped my feet back into my sandals and headed for the front door. Mama must be asleep in front of the TV, or she would have let them in or at least called me.

"What's that?" Mama opened her eyes as I reached the door.

"Someone's here," I answered, pulling it open. "Looks like you've got company."

Brian stood on the other side, the two wallet photos of Caleb and Megan in his hand. "You forgot these last night, so I figured I'd run out here and return them. Hi, Mrs. McCormick. How are you?"

"You didn't need—" I looked from Brian to Mama, who was gaping open-mouthed as I took the pictures from Brian's outstretched hand.

Chapter 32

I took the photos Brian held out. "Thanks, but you didn't need to drive all the way out here. I was going to call you."

"Well, look who's here," Mama trilled behind me. She lowered her footrest and shifted forward in her seat to stand. "Hello, Brian. Come on in."

I stepped back as Brian came inside. "Don't get up, Mrs. McCormick. I can only stay a minute. Kate was showing me photos of her grandkids last night, and I guess we laid them on the table and forgot them."

Mama remained upright in her chair, looking from Brian to me, her eyes a question mark.

"I was using Brian's computer to check my e-mail," I explained. "The ones at the library are always in use, and Brian offered…" I stopped, unsure how to proceed. How could Brian have offered if I hadn't been in contact with him? I hadn't told Mama about the phone call I'd made during her shower.

"Oh." Mama waved Brian toward the sofa. "Well, have a seat and visit a while. What's your hurry?"

Brian looked at me.

"Yes, sit down," I echoed. "Would you like some iced tea?"

"No thanks. I really can't stay." Nevertheless, Brian took a seat on the sofa, and I crossed the room and sat on the armchair beside the window. Did Brian know he was spilling secrets I'd been keeping from Mama? What else would he innocently divulge?

Mama settled back into her recliner and beamed at Brian. "That was good of you to let Katie use your computer. She keeps fussing at me about getting one for myself, but I don't have no need for such a contraption. One of my neighbors has one, and it just sits there. She never even turns it on. I know she'd let Katie use it any time she wanted and save her driving all the way into town."

I felt my face growing warm, beads of perspiration forming on my forehead. Guilt for all my omissions in what I'd told Mama the day before? Or just a menopausal hot flash? "I told you I don't feel comfortable bothering Mrs. Ramsey. And Brian had said I had a standing invitation to use his computer any time I wanted. Plus I had other things to do in town, anyway."

"Glad to do it," Brian added. "Besides, any time I get a chance to have a real meal instead of a TV dinner like I usually eat, I jump at it."

Mama's eyebrows shot up. "Katie didn't say—"

"She didn't tell you? After she finished her work on the computer, we went to Grandma's Kitchen out by the interstate and had chicken and dumplings."

I jumped up from my chair and then realized I didn't have anywhere to go. Brian had already said he didn't want a drink. I laid the pictures that I'd been holding on a shelf beside the TV. "You didn't need to come all this way," I said again. "You could have returned the pictures on Sunday at church. There wasn't any rush."

"Oh, it's not that far." Brian's smile suggested this was a normal, neighborly drop-by visit. "I hadn't been out this way in years. Just wanted to see if I could still find your house."

Still find it? To my knowledge, Brian had never been to this house before. With the Internet, it was easy enough to find any place these days, but before all these dirt roads were named and house numbers assigned for 911 emergencies, finding our house on a dirt road with no address except a rural route number was just about impossible without somebody giving specific directions about turns and landmarks. When had Brian "found" this house before? Had he driven past my house back when we were in high school, hoping for a chance sighting of me, hoping to run into me "accidentally"? The thought brought back my own high school fantasies — Brian showing up unannounced at my front door, and then the two of us strolling down past the pecan trees to the pond, him reaching for my hand once we were out of sight of the house. But my fantasies had always stopped with a kiss; at seventeen, a kiss was the ultimate romantic ending to all the books I'd read and the movies I'd seen.

Brian was standing and making motions to leave. "Guess I'd better mosey on home. I'm glad to see you got that sling off your arm, Mrs. McCormick. I guess you won't be needing Kate here much longer."

"That's right. I keep telling her I can take care of myself just fine and it's high time for her to get back home to her own house and husband." Mama leaned forward again and put her hands on the arms of her chair to push herself up. "Thanks for stopping by, and come again, any time."

"You stay put, Mama. I'll see him out." I followed Brian to the door and stepped outside with him, pulling the door closed behind me. A dark cloud covered the sun, and a rumble of thunder sounded in the distance. "Looks like we might get finally some rain," I remarked, looking up at the sky. I crossed the porch with Brian and walked with him to his car. "Thanks again for returning the photos, but you didn't have to make a special trip."

Brian reached for his door handle. "No problem. So you didn't you tell your mother you were coming to my house to use my computer? Why not?"

"No reason, except I'm a grown woman and I'm not used to accounting for my every action — reporting to somebody about everywhere I go and everything I do. And I'm sorry about last night. I didn't mean for that to happen. I really didn't."

"Right." Brian didn't look at me. "You're the one keeping secrets from your mother, and now it's my fault for misreading the signals? You called me, remember? And what was all that hair tossing stuff at the restaurant about?"

"I didn't mean…" I stopped and started again. "I guess I was a little bit jealous after seeing you with that woman, and I wanted to —"

"Sure. Sure. I get it. You go out with your husband, and I'm not supposed to—"

"I know it doesn't make any logical sense. I know it's forty-some years too late." I stepped back as Brian opened his car door and slid into the driver's seat. "It's not that I didn't feel something. That I don't feel something. It's not that at all. It's just that I'm married, and this fantasy I have in my head—that's all it can be, a fantasy. I have a husband waiting for me at home, and I can't risk—"

"Hey, I get it. Okay?" Brian stuck his key into the ignition. "I need to get home."

I caught the edge of his car door before he could slam it shut. "I thought we were friends. Can't we still be friends?"

Brian started the engine without answering me.

"One more thing." I held onto his car door, not wanting him to leave yet, not wanting this sour churning in my stomach to be the way we left it. "When were you ever at this house before?"

"Oh, that." Brian's tone was so casual and flippant that it shredded every fantasy I'd ever had. "I brought the boys out here a time or two to pick up pecans. That was when they were little and they loved to earn some extra spending money. Your folks didn't have anybody to pick them up, so they asked at church and several of us brought kids out here. They got paid half the going price for all they picked up. They had fun and everybody profited."

My fantasy balloon thoroughly deflated, I stepped back and watched Brian drive away.

I had no desire to face Mama's inquisition, but a zigzag of lightning and a loud rumble of thunder drove me back to the safety of the covered porch. Rain began falling as I crossed the porch to the front door. I hesitated for a moment, hand on the doorknob, caught between the weather outside and Mama's questions awaiting me on the inside. Finally, I pulled the door open. I had nothing to apologize for, nothing to explain.

Mama was standing by the front window, and as I entered she turned toward me. "Rain's coming."

"Yes," I agreed. "Looks like a soaker, finally." So Mama had been watching Brian and me from the window. Well, there had been nothing to see, at any rate. And she wouldn't have been able to hear any of our conversation. Best to dive right in, treat Brian's visit as nothing more than a neighborly act of kindness. But why had Brian driven all the way out here to return the photos? He hadn't even called first to say he'd found them. Had his intention been to deliberately expose me to my mother? Had he suspected that she didn't know about my visit? And he'd made sure to mention our dinner out, too, for good measure. Certainly I had left him angry and hurt last night by running away with no explanation, and it seemed plausible that this visit had been his retaliation. If that was the case, then fine. In one more week I'd be gone and Brian would be out of my life.

"Well, that was a nice surprise, wasn't it? I didn't expect Brian to drive all the way out here, though. I was going to call him and tell him to bring the photos to me at church on Sunday."

Mama walked toward the kitchen. "I know you're a grown woman, and your business is your business, but I just don't understand why you didn't tell me—"

"Tell you what?" I followed her, determined not to let her put me on the defensive or make me feel guilty. "That I was going over to use Brian's computer? What's wrong with that? The ones at the library are always in use, and I felt more comfortable asking him than going back over to Mrs. Ramsey's."

"It's not just that," Mama said. "It's everything lately. Like Monday when you were gone all afternoon and when I asked who you were talking to, you wouldn't tell me. I just don't understand."

I flung open a cabinet door just so I could slam it shut. Why did Mama have to be so nosy? It was exasperating. "I told you I ran into a friend from high school and we got to talking. But it wasn't Brian. There's nothing going on between me and Brian. If you don't believe me, you can call him up and ask him."

"Well, I never said there was. But why all the secrecy? You were never this way before."

261

By now the rain was coming down hard outside, beating against the roof. I wished I could confide more in Mama, tell her I wasn't keeping any secrets from her, but that wouldn't be true. And there was no way I could tell her what I'd been doing, not with her and Lonnie P.'s mother being such old friends. Of course, if things played out as I hoped and I managed to expose Lonnie P. as the murderer he was, she'd have to know eventually, and then what? Would she stand behind me, or would she be devastated? I honestly didn't know. Here in this little closed-off community where loyalties and feuds were carried down from generation to generation, I didn't know what to expect, not even from my own mother.

Mama had opened the catch-all drawer and was rummaging through it, not looking at me. I walked over to her, still angry but contrite, too. "It's like you said, Mama—I'm a grown woman, and I'm accustomed to coming and going as I please. I'm not used to being grilled about every little thing I do—where I go or who I see. What are you looking for?"

Mama brought up a small screwdriver. "This. I need to change the battery in my bedroom clock."

"Want me to do it for you?"

"No, I can do it myself. I'm not entirely helpless, you know."

"Okay then." I walked to the back door. "Look at that. The rain's making a gully out in the lane. I can't remember the last time it rained this hard."

Mama walked over and looked with me, and I put one arm around her shoulder as another tremendous clap of thunder shook the house. "Some thunderstorm, huh? You wished for rain, and now you've got it." I didn't want to ruin Mama's friendship with Mrs. Ramsey, but I knew too much to think about turning back now.

Later that evening while Mama and I were watching *Jeopardy*, the phone rang. Mama answered, and then held the phone out to me.

"For you."

"Who is it?" It was about the time Russell usually called, so I took the phone, expecting to hear his voice, but it was Delia.

"Hi, Delia. I was planning to call you in a little while. Anything new?" I took the cordless phone into the hall away from the TV.

"You got any calls lately?" Delia asked. "From anybody warning you not to ask questions?"

"No." My stomach tightened. "Who knows I'm asking questions?" Had word gotten around town somehow about what I was doing?

"I got a call today," Delia answered. "A message left on my answering machine while I was at work. Somebody telling me I'd better stop asking questions or I'd be mighty sorry."

"Who was it?" My heart began to beat faster.

"He didn't say. But a man, for sure. A white man."

"Lonnie P.?"

"I don't know. Maybe."

"Did you keep the message?"

"It's still on there. I'm keeping it for Marcus to hear."

"Marcus?" I didn't recognize the name.

"Deputy Marcus Boyd. He's the one running for sheriff against Kip Hardwick. I want him to listen to it."

"Oh." Now the name came back to me—the young black man whose face I'd seen on ads in the *Gazette* and posted around town. "Don't delete it. I'm coming over there right now."

"You don't need to do that. I called Marcus' house and Denita— that's his wife—said he's on duty tonight, but she'd tell him to swing by when he gets a chance."

"Is John there with you?"

"He's down at Theo's shop helping him change out an engine, but he'll be home soon."

"You tell him about the message?"

"Not yet. See, he's not from around here, and he don't know nothing 'bout all that mess in the past. Marcus will be coming by any minute now."

"You have to tell John. If you're in danger, he'll have to know. Anyway, I'm coming. I want to hear the message. I'll be there in twenty minutes." I ended the call, picked up my purse, and headed for the front door.

"Mama," I called over my shoulder. "I'm going to Delia's. Something came up. I'll be back in a little while."

"To Delia's? At night? What's going on? It's Silas, ain't it? He's wandered off again."

I hurried out without answering. If the call had been from Lonnie P., there was no telling what he might do to prevent talk about his role in the fire. Would he actually show up at Delia's and threaten her in person? Surely he wouldn't physically harm her; he just wanted to scare her away from asking any more questions. If he did confront her, I had no idea what I'd do or say to him, but I knew I had to be there. I had failed to come to Delia's aid all those years ago when we were both sixteen, and I couldn't fail her now.

Chapter 33

Wednesday, August 9—Thursday, August 10, 2006

Fifteen minutes later, I was banging on Delia's door. "Any more phone calls?" I asked as she let me in.

"Just the one I told you about. I didn't mean for you to come all this way. I only called to see if whoever left that message on my machine had called you, too."

I listened intently as Delia replayed the message several times. The words sounded muffled, as if the caller was trying to disguise his voice. "It has to be Lonnie P. There's nobody else it could be. But how could he have found out? Who would have told him?"

"Nobody I talked to would say anything to a white man, least of all to Lonnie P. Ramsey." Delia spit out the name as if it were poison. "I figured you might know."

"Me?" I was at a loss for coming up with any names. The only person I'd talked to about the fire was Jesse, and he had sworn me to secrecy. Who else? I'd told Brian my suspicions weeks ago, but hadn't mentioned Lonnie P. or the fire since our visit to the newspaper office. Brian was upset with me, true enough, but surely he wouldn't have gone to Lonnie P. And if he had, he would have implicated me, not Delia. I hadn't given Brian Delia's name, only said that she was the daughter of my father's sharecropper, and I'd given no indication that I'd solicited her into helping with my search.

"Have you uncovered anything new?" I asked. "Anything that might be getting close to the truth of what happened, that might implicate Lonnie P.?"

"No, not really. Everybody 'round here has heard talk of two white boys seen running away from that house, tearing through folks' yards, but nobody knows who they were. Back then folks in this neighborhood didn't know white people by name 'less they worked for 'em or they was somebody important or something."

That may have been true in town, but in the country whites and blacks knew one another, for families shared work and mingled in the fields and at the tobacco barns. Theo and Jerome had worked for Lonnie P.'s father on his tobacco-gathering days—Delia, too, before that spring night that changed her life (and mine) forever. If Theo had seen anything, he would have recognized Lonnie P.

"What about Theo?" I asked. "Did he see the boys?"

"Theo? He couldn't have been there. There ain't no way my daddy would have let him go off into town if there was going to be trouble. You know my daddy."

"He was there," I said. "Theo and Jerome both. They snuck off from home sometime after supper and hitched a ride into town. They both knew Lonnie P. If they saw something—"

"You sure about that?" Delia looked doubtful. "I never heard Theo mention nothing 'bout that night."

I laughed. "I'm not surprised. They got in plenty of trouble for sneaking off, believe me. But talk to him. Ask him if he saw anything."

The sound of a car coming down the street interrupted our conversation for a moment, but the noise continued past Delia's duplex, the thrumming bass of a stereo following it down the road. "Nobody chased after the boys?" I asked when it had passed.

"Everybody was too busy trying to save that woman and her two babies. You could hear her screaming, they said. And somebody had to hold back that preacher to keep him from going in and getting burned up hisself."

I grimaced, imagining the scene. "It's awful to think about even now, isn't it?"

"If Lonnie P. did that, then he deserves to burn the same way." Delia's lower lip jutted out in that old way I remembered from childhood. "He can't scare me none with his weasly old phone call. He ain't even man enough to come out here and tell me face to face."

"Yeah," I added. "If he thinks his threats are gonna scare us off, he's got another think coming." I circled one arm around Delia's back, my words emboldened by our shared contempt for Lonnie P. Ramsey. "I learned something this week, something I can't tell you about right now, but I know somebody who can put Lonnie P. at that fire. All I need is a few more days to convince him to tell what he knows."

"Who?" Delia asked.

"I can't say. He made me promise, but—"

Another car came slowly down the street and pulled into the parking spot in front of the duplex. Delia lifted a corner of the curtain to look out. "It's John."

I tightened my arm around Delia. "You call me, you hear, if anything else happens. Anything at all. Promise? You have to tell John what's going on. And talk to Theo, okay?"

Delia nodded, returning my hug as John came in the front door. After introductions and a few moments of explanation, I said goodbye and headed home. I wasn't frightened, exactly, but my adrenalin was pumping. Now that Lonnie P. was feeling pressure, not just from Delia's line of questioning, but from the newspaper article, too, something was bound to happen. I had to get my information to somebody before he discovered I was behind the questioning. But I didn't have enough to go on yet, not without revealing what Jesse had told me. And even if I'd had Jesse's cooperation, going to Kip Hardwick was out of the question. I'd have to go to Tallahassee, try to convince someone from the state attorney's office that a crime had been committed and needed to be investigated.

The only bit of comfort out of the evening was that Delia and I were friends again, and that was something I wouldn't trade for any amount of money.

The next morning I drove Mama and myself into town for our nine-o'clock appointment at the beauty parlor—both of us with Linda Jo, the beautician that Mama had been going to for years. I went first for my trim and was finished by nine-thirty, so I had a couple of hours to myself while Mama underwent the full treatment. "I'm going to walk around downtown," I told her as she followed Linda Jo to the shampoo station. "I'll check back in on you after a while."

The fire station was not that far away, so I headed in that direction. I had no clear plan in mind, but maybe some bit of information would fall into my lap. A young man in the open bay area was winding a fire hose into place. "Hi," I called to him. "I'm looking for information about someone who used to be a firefighter here in the early '60s. Do you have records going back that far?"

"Um-m, I don't know," he answered. "Go inside and ask Fred. He'll know anybody who was ever a fireman here. He's in the office."

I walked to the door he indicated and pushed it open. An older man—at least a decade my senior would have been my guess—sat behind a metal desk with a wall of gray filing cabinets behind it. An old copy machine in the corner and another folding chair completed the small room's furnishings.

"Hello. Fred?"

"That's me. What can I do you for?" Placing both hands on his desk, he pushed himself up from his chair and stuck out his hand.

I returned his handshake. "I'm interested in finding out the names of the firefighters who were at this station in the early 1960s. For a project I'm working on."

"You must be one of them genealogy people putting together that county history book. I heard about that." Fred pulled open a file cabinet drawer, closed it, and pulled open another. "Well, you come to the right place. I can tell you anything you want to know." He laid a fat folder of papers on his desk and sat. "Pull up that chair over there and sit a spell. The gal who used to be our secretary was a stickler for keeping records of everything that went on here. She was forever clipping things out of the newspaper and snapping pictures. Said she was gonna make a scrapbook for us showing our history, but she up and died on us before she got around to it. I was glad to hear somebody wanted to collect all this old history and put it in a book."

I pulled the other chair up to the corner of the desk near the folder and sat. "Were you here in the sixties?"

"Sure. Started working here in '55, and I been here ever since. 'Course I retired from firefighting years ago, but I got this place in my blood. Can't stay away." He opened the folder and fanned a few of the papers across his desk. "I'm strictly volunteer these days, but I answer the phone and keep up the records. And I'm proud to say I'm doing just what Loretta—God rest her soul—would have wanted. I don't throw nothing away."

My eyes greedily searched the papers that I could see on the desk, but they were upside down from my perspective, so reading was hard. Would the official fire reports be part of these records? Would I actually be able to read the report and see photographs of what the firefighters found at the scene? I had no idea if I could trust this man enough to ask about that specific incident. He thought I was here as part of a group putting together a county history, so it was probably best to play along with that assumption.

"Could I look through those?" I asked. "Maybe make some copies? Do you have photos of the firemen from that time? I was in high school in the early '60s—graduated in '62—so I'm especially interested in that time period."

"Sure. There's a picture here somewheres of everybody in front of our new fire engine right about that time." He shuffled through the papers and took a large 8" by 10" photo out of the folder. "Yep. Here's the date on the back. March 1961." He laid it on the desk facing me. "That's me right there."

I picked it up to examine more carefully.

"That was right after we got that new fire engine," Fred explained. "See how we're all busting with pride?'"

"I see." I turned the picture over and read aloud, "March 1961—the Pine Lake fire crew with their new engine," followed by the names of all the men pictured, from left to right. I scanned through the last names—Bass, Harris, Collins, Renfroe—but only a couple of them seemed familiar. The next-to-last name on the list was Johnny Simmons. Was he any relation to Brian Simmons? I turned the page over to look at the young man second from the right. He was tall like Brian and had the same dark hair, but his muscular build and the hint of swagger in his eyes, his brash, confident smile, the sexy dip in his hair over his forehead, were nothing like the serious, brainy Brian—either from high school or the present day.

"Johnny Simmons," I said. "Do you know if he's related to Brian Simmons? Teaches at the college?"

"Sure. Johnny is Jake Simmons' kid brother. That makes him Brian's uncle. Me and Johnny's the same age. Boy, we had us some times back in the day." Fred chuckled, put both hands behind his head, and leaned back in the chair." Johnny was a hell-raiser back then, but times catches up with all of us, I guess. He's a grandpa now, just like me. Married the Corby girl, you know."

"Brian and I are the same age," I explained. "Same class in school. But I didn't know his family—just him."

"Johnny, like I say, was the kid brother. He come along at the tail end of the parade, after all the others was near 'bout grown, so he had lots of folks telling him what to do. Not that he listened to any of 'em." He laughed again.

I didn't want to arouse any suspicions by pursuing the subject. I pointed to the photo. "Snazzy-looking fire engine. I can't believe how old-fashioned it looks now. And how old that makes me feel. Can I make a copy of this?"

"Sure. Help yourself."

I copied the photo, both front and back, and then looked through the other papers in the folder, all in somewhat reverse chronological order, with newer additions on top of older ones, and made a few more copies—mostly of roster lists and photos. The newspaper clippings about the fire of June 1962 were stuffed into the folder, along with clippings reporting other fires, but I didn't see any official fire reports. Those must be kept separately, under lock and key. A subpoena would make them available, though. I could only hope that the official report would not be a whitewash like the newspaper article. Not wanting to push my luck any further, I thanked Fred for his help.

"Any time. Tell them genealogy people we're happy to cooperate any way we can. I'm gonna buy one of them books when it gets published, too."

"Thanks again. I really appreciate it. And I'll tell them what you said." I smiled and hurried away before I found myself inventing more lies.

After stashing the papers in the trunk of my car, I walked into the beauty shop to check on Mama's progress. She was under the dryer, an open magazine in her lap. Catching her attention, I waved and stepped back outside, meandering around the two blocks of downtown, window shopping. It wasn't until my second circuit of the area that I noticed the discreet, elegant script on a sign affixed to what used to be the bank—before the bank had to move out of downtown to find room for all those drive-thru lanes and ATM parking. "Flanders and Bixby, Attorneys at Law." I was a couple of steps past the sign before the names registered in my mind, and forward momentum kept me going for a few more steps before I slowed and stopped. Mama would be under the dryer at least an hour before her perm was ready to be combed out. This was my opportunity.

But what would I say to Ken Flanders? I couldn't tell him what Jesse had told me, and Delia hadn't found anyone who could identify either of the boys seen running from the fire. But she hadn't talked yet to Theo. I had to find out if Theo had seen anything. Besides, how was I to know I could trust Ken Flanders? I was pretty sure that he and his wife were the couple who had talked to Lonnie P.'s mayoral opponent, but I wasn't positive. Theo, though, I knew I could trust. Theo was like family. I hurried to my car and drove to Martin Luther King Boulevard where Maggie and Delia had told me I would find Theo's shop.

Chapter 34

I recognized Theo the minute I walked inside, not because he looked like the skinny teenage boy I remembered, but because he looked so much like Silas—the same broad shoulders and high forehead, the same purposeful stride as he came toward me with a welcoming smile, wiping his hands on a blue mechanic's cloth as he approached.

"Hey, Theo. I'd know you anywhere. Let me give you a hug."

The smile on Theo's face metamorphosed into a wary puzzlement. He stopped a few feet away, out of my reach.

"Sorry." I couldn't help laughing at his expression. "You don't know me, do you? It's Katie. Katie McCormick."

The wariness dissolved, and Theo's rich laugh, so like his father's, filled the cavernous room. "Katie McCormick. Mama said you'd come out to visit her. Where you been keeping yourself all these years?"

He crossed the last few feet, and I reached out my right hand for a handshake. "I can't get over how much you look like your daddy." I shook my head in amazement. "It's like going back thirty years—more than that, must be forty years—since I last saw you."

We reminisced for a moment about old times before I brought up the subject I had come to discuss. "Are you busy? I don't want to keep you from your work, but I came to ask you a question."

"I can spare a few minutes." Theo glanced behind him at a young man who was bent beneath the open hood of a car. "What's up?"

"Can we go into your office?" I had noticed a glassed-in cubicle off to the right.

"Okay. Sure." Theo's friendly demeanor grew more solemn. "Something wrong?"

"No. No. Everything's fine." I followed Theo into the office and pulled the door closed behind me. "I just didn't want to be overheard. I don't know if Delia said anything to you yet, but this concerns something that happened years ago. Back when we were teenagers."

"No." Theo shook his head. "Delia ain't said nothing to me—you mean when she got hurt and moved away?"

"No, not that." Did Theo know any more about what had happened to Delia that night than I did? He would have been about fourteen at the time—old enough to have been aware of her bruises and to have known from her behavior that something was wrong—but too young to be included in family discussions or confidences. Silas and Maggie had probably explained Delia's departure from the family with the same cover story they'd told the rest of the world—a sick grandmother who needed Delia's help. But the true story, whatever it might be, was for Delia to tell, not me. That wasn't why I was here. "No. This is something that happened a couple of years later, in June 1962."

Theo motioned for me to sit in the folding chair, and he perched on one corner of the small desk. "June 1962? Let's see, I would have been—"

"Fifteen? Sixteen? I'd just graduated from high school."

"Sixteen." Theo nodded. "What happened then?"

"You remember that Juneteenth celebration in town with all the fireworks? When that black preacher's house burned down?"

Theo crinkled his brow, and I could tell that he hadn't thought about that night for a long time—decades, maybe.

"I remember you and Jerome sneaked away from home and hitchhiked into town."

Theo nodded again, smiling. "And we got a licking for it, too."

"Well, rumor is that two white boys were seen running away from the house after it caught fire. You know anything about that?"

Theo shook his head. "Some folks say that's so, but I don't know nothing about it."

Theo's answer doused all my hopefulness. "But you were there, weren't you? You didn't see anything?"

"Me and Jerome was over at the church, all right, up around the fireworks, trying to figure out how we could get our hands on some of 'em. When somebody yelled there was a house on fire across the street, we took off running. See, we didn't want to get in no more trouble than we knew we was already in. We was just boys then, and we figured we'd get blamed for whatever had gone wrong. We didn't stop till we got clear to the junkyard, where we sat down under a big oak tree to catch our breath."

The junkyard. That was where Jesse had waited. "Did you see anything at the junkyard? A car? Any people?"

Theo furrowed his brow and thought for a minute. "Let me think. That was a long time ago. Me and Jerome was hunkered down, breathing hard, and we could see the light in the sky from the fire, smell the smoke, hear popping sounds every once in a while. We was scared near 'bout to death—thinking about how we was ever gonna get home and what was gonna happen to us when Daddy found out what we'd done, how he was gonna blame us for starting that fire."

"Did you hear the fire truck?" I asked.

"Yeah, we heard a siren. I remember covering my ears, trying to shut out the sound of it." He grinned. "I wanted it to not to be true, wanted to wake up in my own bed at home and have it all be nothing but a dream."

"Anything else?" I asked. "Think back. Did you hear or see a car parked near the junkyard? Somebody driving away?"

Theo tapped his forehead with his fingers. "Let's see." Then his expression brightened. "Hey, there was a car there. Parked just outside the gate. How'd you know about that? We heard a motor start out right close nearby, and we nearbout jumped out of our skin. I peeked around the tree, and I seen two white boys jump into this big ole light-colored car and then whoever was driving burned rubber getting out of there. I figured they'd climbed the fence and was in there stealing parts for their cars, and the fire—or something—spooked 'em. The way that car took off, they was as scared as me and Jerome." Theo laughed, remembering, and then sobered. "It wasn't till later we learned about the woman and the two little children." He shook his head. "I don't know what happened, but I know me and Jerome didn't have nothing to do with it. Neither one of us laid a hand on a firework that night."

"Did you get a good look at the boys?" I asked. "Did you recognize either of them?"

Theo nodded. "One of 'em was Lonnie P. Ramsey. I remember thinking that if Lonnie P.'s daddy knew he was in the junkyard stealing car parts in the middle of the night he'd be in bigger trouble than me and Jerome." A grin spread across Theo's face. "I didn't know the other one."

"You're sure it was Lonnie P.? You'd swear that in a court of law? It was nighttime."

"I never told on him, but sure, I know it was him, all right. That fire lit up the sky like daytime. Gosh, I hadn't thought about that night in ages. Why you asking about it now?"

"Thanks, Theo. You've been a great help." I looked at my watch. "I have to run pick up Mama at the beauty parlor, and I know you need to get back to work. Don't say anything about our conversation to anyone, okay? I'll explain it all later. Oh, if Delia asks you any questions about that night, you can tell her what you told me. But nobody else, understand?"

"Sure. I guess."

I left Theo looking thoroughly puzzled, but I was so exhilarated that I practically danced out of the shop. I could picture Theo and Jerome crouching beneath the tree, afraid of punishment for something they hadn't done. Theo had no idea what he knew or how much help he was going to be to me and Delia.

When I returned to the beauty shop, it was after 11:30, and Linda Jo was combing out Mama's perm. Since all my running around had left me famished, I talked Mama into a quick lunch of fast-food cheeseburgers and fries before we headed home. It had been a gratifying morning, and I had accomplished quite a bit without making Mama suspicious or having to lie to her about my whereabouts. But where did I go from here? Theo must be scratching his head over our conversation, but I'd promised to keep Jesse's confidence, so I couldn't reveal too much too soon. Theo's testimony, without Jesse's, would be worthless, but together they would be strong evidence against Lonnie P. I'd have to convince Jesse to talk—there was no way around it. In the meantime all I could do was leave it to Theo and Delia to share their information and draw their own conclusions.

Mama was quiet on the drive home, occasionally touching the unfamiliar springiness of her new perm and questioning whether she had done the right thing, but after I reassured her for the third or fourth time that it looked fine, she lapsed into silence, allowing me time to think. Fred, at the fire station, had been a lot of help, and I now had a complete roster of firefighters in 1962. But nobody on the list was personally known to me, so I had no idea whom I could trust. The only name that had jumped out at me was Johnny Simmons, uncle to Brian, but talking to him wasn't an option. I couldn't approach him cold—a total stranger—and getting to him through Brian was out of the question, now that Brian and I had ended our friendship on such a disastrous note. Besides, if Brian had not wanted me asking questions about the fire, then it wasn't likely that his uncle would be any more receptive.

But why had Brian been so adamant about my dropping any investigation into the fire? Was it because his uncle was involved in the cover-up? That would certainly explain a lot about Brian's attitude at the newspaper office. Had Johnny Simmons talked to family at the time of the fire?

With at least a dozen firemen on the roster, it was highly doubtful that the real cause of the fire had remained a secret. The young firefighters would have talked to wives and girlfriends and to other family members—anybody they wanted to impress with the importance and danger of their jobs. There would have been talk of gas—of a gas can, even—for neither Jesse nor Theo nor any of the people Delia had talked to had mentioned seeing anyone carrying a gas can on the run back to the car. It was much more likely that Lonnie P. had left it behind. Someone would have found and retrieved it later. One of the firemen? Or someone from the sheriff's department? Perhaps Lonnie P. had slung it away from the house into a back corner of the yard and someone from the neighborhood had found it? I couldn't get my hopes up in that direction, though. After forty-four years, hard physical evidence like that was too much to wish for.

But if Johnny Simmons had talked to family about what was found at the scene, Brian would have known years ago that the fire had been deliberately set. I could picture Johnny over at Brian's parents' house for Sunday dinner—the recent fire the main topic of conversation, with everybody firing questions at Johnny about what the firefighters had found when they arrived on the scene: how high the flames had been shooting, how frantic the crowd had been, how many men it took to hold back the preacher, how the house's roof was already collapsing, the walls already an inferno of red flame and black, charred wood. Surely there were questions about the cause—about how a house could go up that fast and that furious, the entire house in flames almost instantaneously, with no time to save anyone.

Johnny would have been the center of attention, royalty holding court, and he would have reveled (as any young man would) in being privy to information that hadn't been made public. And Brian would have been there, not contributing to the conversation, feeling himself above all that sensationalist gawking at tragedy and hero worship of an uncle not that many years older than himself, an uncle whose education had most likely stopped at Pine Lake High School, but listening, surely, listening with a scientist's curiosity, to Johnny's description of the cause of the fire, knowing already that the public explanation of an errant firework couldn't possibly have set the entire house ablaze that fast or that completely.

I could picture Brian at that table as clearly as if I'd been there myself. And I understood with certainty that Brian knew, and had known for years, that someone had deliberately set that fire. He'd known all along that the newspaper account wasn't true—couldn't possibly be true. And he had kept silent. What did that say about Brian? And about everyone else in town who'd known and kept silent? Had Brian and the others known the identity of the culprits? Surely they had been aware that Sheriff Otto Hardwick had been behind it. Had he been so powerful a force in the town that nobody could speak up against him? Or had the mood of the times been so ugly that nobody cared about the deaths of three black people?

The fire had accomplished its goal — it had driven the preacher out of town and ended any further demonstrations by the local black community — so had everyone decided that the deaths were an unfortunate but necessary trade-off to keep the local blacks in their place and maintain domestic tranquility?

By the time we arrived home, my spirits had sagged to their lowest ebb. What if I had discovered nothing at all that wasn't already well-known throughout the town and county? What if exposing Lonnie P. as an arsonist and murderer caused nothing but a shrug of the shoulders? What if the town had elected him mayor knowing full well his role in the fire but not caring about "that little episode" in his past?

I left Mama checking out her new hairdo in her bedroom mirror and gathered up a load of dirty laundry, still turning over the facts in my mind and trying to connect all the dots. Lonnie P.'s role in the fire couldn't be that well-known, or he wouldn't have warned Delia to stop asking questions. And Jesse's participation — unknowing as it was — in that night's events was not public knowledge either, for his family knew nothing about it, and he was fiercely determined that they not find out. Perhaps Sheriff Hardwick had kept a tight lid on the identities of the boys to keep himself from being associated with them or the fire. People would have whispered and wondered who and how, but nobody would have wanted to know for sure, because to know was to take on a burden that nobody wanted to have eating away at their consciences for the rest of their lives.

I turned on the washer, poured in the detergent, and waited for the tub to fill before adding my clothes, still trying to sort out the thoughts running through my mind. Even if the deliberate setting of the fire was known at the time, most of the adults of 1962 — my parents' generation — had passed on, and my own generation had seen so many changes that our attitudes had evolved and mellowed over the years. And the younger people, people like Marcus Boyd, who was running for sheriff against Kip Hardwick, and the young man running against

Lonnie P. for mayor, having never lived through those ugly years of segregation, had never even been exposed to the "rules" that my own childhood had been so dictated by.

Many old cases of murder against blacks had been reopened recently, and people had been convicted — people whose identities had been known for years, people who'd never been tried before because witnesses wouldn't talk, but now were breaking their long silence. The same could happen here. And I would be the one to make it happen.

Was I up to the task?

Another week up here and I would be leaving, going back to my own life and family, where all this old horror could be relegated to a back recess of my mind. It wasn't my problem, and I didn't have to deal with it. But, with a sinking feeling, as I pushed the clothes into the washer, sensing them grow heavier in my hand as they took on the weight of the sudsy water, I realized I couldn't walk away. The task was mine, whether I wanted it or not, and justice for Delia and for that woman and her two babies had settled squarely on my shoulders.

Chapter 35

Thursday, August 10—Friday, August 11, 2006

Later that evening after the supper dishes were done, I walked outside with my cell phone to call Delia. "I talked to Theo this morning," I told her when she answered. "Did he say anything to you about it yet?"

"Sure did. He said you came by his shop this morning and left him plumb bamboozled." Delia chuckled. "What did you say to him? He couldn't make heads or tails out of it."

I laughed at Delia's befuddlement. "I know I left him confused, but I didn't have time to explain. I asked him if he'd seen two white boys the night of the fire, and guess what? He saw Lonnie P. running and jumping into a car at the junkyard. Recognized him clear as day. He said there were two boys, and they looked like they'd been spooked by something. Said the car burned rubber getting out of there. He thought they'd been stealing car parts from the junkyard, but I know differently. Theo doesn't know it yet, but they were running from setting that fire, and Theo can positively identify Lonnie P. as one of them. Isn't that great?"

"The junkyard? That's a long way from the church, so that don't prove nothing."

"Not that far if you cut through people's yards. Besides, Theo's story fits perfectly with what I already know from another source. He made me promise not to tell anyone, so I can't say anything yet, but if I can convince him to talk—"

"And how you gonna do that?" Delia asked. "Hogtie him and force him to spit it out? Nobody in this town wants to go up against Lonnie P. It ain't safe."

"Speaking of safe, have you had any more phone calls?"

"Nothing else yet. Marcus stopped by last night and listened to the message, and I told John a little bit about the fire and about what happened to me. Theo's coming over tonight to find out more about what's going on, so I guess it's time I stopped keeping secrets and told him all of it, too. I just don't want John or Theo running off and doing something crazy. That's what I'm most afraid of—that one of them will do some fool thing and get himself killed."

The fear in her voice made me uneasy. "We have to work fast and get Lonnie P. behind bars where he belongs before anything happens. Are you alone?"

"No. John's here, and Theo's on his way over. He'll be here in a few minutes."

"You want me to come?" I asked. "I want to come, too." I had to fight the urge to spill everything I knew, everything that Jesse had told me down at the old turpentine camp. I'd made a solemn promise not to reveal a word of what he'd said, but, still, it was so tempting.... I wanted to give the entire story to Delia like a birthday or a Christmas present— lay it at her feet to make up for all the years of cowardice and silence.

"No, you don't need to do that. You stay home. I can tell Theo everything he needs to know."

"Okay." I swallowed my disappointment. "But if anything happens; if you get any more phone calls or anything, you promise to let me know?"

"Okay. I promise, but I 'spect I know better than you how to take care of myself. Don't you go worrying 'bout me, you hear?"

"Sorry. I'm so wrapped up in this thing that it's like a dog worrying a bone. I can't let it go for a minute. You know what I did today, besides talking to Theo?"

"What? Tell me you ain't gone and done something foolish."

"I went to the fire station and got a list of the firefighters from 1962. A group picture of them, with all their names on the back."

"You stole it right off the wall?" Delia's tone was a mixture of wonder and warning.

"No. Of course not. An older man there—Fred somebody—was very helpful. He let me make a copy. He thought I was one of the people compiling a county history book."

"Girl, you better be careful, or you're gonna be the next one in big trouble. Lonnie P. ain't gonna put up with this nosing around in his business."

"Oh, I didn't say a word about the fire. Fact is, I didn't even tell him my name. For all he knows, I'm somebody from the genealogy group. Besides, I'm not afraid of Lonnie P. Ramsey. What's he gonna do to me?" My words sounded braver than I felt. Delia, at least, had John and Theo to confide in, and I had nobody. I couldn't tell Mama, and with Russell two hundred and fifty miles away and completely unaware of what I was planning, there was no protection from that direction either.

"Theo's here. I gotta go." Delia disconnected, leaving me feeling unanchored, drifting in midstream without an oar. I paced the driveway in the gathering dusk. Summer was drawing to a close; in less than a week I'd be going home to work and normalcy. I had only a few days left to tie up the loose ends, to get enough solid evidence to turn over all I knew to a state prosecutor.

I needed to talk to a firefighter. But which one? Pick a name out of a hat? What would be my pretext for asking about the fire? Delia was right. I needed to be careful, for I had no idea who might be a friend or an enemy.

Jesse was still my best source of information, but how could I convince him to reveal what he had told me? I'd have to find someone he felt he could trust implicitly. Who would that be? His sister? If I could convince him to tell Joanne, surely she would urge him to make his story public. The president of the community college would not want a murderer running the town, would she? If Joanne told Jesse to tell his story to a prosecutor, he'd listen to her. Or maybe I could convince Jesse to talk to Ken Flanders. First, though, I'd have to find some excuse to talk to Flanders myself and see if my instincts about him were right.

The next morning was a Friday, Mama's regularly scheduled day for her physical therapy session, and her range of motion was so much better that the therapist had promised to release her after today's session, provided she continued doing her exercises at home. I dropped Mama off at ten o'clock, promising to be back by eleven on the dot. That gave me a precious hour to myself — less than that factoring in travel time — but time enough for a quick dash into the law offices of Flanders and Bixby.

All I wanted was a quick impression before recommending Ken Flanders to Jesse. I needed to know if Ken and Millie Flanders had been the couple who had spilled the news of Lonnie P.'s lie to his mayoral opponent. Beyond that, I had no clear motive for the visit, no ready story on my lips.

When I walked inside, a young woman looked up from the keyboard she was typing on behind a chest-high partition separating her from a small waiting area. "Hello. May I help you?"

"Um, I wanted to speak to Mr. Flanders for a minute. If he isn't too busy."

"Do you have an appointment?"

"No. I'm not a client. I'm, um, a friend."

The young woman narrowed her eyes and gave me an appraising look. Did she think I was here for an assignation with Ken Flanders? Or some poor soul who needed to appeal to a lawyer's mercy for services I couldn't pay for? I felt my courage seeping away.

"Your name?"

"Um, Kate Riley. I'm in town visiting my mother for a while, and I walked by and saw his name on the sign outside. He probably won't remember me, but we went to school together, and I wanted to say hello. I was in his sister's class, and we're planning a class reunion, our forty-fifth next year, and I thought he might be able to tell me where she was and what she was doing now. Five minutes. If he's not busy."

Uh, oh. Here I was making up fibs again. Of course Ken Flanders wouldn't remember me. He had never known me. But I had known his younger sister Phyllis.

"Phyllis Flanders," I said hopefully. "I haven't seen her in years. But if he's busy, that's okay. I just saw the sign outside, and thought…"

The young woman pushed a button on her desk. "Mr. Flanders. Someone here to see you. An old friend visiting from out of town. Do you have a minute?"

"Sure. I can spare a few minutes. Send him in."

"It's not—"

"Hey, don't tell me. I like surprises."

The secretary pointed to a corridor behind her. "First door on the left."

After giving a light tap and hearing a hearty "Come in," I pushed the door open. "Ken? Hello." I walked toward the desk and stuck out my right hand. "I'm sorry to barge in like this, but I was walking by and saw your name on the sign outside."

Ken Flanders stood and returned my handshake. He was short, with thinning blonde hair and pale blue eyes, portly, with a paunch that extended over his belt. "Hello." He smiled broadly and motioned for me to sit. "Hey, it's great to see you. How long has it been?" It was obvious from the too-high arch of his brows and the too-hearty cheerfulness of his voice that he had no idea who I was.

We both sat. "I'm sorry. You don't know me. I'm Kate Riley. Used to be Katie McCormick. I was in your sister Phyllis' class in school. We were on the newspaper and yearbook staffs together. I'm up visiting my mother, and I saw the name Flanders on the sign outside, and it made me think of Phyllis. How is she? Where does she live now?"

We talked for a few minutes about Phyllis before I changed the subject. "You were what, two years older than us? I didn't really know you in high school, but I heard your name mentioned a lot. Student Council, Honor Roll—that sort of thing. It's great that you became a lawyer and came back to Pine Lake to practice. Most folks would have headed off to a big city. I haven't lived here myself since I graduated from high school."

Ken leaned back in his chair and folded his hands across his paunch. "I moved away for a while, but Millie—that's my wife—she wanted to go back to work once the kids were school-age, resume her career, you know. And her folks (mine, too) were clamoring for us to come back so they could get to know the grandkids. Promised they would baby sit all we needed. She applied for a job at the college and got hired, so we moved back, and I opened up this practice."

"Looks like you're doing well." I looked around at the expensive furnishings and framed certificates on the walls.

"I'm doing okay." Ken followed my gaze around the room. "I started out as the young idealist, thinking I was going to devote myself to all the poor and downtrodden—those who don't get a fair shake from the law—and I still do some of that, but mostly it's civil cases like divorce and child custody and wills and such. Not enough criminal cases in a little place like this for me to ever make a name for myself, but I'm happy. What about you? What do you do?"

I explained my job as school librarian and checked my watch. Ten twenty-five. I didn't have much time left. "When we were growing up here, everything was segregated, and the races didn't mix much at all. It's so refreshing to come back and see how much things have changed. You must see the differences a lot in the legal system."

"Yes and no." Ken paused as if choosing his words carefully. "Of course, there's no more legal segregation, but there's still plenty of social division. Then there's the economic divide, too. And there's no longer the stable family structure we used to see, which leads to all sorts of problems—kids growing up with no discipline, drugs and guns a part of their daily life. We got that here, same as everywhere else."

I nodded. "I know. It's so sad to see kids growing up on the streets. I grew up on a farm about ten miles north of here, and everybody I knew had a mother and a father. That went for the black families, too. Everybody in the family had regular chores, and on Sunday mornings everybody went to church."

I saw Ken glance at his watch, and I quickly stood. "I'm sorry to be taking up your time this way. I know you have work to do."

Ken stood, too, and walked around the desk. "No problem. I needed a little break. It was nice talking to you, and I know Phyllis would enjoy hearing from you."

"I'll just let myself out." Across from where I was standing was a window, and through the window a campaign sign for Lonnie P. Ramsey was clearly visible. I motioned toward it. "I've been seeing those signs everywhere I look. From what I hear, Lonnie P. is big man in town. Funny thing is, though, I never pictured him staying in Pine Lake. I'd have thought he'd have bigger fish to fry."

"You knew Lonnie P.? He was in my class in school."

"Everybody knew Lonnie P. How could you not?"

Ken chuckled. "I guess that's so. He always liked the limelight, that's for sure. Still does."

"You voting for him?"

"Not me. I'm supporting Hal Crawford. Young fellow with a lot of good ideas. But he won't win. Lonnie P.'s got too many people sewed up in his pocket."

"I'm glad I don't live here. Too much coziness for me." I started toward the door. "Thanks for taking the time to see me. And I'll e-mail Phyllis as soon as I get back home."

As I retraced my steps to the lobby, I was surer than ever that my instincts had been right, that Ken and Millie Flanders were the couple who had alerted Hal Crawford to Lonnie P.'s lie about serving in Vietnam. I was confident that I could count Ken as an ally. Now if I could only convince Jesse to do the same.

As I pushed open the front door, my purse strap caught on the door handle, and I reached to unhook it.

"Little Katie McCormick," a voice boomed a few feet away. "So you're still with us. What brings you downtown on this beautiful August day?"

I turned around to see Lonnie P.'s grinning face looming over me, his eyes pointedly shifting focus from my face to the lettered wall sign beside my shoulder.

"Um, just signing some papers for Mama," I stuttered. "She's having her last therapy session today." I looked at my watch. "I have to pick her up right now."

"Well, I know she's enjoying having you up here with her for a nice long visit. You be sure and tell her I said hello."

"Thanks. I will."

"I guess you'll be heading home soon, back to the hubby and all."

"Yes, next week, in fact." I glanced again at my watch. "Sorry, but I have to run."

"Well, y'all take care, hear?" Lonnie P. called after me as I rushed away. "And come back any time. Pine Lake's always glad to have visitors."

It wasn't until Mama and I were heading home that I had time to think about my encounter with Lonnie P. Obviously, if Ken was supporting Hal Crawford for mayor, he and Lonnie P. were not friends. And if I had figured out the identity of the couple who had snitched on him about his military record, Lonnie P. would have known, too, and Ken would have become Number One on his enemies list. Would Lonnie P. be wondering what I was doing talking to Ken Flanders?

And if he knew that Delia was asking questions, how soon before he connected me with her? Weeks ago, when Delia and I had been having lunch in the barbeque restaurant and he'd walked in, cruising from table to table and giving his campaign spiel, Delia had already made her escape before he came to my table, and then he hadn't recognized me as anyone he knew, so I felt safe there. But since then I'd run into him twice, both completely unexpected encounters, and who knew when or where he'd pop up again? I'd have to make sure from here on out that I wasn't seen anywhere in public with Delia. And I couldn't be seen going back to Ken Flanders' law office, certainly not with Jesse Stutts in tow.

The dangers of "messing in Lonnie P.'s business," as Delia had put it, were real, but I wouldn't let myself be scared off. I'd only have to be more careful, that's all. Lonnie P. didn't know it yet, but for maybe the first time in his life he was up against somebody who wasn't the least bit intimidated by his power and couldn't be bought off with his money. I wouldn't stop my search until I'd found a way to make him pay for what he'd done.

Chapter 36

By three o'clock that afternoon, I had driven myself crazy with worry over what Lonnie P. might know or at least suspect. He was bound to start making connections soon if he hadn't already, and I had to stay one step ahead of him. I needed to talk to Jesse again, try once more to convince him to share what he knew.

I got my purse from my bedroom. "Mama, I just remembered our books are due at the library. I forgot them this morning. I'm going to run by there and return them."

Mama raised her eyebrows. "You'll use more gas to get to town than the fine will be. Why not wait and return them tomorrow? Or next week?"

"I'll go now. I'm tired of sitting around anyway, and I can check my e-mail while I'm there. And if you give me your library card, I'll pick up a few books for you to read next week after I'm gone."

"You make me tired with all this running around." Nevertheless, Mama pushed herself up from her chair and plodded down the hall, returning in a minute with her card. "I hope you're not doing this for me. Why don't you sit down and rest a while? You been going a mile a minute ever since we got home."

"I like being active. I'll be back by suppertime." I gathered up the library books and hurried away before Mama could make any more protests.

The dirt road leading to Jesse's house was as bumpy and as empty of traffic as before. I stopped at the entrance to his driveway to check out the number of vehicles parked beside the house. Both the car and truck were there, which meant Jesse's mother was home. Jesse would not have told her about his involvement in the fire, but she'd been home on my first trip out here, and he'd gone inside to tell her he was going to show someone around the old turpentine camp. And on Monday, my second visit, her car was back at home when I'd dropped Jesse off. Had she seen me at the wheel either time? And if so, would she buy another trip to the old turpentine camp? Or would she think that her son, at sixty-plus, had finally acquired a female paramour—something she'd probably longed for all these years?

I pulled into Jesse's driveway and stopped behind his truck. As I was planning what I'd say to his mother if she answered the door, I saw Jesse get up from the front porch swing and come toward me.

I rolled down my window. "I'm sorry to be such a bother, but I really need to talk to you. I've found someone else who saw Lonnie P. that night—saw him and another boy getting into a car at the junkyard. He didn't know the other boy and didn't see you, but he said the car took off in a hurry, spinning its wheels and kicking up gravel."

Jesse's eyes narrowed with suspicion. "You promised you wouldn't say anything. I thought I could trust you."

An odor of alcohol clung to him, and a sudden movement of one hand caused me to raise my left arm as if to ward off a blow. "Honest to God, I haven't told a soul. This other person—he doesn't know you, knows nothing about your part in all this. He was just a kid then, and has no idea what he saw. He thought it was some teenagers who'd climbed the junkyard fence to steal car parts and then got spooked by the fire. That's all."

"I didn't see nobody at the junkyard that night." Jesse's words were a little slurred. "You're making this up to get me to talk."

"No. Honest. He and his brother had sneaked away from home to go to the big celebration, and when the house caught fire, they took off running. They were afraid they'd get in trouble, get blamed for the fire, even, if their father found out they were there. By the time they got to the junkyard, they were out of breath, so they stopped to rest beneath an oak tree."

"How'd you find out about this person, whoever he is?"

"He lived on our place at the time. He's the son of the man who sharecropped for my father. I don't want to name any names, but I've known him since he was practically a baby. And he knows Lonnie P. He used to work sometimes for Lonnie P.'s daddy, especially in the summers. You know how everybody traded work when it was tobacco-gathering time."

"So he's gonna talk? You're gonna pursue this?"

"That's up to you. You're the only eyewitness who knows what happened that night. Lots of people at the church saw two white boys running away from the house, but nobody knows who they were — or at least nobody's willing to name names. We need you to supply those names."

Jesse shook his head. "I already told you, I can't put my family through this. My mama's eighty-eight years old, and her health ain't so hot. And Joanne's finally got her job at the college that she worked so hard for. I can't do it."

"Tell Joanne," I said. "Tell her what you told me and see what she says. Ask her what she thinks you ought to do."

"This was all forty-some years ago. What's the point of bringing it up now?"

"To give yourself some peace of mind. You said yourself it's been weighing on you all this time, that you couldn't look at Lonnie P. without wanting to kill him. Take that weight off your shoulders. Let the law deal with it."

Jesse half-turned away from me, looking into the distance. "I wish I'd never told you nothing. You promised it was just between us, and I was dumb enough to believe you." He brushed one hand across his chin. "Anybody asks, I'll deny I ever talked to you. Just go away and leave me alone, okay?"

"Okay." I shifted the gear into reverse. "But think about it. That's all I ask. Talk to Joanne."

I drove away, my spirits sinking as I made my way back into town, the August dust billowing around my car. I'd pushed Jesse too hard, and now he was backing off even further than before. Without his cooperation, I had no case. I might as well go back to Mama's and start packing my bags for home. Nobody else in town seemed to care that they'd elected a murderer for mayor, so why should I? I didn't even live here, so why was I getting so worked up over something more than forty years in the past?

Because I owed it to Delia, that was why. But my inquiries were starting to put Delia in danger, and I certainly didn't want to be the cause of any further injury to her. When I'd first told her about my suspicions, she'd been reluctant to get involved, wary of the details of her attack becoming fodder for public scrutiny, and had only agreed because I insisted. And now she was the one Lonnie P. was aiming at. Oddly enough, he hadn't yet learned that I was behind the questioning. It was as if I were hiding behind John Wayne all over again and letting Delia take the brunt of Lonnie P.'s ire. But what could I do? My search was stymied. I'd promised Jesse not to reveal any of what he'd told me, and I had no other evidence placing Lonnie P. at that fire.

I'd have to go to Delia and tell her that I'd run into a roadblock, that my one eyewitness wouldn't talk and that the investigation was hopelessly stalled because of my promise of confidentiality. Would Delia be angry at me for letting her down? Disappointed? Or would she be relieved to have the case closed? She and John were talking about moving soon to Tallahassee to be near her oldest son, still close enough to Pine Lake to help out when needed, but far enough away to escape the daily reminders of her life here, so it wasn't likely that she'd ever have to see Lonnie P. Ramsey's face again.

Granted, she'd already told Theo and John all that I'd told her about the fire and maybe something about Lonnie P.'s role in the attack on her two years earlier, but they wouldn't talk without her permission, and Jesse clearly had no intention of making his knowledge public. The only other person who knew about my suspicions was Brian, and he had warned me weeks ago at the newspaper office to back off my investigation. Maybe he'd been right; maybe I should have paid more heed to his warnings.

Ever since my lunch with Delia at the barbeque restaurant, I'd been nurturing my revenge, growing stronger and more determined with each new revelation, but now that I felt it slipping away from me, I felt a strange sense of lightness. I didn't have to go through with this investigation. I could forget it right now, go home to Russell, resume my quiet, ordinary life, and put this whole crazy episode out of my mind.

The clock in my car read 3:56. Almost four o'clock, time for Delia to get off work. I'd run by her duplex before going home and talk to her about what was happening—ask her advice about what to do now. I'd have to give her another half-hour or so, though, for she'd go by the Alzheimer's Center to pick up Silas and take him home to Maggie before going home herself. And she was sure to spend a few minutes talking to her mother, so she wasn't likely to get home before four-thirty, four-forty-five. I'd told Mama I was going to the library to return the books and check out some new ones for her, so I could pass the time there. Surely I wouldn't run into Lonnie P. at the library.

I picked up a couple of novels from the new books shelf that I thought Mama might like—something to occupy her time after I'd gone home, back to my own house and belongings, my old, regular life. Could I really be leaving next week and putting aside all the things I'd learned in the past month? Leaving a murderer not only unpunished but in charge of Pine Lake? The possibility seemed unreal, but then so did all the facts I'd uncovered, as if the events of these scorching summer weeks had been some sort of fevered dream.

After checking out the books and returning to my car, I noticed that my gas gauge was hovering just above empty, so I drove to the nearest gas station, filled up my tank, and went inside to get a cold Diet Coke. Four thirty-five. Delia should have arrived home by now, but I'd give her a few more minutes to kick off her shoes, check her mail and phone messages, do whatever she did to make the transition from work to home.

I circled slowly around town, sipping my drink and mentally saying goodbye to all the places and people that had been so much on my mind these last few weeks — goodbye to the beauty shop and the fire station and the law offices of Flanders and Bixby, goodbye to the rehab center where Mama had had her therapy sessions, goodbye to the park and the courthouse, goodbye to the movie theater and the old high school that I'd graduated from, abandoned now for the new high school out past the community college, goodbye to Gail and Gary and to Brian and all those long-ago fantasies, goodbye to Pine Lake and to all its ghosts and ugly past.

At least I had accomplished part of my goal. Delia and I were friends again. I had confessed my failure in the movie theater all those years ago, and she had understood and forgiven me. But I still hadn't told her the worst part — the part that was unforgivable — and now that I had failed in my quest to make Lonnie P. pay for that night and for the deaths of that young mother and her two children, that memory could never be revealed or atoned for. It would have to remain forever unspoken between us.

As I approached the street leading to the AME Church and to Delia's duplex, I slowed to a stop at the corner to read the huge hand-lettered sign announcing a community fish fry to be held at the church on Saturday, August 12. The 12th was tomorrow. The menu, written in vivid magic marker swishes of red and blue, included fish, hushpuppies, grits, coleslaw, baked beans, and homemade cakes and pies. My mouth watered at the thought. Would Delia and John be going to the fish fry? Could I come? I'd have to remember to ask Delia about it.

When I pulled into the drive behind Delia's car in front of Unit 2A, my car clock read five o'clock on the dot. I jumped out and rang the doorbell, but there was no answer. I waited a minute and knocked. No one came to the door. She must be taking a shower. I waited a while longer before trying again. Still nothing. I walked to the front window, but the curtains were drawn and I couldn't see inside. Perhaps she and John had gone somewhere together in his car? I pulled out my cell phone and called her house number and then her cell phone number, but there was no answer to either one. An uneasy feeling began to build in me. Had something happened? Had Lonnie P. carried out his threat?

Uncertain as to what to do next, I walked back to my car. I had no number for Theo programmed into my phone, but his shop was only a few minutes away. I'd go there and see if Theo knew where she was.

As I backed out of the drive, I noticed something across the street, beside the church, a small patch of something bright glinting in the sun in the very back of the church parking lot, behind a line of trees. No cars were in the lot—all was empty and peaceful. The bright light seemed eerie and out of place. The uneasy feeling that had been gathering sharpened into a stab of fear. Something was wrong. I pulled into the church parking lot and drove back toward whatever was producing the glint.

It was the chrome front grille of a car—a big, late-model expensive car—backed into a narrow shady lane behind a strip of trees so that it wouldn't be visible from the street. Just the sort of car Lonnie P. would drive. But where was he? And where was Delia?

I jumped out and ran around the car and down the lane, calling Delia's name, but there was no answer. After a few yards, I realized I had entered a shady, well-kept cemetery. Oak trees draped with Spanish moss and marble monuments green with age cast graceful shadows across the graves, but there was no place here to hide—not in broad daylight. And how would Lonnie P. have gotten Delia into the cemetery? She would not have gone willingly, and there was no way Lonnie P. could have dragged her out of her house (or more likely her car, since she would never have opened her front door to him), all the way across the street, through the church parking lot and into the cemetery without someone seeing or hearing something. Delia would have been fighting and kicking and screaming bloody murder all the way.

She wasn't here. Some sixth sense told me that. But where? Had Lonnie P. been lurking around her house, waiting for her to arrive home? Had she unlocked her door, gone inside with a handful of mail or maybe a bag of groceries, and been followed inside by Lonnie P.? Maybe they were both inside the duplex, Lonnie P. keeping Delia from being able to cry out.

I retraced my steps, frantic now with worry. Should I call 911? I knew nothing yet. The car might not even belong to Lonnie P. Maybe the church's minister had parked there in the shade so his car would be cool when it came time to go home. As I returned to the spot where I'd left my car, I gave one last call. "Delia!" A sound came from the direction of the church, a dull thud as if something had been thrown against a wall or a door. Could they be in the church? What would Delia be doing inside the church on a Friday afternoon? I ran to the back door and pushed it open. "Delia?"

"Delia!" I ran across the room, giving one knee a painful knock against a pew, and grabbed wildly for the beefy arm of the man who slammed Delia once more against the wall. "Delia, it's me. I'm here. I'm here."

Chapter 37

Lonnie P.'s arm jerked back, throwing me off balance and knocking me into the side of a pew, but my diversion gave Delia enough time to slide sideways out of his grasp. She slumped against the wall, catching her breath.

Lonnie P. turned to look at me, the shock of my presence registering in his eyes. "Katie? What the heck?" He held both hands up toward me, palms outward. "Sorry. You okay?" He glared over his shoulder at Delia. "It ain't what it looks like. I came here to deliver a little message, and she comes clawing at me like a wildcat. I just pushed her away, that's all. I didn't hurt her none." He wiped his hands together as if disposing of the whole business. "I'll be going now."

I rubbed at my hip, sure to be a nasty bruise by tomorrow, and took a step toward Lonnie P. "Delivering a little message, huh? Well, I have a message for you. If you ever touch Delia again, I'll kill you. Myself. With my bare hands." I held up two clenched fists, shaking them in his face.

"Whoa, little lady. Don't get your dander up." Lonnie P. laughed as if it were all a big misunderstanding. "I know this gal used to live on your place, but I didn't know the two of you were such bosom buddies. Anyways, she's the one started it, going at me like she did. I didn't do nothing to her. Now I'll be moseying along." He started past me, as if what I'd seen with my own eyes hadn't happened, as if the shove against the wall had been nothing more than swatting a biting mosquito. "As for you..." He turned back to face Delia. "You better remember what I said if you know what's good for you."

Delia had scrambled to her feet. "I'm just getting started good," she said, still catching her breath. "You don't scare me none."

"You don't come here and shove my friend around and then pretend it's nothing." I stepped between Lonnie P. and Delia. "What are you doing here anyway?"

"Never you mind about that. It's between me and her." He jerked his thumb toward Delia. "She knows why I'm here."

I kept my eyes locked on Lonnie P. So it *had* been his voice on Delia's answering machine. I was positive of it now. But so far he didn't seem to know that I was involved in the questioning about the fire, and I wanted it to stay that way for a while longer. "I don't know what you're talking about, but if you ever touch Delia again, if you harm her in any way, I'll come after you. You can put that in your pipe and smoke it."

"Humph! She's the one spreading lies all over town. You tell her she'd better keep her big mouth shut if she knows what's good for her." Lonnie P. turned and started toward the door.

I pretended ignorance of what he was referring to. "It seems to me the one telling lies is you. You're gonna saunter right out that door like you didn't do a thing, like none of this is your fault? Delia was just begging you to throw her against that wall, I guess, just like she was asking for you and your cronies to attack her that night in 1960? She deserved it then, too, huh?"

Lonnie P. stopped. "What night? Now you're as crazy as she is. I don't know what you're talking about."

Delia shook her head at me, not wanting me to bring up that long-ago attack. Okay, I could understand how she wouldn't want me throwing it in her face in front of Lonnie P. He had already humiliated her enough. But my anger was building, and I couldn't hold back.

"You know what night I mean. At the movie theater. I was there. I heard what you said to your friends. Delivering a message that night, too, weren't you?"

"I don't know what you're talking about." Lonnie P. looked from me to the door, as if trying to decide whether to walk away or stick around and see exactly how much I knew.

300

I pushed my advantage. "You want me to tell the whole county about it? You want them to know what kind of fine, upstanding citizen they elected for mayor?" I was wound up now and couldn't stop. "I think I'll go down to the newspaper office and give them another scoop for next week's paper. Tell them exactly what happened that night."

Lonnie P.'s face turned a furious red. "I don't know a thing about any night at the movie theater. And if that hussy told you I done something to her, she's gonna find herself in more trouble than she already is." He glared at Delia, who had gotten quiet at my mention of the attack. "You putting these lies into her head? You tell her I never touched you—not today or any other time. Tell her right now, or I'll serve your sorry black ass up on a platter."

He took a threatening step toward her, but Delia didn't give any ground. As she glared back at him, I could see that my outburst had awakened her own long-pent-up fury. "I'll tell her no such thing. Because you did it. I clawed you and I bit you and I fought you, but you did it. You and them other boys."

Lonnie P. took another step toward Delia and raised one arm. "Lying bitch. You got no proof. Who do you think is gonna believe the word of a nigger hussy against mine?"

"You don't know what I got," Delia retorted.

"That's right." I kept myself between Delia and Lonnie P. He might think he could get away with roughing up Delia, but he wouldn't dare hit me. "You don't know what we've got." With my adrenalin pumping at full throttle, I felt no fear, and with Delia behind me, I knew the two of us could take him down if we had to. My fury at him for what he had done to Delia was a fresh as if it had happened last night.

Lonnie P. backed away, setting his jaw in a scowl. "I don't know what the two of you cooked up, but this ain't going to work in a court of law. You think Kip Hardwick's gonna take your word over mine? I'll swear on a stack of Bibles that I never touched that hussy, and I'll have the whole county behind me. If you say otherwise, you're gonna find yourselves under arrest for making false statements. I'll see to that personally."

"Who said anything about Kip Hardwick?" I sneered at him. "You think we need Kip Hardwick to handle this? From what I hear, folks in this neighborhood have their own way of getting justice. Maybe we'll just call in some reinforcements right now." I pulled out my cell phone and punched a few numbers.

"That's right," Delia echoed. "And when Marcus Boyd gets elected sheriff, things are gonna change all over the county. You better get ready for it."

"Give me that." Lonnie P. grabbed for the cell phone in my hand, but I tossed it to Delia, and Delia slipped it down the front of her blouse, pushing it into the center of her bra.

"Too late," I said, grinning at Delia's clever move. "I already called Theo when I found Delia's car at home and her not there. He should be here any minute."

As if on cue, the sound of a car's tires on gravel came in through the half-open back door.

"That must be him now," Delia said, rising to her full height and looking Lonnie P. straight in the eye. "You still want that phone, you'll have to come get it."

"You two are in deep trouble." Lonnie P. turned to eye the back door, panic causing his voice to rise into a higher register. "You ain't seen the last of me, not by a long shot."

"We're so scared," I taunted, now that relief was at hand. I hadn't called Theo, but somebody was outside, walking up the back steps.

Lonnie P. headed for the nearest closed door, off to one side of the main sanctuary, and disappeared behind it just as a woman walked in from the back, her hands laden with plastic bags.

"That ain't Theo," Delia muttered, grinning as she looked at the closed door Lonnie P. had disappeared behind. "It's just Althea, bringing some plates and things." She hurried over to Althea. "Here, let me help you with all them bags. You got any more outside?"

I sank onto a front pew, weak with relief now that the encounter with Lonnie P. was over. After a minute or two, Delia and Althea emerged from the kitchen, and Delia introduced me as an old friend, her manner giving no hint of the scuffle that had taken place a few minutes ago. "We're getting ready for the big to-do tomorrow," Delia explained. "You can come if you want." She and Althea filled me in on the details of the fish fry, a yearly event that brought out the whole community and raised money for the church.

"Sorry I have to rush off," Althea apologized, "but I gotta get home and start cooking. We'll have tons of food coming in here tomorrow, and enough fish and hushpuppies to feed the whole county. You come eat with us, hear?'

"Thanks. I'd love to. Can I come early and help you get everything ready?"

"We don't turn down no offers of help," Delia said, and Althea echoed the sentiment.

As Althea disappeared through the back door, Delia sat on the pew beside me and exhaled a deep breath. I shifted my weight to relieve the pain in my hip and grinned at her. "Wow, that was something, wasn't it? We're both gonna be sore as all get-out tomorrow." I stretched out my legs beside Delia's, my light coloring contrasting with her dark. "Are you okay? Did he hurt you any?"

"I'm fine. It's a good thing you came along, though. And Althea. Wonder why Theo ain't showed up yet."

"I never called him," I confessed. "I was just bluffing."

"Oh, girl, you had me fooled, too. I guess you want your phone back." She pulled out the phone and handed it to me.

"Thanks. Did you see Lonnie P.'s face when he thought it was Theo at the door?"

"I sure did." Delia chuckled. "I thought he was gonna wet his pants." Then she pointed toward the door Lonnie P. had gone into. "That room over there? It ain't an exit. It's the children's nursery. Only way out is through a window."

"Really? You think he's still in there?" I put my hand over my mouth, suppressing a nervous laugh. "You think he can hear us?"

"My bet is he's long gone. Theo's not somebody you want to mess with. I bet he squeezed out that window like toothpaste. You wanna go see?"

Before I could respond, the answer came from outside in the parking lot. A big, low silver car sped through the gravel and raced past the side window. "There he goes." I leaned back against the pew, feeling another rush of adrenalin at his departure. "We showed him, didn't we? What you did with the phone—that was priceless. What made you think of that? I'd never have had the nerve."

"Girl, you ain't lived my kind of life. Things I could tell you would curl your hair." Delia smiled. "Make it as kinky as mine." She touched her hair and then rubbed at a spot on one shin. "Lordy, when you come busting in here a while ago, I never was so glad to see anybody in my life. You appeared out of nowhere, like you were my guardian angel or something. How'd you know I was here?"

"I was in town and decided to drop by and talk to you for a minute. Your car was home but you weren't, so I started getting worried." I recounted the sequence of events leading up to me finding her in the church. "But what were you doing here? And more to the point, what was Lonnie P. doing here? How did he find you?"

"Lordy, I don't know. Like Althea, I was bringing over some bags of paper plates and napkins for the fish fry tomorrow. I was planning to pull in right beside the church and drop 'em off, and then I drove up in my driveway like always, forgetting all about what I was going to do." She laughed, lifting both hands into the air and bringing them down on her lap. "Old age catching up with me. So then once I was already home and had cut the engine off before remembering the bags of stuff, I decided to walk over with 'em, get my exercise, you know."

She sighed. "I don't know where Lonnie P. was, but I guess he was hiding somewheres, waiting around for me to come home. I put the bags in the kitchen over there and then checked to see what else had been brought in, and I was walking out to leave when I heard footsteps. I figured it was another one of the women bringing stuff, so I called out, "Hey, come on in," and I walked back in here and there he was. Started in on how I'd better stick to my own business and stop asking questions all over the neighborhood, and then I gave him some lip. You know me."

"That I do." I nodded at Delia's chuckle, remembering all too well the old childhood feistiness that had so frightened Silas and Maggie.

"Well, one thing led to another," she continued, "and next thing I know he's got me shoved up against the wall. That's when you come running in screaming like a banshee." She chuckled. "Gracious sakes, girl, I couldn't believe my eyes when you stood right up to him and said all the things you said."

"I meant them, too." The image of Lonnie P.'s hands on Delia, the dull thud of her body hitting the wall, made me angry all over again. "If Lonnie P. ever touches you again in any way, I'll kill him."

"Thanks, girlfriend." Delia patted my hand. "I can't imagine you killing anybody, but I appreciate the thought all the same."

"I could do it if I had to. I'd do it for you." I turned my hand to clasp Delia's and gave it a squeeze before letting go, feeling warm all over at her use of the word "girlfriend" to describe me. For how many years had I been yearning to regain that closeness we'd once shared? Delia was the nearest I'd ever come to having a sister. "I don't think we have anything to worry about, though. Lonnie P.'s got too much to lose, and he knows now I'm onto him. Something happened to you, he'd be the number one suspect. I'd make sure of that."

"And who would you report him to?" Delia asked. "Kip Hardwick?" Her voice was heavy with sarcasm.

"No. The state attorney's office in Tallahassee. That's where I'm taking all my information about the fire. First thing Monday morning. You can come with me, and we'll tell them everything we know, including what happened today."

Delia shook her head. "I gotta work on Monday. And like I told you before, I don't want mention of what happened to me back then to get out in public. I got family to think about."

"I already gave you my word on that. I'm sorry about bringing it up with Lonnie P., but he made me so angry that it just spilled out."

"It's all right." Delia crossed her arms in front of her. "I been wanting to tell him off about that night for years, so it felt good to get it off my chest."

We sat in silence for a moment, still trying to shake off the last vestiges of our nervous energy. I'd given Jesse my word, too. What did that leave me to tell the state attorney's office? Not much, but I had to go with it. Not to follow through was to let Lonnie P. go on intimidating Delia and anybody else he considered beneath him. I didn't think he'd risk his public image by doing her any real harm, but what did I know? My skin wasn't black; I'd never known the kind of discrimination that Delia had, never been demeaned with racial slurs or regarded as some dumb, less-than-human species who must be kept in her place by whatever means necessary.

And who's to say that instead of coming after Delia himself next time that he wouldn't send some hired, slavish goons to do his dirty work for him, much as he'd used Jesse all those years ago? No, Lonnie P. hadn't changed a bit since his teenage years; he'd shown his true colors today, and he would get what was coming to him. I'd see to that, regardless of the consequences. He'd never hurt Delia again, not while I was alive and breathing. And to think that only an hour ago I had been ready to go home and forget the whole thing, to let Lonnie P. walk away free. What on earth had I been thinking?

I grimaced at my throbbing knee as I stood and reached for Delia's hand to help her up. "Come on, girlfriend. Let's get out of here. We've got a busy day ahead of us tomorrow."

Chapter 38

Friday, August 11—Saturday, August 12, 2006

In spite of her protests, I drove Delia home across the street. "I'm staying with you until John gets home, and that's final," I said. "I'm the one who got you involved in this, and it's my fault that Lonnie P. is taking it out on you. I'm sorry. I should have been the one asking questions."

"Don't go blaming yourself." Delia waved off my apology. "I want to see him hog-tied and roasted same as you. I just wish I knew how he found out. Somebody talking without paying attention to who's in earshot, I guess."

"Probably somebody gabbing on their cell phone. It's astounding to me the things people say into phones out in public, like they're having a private conversation and they forget everybody around them can hear every word they say."

When John's car pulled up a few minutes later, I said my goodbyes, promising to be back first thing in the morning to help with the fish fry and leaving Delia to tell John as much or as little as she wanted about our confrontation with Lonnie P. in the church.

Once I was on the road, I made a quick call to Mama to apologize for being so late and then spent the rest of the drive home worrying about what Lonnie P. might do to Delia if he caught her alone again. His intention this afternoon obviously had been to intimidate her into dropping the subject of the fire, but my coming along had escalated the situation by several notches. Now that I'd let slip the fact that I was aware of his teenage attack on Delia and that I was determined to stick up for her, he had to be apprehensive about my role in the questions about the fire, and my interference today had likely put Delia in more danger instead of less. Even worse, with the weekend just beginning, there was nothing I could do to report my findings to the state attorney's office before Monday morning.

I turned my focus to tomorrow's fish fry. The entire black community would be sure to turn out, but what about the white one? As a fund raiser for the church, the fish fry couldn't be viewed as a political rally, but such a large community event would be a natural drawing card for all the local candidates. Would Lonnie P. show up, after what had just happened? What about Kip Hardwick? I couldn't imagine that either of them had much, if any, support in the black community, but what about their opponents? Surely Marcus Boyd would be there. I was looking forward to meeting him or at least getting a good look at him. And what about Hal Crawford, the young man running against Lonnie P. for mayor? Maybe Ken and Millie Flanders would come. And someone from the local newspaper. Would it be the same reporter who'd exposed Lonnie P.'s lie about serving in Vietnam? Who else? It might be a good way to gauge the sentiment in the county and see how many people I might be able to count on when Lonnie P.'s crimes were finally exposed to the bright light of public scrutiny.

The next morning dawned sunny and clear with the temperature already near eighty degrees at seven o'clock and no rain in the forecast. I dressed for the August weather in a loose white cotton shirt, khaki knee-length shorts, and sandals. I'd asked Mama the night before if she wanted to go to the fish fry at the AME church, but she had declined, as I had known she would.

"Sit outside in this heat?" she had said. "No, thank you. And at the colored church? What if you're the only white person there? There's no telling what trouble there might be. All this meanness in the paper every week—drug dealing and stealing and shooting and what have you."

"Oh, Mama, you're being paranoid. We're going to be on church grounds in broad daylight. There won't be any trouble."

Mama had waved her hand dismissively. "You're gonna do what you want, I guess, but I'm too old for this new-fangled mixing of the races. It seems to me things was better the way it used to be."

"Better for you, maybe," I said. "Not better for the black people." I wanted so badly to tell Mama what had happened to Delia all those years ago to make her leave home, but I'd promised Delia not to tell a soul. So I had bitten my tongue and gone to bed early, taking two ibuprofen tablets for my sore hip and knee and hoping I'd feel better in the morning.

I arrived at Delia' duplex promptly at nine, pulling in behind her parked car. Across the street, men were sticking long PVC poles with tarps attached to their tops into the grassy lawn in front of the church, making a long row of shade for the folding tables that I could see stacked in the back of a pickup. After getting no answer to my knock on Delia's door, I walked across the street.

"Hey, Katie," someone called, and I looked over to see Theo unfolding a table. "Delia's inside if you're looking for her."

"Thanks." I waved back. "Nice weather, isn't it?"

As I walked into the kitchen, Delia and two other women were taking plates and napkins and utensils out of their wrappings, stacking and counting and arranging. Delia made introductions as another woman came in carrying a huge bowl of coleslaw and put it in the refrigerator.

"What do you want me to do?" I gestured down at my clothes. "I'm all ready to work." Compared with them, I felt vastly underdressed for the occasion. Delia was wearing slacks and a nice floral blouse, but two of the women were wearing their Sunday dresses beneath big bib aprons. I was the only one with my knees showing.

Delia handed me some plates to unwrap. "Here. You can finish opening these, and I'll start mixing the batter for the hushpuppies. We won't start cooking the grits for a while yet." Two huge pots sat on the stove, apparently awaiting the big bag of Dixie Lily grits on the counter.

As Delia rummaged in a cupboard for a mixing bowl, a young woman came in bearing a coconut cake on a fancy cake stand, followed by two little girls each holding a sweet potato pie, and there was a flurry of activity as items were rearranged on the counter to make room. Beside the sink, someone was chopping onions, and the aroma of baked beans wafted from the oven. It was still a good two-and-a-half hours before lunchtime, and my mouth was watering already.

By ten-thirty all the preparations had been made. Tables and chairs had been set up outside, all the paper goods were organized and ready, huge coolers of crushed ice and commercial-sized containers of sweet iced tea were in place (no unsweetened option available here), and the kitchen was overflowing with food—too much to fit in the refrigerator and on the counters. The desserts had been moved into the main sanctuary, lined up on pews until time to take them outside to the dessert table.

Meanwhile, in the churchyard, the men had been heating up the huge cookers of oil for the fish and hushpuppies. The task of the actual frying was left to them, but the women were responsible for breading the fish and getting it ready for the fryer, along with mixing the batter for the hushpuppies and ferrying everything out to the men, who were clumped around the cookers, laughing and talking and supposedly keeping an eye on all the kids who were chasing one another across the lawn.

Nearly everyone who brought food had stayed around to help and visit, so there were more people than the kitchen would hold. "Go on outside and get some fresh air," Delia told me. "You can take this pan of fish out to the menfolks. They should be about ready to start frying."

After handing off the fish to the men, I bought a meal ticket at the table that had been set up near the parking lot and then walked along the row of eating tables as if inspecting them, stopping occasionally to adjust the position of a folding chair. So far I was the only white person here, and I felt a little uneasy at that fact. Had Mama been right? Would I be the only white person attending? Who was it who had said that churches were still the most segregated institutions in America? I was also the only adult with bare knees, which made me feel even more conspicuous.

"Hey, Katie." Theo was walking toward me. "It was good of you to come and help out." He held out his right hand and instead of shaking it, I clasped it in both of mine for a few seconds.

"I'm enjoying it. I can't get over how much you look like your daddy."

Theo grinned. "Everybody tells me that. He'll be here later today. I'm going to pick up him and Mama when it's time to eat and bring 'em here for a little while. He can't stay long; being in crowds makes him nervous, but Mama's looking forward to it."

"That's great. I talked to your mom already, but I haven't seen your dad yet."

Theo lowered his voice, although nobody else was near us. "Delia told me about what was going on. You're a brave lady, doing what you're doing. I just wanted to say 'Be careful.' I don't want to see you get hurt."

"Oh, I'm not worried about that." Had Delia told Theo about our encounter with Lonnie P. inside the church yesterday? I didn't think so, but I wasn't sure. "I have to go home next week, so I'm going to miss all the fireworks when this town blows up with what gets uncovered. I'm worried about Delia, though. You and John will watch after her, won't you?"

"Sure we will. And I'm ready to testify in court. You be sure to tell whoever you talk to that I'm ready to help any way I can. If I'd known earlier what he'd done to Delia..."

Theo's eyes blazed, and I laid one hand on his arm. "She didn't want anyone to know. Still doesn't. I'm going Monday to the state attorney's office in Tallahassee to tell them everything I know about the fire. I don't expect anything to happen immediately, you understand, but I hope it's at least enough for them to decide to investigate further."

"I'll come with you if you think it'll help," Theo offered. "My oldest boy works with me, and he can take care of the shop."

"Really? Hey, that would be great. I was planning to leave early so I'd be there when they opened at eight."

We made plans to meet at Theo's shop at seven o'clock on Monday morning, and by the time Theo walked back to join the men, the first batch of fried fish was being lifted from the cookers. At the same time Althea came across the churchyard with another pan of prepared fish, as if every step of this operation were synchronized down to the second.

The church parking lot was filling up fast, and new arrivals were parking along the street. I headed back inside. It should be about time to start carrying the food to the outside tables, and all hands would be needed for that task.

When I emerged again a few minutes later, carrying a dish of baked beans, the number of people in the churchyard seemed to have nearly doubled, and among the crowd I spotted several other white people besides myself, in groups of twos and threes, making their way across the grass to the ticket table. One of the men I recognized, even from this distance, as Ken Flanders, which meant the woman with him must be his wife, Millicent (or Millie, as she was known now). And she, like me, was wearing shorts that fell just above her knees. I felt so grateful that I could have hugged her. I put my dish of beans on the serving table and headed in their direction.

"Hello, Ken." I lifted my hand in a wave. "Good to see you again."

"Hello." Ken smiled with recognition. "Good to see you, too." He turned to his wife. "Honey, this is a friend of Phyllis's from high school. She stopped by my office yesterday to say hello. You're, um-m—"

"Kate. Kate Riley." I turned my attention to his wife. "Hi, Millie. I used to be Katie McCormick. I was two grades behind you and Ken in high school, so you probably don't remember me."

Millie paused, thinking. "Weren't you on the newspaper staff? Sophomore class reporter?"

"Yes. I'm surprised you remembered. And you were the editor that year. I followed you two years later as editor my senior year. Good old *Pine Lake Tiger Growl.*"

Ken paid for their two tickets, and I instinctively reached into my pocket to make sure the ticket I'd bought earlier was still there. We talked for a few more minutes about high school memories until we were interrupted by another couple approaching. The woman, who looked to be a few years younger than Millie and me, was wearing spike heels, dressy black pants and a fitted black-and-white-checked top. The man with her was in jeans and T-shirt.

As Millie introduced us, I remembered where I had seen her before, at the restaurant when Gail and I had lunch. "Kate, this is Joanne and Mike Jameson. Joanne is our president at the college, which makes her technically my boss."

Joanne smiled and waved one hand as if to pooh-pooh this notion as Millie continued. "Joanne, this is Kate Riley, used to be Katie McCormick back in the day, when we were a lot younger and spryer." Everyone laughed, and as I greeted Joanne and Mike, something in Joanne's eyes when Millie said my name, a slight arch of her eyebrows and an opening of her mouth in the shape of an "O" suggested some recognition that took me by surprise. I had no recollection of Joanne from high school, but had she known me? Gail had said Joanne was several years younger than us, but "several" could have been only two or three.

We continued talking until Ken noticed that a food line was beginning to form. "Hey, looks like the food's ready." He rubbed his ample stomach. "Y'all coming?"

"Sure," Mike answered. "Smells terrific, doesn't it?'

Ken and Millie started for the line, followed by Mike. "Aren't y'all coming?"

"Go ahead," Joanne answered. "I need to sit down for a minute. My feet are killing me. I never should have worn these heels. Kate can keep me company, and the rest of you can save us a place in line. We'll join you in a little while."

"I told you not to dress up in the first place," Mike said. "Look at Millie. And Kate."

"True. But I have an image to uphold." Joanne winced as she pulled off one shoe and then the other. "Go on. We'll be there in a minute."

Mike hurried off to catch up with Ken and Millie, and I followed Joanne to the row of tables and chairs. Nobody else was around, for everyone was heading for the food line.

Joanne sat and dangled her shoes from one hand. "Wow. That's a relief. Sit down with me for a minute. You're the person who's been talking to my brother."

"Yes." But how did Joanne know about that? Had she kept me back to tell me to leave her brother alone? My stomach clenched and I became aware of the ache in my sore knee as I lowered myself into an adjoining folding chair. "Jesse talked to you?'

"He called me last night. He'd been drinking pretty heavily, so he wasn't making a lot of sense."

"What did he tell you?" I could hear a quaver in my voice, and I felt like a pupil who'd been called into the principal's office for some infraction. I coughed to clear my throat.

"He was scared. Said he'd told you some things he hadn't ought to have said, and now he was afraid you were going to make it public. When I asked him what he was talking about, he told me this long, complicated story. I didn't know whether to believe him or not."

"It's true," I assured her. "All of it." I paused and coughed again to regain control of my voice. "I tried to convince him to tell his story to a lawyer, but he didn't want to. I told him to talk to you, to get your advice."

"I'm glad you did. If this is all true, if that fire really happened the way Jesse said it did, then this needs to be exposed. We don't need a murderer in charge of our town. Kip Hardwick has been bad enough, and now this. What are you going to do now?"

I told her about my planned trip to Tallahassee on Monday morning. "I promised I wouldn't betray Jesse's confidence, so there's not much I can tell them, but I can't let this go."

"I want Jesse to go with you. Mike and I are going over there this afternoon right after we leave here and I'll try to convince him that he needs to cooperate with anyone who wants to question him. Everybody who knows him knows he doesn't have a mean bone in his body. He got sucked into something he couldn't handle, and now I'll make him see that it's up to him to set things right. He's got to get this off his chest. I've wondered for years what was eating at him so, and now I know."

A huge wave of relief flooded over me. "Thank you. You don't know how much I appreciate this. Let me give you my phone number so you can call me after you talk to him."

By the time we had exchanged phone numbers, each of us programming them into our cell phones, the first people in line had filled their plates and were headed toward the tables. Ken, Millie, and Mike had moved up so that only a dozen or so people were ahead of them. Joanne put her shoes back on. "Mike did warn me not to wear these," she conceded, "but stubborn me, I wanted to make a good impression, so it's only right that I suffer for it."

We walked over to join the others in line, our secret safe between us.

Chapter 39

As I placed my heaping plate of food beside Joanne's and Millie's, with Mike and Ken across the table from us, I realized that I hadn't seen Delia since I'd last come outside an hour ago. All the food had been brought outdoors, so there was no need for anyone to have remained in the kitchen. Theo had left to pick up Silas and Maggie, and John was still in the group of men clustered around the fish cookers. A sudden sense of panic gripped me, which I told myself was nonsense. There was no way Delia could have been alone in the middle of such a crowd. Nevertheless, I had to reassure myself.

"Excuse me for a minute," I said to Joanne. "I need to run inside. I'll be right back."

"Sure. We'll save your spot."

The sanctuary was dark and cool, and after the bright light of outdoors, I couldn't see anything at first. Then a voice called out. "Hey, Katie, where's your plate of food? You better get in line before it's all gone."

I took a few steps forward, waiting for my eyes to adjust to the dimness. "Delia? What are you doing in here? Everybody's outside."

By now I could see Delia sitting on one of the front pews, a plate of food in her lap, surrounded by nearly a dozen other women, all eating in cool comfort, their plastic cups of iced tea on the floor in front of them.

"The smart ones ain't," she replied. "Go get you a plate and come join us."

"I have a plate outside already. I didn't mean to run off and desert you, but I ran into some people I knew back in high school and they invited me to sit with them."

Delia reached for her tea. "Don't you worry none about that. We had more people in that kitchen than the fire department allows in the whole building, just about. You go on and enjoy yourself. Eat your fill."

"Oh, I intend to. Thanks. I'll see you later."

When I got back to my spot beside Joanne, another family group had joined our all-white table—a young couple with two small children—all the white people clumping together like sheep in a meadow.

Ken introduced me. "Kate Riley, meet Hal Crawford and his wife Rachel. Hal's the young fellow I mentioned yesterday who's running against Lonnie P. Ramsey for mayor."

"Glad to meet you." I extended my hand across the table, shaking first his hand and then his wife's. "Good luck with the campaign." I looked at the two children, a boy of about six seated between his parents and a younger girl on the other side of her mother, so close that she was halfway in her lap. I directed my question to the little girl first. "And who are you?"

The girl ducked her head into her mother's side and didn't answer. I looked at the boy. "I guess she doesn't have a name. Do you have one?"

The boy giggled. "I'm Jacob. And she's Maddie."

"Well, hello, Jacob and Maddie. I have two grandkids about the same age as you, but they don't live here. I bet they're pretty unhappy about missing out on all this good food." I dug into my plate, and all was quiet for a while as everyone else did the same.

All the tables were filling up, and some people had taken plates over to the front steps of the church. Others found shady spots on the grass beneath the three big oaks that grew between the street and the row of covered tables. There were still three vacant seats at our table—two beside me and one at the end beside Maddie, but everyone seemed to be overlooking them—glancing at them and then moving on somewhere else.

"Hey! Mind if we join you?" A loud, hearty voice boomed behind me.

"Marcus! Imagine running into you here!" Hal boomed back. "Get yourself right on over here, but no politicking, mind you. Remember we're on church property here."

"I won't if you won't." Marcus set his plate down one spot away from me, leaving the space beside me for his wife. "Lissa, you sit over there beside Maddie. Keep her company."

A little girl about the same age as Maddie—about four, I'd guess—scooted around her parents, her plate tilted precariously, a smile on her face that was the brightness of a hundred megawatt light bulbs. Her hair was plaited into a dozen or more braids, each adorned with a colorful barrette at the end, and they swung in the sun as she pirouetted, nearly spilling her food. My head spun with the image—remembering another scene of a four-year-old Delia jumping off the back of Daddy's pickup right in front of me—looking at me with that same eager expectation, as if she were waiting for me to give her the world as her personal present.

Maddie, I could see, was as enchanted with Lissa as I had been with Delia. When Lissa plopped her plate down beside Maddie's, Maddie sat up straighter and gave Lissa a shy smile.

Meanwhile, Ken was introducing me to Marcus and his wife Denita. "I guess you're not up on local politics," Ken said to me, "but Marcus is running for sheriff against Kip Hardwick."

"I heard about that. And I've seen the signs everywhere." I leaned forward to get a better look at Marcus. "I hope you win."

"Thanks. I'm trying my best to collect votes."

"I got fruit punch," Lissa was telling Maddie. "You got plain ole tea."

Maddie looked at Lissa's bright red drink, and her face fell. Tears began to pool in her eyes, but she was trying her hardest not to cry.

"You want fruit punch?" her mother asked. She looked over at Denita and Marcus beside me. "We didn't see the punch when we got our drinks."

Maddie nodded, and then Jacob chimed in. "Me, too. I want some, too."

Rachel pushed back her chair to stand, but Marcus spoke up. "Hey, let me. Two fruit punches coming up. Be right back."

He sauntered off and I could see him speaking to people along the way, clasping someone on the shoulder, waving, calling to someone else in the distance. Something in his bantering tone sounded awfully familiar. Where had I heard that voice before? Then it came to me. At the ATM at the bank, the day I got in line behind Delia. Marcus had been the deputy behind me, the man who'd called out Delia's name, who had joked with her as I stood there overcome with all those old feelings of shame and guilt. And now here I was running into him again. My time up here with Mama had come full circle, and it was almost time for me to go. But not before I took my story to the state attorney's office. Would Joanne be able to talk Jesse into going with me and telling a prosecutor what had happened that night? Beneath the table I crossed my middle finger over my index finger for good luck.

By the time I'd cleaned my plate and made a trip to the dessert table, I was so full that I could hardly move. Soon afterward, Ken and Millie and Mike and Joanne said their goodbyes, and I was left at the table with the two young mothers, Rachel and Denita, while their husbands made the rounds of the crowd, shaking hands and exchanging greetings. Jacob had run off to play with some other boys, and Maddie and Lissa had their heads together, whispering and giggling.

"Excuse me," I said. "I see someone over there I want to speak to. It was nice meeting you and your families. Tell your husbands I hope they both get elected."

I headed to the table where Theo sat with Silas and Maggie and a crowd of others. "Hi, Maggie." I clasped one of Maggie's hands in both my own. "It's good to see you again. I tried to get Mama to come with me today, but she didn't want to sit out in the heat."

"I don't blame her one bit." Maggie smiled up at me. "It's good you came out, though."

"Oh, I wouldn't have missed all this good food for anything. I'm so stuffed right now I'm about to pop." I looked at Silas beside her, but he showed no sign of recognition. Sitting in a wheelchair, his plate of food hardly touched, he was a shrunken shell of the man I'd once known. I didn't know what to say to him.

Maggie leaned toward him. "Silas," she said, "this is Katie McCormick. You remember little Katie."

I touched Silas's gnarled hand lightly with my fingertips. "Hello, Silas. It's been a long time. It's good to see you again."

Silas didn't respond.

"He's tired," Theo explained. "I'm taking him home soon. I want you to meet my family." He introduced his wife and his oldest son and the son's wife and their children—a table full of people whose names I couldn't keep straight. I talked with everyone for a few minutes and then excused myself to refill my cup of iced tea.

The crowd was beginning to thin as people headed for their cars out of the afternoon heat, but stragglers were still arriving, and as I walked past the food-laden tables, I could see that there was still plenty of food for the latecomers.

"Hello." A young woman I had noticed earlier taking pictures of the gathering smiled as our paths crossed. "Are you enjoying the fish fry?"

"Yes. Very much." I smiled back. She looked to be maybe in her early thirties, long blonde hair pulled away from her face with a hair clip, friendly blue eyes, and casual navy Capris and white cotton-knit tank top. I had noticed earlier that she, like me, seemed to have come alone.

"I don't think we've met," she said. "I'm Charlie Bascom Sims." She stuck out her hand.

Momentarily taken aback, I hesitated a split second before returning her handshake. "You're Charlie Bascom Sims? Editor of the *Gazette*?" The image I'd had in my mind of a male Charlie Bascom Sims, a younger, more laid-back version of Mr. William C. Bascom, jarred with the slim, attractive woman in front of me.

She laughed. "That's me. You must not live here."

"No, I don't. I used to, a long time ago. I'm up for a few weeks this summer visiting with my mother. I'm Kate Riley. I saw the name 'Charlie Bascom Sims' on the masthead of the paper, but I assumed—"

"That I was a man?" She smiled again. "My real name is Charlene, but I've been Charlie since I was a kid."

"Your grandfather was editor when I was growing up here," I said. "I guess he was your grandfather. His son Charles was in my class in school. Are you related to Charles?"

"He's my dad. I'm the third of three girls. That's about the time he gave up on having a William Charles Bascom, V, I guess. Hence the Charlie. Neither of my sisters was interested in the newspaper business, but it was in my blood from the beginning, so when my grandfather retired a few years ago, he turned it over to me. And I love it." She patted the camera hanging from a strap around her neck. "I've been so busy taking pictures and getting names and quotes that I haven't had time to eat yet. Have you eaten already?"

"Yes. I couldn't hold another bite. But there's still plenty of food left. And no line to speak of. Enjoy."

"Would you like to keep me company? Since we both seem to be here alone." She smiled again. "You can tell me what my dad was like in high school."

"Sure. I'd love to." I pointed to a table that was now completely vacant. "Let me carry your things over there, and I'll wait for you while you get a plate."

I walked to the table and sat, piling Charlie's camera and bag onto the chair beside me. So Charlie Bascom Sims was a woman, and she had been the one to approve the exposé of Lonnie P.'s lie about serving in Vietnam. Another person to count in my corner.

I sipped my tea and looked over the crowd while I waited for Charlie to return. Hal and Marcus were both still making the rounds, being sure to greet every person present. No sign, though, of Lonnie P. or of Kip Hardwick, their opponents. After yesterday's incident, Lonnie P. was sure to know that his involvement in the fire wasn't being discussed only in the black community, but that I knew about it, too. He had to be trying to cook up some scheme to stop us from talking, but what? I had no idea, but I knew that he wouldn't simply sit back and wait meekly to be exposed.

Charlie was headed toward me with her plate in one hand and plastic cup in the other when my cell phone rang. I looked at the caller ID. Joanne Jameson. She'd hardly had time to even get over to Jesse's house yet, so surely she hadn't already convinced him to tell what he knew. A feeling of dread swept over me. Had something happened to Jesse?

"Hello?'

"Kate? It's Joanne Jameson. Jesse's sister?"

"Hi, Joanne. Did you already talk to Jesse?" I tried to make my voice sound calm, but something in her tone raised the hairs on my neck. "Is something wrong?"

"I've just been to my mother's, and Jesse wasn't there." Joanne's voice was bordering on frantic. "He left early this morning to go down to the river to see if the fish were biting. The worst part is, though, my mother says Lonnie P. Ramsey came by her house about half an hour ago in his pickup, wanting to talk to Jesse, acting all friendly-like, saying what good friends they used to be in high school, and such hogwash, and Mama, not knowing anything about what's going on, told him he could find Jesse down at the river—even gave him directions to Jesse's favorite spot, the one he and Mike always go to. Mike and I are on our way there right now. I thought you'd like to know."

A chill ran up my spine. Jesse was the only local witness who knew exactly what had happened the night of the fire. Did Lonnie P. think that he could become Jesse's new best buddy and flatter him into not talking? His ego would make him think that all he had to do was pull his "old friends" act and Jesse would fall right in line. And what if Jesse didn't respond the way Lonnie P. expected him to? A private, out-of-the-way spot on the riverbank was a perfect opportunity for an accident. With Jesse's known reputation for drinking, an accidental drowning wouldn't raise much suspicion.

Charlie set her plate on the table.

"I'm heading that way right now," I told Joanne over the phone. "Let's just hope we find them before something happens. I'll call you back for directions once I'm on my way."

"What's going on?" Charlie asked.

"I'm sorry. I hate to rush off, but I have to go find a friend."

"Is someone lost?"

"Not lost, no. But in danger. I really have to go."

"Can I come with you?" Charlie's newspaper instincts were kicking in. Having her there with her camera and recording equipment might be invaluable. If we could get Lonnie P. on tape, we'd have the evidence we needed. "Sure. Bring your plate and cup with you. I have to talk to someone first, though."

I grabbed her camera and bag and headed toward Theo, who was still at the table with his family. "Theo, I need you to come with me. Quick. Can someone else take your parents home?"

"Delia?" Theo was at full alert.

"No. Someone else. Can you come?"

"Sure." Theo handed his car keys to his son. "You take Grandma and Grandpa home in my car, and then come back here, okay?" He turned to his wife. "If I'm not back by the time the rest of you are ready to leave, you drive on home, and I'll meet you there."

Theo hurried off with me and Charlie toward my car. "What's going on? Where are we going?'

"To the river. I'll explain once we're in the car."

Charlie climbed into the back seat with her uneaten lunch and I piled all her equipment in after her. Theo sat up front with me. As soon as I was on the road, I pulled out my cell phone and dialed Delia's number.

She answered with a laugh. "What, girl, you too stuffed to walk inside the church and talk to me? You got to call me from outside?"

"It's Lonnie P.," I explained. "Remember I told you I had a witness who knew what happened the night of the fire? Who could put Lonnie P. at the scene? Well, Lonnie P. is with that witness right now. His sister just called me. Lonnie P. followed him down to the river where he had gone fishing—some little private out-of-the-way spot that hardly anyone goes to. We have to find them before something happens."

"Lonnie P. Ramsey? Our mayor?" Charlie asked from the back seat. "What's going on?"

"Get John," I told Delia over the phone. "And come down to the river. The sister and her husband are already on their way. I have to call her back and get directions to where we're going. Then I'll relay them to you once you're on the road. The sister is pretty sure she knows where we'll find them. Oh, I've got Theo and the editor of the newspaper in the car with me."

"Theo's with you? I'll get John right now. You call me right back, you hear?" Delia was all business. I hung up and called Joanne again to get directions, repeating them out loud so that Theo and Charlie could help me remember.

"I know where it is," Theo said. "I been there before. The road ends about two-three hundred yards from the riverbank and you have to walk in through the woods. Nice little sandbar there right in the curve of the river."

I turned onto the highway, watching my speedometer so that I didn't get stopped for speeding. Charlie was itching to know more about what was going on, so I explained the situation as concisely as I could, concentrating strictly on the fire and not mentioning anything about Lonnie P.'s attack on Delia and not giving away Jesse's name, in spite of the fact that it would soon become a moot point, regardless of what we found once we reached the river.

"Forty-four years ago?" Charlie said. "That was way before I was even born. You're saying a house was deliberately set on fire with a woman and children inside? With the sheriff's knowledge and direction?"

"That's right," I said. "You're too young to remember what things were like back in those days, before integration. Theo and I remember, though, don't we?"

Theo nodded. "Sure do. I hope we get there in time, knowing Lonnie P. and what he's capable of."

"I don't know him that well," Charlie said. "Mostly by sight and reputation. He's full of himself, that's for sure. But everybody talks about all he's done for this town, with the new hospital wing and that Rambling Acres neighborhood and golf course he developed. I can't believe he could have committed murder. Are you sure it was him?"

My phone rang again. It was Delia. "You got directions to this place we're going?"

"I'll let you talk to Theo. He says he knows where it is." I handed the phone to Theo so that I could concentrate on my driving. My insistence on making things right with Delia had not only put her in danger, but had now endangered Jesse as well. I pushed the gas pedal as far down as I dared. We had to get to that fishing spot before another tragedy occurred.

Chapter 40

By the time I turned onto River Road, my heart was pounding. With one strong man in each of the three cars, we had more than enough people to overpower Lonnie P., but what if we were too late? He'd had a good half-hour's head start on us, and I had no idea what sort of welcome Jesse might have given him when he'd shown up so unexpectedly, oozing with buddy-buddy camaraderie. Jesse had told me that he hated Lonnie P. enough to want to kill him, so it wasn't likely they'd had a friendly encounter. Had there been bitter words between them? I feared the worst.

Whatever was happening or had happened, if we all bolted onto the scene en masse, we'd immediately cause Lonnie P. to close down. Anything he'd said or done, he'd deny, and with no witnesses, it would be his word against Jesse's. And whom would Kip Hardwick choose to believe: Pine Lake's most deep-pocketed philanthropist and mayor—or the town drunk? We needed to sneak up on them unawares, have Charlie turn on her video camera, and catch him in the act. I called Joanne again. "Hi, it's Kate. Are you there yet?"

"We're turning off on the dirt road right now. Their trucks should be around this next corner. Hold on a second. Yes, there they are. Jesse's old Ford and a shiny new red something or other."

"Great. We'll be there in a couple of minutes. Wait for us, will you? We want to sneak up on them, catch Lonnie P. unawares. I have Charlie Bascom Sims, editor of the *Gazette*, in my car, and she has her video camera. I'm hoping she can get something on tape."

"Whoa. You have Charlie with you? How'd that happen?"

"It's a long story. I'll fill you in later."

Joanne agreed to wait, and when I turned onto the dirt road, the red clay dust raised by Mike and Joanne's car had not yet settled back down, so I knew we weren't far behind them. I asked Theo to call Delia again and see where they were.

"They just turned onto River Road," he reported. "They're less than five minutes away."

I pulled in behind the red pickup, blocking Lonnie P.'s escape route. "Good. Tell her we'll wait. Let's do some quick planning in the meantime." I jumped out of my car, followed by Theo and Charlie, and joined Mike and Joanne, hoping that the woods between us and the river were thick enough to block the sounds of our cars and our voices.

"Let's send in Mike first," I said. "Mike can say he heard Jesse was down at the river fishing, and he'd come to see how the fish were biting. Charlie can sneak along behind with her camera. That way if anything's going on, if Lonnie P. and Jesse are talking, or arguing, she can get them on tape before they're aware that she's there. Then Lonnie P. can't deny his own words. The rest of us can bring up the rear." As much as I wanted to be present for whatever was going to happen, I didn't want Lonnie P. to see me or Delia, not until we had him cornered, at least. Our presence would be a certain sign that he was trapped, and I didn't want to spring the trap prematurely.

By the time we'd worked out our plan, Delia and John had pulled up, and I quickly relayed it to them. Mike started off first down the path, with Charlie a few feet behind. The rest of us hung back, giving them a few minutes' head start before we followed, with John and Theo in the lead in case they were needed, and Joanne, Delia, and I bringing up the rear. There was no further conversation, all of us trying to walk as quietly as possible and keeping alert for any noises coming from the riverbank.

We'd gone about a hundred yards along the path when we heard someone call out a greeting. I couldn't make out the words, and I didn't hear an answer. Had Mike reached the sandbar? And who was he calling to? Was it Jesse or Lonnie P.?

We continued cautiously along the path, which was beginning to slope downward. All three of us women were in open-toed sandals—Joanne, still in her pants suit, had either gone home and changed shoes or had brought sandals in the car—so we were all watching our feet so as not to stub a toe on a root. Then Theo, in the lead, put up a hand to indicate we should stop. He pointed, and through the trees I could catch glints of the river below and a narrow strip of sandbar. No men were visible, but a breeze was blowing off the river toward us, carrying the sound of their voices. We remained silent, listening, trying to decipher individual words.

"Where's Jesse?" I heard a voice ask. That had to be Mike. And he had to be talking to Lonnie P.

The answer was muffled. Lonnie P. must have been facing away from where we were standing.

Mike spoke again—something about "truck" and "fishing." I could catch only a random word or two, but Mike must be telling Lonnie P. about seeing Jesse's truck and knowing that he had come here to go fishing.

Again, the answer was not audible. Had Lonnie P. already done something to Jesse? Had he hurt him? Pushed him into the river? I arched my eyebrows at Theo as a question of what to do now, and he pointed down the path. Following his finger, I saw Charlie below us, half-hidden behind a tree, her camera steadied against the tree trunk. I hoped she was close enough to get whatever Lonnie P. was saying on her video recorder.

As I looked again toward the sandbar, a man's back came into view, someone walking toward the water. That had to be Mike; he was too tall and lean to be Lonnie P. Was he looking for Jesse? Had Lonnie P. pointed him out on the riverbank, or had he denied seeing Jesse at the river at all? I still couldn't see Lonnie P. Then a branch cracked somewhere below, and I could see Charlie moving around the tree and then disappearing. More branches snapped as someone moved up the path, closer to where we were all grouped.

Theo and John took a few steps forward, motioning for us to remain where we were. They had not gone far when I heard Theo's voice. "Hold it right there!"

Lonnie P. was scurrying up the pathway, breathing hard and sweating profusely. Theo and John stepped apart, each grabbing one of his arms and stopping him in his tracks.

He looked up the path, straight at Delia and me, as Joanne dashed past the group of men, headed down the slope to join Mike in the search for Jesse. "You again," he spat at me. "Why ain't that a big surprise? I didn't do nothing to that queer bastard. He ain't even here!" His shoes squished with water as he twisted his body, trying to break Theo and John's grip, and I noticed that both pants legs were wet up to his knees. "You coons better let me go right now, or I'm gonna have the law on the whole lot of you!"

He looked at me. "I should'a known you were the one behind all this. Miss High and Mighty. All I got to say is you don't know who you're messing with. This town is gonna chew you up and spit you out—just like you deserve for sticking your nose where it don't belong."

"We'll see about that." Beyond the three men, I could see Charlie ascending the path, stealthy and silent as a shadow, her video camera still recording. "I see you've been taking a little wade in the river, in your shoes."

Lonnie P., whose back was to Charlie, had not yet become aware that his every word and move was being taped. "So I slipped," he said. "Last I heard, that ain't a crime." He twisted again, trying to get loose. "Get your filthy hands off me, niggers," he snarled, losing his balance and falling to one knee.

"You ain't going nowhere till we see who we come to find," Theo said, giving him a jerk upright. "You better tell us where he is if you know what's good for you."

"His name's Jesse," I said. "Jesse Stutts." There was no need to try any longer to keep Jesse's name a secret. "He was with Lonnie P. the night of the fire, and he knows exactly what happened."

"Hah!" Lonnie P. sneered. "Not no more he don't."

"What?" I asked, panic setting my heart to racing again. "What did you do to him?" Had he killed Jesse already?

Charlie stepped off the path and behind a tree as Theo twisted Lonnie P.'s arm behind his back and he and John turned him around facing the river. "You know where he is, you're gonna show us, right now," Theo growled. "And if you did something to him, you're gonna be in jail before the sun sets today."

Pushing my way past John and Theo, who were half-dragging Lonnie P. down the path, I raced toward the river to join Mike and Joanne in the search for Jesse. Whatever had happened to him, it was my fault. I was the one who had started this whole train of events. Mike and Joanne had moved out of sight, but I could hear them off to the right, alternately calling Jesse's name, the desperation in their voices rising with each repetition. To the right of the sand bar, a rocky ledge marked the boundary of the river at its high point, and I scrambled onto the rocks to get a better view of the water in both directions. A movement in the center of the river caught my eye, something brown moving downstream in the current. Mike and Joanne had seen it, too, for both were already heading in that direction, stumbling along the narrow strip of sand and brush that lined the river bank. I ran after them, panting for air.

Before I reached them, Mike had kicked off his shoes and jumped in and was swimming out toward whatever was there. If that was Jesse, he had already been in the water for how long? Fifteen minutes? Half an hour? Longer? Even if he was a strong swimmer, fatigue would have weakened him quickly in those heavy wet clothes and shoes. And what if he was injured? "Should I go after them?" I called to Joanne. My swimming skills were rusty, but I had to help.

"Mike will get him," Joanne reassured me. "He was a lifeguard in college, so he knows what he's doing. Knows CPR, too. Let's keep going down this way, and Mike can bring him to us—if it's him."

Relieved at Joanne's trust in Mike, I followed her along the bank, both of us keeping our eyes on Mike, who had reached and grabbed the brown bundle and was letting the current take him farther down the river while he angled toward shore. We caught up with him as he reached the riverbank and helped to pull Jesse's limp body onto the narrow strip of sand. "He's been hurt," Mike said. "Look at his eye."

An ugly black bruise surrounded Jesse's left eye, and his upper lip was swollen and raw-looking. He seemed unconscious.

Mike fell to his knees and took a few deep breaths to recover from his exertion before going right to work, clearing Jesse's airway, checking his pulse, and then beginning CPR. I scrambled back up onto the rocky ledge to signal to the others where we were, and they soon joined us, Theo and John still half-dragging Lonnie P. along, Charlie following with her camera, and Delia bringing up the rear.

Joanne pulled her cell phone from her pocket and shot a dangerous look at Lonnie P. while pressing 911. "If my brother dies, you're responsible."

Lonnie P. twisted again, but he couldn't break Theo and John's hold. "I ain't done nothing to him. I just came to the river to go fishing. I didn't even know he was here."

Mike was performing chest compressions on Jesse, Joanne was talking on the phone to the 911 dispatcher, Charlie was still filming, and Lonnie P. was still sputtering and denying everything. I kept my attention focused on Jesse, repeating over and over under my breath, "Let him breathe. Let him breathe. Let him be okay."

"They're on their way," Joanne said. She knelt opposite Mike at Jesse's other side, telling him everything was going to be okay, that she was here and help was on the way. I kept checking my watch. Two minutes. Two-and-a-half. The second hand was approaching three minutes when Jesse sputtered and coughed, a stream of water coming out of his mouth. Mike quickly turned Jesse's head to the side to let the water dribble out and checked his pulse again. "Heart's beating strong," he said to all of us assembled. "He's gonna be okay." He turned back to Jesse. "Jesse, old boy, you had us all scared there for a minute. Go ahead, get all that nasty water out of your lungs." He turned Jesse on his side and patted his back. "Cough it up."

Jesse coughed up more water and took a deep, raspy breath. "Lonnie," he began, and then stopped, exhausted.

"Just rest," Joanne said. "We're here, and everything's going to be okay. Don't try to talk yet. There's plenty of time for that. Lonnie P.'s in custody, okay? We'll make sure he goes to jail for this."

At the mention of his name, Lonnie P. became belligerent again. "He's lying. I never hit him. He must'a fell in the river all by himself. You ain't pinning nothing on me."

Charlie was still filming.

"Who said anything about hitting?" I wasn't a regular viewer of TV crime shows, but I'd seen enough that I immediately caught the slip-up. "Nobody mentioned hitting. You two get in a fight or something?"

"I didn't do nothing to him," Lonnie P. reiterated. "Didn't hit him, didn't push him, didn't do nothing. I don't know nothing about how he got out there in the river. Probably drunk as a cooter, like he usually is. You see all them beer cans back at the sandbar?"

"His mother told you he was here," I said. "You went by his house looking for him, and his mother told you where to find him. You parked right by his truck and walked in through the woods. You can't deny any of that, can you?"

"I already told you I never saw him. Didn't know whose truck was parked there. I just came to relax a little myself—see if the fish were biting, that's all."

Joanne glared at Lonnie P. "You calling my mother a liar? I don't think she'd appreciate that one bit."

"That's how your pants and shoes got all wet," I added. "You waded out to catch fish with your bare hands? I saw only one fishing pole back there."

Lonnie P. swiveled his head toward Charlie. "Turn off that damn camera right now, I told you, or you're gonna find yourself tossed out on your butt in front of that pansy newspaper office of yours. Nobody in town can stomach the thing any more, now that you started running the show. Anybody tell you that, Missy?"

So Lonnie P. had finally noticed the camera. Well, too late now. I was sure Jesse would have a riveting story to tell once he was rested enough to tell it. And his face and lungs bore the evidence to go along with it, not even counting the eyewitness testimony of all of us and the video camera documenting his rescue from the river. Jesse was breathing now—heavy and rasping—but regular breaths, his chest rising and falling with each new effort. I knelt beside him and clasped one of his hands. "I'm sorry for getting you into this. I truly am. I didn't mean for anything like this to happen. You don't need to say anything right now. Just one question. Did Lonnie P. do this to you? The black eye and busted lip? Did he push you into the river?"

Jesse nodded. "He said…" Jesse took another raspy breath. "…dead men don't talk."

"I think it's time we got some law enforcement out here," I said. "Let's just hope we get somebody who'll listen. Too bad Marcus is off-duty."

Delia looked at her watch. "He went on duty at three. Denita came into the church at the fish fry and said they had to leave because he had to go in to work. Said she'd come back and pick up her dishes later. It's five minutes after three now."

"Can you ask for him? Does it work that way?" I assumed that you had no choice in who got sent out on a call.

"Watch this." Delia punched in a number and then put on the most obsequious Southern black dialect I'd ever heard come out of her mouth. "Yas, suh, us is got us a situation out here, and we needs Deputy Marcus Boyd to straighten things out. Yas, suh, it's been a fistfight, and somebody's got a busted lip and a black eye, and we needs Deputy Marcus to take care of it, if you don't mind. Yas, suh, thank you, suh. I surely do appreciate it, suh." She was silent for a moment and then Marcus must have come on the line, for her tone changed, and she quickly told him what had happened and where we were. "We got the perpetrator in custody," she told him. "Theo and John are holding on to him, waiting for the handcuffs. Somebody's got a tale to tell you, too, when you get here. Thanks. You'll see all the trucks and cars parked right off the road. Just follow the path down to the river. We got EMTs on the way here, too, so you can't miss us."

Delia and I headed back to the sandbar to meet the EMTs and direct them to Jesse, and a few minutes later they were picking their way along the riverbank, carrying a stretcher and their other equipment, and by the time Marcus arrived in his uniform, Jesse was being prepared for a trip back to the ambulance and on to the hospital.

The emergency technicians wouldn't allow Marcus to question Jesse at the scene, not until he'd been checked out thoroughly at the hospital, but Jesse did say enough to provide cause for Marcus to arrest Lonnie P. and lead him back to his patrol car in handcuffs, reading him his Miranda rights along the way. Charlie followed with her video camera still recording, and the rest of us made a small jubilant parade in their wake. Delia, beside me, burst into a spirited rendition of "We Shall Overcome," and as Theo and John chimed in, I caught Delia's hand and swung our joined hands high in the air in triumph.

Chapter 41

Mike and Joanne followed the ambulance to the hospital while the rest of us remained behind Charlie as she filmed Marcus leading Lonnie P. to his patrol car. In spite of having been read his Miranda rights, Lonnie P. was still spewing—going on about contacting his lawyer and suing everybody in sight for invasion of privacy, kidnapping, and false arrest. "You're gonna lose your job over this," he assured Marcus. "I'm the one in charge of this town, and don't you forget it. Kip Hardwick ain't gonna put up with this kind of treatment of an elected official. I didn't have nothing to do with Jesse Stutts being in that river. I never even saw him there. He got drunk and fell in, most likely."

Marcus opened the back door of his patrol car. "Whatever you say, Mayor. We'll get it all straightened out down at the station. Hope you find it comfy back there." He assisted Lonnie P. in getting into the back seat and then called the sheriff's office for investigators to be dispatched to process the scene for evidence.

"Are we free to go?" I asked. "Or should we wait? In case they want to talk to us or see Charlie's video?"

Marcus looked toward Charlie, who had lowered her camera. "What's on the tape?"

"Everything," Charlie told him. "The whole story. From the minute we arrived at the river until you put the handcuffs on Lonnie P. It's all here."

"I'll need that for evidence. May I take it with me now?" Marcus asked. "Or I can get a subpoena."

Charlie took the tape out of the camera and handed it to him. "Sure, but can I get it back? I need it for writing my story for the *Gazette*, and for getting to Channel 6 news in Tallahassee. They rely on me for local news from this area. I have video of the fish fry on there, too, and they were going to run a clip of that later tonight or tomorrow."

"Thanks. We'll take a look at it and make a copy for you, though I don't know if the fish fry will make the news tonight. Soon as my arrest report gets logged in, this place will be swarming with reporters from *The Tallahassee Democrat* and news crews from the Tallahassee TV stations." Marcus reached into his car for a clipboard. "I'll need written statements from everybody here, but I'd appreciate it if nobody talks to any media people quite yet, till we see the tape and I know exactly what's going on. I'll be calling each of you in for interviews, so you'll get your turn to talk then."

We all nodded in agreement. I hadn't considered what big news Lonnie P.'s arrest would generate. Would the Tallahassee stations really cover it tonight? Six o'clock was only two-and-a-half hours away. I couldn't quite comprehend how quickly everything was happening.

After the other officers arrived to inspect the scene and we finished writing our statements, we were free to go. Charlie and I got into my car so that I could return her to her car at the AME church. Theo decided to ride back with Delia and John so they could drop him off at home. Marcus would be calling us later tonight to arrange for individual interviews.

Charlie settled into the passenger seat beside me. "Wow! If you'd told me this morning that by the end of the day I'd be covering an attempted murder by Pine Lake's mayor, I'd have never believed it in a million years. This is all so surreal. Can you tell me again how you knew Jesse was a witness to that fire back in the 1960s? How all this came to be brought up again after all this time?"

"I don't know if I should. Marcus said —"

"His instructions were not to talk about today until he knew himself what was going on. He didn't say anything about talking about something that happened forty-some years ago. Besides, the next issue of the *Gazette* won't be out until Wednesday. By then the story will be all over the news, and who knows what kind of misinformation will be out there. I just want to make sure I get the facts straight, and you seem to be my best source." She looked over at me and smiled. "Agreed?"

"Sure, I guess so." Now that there was no longer any need to protect Jesse's confidence, it was time to step up and take responsibility for my actions. There could be no more hiding behind cardboard figures or keeping silent out of fear for my own well-being. I'd been cowed for far too long by society's expectations.

Charlie reached into her purse. "Mind if I tape you?"

"No, I guess not." I took a deep breath and began to recount for Charlie the entire sequence of events as they had unfolded. I told her about my visit with Lonnie P.'s mother and how I had come to connect the fire to Lonnie P. and to Jesse and to a third person, Cole Tanner, who lived now, as far as I knew, in California. I told her about coming to the *Gazette* office and making copies of the 1962 newspaper accounts of the fire and how those articles had further aroused my suspicions about the fire's cause. "We talked to a young woman there, a college student," I said. "She let me look at the issues I wanted."

"That was Emily," Charlie said. "She told me about someone coming in to look up some genealogy information, but she said it was one of her college professors and his sister, I think. That was you?"

"Yes. I went there with Brian Simmons. We're not related. We're old friends, going back to our high school days at Pine Lake High, and I asked him to go with me rather than going alone. Moral support, more or less."

"Oh, yes. Emily is a great fan of Dr. Simmons. Was he in on your discoveries? Is he someone I should talk to?"

"Oh, no," I quickly assured her. "He didn't even know what I was looking for when I asked him to meet me there." I thought back to our visit to the newspaper office and how antsy Brian had been the whole time we were there, so afraid that Emily would find out about my search and connect him with it, so insistent that we leave and that I drop the subject of the fire immediately. And then there was my discovery at the fire station—the photo from 1961 that included a young, rakishly handsome Johnny Simmons, uncle to Brian. There had to be something there that Brian wasn't telling, but I didn't know what it was and I didn't want to antagonize him further by exposing him to examination by Charlie.

"Brian wasn't a part of any of this," I reiterated. "He doesn't have any information about the fire." After our parting scene at Mama's, I shrank from the thought of talking to him again, but if there were any questions to be asked, I'd have to be the one to ask them, much as I hated to put myself in that position. I quickly moved on to my meeting with Jesse and our conversation at the old turpentine camp. "He had been holding it in for so long," I concluded. "He was itching to tell someone, and I just happened to be the right person at the right time."

"Wow." Charlie was silent for a moment, letting it all sink in. "You think he'll tell all he knows? After all, he would be implicating himself."

"After Lonnie P. tried to kill him to shut him up? He'll talk, all right. Joanne will see to that. The reason she and Mike were going over to visit him this afternoon was to persuade him to tell the truth. If they hadn't gone when they did..." I trailed off, not wanting to think about what would have happened if Joanne hadn't gone to her mother's as promptly as she had and if we hadn't all rushed to the river and found Jesse so quickly. A few more minutes, and it would likely have been too late.

After dropping off Charlie, I headed home. As badly as I wanted to visit Jesse in the hospital and tell him again how sorry I was, I knew I had to tell Mama what was going on before she heard about it on the six o'clock news.

Mama sat in stunned silence as I spent nearly an hour telling her all that had happened in the last few weeks. "So that's the whole story," I concluded. "I'm sorry I seemed so secretive when you started asking me where I'd been or who I'd been talking to, but I couldn't tell you anything until now. I've known in the back of my mind all these years that Lonnie P. was responsible for whatever happened to Delia that night that nobody ever talked about. I knew, even back then, that the story about a sick grandmother wasn't true—that the reason for Delia's leaving and staying away all those years was connected to whatever happened that night." I'd told Mama about seeing Delia come into the movie theater and what the boys had said, but I hadn't told her about what I'd witnessed later that night from my bedroom window. Some things were too horrible to confess, even nearly half a century later.

I stood and paced the floor. "Delia and I were so close when we were little, and then when the chips were down, I failed her. Coming back here and seeing her again opened up all that old guilt I'd been pushing aside for years. So when I began to suspect that Lonnie P. killed that mother and her two children, I had to act on my suspicions. You understand that, don't you?"

Mama didn't answer.

"I didn't mean to put anybody in danger. I guess I wasn't thinking about what might happen."

"This will kill Thelma," Mama finally said. "Her baby. She's so proud of all he's accomplished."

"I'm sorry." I truly was sorry for the pain that Lonnie P.'s mother and all of his family were going to be put through. "It was bound to come out, sooner or later. There have to be other people in town who know what happened that night, who've been keeping it covered up all these years. If it hadn't been for me, someone else would have exposed him eventually. Do you really want a murderer in charge of Pine Lake?"

Mama sighed. "Back then lots of people did things they wish they could take back now. Everybody was running scared, and they felt like they had to protect their way of life."

"Lots of people?" I asked. "Did you or Daddy beat or kill anybody because they were black? Did Daddy join the Ku Klux Klan? Did either of you ever mistreat Silas or Maggie or anybody in their family?"

"Of course not. You know we didn't." Mama twisted her hands in her lap. "You know what I mean. Times was different back then; people do things when they're scared that they wouldn't do in ordinary situations."

I didn't answer, but I could feel myself back in that movie theater lobby, hiding behind that John Wayne cutout, praying desperately not to be detected. I hadn't called anyone names or made threats or hurt anybody, but later that night I had crouched at my bedroom window, frozen in fear, unable to scream or move. If sin included sins of omission as well as commission, then Mama was right, and I was just as guilty as those other people Mama was referring to.

At six o'clock the lead news story was the arrest of Pine Lake Mayor Lonnie P. Ramsey on attempted murder charges. A brief interview with Deputy Marcus Boyd followed, announcing that there had been an altercation at the Withlachoochee River between Mayor Ramsey and fellow Pine Lake resident Jesse Stutts and that Mr. Ramsey had attempted to drown Mr. Stutts in the river. It was only though the intervention of Mr. Stutts' brother-in-law, Mike Jameson, who had gone to the river looking for Mr. Stutts, that he was rescued. Stutts was presently in Pine Lake Hospital with facial injuries. That was it—with promises of more details at eleven. None of the video was shown, and no other names were mentioned, so I had not yet been associated with the case. But that, I knew, was only a temporary reprieve. As soon as Marcus familiarized himself with the facts of the case and interviewed Jesse and those of us who were present at the scene, my role would become public news, and I wouldn't be able to avoid the spotlight.

I looked at Mama's drained face. What was she thinking right now? The adrenalin that I'd been running on all afternoon was winding down, replaced by a burden of guilt for what I might have done to her standing in the community. Her friendship with Mrs. Ramsey was, of course, irreparably dissolved, but would that extend to her other friends and neighbors? Would my actions make her a pariah in the community? And would she ever forgive me for what I'd done?

I didn't know.

Chapter 42

When the weather report ended — more hot, humid August weather with a chance of an afternoon thunderstorm — I walked onto the front porch and pulled out my cell phone. I'd admitted my involvement in Lonnie P.'s undoing to Mama, but Russell still had no idea of the machinations I'd been up to during the last few weeks. While I was still in a confessional mood, it was time to come clean with him, too.

I spent the next half-hour filling Russell in on everything that had been happening, not letting his frequent exclamations of "What? Are you crazy? And "You could have been killed" deter me from finishing my recitation.

"You have to come home right now," he demanded when I finally ran out of steam. "What if this guy bonds out of jail? What happens then?"

"I don't know." I was so relieved that Jesse was alive and okay and that Lonnie P. was under arrest that I hadn't given any thought to what happened next.

"Tomorrow morning," Russell said. "I want you to pack tonight and be on the road early tomorrow morning. If you're not home by noon, I'm coming up there."

"I can't do that," I protested. "The sheriff's office will be calling me in for an interview, so I have to stay here. I was planning on coming home Wednesday, anyway. Mama finished her last therapy session on Friday, and I was going to do laundry and grocery shopping on Monday and Tuesday and head home Wednesday morning so I'd have a few days to take care of things there before I go back to work next week. You don't need to worry about me. Nothing's going to happen between now and Wednesday."

"Then I'm coming up there. I'll take a few days off work. You and your mother aren't staying alone in that house. You say this guy tried to kill somebody today, and you don't think he's coming after you?"

"He's in jail."

"That means nothing. If he's as well-off as you say, he'll be out tomorrow. And even if he isn't, he has friends, doesn't he? It's nearly seven now; I'll need a few minutes to pack a bag, but I'll be there in four-and-a-half hours, by eleven-thirty. I'll call you back once I'm on the road."

"There's no need," I began, but Russell had already hung up. I could picture him tossing a few clothes into a bag, grabbing his toothbrush and shaving supplies from the bathroom, slipping on his shoes, and heading for the door. He'd be out of there in ten minutes, maybe less.

Meanwhile, all I could do was sit and wait for him to get here and chew me out for putting myself in danger. I walked back into the house. "I called Russell," I told Mama. "He's on his way here right now. I told him he didn't need to come, but he said we weren't staying in this house alone tonight." I shrugged as if Russell's worries were completely unfounded, but some of his fear was beginning to rub off on me.

Within fifteen minutes Russell called again to tell me he was on his way, adding more admonitions about locking doors and not answering any knocks.

"You're being paranoid," I said. "My name wasn't mentioned on the news. Nobody knows I'm the one who put the puzzle pieces together."

"The guy who was arrested knows," Russell shot back. "And he's the one you gotta worry about. He'll be talking to people tonight from the jail."

"All jail calls are recorded, you know."

"You think that matters? Any information he wants to get out, all he's got to do is tell his lawyer. People like him have lawyers that are as crooked as they are."

"You're the crazy one," I said. "Nothing's going to happen."

"I hope you're right. I'm burning rubber to get there as fast as I can, but there's a lot of miles of road between us. Don't open your door to anybody till I get there."

A few minutes later the phone rang again. This time it was Marcus. He had reviewed the videotape and read everyone's written statements and he wanted me to come to the sheriff's office to answer a few more questions.

"Tonight? You want me to come right now?" I was astounded again by how quickly everything was moving. "Sure, I guess so." Then Russell's warning echoed in my ear. "I can't leave my mother alone, though. Can I bring her with me?"

On our way into town, I called Russell again to let him know where I was. "I'll call you back as soon as I'm finished with the interview," I promised.

After Russell and I disconnected, I turned to Mama. She was staring straight ahead, hands folded primly in her lap. We hadn't talked since the six o'clock news report, and the silence was becoming uncomfortable. "I hope you understand why I had to pursue this," I began. "Seeing Delia at the barbeque restaurant when Lonnie P. came sauntering in that day we had lunch together, that decided it for me. Take every fear you've ever had and every bit of hate you've ever felt and roll it up in a ball, and that's what it was like for her."

Mama opened her mouth as if to answer, but no words came out. I could see her lower lip tremble a little as she closed it, leaving whatever she'd been thinking unspoken. I had to remember that I'd been living with this knowledge for nearly a month and Mama was being exposed to it for the very first time. I couldn't blame her for being overwhelmed with everything that was happening.

While Mama waited in the lobby area of the station, I sat across from Marcus and a young white deputy in a tiny interrogation room, acutely conscious of the camera focused on me, and related for the fourth time that day everything I'd already told Charlie, Mama, and Russell about my pursuit of the truth about the Juneteenth fire. The two young men listened intently, occasionally interrupting to ask a question or get me to clarify a point, showing no emotion except for an involuntary grimace as I relayed Jesse's description of Lonnie P.'s amped-up excitement at the "bonfire" he was about to light.

"The rest is on the video," I finished up. "Lonnie P. must have thought he could flatter or intimidate Jesse into not talking, and I guess it didn't work. You'll have to get the rest of the story from Jesse."

Both men stood and thanked me for my time before ushering me back to the lobby, giving no hint of what emotions might have been aroused by my account. Both deputies were too young to have ever experienced segregation. By the time they were born, Martin Luther King Jr. was already dead, and the civil rights marches and the dogs and water hoses were nothing more than a couple of pages in a history textbook or an old, grainy black-and-white newsreel that belonged to some distant time and place. Had either of them, I wondered, ever had any reason before now to connect those images to Pine Lake, to the world they'd grown up in and thought they knew?

When I returned to the lobby, Delia, John, and Theo were all there, waiting to be interviewed, making small talk with Mama, who looked frail and lost among the three black faces.

"I'm sorry about dragging you into all this," I said as we got into my car. "Believe me, I've spent a lot of time these last few weeks thinking about how this was going to affect you."

"The one it's going to affect is Thelma," Mama said. "She's already had one heart attack, and this is likely to give her another one."

I started the engine. "I feel bad for Mrs. Ramsey, too, but I hope you understand why I had to do what I did. Lonnie P. deliberately killed that mother and those two babies, and this whole town has been covering it up and not only letting him get away with murder, but actually rewarding him for it by electing him mayor. Is that the kind of place you want to live in? The kind of place people ought to be raising their children in?"

"I didn't know anything about that fire," Mama answered, "and neither did your daddy. We thought it was an accident, same as everybody else."

"Oh, Mama, I'm not accusing you." I laid one hand on her knee. "I know you didn't know about it. But there have to be lots of people in town who did. Friends of the sheriff. The fire department. People like that." People like Johnny Simmons, I thought, uncle to Brian Simmons. And what did Brian know about that night? About the fire? What had he wanted me not to find out?

I reached for my cell phone to call Russell. It was a quarter-to-ten, and Russell was on the I-295 bypass around Jacksonville, slowed by heavy Saturday night traffic, and still two hours away.

When we arrived home, Mama, tired from the excitement of the evening, went on to bed, but I paced the floor in the living room, waiting until time for the eleven o'clock news. I still hadn't heard anything from Brian, so maybe he hadn't seen the six o'clock report. It was Saturday night, after all; maybe he was out again with the lovely blonde-from-a-bottle Shauna. So far, so good. Should I call him and tell him what was happening, or should I wait for him to find out? If he was out on a date, I certainly didn't want to intrude. Besides, the news hadn't mentioned my name or said anything to connect Lonnie P.'s arrest with me, so there was no proof yet that I had gone behind his back and continued my investigation despite all his sage counsel against it. I'd wait for Russell to get here before dealing with Brian.

The eleven o'clock report didn't divulge any more details about the altercation at the river than the earlier report at six, but it did suggest that the attempted drowning was linked to a fire forty-four years earlier, in June of 1962, that had killed a young black mother and her two small children, a fire that had been attributed, at the time, to an exploding firework, and was now suspected to be arson. The president of the Leon County NAACP, who had been contacted for a quote, announced that his organization would be into looking into the fire, and if it was determined that the facts justified filing criminal charges, they would put all their resources into bringing attention to the case and making sure that justice was finally served, however delayed it might turn out to be.

What had I set in motion? And how many people would be implicated before it was all over? Russell's warnings rang in my ears. Maybe I should be afraid. I checked my watch. Eleven-twenty. I turned off the TV so that I could listen for the sound of Russell's Ford Explorer pulling into the drive.

I turned on the porch light, checked the locks on the front and back doors, and wandered around the house in my bare feet. All was quiet in Mama's room, and the only outside noises were the normal ones of crickets and tree frogs. Five minutes passed, then ten. Eleven-thirty. Russell would be here any minute now. I sat back down and picked up one of the library books I'd checked out for Mama yesterday while I was waiting for Delia to get home from work. Had it been only yesterday that I'd heard the thud of Delia's body against the wall of the church and rushed in to see a furious Lonnie P. threatening to hurt her if she kept asking questions? It seemed that days, even weeks, had passed since then—a long nightmare that kept relooping itself and wouldn't end.

A light flashed through the front curtains, and a vehicle turned off the road and pulled up to the house. Thank goodness. Russell was here. I rushed to the front door, flung it open, and stepped outside.

Chapter 43

I was already down the steps before it dawned on me that the vehicle that had pulled up behind my car was not Russell's black Ford Explorer, but a similar-sized silver-colored Isuzu.

Brian stormed out of the driver's seat. "You didn't leave it alone, did you, Kate? You just had to stick your nose in where it didn't belong. I told you—"

"Hi, Brian." I tried to keep my voice calm. "I assume you saw the eleven o'clock news."

"You're darn right I saw the news. What in blazes do you think you're doing?" Brian stalked toward me. "I told you to leave that fire alone. Maybe you don't have to live here, but I do. I have two more years to go before retirement, and I don't want anything to mess that up."

"How is Lonnie P.'s arrest going to mess up your retirement?" I was truly perplexed at Brian's reaction. "I don't see the connection."

Brian shook his head with disgust. "Trust me, Kate, you bit off more than you can chew with this little episode. When you play with fire, you get burned. That's a foregone conclusion."

"Burned? How?" I still didn't know what Brian was talking about. "I didn't have anything to do with that fire." I paused and looked at him. "Did you?"

Brian didn't answer me.

"Did you?" For the first time ever, the possibility popped into my head that Brian could have had something to do not only with harboring information after the fact but with actually setting the fire. But that was impossible. Jesse had said only he, Lonnie P., and Cole were involved, and they were the only three who had been whisked off to join the army the next morning. Nevertheless, a shiver ran down my spine. "What's going on?" My voice was shaky. "What's this all about?"

Brian's face seemed to grow paler as I waited for an answer, the blood draining from it and leaving it a ghostly white against the surrounding darkness.

"Tell me," I urged. "There's something I need to know, isn't there?"

"Kate? Is that Russell?" I looked behind me to see Mama coming across the porch. "Sounded like somebody yelling out here."

A dog started barking in the distance, and a second set of headlights turned into the drive, blinding me for an instant. With all the confusion, I didn't know which way to turn or look.

Russell barreled out of his vehicle and headed straight for me. "What in heck is going on?" he demanded. "What's *he* doing here in the middle of the night?" He held up one fist and shook it in Brian's face. "If you touch one hair—"

"Hey, Honey, it's okay. He's not here to hurt me." I grabbed at Russell's arm. "Everything's fine."

Taken aback by Russell's threatening posture, Brian backed up a few steps toward the safety of his Isuzu.

"What's he doing here then?" Russell demanded again. "It's nearly midnight." He looked at Brian and back at me, suspicion growing in his eyes.

"No," I insisted. "It's not what you're thinking." I needed to defuse the situation quickly. "He found out about the arrest on the eleven o'clock news, and he showed up two minutes ago to chew me out for getting involved. Same as you did. That's all."

Russell put one arm possessively around my shoulder. "I don't need anybody driving out here in the middle of the night to talk to my wife," he told Brian. "I'm here now, and you can just go on back home. I got things covered."

Brian reached for the Isuzu's door handle. "Okay, buddy. You got it covered. Glad to hear it. Your wife is playing with fire here. She has no idea what she's got herself into. I came out here to warn her, that's all."

"Wait a minute." I didn't want Brian to drive off without telling me why he was so upset. By that time Mama was coming down the porch ramp in her nightgown.

"What's going on?" she asked. "Why is Brian here? Hello, Russell. I was sleeping and heard noises. Sounded like somebody yelling."

"Sorry, Mama. Brian came to tell me how much trouble I'm causing everybody." I turned back to Brian. "And exactly how is it I'm playing with fire here? What is it you're not telling me?"

Brian looked at the three of us lined up against him. He was clearly outnumbered. "I'm leaving. I hope you're happy about what you've done to this little town, dragging up old skeletons and making us the butt of national attention. You can run back home and escape it, but those of us who live and work here are gonna suffer — your mother included. Lonnie P.'s influence in this place casts a wide net." He looked at Mama. "You know how it's going to be, Mrs. McCormick. All the news crews going around town talking to everybody, digging up old bones, shaking the rafters looking for clues, wanting to know everybody who was involved. And Lonnie P. will be spewing off names left and right, blaming everybody but himself — people who've devoted their whole lives to this place — and now they'll be ruined."

"People like your uncle?" I asked. "Was the fire department in on the cover-up, too?"

"What do you know about my uncle?" Brian asked.

"I did my homework. I know he worked for the fire department back in 1962. The firemen knew it wasn't a firework that caused that fire. They took their orders from Sheriff Otto Hardwick, didn't they? 'Write it up as an accident. Don't mention the gasoline that had been poured all around the house.' What happened to the gas can Lonnie P. left at the scene? He didn't have it with him when he got back to the car where Jesse was waiting, so it got dropped somewhere along the way. Who found it and made sure it didn't turn up as evidence?"

"I don't know anything about a gas can," Brian said. "My uncle said it was an accident—an exploding bottle rocket and an old house with overloaded circuits and frayed wiring. Nobody had reason to believe any different."

"Nobody?" I asked. "You were the science whiz of Pine Lake High School. Our valedictorian just a week before. You knew something wasn't right about that story, didn't you? And you've been harboring that secret all these years. It's been eating you up, too, or you wouldn't have driven all the way out here at midnight to yell at me about ignoring your advice and exposing Lonnie P. for the murderer that he is."

"I had nothing to do with that fire," Brian insisted. "Nothing. I had no idea Lonnie P. was planning to burn down that house."

"But you're holding something back." I was sure there was something Brian wasn't saying—something that had brought him ten miles out here to my mother's house in the middle of the night to take out his frustration on me. "What is it?" I tried to think what it could possibly be. Brian had said he had no idea Lonnie P. was planning to burn down *that* house—so did that mean Lonnie P. had asked Brian about burning something else? Maybe a question about combustion—something a science whiz would be expected to know—especially a science whiz whose uncle was a firefighter?

"Lonnie P. probed your brain for information," I guessed. "Sometime before the fire, he had a conversation with you about the best or the fastest way for a fire to spread, didn't he? How somebody would go about setting fire to an old building that he didn't want any more? Something like that. Didn't he?"

Brian's expression told me all I needed to know. "He said his father had an old shack out in one of his fields he wanted to get rid of. He wasn't using it any more and wanted the land for more crops. Lonnie P. was going to set fire to it and watch it burn. Wanted to create a big spectacle while he was at it, he said, and wanted me to tell him the best way to do it—how to create the hottest flames so it all went up fast without a lot of clean-up involved. I believed him. Why not? I didn't have any idea what he was planning." Brian's eyes relayed a silent appeal for understanding.

Russell whistled in appreciation. "Whew, Katie-did, you're good, aren't you? How'd you know that?"

Russell's use of Daddy's old nickname for me brought a lump to my throat. "Brian beat me out for class valedictorian," I said. "By one class grade. I got a B in chemistry and he got an A. Only subject he bested me at."

"Smarty-pants." Russell grinned at me. "Least Lonnie P. didn't come running to you for advice about burning down a house, so you can be happy about that."

I looked at Brian, sympathy now overtaking indignation. "It's not your fault," I said. "Whatever you told him, you're not to blame for what happened. He used you, just like he used Jesse. Like he used anybody he could get away with using. Nobody's going to hold you responsible for anything to do with that fire. So don't go blaming yourself." I felt such empathy for Brian that I wanted to go over and give him a hug, but I held back, not wanting Russell to take it the wrong way.

"I didn't know anything about that fire," Mama said, her voice startling me since I'd almost forgotten she was there, "but that night when Delia got hurt, me and Roy knew something bad had happened. Roy asked Silas about it, and Silas wouldn't tell him a thing. I'm ashamed to say it now, but I never asked Maggie a word about it—just pretended to believe Maggie's story that Delia was sick with a fever. Buried my head in the sand and didn't want to know."

"It's all right, Mama." I put one hand on her back. "Those were scary times back then. All of us did things we're not proud of."

But Mama wasn't finished. She stood up straighter. "Then when that fire happened, and Lonnie P. and them other boys up and joined the army right soon afterward, I never put two and two together. I just went about my business and didn't ask questions. It took Katie coming home after all these years to make the connection."

On my other side, Russell put one arm around my shoulder. "Couldn't stay out of trouble, could you? I let you out of my sight for a few weeks, and you're off chasing down murderers."

I gave him a dig in the side with my elbow as Mama continued talking. "Too many people have been letting Lonnie P. get away with things for way too long. I been knowing Thelma Ramsey all my life, and that boy ain't been nothing but trouble and worry to his mama since the day he was born. Katie may have stirred up a heap of trouble, all right, but she done the right thing, and I'm right proud of her for it."

"Thanks, Mama." I laid my head against hers as my eyes filled with tears. "I appreciate that."

On my other side, Russell tightened his arm around my shoulder. "Me, too," he echoed. "I'm right proud of her, too."

Brian was silent, his hand still on the door handle of his Isuzu as if prepared to escape at any moment. I pulled away from Mama and Russell and crossed the few feet of distance between us. "Wait," I said, laying one hand over the hand that was grasping the door handle. "Don't go yet. We've both been carrying around a bucket load of guilt for all these years. I wish you'd told me before, and we could have shared the load."

Brian lifted his hand, shaking mine off. "I thought you'd dropped the subject like I told you to."

"You thought I'd let Lonnie P. get away with murder? Let him go on running this town and buying everybody's silence with his money? Don't you see it's time to bring all this ugliness out into the open—time for Lonnie P. to be held responsible for all the things he's done over the years? Nobody's going to blame you for anything—no more than they're going to blame Jesse. And if he used you and Jesse, who's to say how many other people he's used over the years and then intimidated into keeping quiet? You're not going to be the only one. People will be coming out of the woodwork to air their grievances. I guarantee it."

While I was talking, Russell had walked over and stood beside me. He stuck out his right hand toward Brian. "Kate's right, you know. You seem like a decent guy. I don't know this Lonnie fellow, but he sounds like a real snake in the grass."

Brian hesitated before shaking Russell's outstretched hand, and I wondered if he was remembering the same thing I was — the kiss in his living room, which I'd broken off in the nick of time. "Thanks," he told Russell, and something in him seemed to relax a little. "I hope you're right."

"He is," I assured Brian. "Nobody's going to blame you for any of this."

Brian reached again for his door handle. "I tried my darndest to talk her out of pursuing this," he told Russell. "Told her how much danger she was putting herself in, but she wouldn't listen."

"I know." Russell put both arms around my waist from the back and pulled me against him, rubbing his chin on the top of my head. "When she decides to go after something, there's no changing her mind, that's for sure. You should'a seen how she went after me forty years ago. I tried to escape, but she wouldn't leave me alone."

I crossed my arms on top of Russell's and slapped at one of his hands. "That's not true, and you know it. I never chased after you or any other man. Ever." My eyes met Brian's. If I had made my feelings known about Brian back in high school, would my life have turned out differently? I didn't know, but I was happy with the choices I'd made. I couldn't imagine being married to anyone besides Russell. "Don't go feeding Brian a bunch of tall tales. You did the chasing, not me. Now let's get inside out of all these mosquitoes."

As Brian drove off, I remained in Russell's embrace. Whatever happened next, I'd be okay. We'd all be okay.

Epilogue

Friday, July 20, 2007

Now that the jury has spoken and Lonnie P. Ramsey has been found guilty of the attempted murder of Jesse Stutts, I can finally rest easy, knowing that he will spend the next few years, at least, behind bars. The trial of Lonnie P. and Cole for arson and murder in the forty-five-year-old case of the Juneteenth fire is still ahead of us, set for sometime in 2008, but I'm confident justice will prevail in that case, too. Jesse has been given immunity in exchange for his testimony against Lonnie P. and Cole, so no charges will be brought against him, which is a great relief not only to him but to me, seeing that his near-drowning is already on my hands.

Looking back to a year ago, it's hard to believe that the events of last summer even happened, much less that I instigated them. The entire episode seems like a dream or something I read about in a novel. Every day I question myself as to how I could have set all those events in motion—quiet, reserved librarian that I am, who had never so much as caused a ripple before or since in social or political waters.

After that night of Lonnie P.'s arrest, Russell and I had remained with Mama for a few more days, waiting to see how things were going to play out, and just as Russell had predicted, Lonnie P. had bailed out of jail first thing Monday morning, free until his trial date, and had immediately begun complaining loudly to anyone who would listen about the indignities of being falsely accused of a crime that never happened. He stuck adamantly to his story that he had gone to the river to see if the fish were biting and had never seen Jesse there at all. According to him, Jesse must have accidentally tumbled into the river and his facial injuries had to be the result of hitting his head against the rocks. All of this was reported on the local TV news out of Tallahassee, and Mama, Russell, and I watched his impossible lies with a sort of horrified amusement.

Of course, the newscasts also reported the story told by Jesse and the rest of us who were present, along with the indisputable facts that the only fishing equipment at the scene was Jesse's, that Jesse's bruised eye bore the unmistakable impression of a fist, and that Lonnie P. had already convicted himself at the scene with his own words. Snippets of Charlie's videotape had been released to the media, including my statement to the others that Jesse had been with Lonnie P. the night of the fire and knew what happened, and Lonnie P.'s snarled answer, "Not no more he don't."

On Thursday morning, five days after Lonnie P.'s arrest and three days after his release on bond, Russell and I had headed home, with Mama in tow. Against all her protests, we had insisted she come with us for her own safety and our peace of mind, and she'd remained with us in Titusville until mid-October, until things had calmed down in Pine Lake and life had gotten halfway back to normal.

In Titusville I no longer had access to the local TV reports from Tallahassee, but we did have all of Mama's mail forwarded to us, including her subscription to *The Pine Lake Gazette*, so I was able to keep up with what was happening. Charlie covered the story with gusto, shredding Lonnie P.'s reputation with a relish that only a woman could have felt— interviewing everyone in town, reporting on every new detail, and instigating a probe into Lonnie P.'s business dealings for prior and current improprieties.

At first Lonnie P.'s friends had rallied around him, excoriating Jesse as a drunk and a liar, but as the NAACP began to pressure the state attorney's office to investigate the cause of the Juneteenth fire and a trial for arson and murder seemed more and more likely, the number of his supporters began to dwindle. Sheriff Kip Hardwick, watching the evidence mount against his grandfather, and up for reelection in what was becoming a fiercely contested race with Deputy Marcus Boyd, had begun backpedaling fiercely to save his own reputation. Soon he was denying any past or present association with Lonnie P. and any knowledge of what had happened back in 1962, two years before he was even born. Other town leaders, seeing where things were headed, followed his example, disassociating themselves from Lonnie P. and denying any knowledge at the time that the fire was anything but a tragic accident.

Whether or not Lonnie P. had ever attempted to draw Brian into his web of blame, I didn't know, but Brian's name never appeared in the *Gazette,* and as I had predicted the night of Lonnie P.'s arrest, more and more people came forward to tell Charlie tales of how Lonnie P. had used or taken advantage of them. Soon Charlie was digging deeper into Lonnie P.'s used car business, not only the one in Pine Lake, but the dealerships he'd owned in the various places he'd lived, and her search was picked up by reporters in Tallahassee, who followed his trail down the East Coast, interviewing people who'd known him or had dealings with Ramsey Ford. The *Gazette* reported numerous customer complaints, such as mileage odometers turned back, body damage and engine problems concealed, bait and switch practices, and the like. Lonnie P. had never been charged with a crime; when the complaints began to mount, he simply closed up shop and moved to a new location farther down the coast, leaving plenty of livid customers behind.

Each new issue of the *Gazette* brought new revelations, and I devoured each one like an addict crazy for her next fix. Once we took Mama home, I started my own subscription so as not to miss out on any new discoveries, and I checked the Internet daily (even sneaking peeks at it from my computer at work) for any mention of Lonnie P. in *The Tallahassee Democrat* or on the websites of the Tallahassee TV stations. In Miami Lonnie P. had switched from cars to real estate, buying a huge tract of worthless swampland and marketing it on slick, full-color brochures to northern tourists as the perfect retirement spot. And since buyers often bought sight unseen, falling in love with the gorgeous, palm-dotted square of paradise pictured in the brochure, he was able to rake in big sums of money before his scheme began to be exposed. That was when he once again pulled a disappearing act—this time back to Pine Lake where he could wave his money around and show everyone who'd ever doubted his abilities that he was rich and successful beyond their wildest imaginings.

I had also stayed in contact with Delia, by phone and e-mail, and was getting weekly reports from her about how the black community was reacting to unfolding events. At first the older people had feared retaliation, but as the tide of the town turned against Lonnie P., that fear turned to hopefulness, and in November, when Hal Crawford was elected mayor with over seventy percent of the vote and Marcus Boyd beat out Kip Hardwick for sheriff (although by a much narrower margin), the cautious hopefulness turned to jubilation.

Not all was as rosy as it might sound—in spite of the charges against him for attempted murder, Lonnie P. had managed to hang on to his position as mayor and had actually received nearly thirty percent of the vote for reelection—and Marcus Boyd had squeaked by Kip Hardwick with a fifty-two to forty-eight percent majority. Still, it was a big change for Pine Lake, a town that had remained mired in the past for generations as the brightest and most ambitious of each new graduating class moved off to greener pastures.

Sadly, my exposure of Lonnie P.'s crimes had ruined Mama's and Mrs. Ramsey's friendship, but nobody else in the community shunned Mama or held my actions against her, and she had even come to enjoy the attention that came from my role in Lonnie P.'s undoing. By the time we took her back home in October, the initial shock of the arrest had worn off, and as more and more details emerged, all those people who had watched Lonnie P. grow up began to cluck and nod and agree that they knew something like this was bound to happen, and, as Mama proudly reported to me over the phone, they never suspected that little Katie McCormick had it in her to be the one who brought it to light. Nobody blamed Mrs. Ramsey, though; all of them had seen the worry and trouble she'd been through, and they rallied around her, knowing that "but for the grace of God" it could just as easily have been they who were in her shoes.

Gail is finally e-mailing me again, after months of icy silence, filling me in on all the juicy details of Lonnie P.'s and Sherri Lynn's divorce proceedings, but I've had no contact with Brian since the night of Lonnie P.'s arrest. Yesterday, however, a notice came in the mail reminding me of our forty-fifth class reunion, only two weeks away. I haven't decided yet if I'm going. I'd like to see everyone, but I don't want to be the center of attention—the person who brought down Lonnie P. Ramsey.

And I don't know if I'm ready to face Brian again. Ever since finding out that he, like me, had been carrying around a truckload of guilt for all these years, I've been feeling closer to him than ever. I keep thinking about him at odd moments, remembering the excitement of last summer—our confessions to one another of our high school crush, our "dinner dates" that came forty-five years too late, the glass of wine and the kiss in his living room. And despite knowing that marrying Russell was the best decision I've ever made in my life, I still find myself having fantasies about what might have been. From this distance, those fantasies are nothing more than harmless pleasure, but it wouldn't do to indulge in them up close.

Russell and I were in Pine Lake last week for me to testify in the trial against Lonnie P., and we stayed three extra days so as to be there for closing arguments and the verdict, so another trip up so soon for the reunion is still up in the air, though Russell says it's completely up to me.

Two days ago Delia called to tell me that she and John had signed the papers that day for the house they'd been looking at in Tallahassee and would be moving in over the weekend. "You have to come visit us," Delia had said, "Soon as we're settled in."

"We'd love to," I'd said, "and you and John have to come visit us in Titusville. You have to come down and see a shuttle launch."

It's Friday afternoon: the weekend is ahead of us. Russell and I have plans to go out to dinner tonight, so I don't have to cook. Upon arriving home from work, I kick off my shoes, pour myself a glass of iced tea, and turn on my computer to check my e-mail. Now that Lonnie P. is finally behind bars, I feel that I've at least begun to make reparation to

Delia for my failure all those years ago. But is it enough? That's the question I keep asking myself. Should I tell her what I saw out my bedroom window that night? Nothing I can say or do now can change or erase what happened that night, and telling her now might ruin that fragile new friendship we've established. Is it worth taking the risk?

I sit down in front of my computer and open my e-mail. There is a message from Delia—a cheery hello and news that she's been packing all week for the big move tomorrow. And there's an attachment—a photo of the new house, Delia says. I open the attachment and stare. There is the new house—a small bungalow style with a covered front porch and a rose bush by the front steps, but it's not the house that I'm staring at. Standing in front is Delia, flanked by two men. The one on the right is John, but the one on the left is the one who draws all my attention—a tall man in his mid-forties, maybe, handsome, smiling broadly, one arm around Delia's shoulder. David? I study his features, and then I know.

I also know I'll never tell Delia what I'd witnessed later that night. "I got family to think about," she'd told me in explaining why the attack could never be made public, and sending me this photo was her way of trusting me, of proving our bond. The best way for me to honor her wishes was with my continued friendship. And my silence.